# TRANSFIGURED

## THE TRANSCENDENT TRILOGY, BOOK TWO

### K. A. RILEY

# A NOTE FROM THE AUTHOR

Dearest Fellow Conspirator,

What you have in your hands is one-ninth of what's called an *ennealogy*, a rare and hard-to-pronounce word meaning "a nine-part series." It's basically three sequential, interlocking trilogies. (Think *Star Wars*, *Planet of the Apes, or* Yukito Kishiro's nine-volume *Battle Angel Alita* cyberpunk manga series.)

Here is the Reading Order for the *Conspiracy Ennealogy*...

#1: **Resistance Trilogy**
  *Recruitment*
  *Render*
  *Rebellion*

#2: **Emergents Trilogy**
  *Survival*
  *Sacrifice*
  *Synthesis*

\#3: **Transcendent Trilogy**
    *Travelers*
    *Transfigured (You are here!)*
    *Terminus*

If you're enjoying the series, please leave a review on Amazon or Goodreads to let your fellow book-lovers know about it. And be sure to sign up for my newsletter at www.karileywrites.org for news, quizzes, contests, behind-the-scenes peeks into the writing process, and advance info. about upcoming projects!

Thank you for reading and for joining in the Conspiracy!

Conspiratorially yours,

*KARiley*

*To the ones brave enough to change.*

# SUMMARY

Embarking on a fresh set of adventures through France and Spain, Kress and her Conspiracy continue their search for fellow Emergents, unsure if they're about to find new friends or the deadliest collection of enemies.

With Noxia and her team of Hawkers hot on their heels, the Conspiracy will come face to face with mind-blowing discoveries, the shocking truth about their dreams, and solutions to mysteries they may wish they'd never tried to solve.

"O God, I could be bounded in a nutshell and count myself a king of infinite space, were it not that I have bad dreams."

— *Hamlet*, Act 2, sc. 2

"*Allons*! through struggles and wars!
    The goal that was named cannot be countermanded."

— "Song of the Open Road," Walt Whitman

# HOME BASE

IT'S quiet in the Arrival Station.

And not a peaceful quiet. More like the kind in that scene in the old horror movies where some teenaged couple is walking down a long, creepy high school hallway and then a little blond girl with pigtails and dead eyes leaps out of nowhere and hacks them to pieces with a pair of long-handled pruning shears.

I'm not exactly expecting a small child to terrorize us. On the other hand, the last time Brohn and I walked hand-in-hand down a long hallway, the building got attacked, and the ceiling pretty much collapsed on our heads.

We went from holding hands to running for our lives.

But this time, things feel safe at least.

Spooky, but safe.

This complex we're in, so we've been told, was once part of one of London's airports.

There are hints here and there of its life before the war—exposed foundations, collapsed walls, exposed metal posts, endless banks of empty window frames, melted slags of steel carts and plastic benches, and old signage for long-gone restaurants, registration counters, and security offices—all traces of the bustling transportation hub this apparently used to be.

Almost all the floors in the rooms and corridors have drifts of red sand pushed up in long dunes along the base of the bent-in and broken walls.

There's a row of smashed-to-pieces escalators and a base of crumbling concrete for a flight of stairs leading up to a second floor we can't really access, even if we wanted to.

Some of the gaping holes in the ceiling have been covered up with planks of wood or panels of blue insulating sheets stretched tight and nailed into place. Other parts of the ceiling in various rooms are exposed, with streaks of the sun's searing red rays seeping through the gaps and cracks like blood from an open wound.

Most of the place reeks of war, neglect, and the total and absolute surrender to the stupid, stubborn cruelty of time.

Outside of the Arrival Station, there are endless heaps of collapsed buildings coated in thick layers of decades-old dust. Long runways, blistered with bubbles of molten tar and over-grown with creeper vines, crisscross the ground in every direction.

In the distance, skeletal remains of a fleet of passenger jets, cargo planes, mag-loaders, and yellow baggage carriers have been swept into a mountain range of fused and melted-together metal.

The building we've been staying in seems to be all that's left. It's bigger than I realized, with more floors and lots of rooms, most of them empty, where Brohn and I have been able to slip away for some alone time.

There's one room way down the hall, on the far side of the building from the one we're in right now. We went in there once.

Once was enough.

Turns out it was filled with open crates of human skulls and bones. The remains were mostly splintered, cracked, and crusted over with patchy cultures of greenish-gray mold. We couldn't tell if they'd been exposed to radiation, contaminated by some virus, or set on fire.

Or maybe some combination of all three.

Either way, the smell was enough to make my throat gurgle and my eyes water.

I nearly threw up before Brohn had the sense to whisk us away, slamming the door shut behind us for good measure.

"The dead can't hurt us," he assured me as we scurried down the hall.

"No. And they can't scare us."

"Then why are you shaking?" he teased.

"Because the dead can still remind us of how temporary we all are."

Normally, Brohn would've countered my pessimism with some alpha male bravado about how tough we are and about how it's no accident we've survived so much. Instead, he simply said, "Good point" and walked on, his arm around my shoulders.

When we sneak away for alone time, we usually come to an old storage room at the end of one of the smaller side hallways on the far side of the building. It's a small, windowless room. It's musty and a little cramped, even after we dragged the stack of broken chairs and the two metal bookcases out into the hall.

But it's a quiet home base for us, and at least it's not filled with crates of dead bodies.

Brohn holds me tight, my face nestled against his chest. We talk in whispers, mostly about our lives back in the Valta.

Half of everything we say begins with, "Remember that time when…?"

Our conversations end with wet eyes and tight throats as we wrestle with the balance between honoring our friends and family by remembering their lives…or hanging onto our sanity by forgetting their deaths.

The mountain town we grew up in is gone, burned to the ground by Krug's Patriot Army. Nearly everything and everyone we knew was wiped out in a series of drone strikes that started when we were six years old and ended a year ago when Krug sent in one last fleet of drones to destroy whatever little bit of the town was left.

Tonight, tucked away in our little supply room of rotten wooden floorboards and a rusted army cot with coiled springs and a thick strip of industrial carpet for a mattress, Brohn and I stay up late, long after Cardyn and Terk call down the hall through cupped hands that we should really get some sleep.

Brohn opens the door and leans out. "We'll be right there!"

But that's a lie. Moments like this are rare, and neither of us wants them rushed out of existence.

Besides, sleep just means I'll have dreams—half of them nostalgic, half of them nightmarish—about our lost lives in the Valta.

Lately, my sleep has been flooded with images of blinding, pinprick lights in walls I can walk through but only part way before I get stuck. In those dreams, I scream for help, but it's someone else's voice that comes out of my mouth.

I can't tell if those are dreams or nightmares.

Trying to stay awake, I sit next to Brohn on the squeaky cot and talk, flashing back again to our time growing up together. To our committees of Neos, Juvens, and Sixteens. To our struggle to survive under a constant cloud of fear.

We reminisce about our years of lessons—all of us kids teaching and being taught by each other—and about Final Feast, the day we graduated into the exclusive club of Seventeens.

That was the day we looked forward to, hoped for, and feared.

"It's what started all this," I say through a glum pout. "It's the day that led to so many people getting killed."

"And saved," Brohn reminds me.

"I guess."

I know he's right. It's easy to forget how much good has come from so much bad.

In the past year, we've had our setbacks and narrow escapes. We've suffered losses at the hands of Krug and traveled through the country where we experienced endless waves of deadly violence, poverty, fear, helplessness, and hopelessness.

We fought our way out of captivity in Chicago, squared off against the combined might of the Patriot Army in Washington, D.C., and even battled Medieval knights in a palace courtyard right here in London, England.

But we managed to survive it all, and, along the way, we even saved a lot of lives, including our own.

"Are you worried?" Brohn asks.

"About being chased by assassins while we blindly run across three foreign countries to break into a secret government facility and rescue kids who might turn around and try to kill us?"

"Um, yeah."

I answer him with a smile and an eye roll.

"You're right," he chuckles. "Granden should have given us a *real* challenge."

Stressed now and fidgety, I stand up to pace, and Brohn gets up a minute later to stop me.

He grips my shoulders and leans down to look me in the eye. "Seriously. Are you okay?"

I slump toward him, breathing a sigh into his chest. "Do you have regrets?"

"Lots." He tilts his head, leans forward, and kisses me. "But not about us."

I feel my face go red as my heart does a happy butterfly flutter.

I tuck my hair behind my ears and ask Brohn why our conversations keep coming back to the Valta.

He pulls me close, his arms strong, gentle, and supportive all at the same time. "I guess it's because in our hearts, it's still home."

## 2

## HELP

Tucked away in our storage room, it's wonderful yet terrifying to feel like Brohn and I are the last two people on earth.

But the feeling doesn't last nearly as long as I'd like.

"It's morning," Brohn says, tilting his head toward the long crease of light at the top edge of the wall where the ceiling has warped and separated from the rest of the building. "We talked through the night."

"Well…" I yawn, "we might have kissed a little, too."

"That we did," he confesses with a blush. "That we did."

He stands and takes my hand in his to help me to my feet.

Staring up at him, I cock my head to the side. "What are you so smiley about?"

He puts his hand on his heart. "Nothing. It's just…"

"What?"

"You make me happy in here."

With a smile I'm sure is going to split my head in half, I leap into his arms to exchange one more lingering kiss before we head down the corridor to the Canteen.

When we arrive, we lean through the open doorway. Except for the normal cluster of round tables, metal-framed chairs, and the long, green-topped counter, the room where we eat our meals and store our weapons is empty.

Cardyn, Terk, Manthy, and Branwynne must still be asleep in the dorm room we share down the hall.

Render isn't around, either.

Ravens are notoriously adaptable birds. They can survive on any continent, in almost any climate or conditions. And Render decided a few days ago that he'd rather stretch his wings and brave the heat outside than stay cooped up with us in the Arrival Station.

I can't say I blame him. The Arrival Station is big, but there's something lonely and somehow confining about its run-down barrenness and echo-y, expansive hollowness.

To add to the feeling of emptiness, Granden, Kella, and Wisp have returned to Washington, D.C. with Lucid and Reverie. That was three days ago.

We haven't heard from them yet.

When I tell Brohn I'm nervous about that, he reminds me about how the communications system here is glitchy at best.

"Glitchy I can handle," I tell him. "It's my stupid imagination I can't deal with right now. I mean, what if—?"

"I'm sure they're fine."

I know he's not sure. We haven't been sure about anything since, well...*ever*. But his words are enough to stop me from drifting into a full-on, heart-clutching panic attack.

A noise catches our attention as we walk, and we pause to peek into a room we've passed by dozens of times but have never been in before.

We step in to find Grizzy lying on her back, buried under a long communications console of flickering holo-lights, black glass, steel, and chrome.

Our host and the sole proprietor of the Arrival Station has baffled me since we first met her more than a week ago. She's body-builder big, shaggy as a molting bear, and gruff in the way that only someone who's had nothing but her own thoughts to keep her company can be gruff.

But I can't help liking the hell out of her.

She's a no-nonsense straight shooter who's dedicated her life to living alone in the Arrival Station as the solitary overseer of one of the last working airports in the country. She's a host, a gatekeeper, and she's quickly become a good friend.

Plus, she has a marvie accent that makes everything she says sound somehow both super smart and down-home folksy.

Nudging aside a rainbow-colored tangle of wires, I kneel next to her feet and ask what she's doing.

"Patchin' up a network of decayed an' burned-out relay feeds. They're kinda vital for stayin' in contact wif as many people as possible. Not that there's many people worth contactin'," she adds, her voice low and hollow from deep within the bowels of the console's monitoring ports.

"Mind if we join you?"

"Sure. Long as you don't mind shootin' one o' me tools up ta me from time ta time."

Brohn says, "It's a deal," and we sit cross-legged on the floor on either side of her feet.

"Will you be able to contact Granden, Wisp, and Kella?" I ask. "They're the ones calling the shots."

"I'll do me best, Love," Grizzy grumbles. "Do ya see a zip-roller out there?"

"Zip-roller?"

"Looks like a little pizza cutter."

Brohn says, "Got it" and reaches under the console to hand the device to Grizzy, who grunts her thanks.

"That there's one tenacious trio," she says over the buzz of the tool and a strobing pulse of yellow-white light. "Granden an' them."

"They're family," Brohn says.

"Literally, when it comes to Wisp," I remind Grizzy.

"Right. Yer fledgler, eh?"

"Fledgler?" Brohn asks.

"Ya know. Yer chabbie. Yer swaddler-sister. Yer mini-moppet."

Brohn and I laugh, and I remind Grizzy that other than her physical size, there's nothing "mini" about Wisp. "She escaped a drone attack that should've killed her. She single-handedly assembled an army of Insubordinates. Oh, and she's led *two* revolutions that've saved lives, liberated cities, toppled a government, and overthrown a dictator."

"She used to be nervous all the time," Brohn adds. "She was always afraid of bad guys coming to get her. Now, *she's* the one the bad guys are afraid of."

Grizzy's deep chuckle rolls out from under the console. "Yeah. I could see that when I first met 'er. Talk about punchin' outa yer weight class. She's a right corker, that one."

Her knee-high, fur-lined boots, which are about all we can see of her at the moment, wriggle back and forth as she murmurs and squirms. She reaches out a hand and pats around on the floor by my feet. "Ya see a titchy charge-inverter down there, Love? Got a line o' red indicator lights on the 'andle."

I rummage through the pile of gadgets and gizmos lying in front of me until I find the tool she described and pass it up to her. "Anything else we can do to help?"

"I'm okay wif the 'ardware. Patched this thing together out o' spit an' polish more times'n I care ta count. Software's another problem, innit? Not a techie, me. I don't suppose either o' ya can talk ta this wankin' communications array and tell it what ta bloody well go do wif itself?"

I mouth the word, "Manthy" to Brohn, but he frowns and shakes his head.

A few days ago, the Auditor asked Manthy if she might be able to help her smooth out a few lines of code in some diagnostic sub-routine she was running.

The day after that, Rain suggested that maybe Manthy could

patch into one of the few remaining access ports of the W.E.D.P. —the Western European Digital Network—to help identify security measures and the exact location of the Processor we're supposed to find in Spain.

Just yesterday, Grizzy was going to try to activate the transponder array in a box inside the front entryway of the Arrival Station.

Each time, we pulled Manthy aside and asked and then begged her to help. Each time, with distant, defiant eyes, she said the same thing: "I can't."

Manthy's a technopath. Her Emergent ability to communicate with local compu-systems and what's left of the world's local and universal digital grids has been impressive and lifesaving.

Unfortunately, that amazing ability resides inside the most mysterious, annoying, and stubborn head I've ever met.

Even at her most relaxed, Manthy has never been the most communicative person in the world. I've known her most of my life, and I can't think of more than a handful of minutes when she didn't have her eyes down and her guard up.

So I don't know if her claim that she can't help means she's lost her ability. Or if she's been transfigured somehow by her recent, dramatic return from the dead. Or if the pain of using her skills—which I know is real—has gotten to be too much.

Or if it just means, for reasons only she could possibly know, she *won't* help.

"What about *them?*" Rain says from the doorway.

Brohn and I look up to see Rain leaning against the door frame, her thumb flicking over her shoulder to where Terk is looming in the hallway behind her.

Although the rest of us switched from our Medieval clothing back into our more familiar tactical combat gear, Rain's decided to keep sporting her silky white top with the red vest, and the plaid, tartan skirt.

I pretend to gag, but the truth is that she looks really pretty, and, to be perfectly honest, I might be just the tiniest bit jealous.

"Who's *them*?" I ask.

"Terk and the Auditor. Well...the Auditor, anyway." Rain slips her glossy black hair behind her ears and turns to give Terk a wink. "No offense, Big Guy. But I don't think you'd be able to fit under there."

I smile at Brohn. "What do you think?"

"Can't hurt to try," he says with a grin and a shrug. He leans over Grizzy's waggling boots and calls into the dark access port. "Hey, Grizzy! What about the Auditor? She's been plugged into the Patriot network back home. She might know how these things work." Brohn looks back over his shoulder. "You *do* know how these things work, right?"

The Auditor's voice hums from the disk on Terk's back. "I won't know until I try to plug in. The protocols might be a lot different here."

Grizzy hauls herself out from under the console. Brohn and I stand as she sits up and wipes a sheen of sweat and streaks of grease from her face and forearms. "Desperate times an' desperate measures, right?"

Ducking down to avoid cracking his head on the top of the doorframe, Terk steps fully into the room. At nearly seven feet tall, with broad shoulders and the left side of his body made up of a patchwork of gears and exposed cables, there aren't many rooms he can slip easily into.

Her graceful voice rolling out in gentle waves, the Auditor asks Grizzy about the status of the communications grid and what help she needs to get it running again.

Before Grizzy can answer, though, Cardyn sidles into the room. His ruddy hair is a disheveled mess. He's got tired eyes, a dirty t-shirt, and his hands are plunged deep into the pockets of his frayed, army-green cargo pants.

"What's up with you?" I ask.

"Nothing."

"Where's Manthy?"

"In the Canteen. Staring at a cup of tea."

"Well, ask her to come join us."

"I did."

"Let me guess…she can't."

Cardyn nods.

"It *does* seem to be her mantra these days."

"What about Branwynne?" I ask.

"Asleep."

"We were just getting ready to see if the Auditor can help Grizzy access the comm-grid."

Cardyn smiles. "Mom to the rescue."

I give him a fiery glare, and he annoys me by returning it with a glossy-toothed smile.

Technically, the Auditor *was* created partly out of my mother's consciousness. And it's true she's been helpful. *Beyond* helpful, in fact. But it'll take more than a few acts of cybernetic heroism for me to think of the disembodied voice wafting out from the glossy black disk on Terk's back as my "mother."

"Do you have a network feed? Or a direct line to the transmitter mainframe?" the Auditor hums to Grizzy.

"Got both, actually."

"Let's try the network feed first."

Grizzy surveys us as Rain stands behind Terk and works with the Auditor to see if they can link her up to the Arrival Station's grid.

"Hey," Grizzy says. "When we're done 'ere, I can return ya ta 'yde Park. If yer sure ya still want ta go back an' all."

"We need to," Brohn says.

Grizzy nods and gives us all a feeble smile.

Brohn reminds her about what she already knows: "We have a mission. A dangerous one. And the Banters and the Royal Fort Knights are our only chance to help get Branwynne back to the

Tower of London before we head south to find the Valencia Processor."

Grizzy nods again. "Girl that age should be wif her parents."

"Not that she needs our help getting to the tower," Cardyn quips.

"That *is* one tough little girl," Terk agrees.

"And resourceful," Rain adds from behind Terk's back. "She thinks fast and moves faster. Did you notice that?"

Brohn snaps the three of them out of their cheery moment of hyper-optimism. "She could still die out there if we don't help her."

Looking like they've been chastened by their stern father, Cardyn, Terk, and Rain hang their heads.

"We need to keep things in perspective," Brohn warns. "We're alive because of a little bit of training, a handful of friendlies, and a whole lot of luck."

"She *is* special, though," I tell Brohn, but he's having none of it at the moment.

He tilts his head toward the wall. "Out there, 'special' just means having a bigger target on your back. We're talking about delivering a twelve-year-old into the hands of a bunch of wannabe royal kids who tried to kill us a week ago."

"I still say we should at least consider taking her with us," I tell him without making eye contact. "On our mission, I mean. She wants to come."

"She *needs* to be with her parents," Brohn says. He offers up a deep sigh and steeples his fingers in front of his chin. "Look, we missed out on the kind of lives we could have had if we hadn't lost our own parents. We became each other's family. We can't deprive her of the right to be with hers."

Rain offers up a teasing smile. "You're not worried, are you?"

"All the time," Brohn admits.

Terk chuckles, and Cardyn says, "Yeah. Right."

13

"Seriously," I ask with a light laugh. "You're *not* worried, are you?"

I'm expecting a typical Brohn answer, a leader's answer... something along the lines of, "It's what I need to tell the rest of you to keep you on your toes." Or, "A healthy dose of worry is what's kept us alive this long."

Instead, he stares at a spot on the floor and says, "Yes."

And it might just be the scariest little word I've ever heard.

## 3

## RETURN TO ROYALTY

"IT'S TIME," Grizzy says the next morning.

"Time for more sleep?" Cardyn asks with a drawn-out, groggy groan. He pulls the tattered sheets up over his head and curls into a ball in the center of his nest of blankets on the floor.

"The Auditor o' yours done her smashin' best. Right good egg, her."

"We should've suggested it days ago," I sigh.

"Nah. Didn't know I needed 'er 'til yesterday."

"Communications are back on-line?" Rain asks, rubbing her eyes.

Grizzy claps her hands and rubs them together. "Good as they're gonna get, anyway, Love. Comes and goes, don't it? Always 'as."

"What about Granden? Did you hear back?"

"Got shot at."

"What?" I stammer, shocked wide awake by her nonchalance.

"Their plane. It got shot at. Somewhere over the Atlantic. Had to put down in Philadelphia before movin' on, 'e says. They're all fine, though. Safe and sound in D.C." Grizzy takes a second to scan our horrified faces. "S'okay. 'appens all the time."

"All the more reason it's not okay," Brohn growls.

"He also says to tell you ya got eleven days."

"Eleven days till what?" Rain asks.

"Till those kids in the Processor get activated."

Terk's mouth hangs open for a second before he says, "Activated? What the hell does that mean?"

Grizzy shrugs. "Don't know, do I? Just tellin' ya what Granden told me."

Brohn and I exchange a look, and I know we're both thinking the same thing: Sheridyn, Dova, Virasha, and Evans—the four Hypnagogics who were "activated" out of our old Processor before being sent to capture us and, later on, to kill us.

Grizzy scratches her head and gives all of us in the room a confused squint. "So what's it mean, anyway?"

"They're going to turn any Juvens they've got, any possible Emergent kids, into human weapons by brainwashing them. The ones they can, anyway."

"An' the one's they can't?"

We don't answer, because we don't need to. It's clear from Grizzy's wide eyes that she knows exactly what's going to happen to the young Emergents who either can't or else won't agree to go along with the En-Gene-eers' attempts to hold power, all while they hide behind the invented Eastern Order.

We saw the same thing with the Deenays and the Patriot Army back home, and it occurs to me that the horrors and lies we thought were local might just be *global*. It also occurs to me that me and my friends might not be the only conspiracy in the world.

"Eleven days," Cardyn says. "That's a good chunk of time. No need to hurry, right?"

When Grizzy doesn't answer, he says, "Right?" again.

Grizzy breaks the bad news. "The message is five days old by now."

"So we've got…" Cardyn does an embarrassingly slow calculation on his fingers. "Six days?"

"More or less," Rain says.

"More like *less*," Grizzy tells us after a strained inhalation. "With the comm-network down, I'd say you have five days…*tops*."

"How long does it take to get to Valencia from here?"

"Before the war and the drones, the Eastern Order and the checkpoints…you probably coulda done it in a day or two by mag-car."

"And now?" Rain asks.

Grizzy doesn't answer, so Rain asks again. "Grizzy, how long?"

"Honestly, Love, I'm not bloody well sure it's advisable."

"Is it possible?" Brohn asks.

Grizzy sighs. "*Anything's* possible, Love. But you got twelve-hundred miles to go, most of it straight through parts you aren't gonna want any part of."

"We don't have a choice," I sigh. "We promised Granden, and the stakes are just too high."

"Kress is right," Rain agrees. "This has always been a high-risk rescue mission. Now, there's a deadline attached to it."

"Which means we need to get going sooner rather than later," Brohn says, slapping his hands to his knees.

"That Auditor o' yours could come in 'andy. I don't suppose you'd mind leavin' 'er 'ere wif me?"

With a wincing groan and a whir of pistons from his left arm, ribcage, and shoulder, Terk lumbers to his feet. "We're kind of attached."

Brohn pushes himself up and starts slipping into his boots. He's bare-chested. The muscles in his arms and legs twitch and flex. He's tanned and toned. His eyes sparkle while the rest of us are still rubbing life into our own eyes, which are crusty and red. He runs his fingers through his somehow perfect hair.

I still can't believe someone who looks like him spent good

chunks of the last several nights with his arms wrapped around someone who looks like me.

Not that I'm ugly or anything. But, unlike my boyfriend, I don't exactly look like a Greek god chiseled out of marble and polished to perfection.

"What about our weapons?" Brohn asks Grizzy, sliding a white-seamed, black compression shirt over his head and tucking it into his pants.

"I wouldn't risk it if I was you. 'Course, if I was you, I 'ope I'd 'ave enough sense ta find some little corner o' the world ta squirrel away in an' live 'appily ever after."

"Not our mission," Brohn says.

"Or our style," Rain adds.

"So what's it going to be?" Terk asks, looking distressed. He pulls on the full-length, baggy-sleeved brown hooded cloak he wore for our last trip into London. "Can we take the guns?" He holds up his flail, the club and chain with a menacing-looking spiked iron ball at the end. "Or do I get to swing this some more?"

"You're in good wit the Royals now. They're the ones what woulda killed ya for 'avin' guns. There's others out there who'll kill ya to have 'em for themselves. So…if ya want ta risk it…"

"We'll risk it." Brohn slings on his arbalest—his mammoth crossbow—and grabs our heavy canvas bag of pistols, shotguns, and assault rifles. "We don't have a ton of ammo, but better safe, right?"

We all murmur our general agreement as we finish getting dressed in a rushed flurry, Granden's updated timetable looming over us and hurrying us along.

Cardyn starts to clip the mag-holster and the twin tomahawk axes to his back but stops when he notices Manthy watching.

"Sorry," he blushes, holding out the holster and the two axes. "These are yours."

"You keep them," she mumbles.

"I can't take your weapons."

"You're not taking them. I'm giving them to you."

Cardyn rolls his eyes. "I can't let you *give* me your weapons."

"I want to travel light for a while. Besides, I've seen you fight. I think you'll need them more than I will."

Off to the side, Terk nudges me. "Hey. Did Manthy just make a joke?"

"I think she did."

"Do you think dying gave her a sense of humor?"

I give Terk a playful punch to the arm before walking over to nudge Branwynne awake. From under her silver-lined insulation blanket, she mumbles at me to go away, which makes me laugh.

Realizing she may have just insulted me in her half-sleep, she bolts up and apologizes. "I'm so sorry, Kress. I kind of forgot where I was."

"Don't worry about it. Sometimes it can be nice to forget where you are."

Blushing, Branwynne clambers to her feet and looks around the room. "Where's Render?"

I can't help but giggle at her youthful energy. In a room full of foreign Emergents—armed and preparing to head back out into the bleak remnants of what used to be one of the greatest cities in the world—all this bouncy, coal-eyed girl wants to know is the status of a six-pound bird.

"He's still outside," I tell her. "He used to sleep with us all the time. I think now he likes to be out there. Kind of a guard for us, keeping an eye on things."

"Can I go get him?"

"Sure."

Beaming and already dressed, Branwynne slings on her red leather jacket and bounces off to track down Render. I'm not sure how she communicates with him, but he's taken to her in a way he rarely does with anyone other than me.

Once we're all armed and dressed in our combination battle-fatigues and Medieval vests, dresses, waistcoats, skirts, and over-sized robes, Grizzy takes us to the tube platform where she loads us onto the single-car train she runs between the Arrival Station and the city.

Branwynne meets us there with Render on her arm, quietly bobbing his head.

I apologize to Grizzy for making her shuttle us into the city again.

But she smiles and shakes her thick mane of hair, which sends a cloud of dust particles into the air around her head. "I 'aven't 'ad reason ta take anyone on this thing in nigh onta a year. Now I get ta run 'er twice in the space of a week. It's me what should be thankin' *you*."

Ducking into the small control room at the front, she throws the train car into gear, and we start on our way.

Although it's a dark and rattling ride, the trip is actually kind of pleasant this time. We know what we need to do, where we're going, and who's on the other end—at least for the first leg of our journey.

Okay, we don't exactly know what roving gangs of desperate, violent survivors might be out there. And, of course, there's always the lingering threat of Noxia and the Hawkers, the deadly Hypnagogic with mind-controlling powers and a team of assassins at her command.

But for once, it feels like we know more than we don't.

There's something comforting about that.

With all of us rested and rejuvenated, the tube car fills with our chatter, and the ride is over practically before I knew it even started.

At the end of the line, we step off the train and onto the dusty platform where we turn to say our goodbyes to Grizzy.

With her hands on the inside of the doorframe, she manages a half-smile and scans us with eyes full of sparkling pride. "Never cared fer company. Never 'ad any company ta care *for*."

I cut her off before she starts to cry, which I know is going to make *me* start to cry. "We'll miss you, too. We'll be back."

She nods, but I can tell she doesn't believe me.

"Why don't you come with us?" I ask. "You used to live in the city, right?"

"That was a long time ago. I got nothin' but bad memories. No. My place is keepin' the communications lines open and the Arrival Station up ta snuff." She drags her sleeve under her nose. "It's been nice watchin' out fer friends 'stead of lookin' out fer enemies."

"If we can find the Emergents we're looking for," Rain says, "we'll need to figure out if they want to come with us or not. Either way, we're going to need to get ourselves back home."

"And you said yourself there's not a lot of options," Cardyn reminds her.

"Not for air travel. My Arrival Station's the only safe game in town."

"Then we'll definitely do our best to get back here," I promise.

"I'd like that."

Brohn tugs my sleeve. "Come on, Kress. We've got a mission to start."

After a chorus of goodbyes and with Branwynne in tow, we make our way back toward Hyde Park and to the Banters who first welcomed us to the city...by kidnapping us.

For our sake and for Branwynne's, it's a reunion we need to have.

It's just not one I'm especially looking forward to. After all, nothing's more awkward than asking for help from the kids who once tried to kill you, right?

## 4

## REVELATION

CLIMBING the crumbling stairs and stepping out into the light, Rain takes the lead, which is a good thing.

Even though we've been down these roads before, I was too scared and disoriented to take note of all the landmarks Rain seems to be using now to help us on our way.

The six of us walk in a loose cluster around Branwynne. Our training and experience kick in as we shift into protective positions on the deserted road, with a couple of us keeping an eye on Branwynne while the others stay on constant alert, scanning for Noxia and the Hawkers.

In our battles to survive both the Banters and then the Royal Fort Knights, Noxia and the Hawkers were a wild card we didn't account for and whose whereabouts and motivations we still aren't sure about.

Noxia, we've agreed, is almost certainly a Hypnagogic. From what we've gathered, that means she's an Emergent like us. Only, unlike us, she draws her abilities from somewhere between the worlds of wakefulness and sleep. That makes her both dangerous and sought after as a tool to be manipulated and used by powerful people who'll stop at nothing to rule over this waste-land of a world.

As we've seen first-hand, she seems to have the ability to infil-trate people's minds and control them. The Hawkers—the team of assassins who keep her company—are some kind of bounty-hunter militiamen whose three-part purpose in life seems to be tracking, capturing, and killing. And they're apparently really good at it.

So either we heard wrong or else we've got nine lives with at least seven or eight of them used up.

We barely escaped from the Hawkers once. Now, here we are, a week later, stepping back out into the open like a pack of dimwitted pygmy antelopes voluntarily offering ourselves up as brunch for a pack of rogue lions.

So I don't blame Terk for whipping his flail out from under his billowing cloak and spinning around when we hear a small clatter of noise from the ruins of an abandoned building we pass.

Pushed along by the wind, a crusty plastic jug skitters over a pile of stones and out into the middle of the street.

"Thought it might be Hawkers," Terk admits with a blush and downcast eyes.

"I wish I knew what they want with us," I confess, although I'm not sure I really want to know the answer one way or the other.

Cardyn guesses they want to kill us, but Brohn isn't convinced.

"We have to remember, we're not just a Conspiracy or a band of rebels or refugees anymore. We're a commodity."

Terk frowns and rubs his neck as we walk on. "A commodity?"

"He means we're a proven product," I explain glumly. "We've gone from experiment to myth to coveted Emergents, ready to be caught, weaponized, and sold off to the highest bidder."

"Just what I've always wanted to be," Cardyn says, clapping his hand onto my shoulder and giving it a good shake. "Merchandise."

Manthy walks past us, her eyes riveted to the ground. "Just be grateful *someone* wants you."

"Hey!"

Terk elbows me again and drops his voice to next to nothing. "See?"

"I think you're right," I giggle behind my hand. "She's either come back with a sense of humor, or else..."

Clipping his flail to its leather strap and tucking it back under his cloak, Terk glances down at me. "Or else what?"

I answer with a shrug and pick up my pace to keep up with Rain.

I don't want to jinx it by saying anything out loud, but I think Manthy might have changed in other small ways. These past few days, hanging around and catching up with each other at the Arrival Station, I think maybe she's started letting down her guard a bit.

With Cardyn, anyway.

After our escape from the Processor, the two of them developed an odd, bickering, and antagonist brother-sister kind of relationship. It's still there. Only now, Manthy seems to be enjoying it almost as much as Cardyn does.

Except for the extreme pleasure of keeping to herself, I've never known Manthy to enjoy much of anything. So I'm thinking Terk might be right. There *is* something different about her. I've decided to keep a closed mouth and open eyes until I figure out if it's good-different or bad-different.

Either way, it's occurring to me that there's all kinds of ways to emerge.

Snapping my wandering mind back to attention, Branwynne sidles up to me, her eyes a disorienting coal-black, except for glossy specks of white from reflected light glinting off the steel and glass of the world around us.

*There's a galaxy in that girl's eyes.*

Dressed in her form-fitting red leather gear and fingerless red gloves, she looks like she's getting ready to jump a motorcycle over a gorge or leap over a line of buses or something.

I ask her if the high temperatures around here ever bother her, but she doesn't answer.

I ask if she's excited about being reunited with her parents at the Tower of London.

She stares straight ahead and doesn't say anything.

When I ask if she's worried about us being out in the open like this with so many potential dangers around, she gives an almost imperceptible shrug.

So I switch gears and thank her for her help defeating the Royal Fort Knights.

She opens her mouth but doesn't say anything.

"You never did tell us how you got into Buckingham Palace like that," I say. "How'd you know we were in trouble?"

She blinks a few times and glances at me out the corner of her galaxy-eyes before looking away.

I try to talk to her about her past, her life, the training she must have had in order to be able to fight like she does at such a young age, but I'm discovering she's nearly as quiet and mysterious as Manthy.

*Nearly*, but not quite: Once the subject turns to Render, she's a total and absolute chatterbox.

Out of the blue, she asks me if I grew up with ravens, too.

"Just him," I tell her, pointing up to where Render is banking and gliding like a surfer on the air's thermal waves.

"He's such a beaut!" She shields her eyes with her hands. "I meant to ask. How come he's got...?"

"The gold armor?"

"Yeah."

"He helped us win a battle back in San Francisco. But he got

25

hurt. Bad." Branwynne's eyes get big, but I tell her not to worry. "His 'armor' is really a system of embedded nano-circuitry."

"Embedded…?"

"It's like crutches for his nervous system. We're all made up of electrical impulses. He gets a boost from the implanted tech. Our friend from back home—Olivia—helped make it. She's a Modified." I flick my eyes back to where Manthy is now straggling off to the side of the road with Cardyn. "Olivia and Manthy. They saved his life."

"And the armor…it doesn't come off?"

"Not without killing him, no."

Branwynne reaches over and runs a finger along my forearm. "This is how you talk with him?"

"My tattoos? They help."

"But you don't need them?"

"I did at first. Over time, I think Render and I have kind of outgrown them."

"Then what are they for?"

"Remember how we passed through that wall back in St. Paul's Cathedral?"

"Yeah."

"How'd you do that?"

"Dunno. It was my first time."

"Really?"

"Yeah."

I hold my forearms out. "Well, these might be able to help me to access the other side."

"The other side?"

"Of this. Of the physical world."

"You can pass through, too?"

"Well, I'm working on it," I laugh. "Eventually, I think I'm supposed to be able to do what you do naturally."

"Mergies aren't natural." Branwynne glances skyward, and I think she's going to attribute who we are to God or to some kind of cosmic accident. Instead, she says, "*They* made us. The scientists. The Deenays and the En-Gene-eers. You were right before. They just needed a new weapon against the Eastern Order."

Brohn's walking on my other side with Rain next to him. I sense their ears perk up at the mention of the Eastern Order.

I exchange a glance with them, and they both nod, giving me the silent go-ahead to tell Branwynne the truth.

Which I do only after a deep breath, knowing the next five words I say are going to be hard for her to believe, next-to-impossible to process, and more horrifying than anything she's ever heard.

I clear my throat to gulp down a knot of nervousness. "There is no Eastern Order."

Branwynne starts to laugh, but something in my voice must register with her because she stops—not just laughing but also walking.

Behind her, Cardyn, who's wandered over with Terk and Manthy, bumps into her and nearly knocks her over.

"What do you mean?" Branwynne sweeps her hand in the direction of the razed city around us. "Who do you think did all this?"

"For us, it was our own government," I tell her. "Our president —Krug—he needed something to keep everyone distracted and afraid."

"So they wouldn't question him," Rain adds. "Or challenge him while he kept scooping up more and more power."

"And since there was no enemy, he invented one. And then when the Eastern Order 'invaded,' he said we had no choice but to go to war."

"And going to war meant spreading lies, recruiting soldiers, and sacrificing citizens," Cardyn says.

Lumbering along behind us, Terk leans forward. "That's where we came in."

"We were recruited," I explain. "Into a secret military training camp. We were supposed to be killed off or turned into human weapons for Krug to use against our own people."

"Instead," Rain chimes in, "we discovered the truth."

"My guess is it was the same here," Brohn says as he starts us walking again. "The lies. The invented enemy. The manufactured war. When this is over…if we can rescue the Valencia Juvens—"

"And not get caught by the Hawkers in the process," Cardyn reminds him.

"Then our next mission will be to come back here and help spread that truth through Grizzy's communications array back at the Arrival Station."

"We can't end this," I tell Branwynne, "we can't set things right until we can get everyone to see the reality behind all the lies."

Branwynne answers with a creased forehead and a blank stare.

Rain points to a narrow laneway formed by the crushed rubble of what—based on the scorched remains of furniture, kitchen appliances, shards of porcelain from smashed sinks and toilet bowls, and a horrifying cluster of human bones—used to be two rows of apartment buildings. "This way."

Branwynne lets out an unamused chuckle as we follow Rain. Her black eyes flash fire and focus on me with a weird, bottomless intensity. "You're really saying our own government did this to us?"

"I don't know. Maybe."

"Could've been *our* government, for all we know," Brohn says.

"Or both," I add. "Or even a third government we don't even know about."

"But why make up an enemy? There've always been enough enemies to go around, right?"

"Enemies almost *always* have to be invented," I tell her.

"And governments have almost always risen to power on the backs of those inventions," Brohn adds.

Branwynne swings her head from side to side, taking in the

carnage around us and the enormity of what we're telling her. She opens her mouth, but nothing comes out except for a choked sob, and then, out of nowhere, she bursts into tears.

Which makes *me* start crying.

Cardyn slips between us and throws his arms around our shoulders. "I know it's a lot to take in," he tells Branwynne. "But we wouldn't be here if we didn't know the truth, ourselves."

"We wouldn't be alive at all if we didn't know the truth, ourselves," Rain calls back over her shoulder.

"Ignorance isn't bliss," I promise Branwynne through a half-laugh as I wipe my eyes with the heels of my hands. "It's just ignorance."

"I think maybe I kind of knew," Branwynne says through a snuffle. "About the Eastern Order. After all, no one's ever seen them, right? It's always just drones."

"Oh, there are real people pulling the strings," I assure her. "Only now, it's the Wealthies, who aren't about to get their hands dirty in the process. They just keep putting up walls they say are supposed to separate the good guys from the bad guys."

"Sometimes I have dreams about passing through walls," Branwynne says.

"Passing through walls?"

"Like I'm going from here into some other version of here. Kind of like we did in St. Paul's."

"Only that wasn't a dream," I remind her, but she just shrugs like she's not so sure.

Manthy is walking next to me now, her head down. She doesn't look up when she says, "Me, too."

"You, too, what?" I ask.

"I dream, Kress."

"Everyone dreams," Cardyn tells her.

Manthy shakes her head. "This is more than that."

"What do you dream about, Manthy?" Brohn asks.

Manthy flicks her eyes sideways like she's afraid someone might overhear her. "The Lyfelyte."

Branwynne fiddles with the zipper of her red leather jacket and takes a deep breath. "The Lyfelyte? The place we went into with those other Emergents?"

"Lucid and Reverie," I remind her. "Yes."

From overhead, Render circles down. I expect him to land on my shoulder like he usually does, but, instead, he hovers for a second in front of Branwynne and then drops down onto her extended forearm.

I drag the backs of my fingers along the tattoos on my arm. "I still don't know exactly what the Lyfelyte is. Not really. Not yet. But I think the answers are in between my tattoos," I say. "And that little black head of his."

"And the Auditor," Cardyn says. "Caldwell said she's the third part of your little puzzle."

"Right."

Branwynne seems relieved by this. Relieved and somehow grateful, although I don't know why. If someone told me the same thing—about the Eastern Order, about having access through dreams to some other, hidden side of life—I think I'd be shocked, confused, and, honestly, probably scared incontinent.

But Branwynne continues to surprise me with her odd combination of innocence, beyond-her-years composure, and plain old bad-ass fearlessness.

Because I've seen her in action, it takes some effort to remember that she's at least five or six years younger than the rest of us. Although she's obviously had her own struggles here in London, she hasn't been through what we have. She hasn't traveled like we have.

At least now she knows the truth like we do.

I'm hoping what we've told her helps. In my experience, the burden of truth crushes as often as it elevates.

My protective instinct has begun to kick in. I've *been* a little sister, but I've never had one. And now I feel like I've got a deeper-level of appreciation for Brohn's relationship with Wisp.

As if to confirm my feelings, Branwynne slips her hand into mine as we walk on, passing into the shadow of the wall around the Hyde Park Settlement. She gives my hand a little squeeze and giggles.

"What's so funny?" I ask.

She doesn't have a chance to answer.

Up ahead, an arrow zings down from one of the makeshift turrets along the towering wall around the settlement and pierces the hard-packed dirt road right next to my boot.

## 5

## WELCOME BACK

Brohn leaps forward while the rest of us leap back, scrambling for whatever cover we can find.

Three more arrows whistle through the air and bury themselves in the ground at his feet.

I scream at him to get out of the middle of the road, but he holds up a finger and tells us to stay where we are and to give him a second.

Waving his arms over his head like a castaway signaling a rescue boat, he calls out to the archers. "We're the Emergents! The Mergies! We were here a week ago!"

Overhead, the archers—three girls in white smocks with red crosses on the front and with their longbows drawn and ready to fire again—pause and exchange a look.

With sudden awareness falling over them, they lower their weapons and burst into smiles.

Turning toward the interior of their compound, one of the girls calls down through cupped hands, "The Mergies is back!"

Cardyn, Rain, Terk, and Manthy rise up from behind the dunes of rubble they leaped over for cover.

Branwynne and I emerge sheepishly from our hiding place

under the remnants of a collapsed marble archway off to the side of the cratered road.

Brohn tugs one of the arrows out of the ground and inspects its bent tip and splintered shaft before tossing it off to the side. "Not exactly a welcome mat, is it?"

"At least they were *warning* shots," I tell him.

"True."

For the next few minutes we mill around outside the imposing, twenty-five-foot-high wall of concrete blocks, jagged sheets of steel, thick beams of scorched wood, and the towering array of discarded junk between us and the inside of the Banters' Hyde Park Settlement.

On high alert for Noxia and the Hawkers, Cardyn and Terk scan the bleak and bombed out neighborhood. We hear voices and see flashes of people creeping around in some of the partially collapsed buildings lining the road around us.

"Is this going to be okay?" Branwynne asks, her eyes darting side to side as she follows the sounds of scuffling and footsteps.

"Sure," Cardyn promises. "We just need to wait a minute. We know the Banters. They'll let us inside." He's grinning and trying to seem relaxed and confident, although he's also sweating and biting his fingernails.

Finally, a break appears in the wall, and a large door on hinges made of thick links of chain groans open.

The sun is high, and the figures who emerge are buried in a deep shadow.

As they step forward into the light, we recognize the first two people instantly: Ledge and Harah.

Last week, Ledge kidnapped us. Then he let us go. Then Harah kidnapped us, put us on trial, and lined us up to get beheaded in a guillotine.

Now these two former adversaries—both of us and of each other—are standing arm-in-arm, as radiantly chummy as long-lost friends.

We recognize several of the others, too, as they step forward out of the looming shadows.

The brother and sister team of Trolley and Chunder.

All-to-Pot.

Bob's-yer-Uncle.

Harah's attendant, Squire.

Mixed in are a bunch of the Banters we fought with and some of the Royal Fort Knights we fought against.

There are even four lumbering, Terk-sized guys toward the back. They're thick-necked and bulgy with muscles, and I'm guessing they're four of the knights we crossed paths with during our last adventure.

The last time we saw them, they were dressed head to toe in red and silver armor. Somehow, they're even scarier in their current outfits of tight white tank-tops, shaved heads, and kilts. They look like the offspring of an oak tree and a bald gorilla.

I think it must take me a full minute to stop staring at them.

The four giants don't move, but everyone else in the crowd offers up hearty waves, which we return.

Standing behind them on the periphery is Ledge's foul-mouthed, wonky-eyed lieutenant, Lost-the-Plot. He's got his arms crossed and his chin down, his eyes bouncing randomly over the crowd of Banters and Royals gathered around Ledge and Harah. His scowl is deep and crooked.

Brohn nudges me. "I guess not everyone gets to live happily ever after."

"Honestly, I don't think that guy has *ever* been happy."

It's true. In our brief experience with Lost-the-Plot, I don't recall one time when he wasn't scowling, pointlessly enraged, or peering around randomly through his drifting, unfocused eyes.

Ledge and Harah, on the other hand, are all focus and joy.

Considering these two used to be at war with each other, and Harah was ready to have us executed after we broke into her palace, it's a happy sight to see.

Ledge summons us forward and shouts out for us to come through the gates. "We ain't gonna bite ya, Mates," he beams. "But we can't leave the gate open. Never know what might try ta weasel its way in, eh?"

Brohn and Rain lead us into the compound with Terk, his flail at the ready, urging us forward as he brings up the rear.

Brohn hangs our black sack of guns over his shoulder along with his arbalest. Guns are strictly forbidden here, and I'm hoping no one notices or asks about the mysterious bulging bag.

Once inside the compound, two girls on either side of the entryway strain against a hand-crank attached to two thick chains.

With a metallic grind, the doors thunk shut behind us, and the girls slide steel beams through u-shaped brackets, sealing us all inside the compound.

Ledge claps Brohn on the arm. "Good ta 'ave ya back, Mate."

"Good to *be* back." Brohn sounds sincere, and he probably is. But I'm pretty sure he hasn't forgotten Ledge hitting him full-force in the neck with a broadsword.

"An' who's this sad-eyed one, then?" Ledge asks with a nod toward Manthy.

Cardyn steps forward and introduces her to the Banters and Royals, who give her curious looks before turning back to the rest of us.

"We're back because of Branwynne," Brohn tells them.

"What about 'er?"

"She needs to get back to the Tower."

"We can get 'er there," Ledge says.

"She's in good 'ands," Harah assures us. "It's not far, and we've got the weapons and people ta keep 'er safe."

"Hawkers?"

"Shouldn't be a problem. We been dodgin' 'em for years now. They stopped trying to get in 'ere. No Mergies to go after, so why bother, eh?"

"All the more reason we need to get going," Brohn explains.

Harah p'shaws this and insists we stay.

"No," Rain says. "Brohn's right. Hawkers have left you alone because you don't have Emergents here for them to go after."

"Until us," I say.

"Right. So we were hoping we could leave Branwynne with you while we try to get to this Processor before the Hawkers figure out we're here and decide to end whatever truce you might think you have with them."

Harah slides her arm around Branwynne's shoulders.

Branwynne smiles up at her, and Brohn breathes a visible sigh of relief.

I'm still worried, though.

We've seen some of what's out there, and we've heard about the rest. Hawkers, Roguers, Scroungers.

"It's crazy," Ledge says as he starts walking along one of the hard-packed dirt paths that crisscross the settlement. "Before, we 'ad two sides at war an' a lot o' wee factions climbin' all over each other for scraps."

"Now," Harah continues, "Those wee factions've gotten bolder than ever. Like they got so used ta all the trouble, they need ta stir it up again just ta...I don't know...feel alive."

"Funny," Cardyn says. "Same thing happened with us. We won. We ended a war. But this lunatic fringe group—"

"The Devoteds," I clarify.

"Right. The Devoteds. They came swooping in *two days later* and tried to stir things up again."

"What is it with people?" Terk asks. He looks around at us like he's waiting for an answer, but we don't have one to give him. "Who prefers violence to peace? Who'd rather have enemies than friends?"

"Maybe they're afraid," Harah shrugs.

Terk scrunches up his face. "Afraid?"

"Of being vulnerable. Of being kind."

"Maybe it's easier for some people to hate," I guess.

"Or maybe they just need a hug," Cardyn suggests with a twinkle-eyed smile.

With their fingers interlocked, Ledge raises Harah's hand to his mouth and kisses it. "We weren't really afraid when we was apart. But now that we're together, there's not a whole lot we can't 'andle."

"Stay a while," Harah offers. "We ain't afraid o' the 'awkers."

"We can't," Brohn explains. "There's a Processor in Spain."

"A confirmed one," I add.

"Right. Every second we delay could have disastrous results. And not just for you. For the Juvens in Valencia, too."

Ledge turns and raises an eyebrow as we walk on. "Disastrous?"

"There was this girl Sheridyn who got flipped in one of the Processors back home," Brohn explains. "She and a bunch of her friends wound up being recruited by Krug and nearly killed us all."

"Krug is your president?"

"*Was*. And no. He was our power-hungry, self-centered dictator."

"What 'appened to him?"

Rain flicks her thumb between our Conspiracy. "We did."

"And this Sheridyn?"

"She could harness radiation," Cardyn says as we continue on our way and as the crowd of Banters and Royals trudges along, leaning in and listening with open mouths. "The Deenays turned her into kind of a human bomb."

"Deenays?" Harah asks.

"Like the En-Gene-eers," I say. "The ones we think were behind it all. The ones who worked for Krug and forced their own brand of evolution on us. The ones who helped set all this in motion. The ones who made Sheridyn."

Rain holds her thumb and finger an inch apart. "She came this close to turning D.C. into a burning lump of carbon."

Ledge and Harah exchange a look before Ledge gestures for us to follow him along another one of the dirt paths, this one leading between tidy rows of white tents and up to Kensington Palace. "So you're saying there's Mergies who can save the world—"

"Or destroy it. Yes."

"Well then, if your mission involves stoppin' 'em, you should probably toddle off, I suppose."

"We know where we need to go," Rain says. "Only…"

"Only what?"

"We don't know where to start."

"You need to get to Spain, you said?"

"Yes. To Valencia. It's where the Processor is."

"Never been ta Spain, me."

"You've never been *anywhere*," Harah teases.

Ledge laughs and says that's true. "But I do know a place they could start."

At the same time, he and Harah say, "Vauxhall."

Cardyn's ears perk up. "My parents were from Vauxhall!"

"That so?"

"So they told me."

"Then I guess this'll be like a little homecoming for you, eh?"

"I don't know if I'd go that far."

"And you can get us there?" I ask.

"We can *direct* you there."

Harah looks oddly sad. "But we don't even feel good about doing that."

Ledge kisses her hand again. "Harah's right. You're safer 'ere with us."

Rain says, "True. But the kids we're looking for aren't safe at all."

"You'll take care of Branwynne?" I ask.

"Sure an' all. We'll get her back ta the Tower."

"And we should get moving ourselves," Brohn says.

"Bollocks ta that. Come inside first. 'ave a rest. Take a breather. No sense caperin' off and gettin' killed on an empty stomach."

The offer is appealing, and we agree to take them up on it.

Comfort is a rare commodity these days.

And we know from experience that it never, *ever* lasts.

## 6

# VAUXHALL

LEDGE AND HARAH lead us past the stables and through the grand double-doors at the front of Kensington Palace.

The last time we were here, we went up a flight of stairs and nearly got killed in an all-red room. This time, Ledge takes us down a narrow, first-floor hallway that opens into a much nicer, much less red room.

"This is our conference room. Blokes from the Settlement what has a grievance come 'ere, an' we all work together ta get it fixed up, right and proper."

"So you need to get to…what was it? Valencia?" Harah asks.

His eyes wide with an excitement he seems to have been holding inside, Ledge tells us he knows someone. He eases into one of the two wide-backed chairs at the head of the table. "Her name's Elisa, but everyone calls her 'Croque Madame.' She's French, I think. Or Belgian. Maybe German? Who knows, eh? But she's been 'ere in Blighty for a good while now. Found a way to make a career of runnin' supplies back and forth. Dover and Folkestone. A bunch o' places in Spain. Part of a whole underground supply crew from what we've 'eard. All very hush-hush, so don't ask me what they do, exactly, or why."

Harah sits down next to Ledge and nods her agreement. "People who know too much around here, especially about the Emergent myths, tend to…disappear."

"We're not a myth," Brohn assures them.

Ledge laughs. "You kinda *were*, though."

"Until you showed up here and turned real before our eyes," Harah grins. She looks at Brohn but catches me glaring at her and wisely averts her eyes.

Terk leans forward. "So…Who is this Croque Madame person? Can we trust her?"

"As much as you kin trust anyone 'ere. She's a runner. One of a bunch. They specialize in dangerous goods. Contraband. Weapons. But you didn't hear it from us. She doesn't always make the trip, 'erself. Could be anyone. Drivers. Security. The works. They haul weapons an' lab equipment an' such down there. If you're lucky, maybe you can track 'er down, snag a ride."

"They start out o' Vauxhall," Harah says. "They take supplies, and then make their way south. Don't ask us how they survive. There's got to be a dozen checkpoints…"

"An' another dozen cliques an' clans o' scrappers, kill ya soon as look atcha."

"But this woman," Cardyn asks. "This…Croque Madame. She *does* survive, right?"

"So far."

"Last we 'eard."

"If she survives, we can, too," Terk says, his voice light with optimism.

"How far is it to Vauxhall?" Rain asks.

"About three or four miles," Harah sighs. "Wouldn't normally take more'n an hour or two. But I don't recommend takin' main roads."

She and Ledge exchange a mysterious look before Harah sighs again, deeper this time. "We both lost people 'tween 'ere and there. Scouting missions. Supply runs. Sometimes just searchin' for someone they mighta known. A few made it back, but what was left of 'em didn't last long."

"Scroungers," Ledge says. "Hawkers…"

"Going *anywhere* means takin' a chance," Harah warns us. "It's why we holed up in the palaces from the early days."

"I'm sorry we don't have more guards to send with you," Ledge apologizes. "It's gonna be 'ard enough makin' sure little Miss Branwynne 'ere gets back ta the tower."

"It's okay," Brohn says. "Taking chances is kind of our specialty."

Squirming in her seat, Branwynne pleads with us again to let her come with us. It's strange to see the girl who not so long ago helped liberate Buckingham Palace now tugging on Brohn's sleeve and begging him to let her join our Conspiracy.

Brohn reaches out, his strong hand heavy on her small shoulder. "Sorry. You're too young."

Rain agrees, although I can tell she's conflicted. "Your parents still need you. And you need them."

Branwynne's wet eyes bounce between Ledge and Harah. "But the Banters and the Royal Fort Knights are reunited. We don't have anything to worry about."

Ledge shakes his head. "The balance o' power just shifted right under our feet, an' the Mergies what made it 'appen, possibly the only ones powerful enough ta keep it from goin' south again, 'ave ta leave us ta fulfill a quest of their own. I'd say there's *plenty* ta worry about."

While Branwynne sulks low in her chair, her arms folded and her dark face in a brooding knot, Ledge and Harah agree to direct us to Croque Madame in the south end of London.

Ledge asks Lost-the-Plot to bring him the City Sketch Book.

Lost-the-Plot grunts up from his chair and lopes across the room. He opens a drawer in a wooden cabinet and comes back with a roll of wrinkled paper. He unfolds it on the table in front of Ledge and Harah, who proceed to show us an old-style, pencil-drawn map of the streets of London.

"Doesn't look like this anymore, of course," Ledge says, dragging his finger along the drawings of streets, laneways, and looping roundabouts. There are big red "Xs" scattered over the map. "Drop-a-Clanger drew this up for us a few years back. Got a funny good eye for maps, 'im." Ledge taps his finger on various parts of the dried paper. "Can't pass 'ere. Road's cratered out. Bridge'll be a bear. And over 'ere, Roguers've staked a claim. Cyst Plague hit 'ere, all 'round Lambeth. Probably not much ta worry about anymore after the quarantine, but I wouldn't take any chances. Be a shame ta get this far and get iced by a leftover bit o' the virus."

"I can get us there," Rain exclaims.

Ledge's eyebrow goes up. "How ya figure?"

"She calls it the Culling," Brohn explains. "Rain has the ability to see choices in her mind's eye. Helps with navigation."

"And makes it impossible to beat her at chess," Cardyn pouts.

Nodding with her eyes darting back and forth over the map, Rain swears she can get us to Croque Madame in Vauxhall. "After that, though, I can't make any promises."

Harah stands up. "You all should get some sleep before you head out."

"We've slept enough."

Terk rubs his hands together. "Brohn's right. It's time for action."

I wonder if he'd be saying that if he hadn't been unconscious while the rest of us were on our previous little misadventure through London.

Cardyn swings his head around, taking in the large, clean conference room. "I don't suppose we could crash here for the night. In the palace, I mean."

Ledge and Harah shake their heads aggressively in unison.

"No one stays 'ere," Ledge reminds us. "Ain't allowed. The palace is for meetings an' emergency purposes only."

Harah puts her hand on Ledge's forearm. "We spent the past five years building a system o' hierarchies we thought would keep us safe."

"Thanks to you and your Conspiracy, we've 'ad a change of 'eart."

"Turns out there's more safety in equality than in inequality."

Brohn nods. "That's um…a profound conclusion to come to."

"For a bunch of kids, right?" Lost-the-Plot snarls through a snarky squint.

"I wasn't going to say that. You've proven yourselves to be better at running things than the adults ever were," Brohn adds.

Mollified, Lost-the-Plot drops his combative grimace.

Ledge gives the tabletop a light slap with both hands as he stands up. "Come on. We'll take you to the East Gate. You can take your chances getting ta Vauxhall from there."

Ledge and Harah—flanked by Lost-the-Plot, Trolley, and Chunder—lead us out of the palace and through their compound.

It takes us nearly an hour on the network of winding paths to get from Kensington Palace to the East Gate.

From there, according to Ledge and Harah, it's likely to be a short but dangerous walk to Vauxhall where we're supposed to track down this Croque Madame person.

As we walk through the settlement, Terk and Rain greet the young Banters and Royals who skip up to us in droves.

Usually the most serious of our Conspiracy, Rain is having a blast as group after group of giggling Neos and Juvens inches closer to ask Terk if it's true he's a Modified. He pushes up the sleeve of his monk's robe to reveal the slender pistons, churning gears, and coiled circuitry of his left arm. The kids lean in but then go skittering away with peals of laughter when the Auditor talks.

A bunch of the older boys and a few of the girls seem

completely infatuated with Rain, who either doesn't notice or else doesn't care. While the Auditor talks, while Terk shows off, and while the younger kids dash and squeal, five or six of the Banters, blushing and wide-eyed, shuffle around Rain in a smitten, hypnotized orbit.

Not that it's any surprise. With her shimmering black hair, her lithe and nimble build, and her dark, penetrating eyes, she's probably about the prettiest girl I've ever seen.

Of course, Rain, always serious and focused, barely acknowledges her admirers, which seems to make them want to talk to her even more.

Meanwhile, Branwynne has finally left my side and is walking between Ledge and Harah. Render's perched on her shoulder and is enjoying having her stroke his feathers.

At one point, I hear Harah say she's sorry to Branwynne, but I can't make out what she's apologizing for.

Cardyn keeps Manthy company at the back of our procession.

I glance over my shoulder from time to time to check on them. Manthy doesn't notice me looking because she's got her eyes down. Cardyn doesn't notice me looking because he's got his eyes on Manthy.

In the middle of the pack, I whisper to Brohn that I'm not sure about something.

"About leaving here?"

I nod, but I can't explain where my reluctance is coming from. After all, we're a Conspiracy on a very specific mission. It's not really my place to second-guess Granden and the task he's laid out for us.

"Actually, I'm kind of with you," Brohn confesses. "I'm having doubts, myself."

My heart jumps up into my throat, and I take a quick look around to see who might be listening. "Should we not go?"

Brohn shakes his head. "I think you know the answer as well

as I do. If we stay, we can live out the rest of our lives with Ledge and Harah and all the Banters and Royals."

"But that's not where we belong," I sigh.

"No. And it's not where we were meant to be."

"You're going to say we were meant to save other Emergents, right?"

"You read my mind."

"Now, if only I could *change* it."

"And what would that accomplish? We'd stay here—"

"And be safe."

"But helpless, too."

"How do you mean?"

"Look, Kress. I have to admit, I'm just as anxious as you are to stop running. To stop traveling. To settle down and quit having to save the world. Hell, you've seen it out there. I'm not sure there's enough of it left to save. And who's to say that what's left is worth saving, anyway?"

"So let's do it. Let's stay here."

Brohn gives me a steely-eyed, furrowed-browed stare. "And give up on Wisp? And Granden and Kella? And what about the Insubordinates, the Survivalists, and the Unkindness? They're counting on us, too. Not to mention the Emergents who might be in the Processors being tortured like we were…or *worse*…even as we speak."

"No," I confess, my chin in my chest. "You're right. We have to do this."

Brohn throws his arm around me and pulls me close as we walk. "We don't *have* to do this. And we don't *need* to. We can tell Granden, Kella, and, okay…even Wisp, that we're out. That we're going to settle down here in London and live happily ever after in this adult-free, brutally hot and perpetually deadly paradise with the Banters and the Royals."

"But that's not an option, is it?"

"Giving up has never been an option for us. We took that off the table a long time ago."

"And that's why we're still alive, right?"

Brohn lets his eyes bounce from Ledge and Harah and to each member of our Conspiracy as we continue along the winding path through the compound. At last, he leans down to me, his voice warm and breathy in my ear. "We're still alive because we refuse to back down. Every obstacle is another opportunity for us to quit."

"But we don't quit."

"We're a Conspiracy. Our job is to resist the urge to quit and to make something meaningful happen in the world, instead."

"Fine," I sigh with a smile. "But promise me something."

"Anything."

"After this...after Valencia and the Processor and any Emergents we might find..."

"Yes?"

"And if we survive..."

"Yeah?"

"Tell me we can go home. Settle down. Get some rest."

Brohn's smile drops, and his features go stern as stone. "I can guarantee a lot, Kress..."

"But?"

"We don't really have a home to settle down in. Not anymore."

I hook my arm into his. "Then tell me we'll find one. Promise me we'll find somewhere...anywhere...we can call home."

Brohn crosses his heart and promises.

I breathe a sigh of relief and promise to hold him to it.

## 7

# FERAL

"This is it."

Ledge signals to the archers in the turret. One of the girls scans the outside of the compound through a pair of infra-red, range-finder binoculars. She gives Ledge a nod, and he tells the two boys by the crank and chain to open the huge door.

The shirtless boys drip sweat as they work the crank around and around until the reinforced gate swings open with a thunderous groan.

Ledge breaks with convention and thrusts a hand out at Brohn, who returns the hearty handshake.

"You stopped us without killin' us," Ledge says. "You stopped us from killin' you."

"Or each other," Harah adds.

"If you can do that..."

"You can do anything."

"We've run head-long into conflict wherever we've gone," Brohn says through a grim smile. "You're proof it's not inevitable. You're the proof that peace is possible."

Cardyn points a pretend menacing finger back and forth

between Ledge and Harah. "Just make sure it lasts. If we have to come back here…"

"We'll be 'ere together," Ledge assures him.

"To welcome you with open arms," Harah adds.

We say a round of goodbyes for the second time and hope it won't be the last time we see each other.

Right before we turn to leave, I lean over and throw my arms around Branwynne and hug her goodbye.

I just can't help it.

She squeezes me back before gazing at me with those eerie white-speckled black eyes of hers. "Someday, let's meet up on the other side, okay?"

"If I can figure out what it is, exactly, and how to get there," I whisper, "then, yes. I'll meet you on the other side."

With our weapons strapped on and our sights set on getting through this next leg of our travels, we step through the gates of Hyde Park and back out into the decimated city of London in search of a woman who might agree to take us deeper into danger.

We've been on the road for about half an hour when a wave of sadness sweeps through me.

Honestly, I don't know what upsets me more: the very real risk of getting killed or the horrible wasteland this once-great metropolis has become.

And these are only buildings and roads that have been destroyed. *Things* can be rebuilt. Replaced. Human life, though, once that's gone, it's gone for good.

Well, at least we thought so…until Manthy.

*What is it about her? There's something just a shade off. Like she's either almost herself or not quite what she used to be. What was it Branwynne said about going from here into some other version of here? I'm not sure what that means, but whatever it is, it almost feels like Manthy's done it.*

Overhead, Render banks and disappears behind the steep roof

of a soot-covered, five-story building with one of its sides blasted away.

I'm just about to try connecting with him when we pass by a gaping opening in the front of what must have been a pub at one point.

Inside, there's an overturned bar, a floor coated in shattered glass, and the crisp, black remnants of benches and tables lying in an entangled overlap at every imaginable angle.

Two bodies, barely recognizable as human, are hanging from the ceiling rafters. They're suspended two feet off the ground by lengths of thick black chains.

"Oh, God," I mutter.

Cardyn says, "What?" and I point to the horrific sight.

We all stop and stare. It'll be evening soon, but there's plenty of light at the moment to make out every detail.

The bodies belonged to kids, probably Branwynne's age by the look of what's left.

Their clothes and skin have disintegrated to the point where we can't tell which is which. A hint of skeletal bone peeks out from behind the last traces of their gaunt faces.

Brohn rushes over to put his hand on my back as I dash to the side and double over to spit up a thin trickle of vomit.

"It's okay," I tell him, wiping my mouth with my sleeve. "Just caught me by surprise."

"Good," Brohn says as he guides me back to the others, who are turning various shades of green, themselves, as they stare at the ghastly scene. "If we ever consider this *unsurprising...*"

He doesn't have to finish. I know being repulsed by the grotesque brutality of pointless violence is a *good* thing.

It's just a little embarrassing, especially after all we've been through, to lose my lunch over it.

Ignoring the smell and the generally shocking nature of the scene, Manthy drags her foot along the floor under the hanging bodies. With the toe of her boot, she pushes aside thick layers of wooden splinters and broken glass. She points down, and we follow her finger to where the word "MERGIES" is written in large, flaking black letters.

Rain kneels down and drags a fingertip through the letters. "Blood."

Terk's eyes drop at the corners, and he looks behind us toward the road like he's expecting the Patriot Army or the Hawkers or worse to come storming in.

Rain stands and brushes her hands on the sides of her checkered skirt before resting one hand on Terk's tree-trunk of a forearm. "Don't worry, Big Guy. Whoever did this is long gone."

"Whoever did this," Cardyn says, "is just as likely to try to do it to us."

Brohn pumps his hands and tells everyone to calm down. "This is scary. I get that. But remember, there are Emergents who are a lot deadlier than we are. For all we know, these kids could've been like Sheridyn. Or worse."

I can tell everyone's nervous, but Brohn's right, and I tell them so. "We've seen kids like Sheridyn up close and way too personal. Whoever did this might've been trying to stop the deadly ones from getting even deadlier. There are good Emergents and bad Emergents out there, after all."

Cardyn spits on the ground, turns on his heel, and starts walking back out toward the street. "You're assuming anyone'll bother to try to tell the difference."

Back outside, we follow Cardyn, who continues striding along the litter-strewn road we've been following.

Even though the image of the two dead kids is probably permanently burned into my brain, I'm finally able to take a breath and focus on where we're going.

"Is it just me," Cardyn asks, "but is leaving the safety of Hyde Park one of the dumber moves we've made in a while?"

"We can't save the world if we're not in it," I tell him.

"Good point. By the way, Kress…?"

"Yes?"

Cardyn directs our attention to the base of a collapsed bridge where a bunch of dark, slender animals are scavenging in a tight knot over what must be a fresh kill. "Who's going to save *us*?"

Terk stops in his tracks. "Is that...coyotes?"

Brohn frowns. "I don't think there's much animal life around here to kill."

"We'll, they're eating something."

"Those aren't coyotes," Rain mumbles.

"Then what are they?" Brohn asks.

"Kids."

I start to laugh but then look more closely as we pass the figures snuffling and scrounging in a crouched circle at the base of the collapsed bridge.

"Oh my God. Rain's right."

Cardyn turns halfway around and blinks hard. "I bet they're the ones who hung those kids up back there."

"Easy, Card," I say. "Let's not panic until we know there's something worth panicking about."

Terk steps forward and reaches out to Rain. "Should we help them?"

"How?"

"I don't know. We have weapons. A few supplies. Maybe we can offer them *something*."

"We have a mission," Rain reminds us. "We can't stop to risk our lives for everyone we come across."

I'm surprised when she's vetoed by Manthy of all people.

Diverging from her "I can't" refrain, Manthy says, "I can," and peels off from our group. Before any of us can stop her, she winds her way through a maze of bricks, broken concrete blocks, and around a tangled mass of rusted rebar.

The group of kids I thought were coyotes stops its rustling. There are a lot of them, younger than us, malnourished, and dressed in thin strips of mud-colored, crusted-over clothes. One at a time, like prey animals at a watering hole, they perk their heads up at Manthy's approach.

Cardyn sprints past us. "We've got to help her!"

In a moment of panic, I realize I don't know if Cardyn means we need to help her to help the kids or help her to not get *killed* by the kids.

Sprinting after Cardyn, who's sprinting after Manthy, Brohn shouts for me, Rain, and Terk to follow him, which we do.

We slide to a stop in a cluster at the base of the broken bridge. Manthy has one hand out toward the kids while she reaches into the small leather pouch on her belt. Inching forward, she extends her open hand to reveal a small mound of her share of our protein cubes.

For a moment, the sniffing, snuffling kids don't seem human. And for a moment, I feel a deep pang of sorrow for them.

The moment doesn't last long.

Instead of bolting away like prey or inching forward to accept Manthy's charity, they turn in a single motion as predators.

Moving as a coordinated pack, they leap at Manthy, who clearly wasn't expecting her good intentions to lead to her getting swarmed by the very kids she'd set out to help.

She shrieks and collapses as they pile on her.

In the same second, the rest of us sprint the remaining distance to help her.

Terk whips his Sig Sauer P320 out of the waistband under his billowing brown cloak, but Rain cries out, "No!" and smacks the gun down.

Terk's not the best shot, and I'm not sure if Rain is protecting Manthy or sparing the kids.

Either way, what looked like a minor confrontation has turned instantly deadly.

Like the two charred bodies we found a couple of blocks back, these kids can't be much older than Branwynne—maybe eleven or twelve-years-old—but they continue to pile on Manthy with the raw desperation of animals protecting one kill and intent on making another.

Brohn and Terk dive right into the middle of the snarling pack and start slinging the kids to the side.

Terk snags one of the Juvens—I think it's a girl—and tosses the slashing wild-child twenty feet through the air. She lands on top of a slanted pile of cement blocks with a shriek and rolls to the ground.

One of the kids clings to Brohn's back, but he has no problem reaching over his shoulder, snagging the thrashing boy by the scruff of his neck, and discuss-tossing him into the side door of a warped and stripped-to-its-bones mag-car.

I reach into my waistband for my gun, but Cardyn shoulders past me.

Accessing his Emergent persuasion abilities, he lets his eyes bounce from one feral kid to the next. With one hand raised, he calls out to the swarming Juvens. "There's enough enemies to go around. We don't need to be each other's."

Other than the kids looking angrier and deadlier than ever, nothing happens.

His jaw tense, his forehead in a knot, Cardyn tries again. "Only the human soul separates the survivors from the savage."

The feral kids regroup and turn their full attention to Cardyn. "They're too wild!" he cries out, stumbling backwards, away from the encroaching scavengers. "I can't reach them!"

In a single blur of motion, they leave Manthy writhing on the ground and scramble over the pockmarked ground toward me and Rain.

Their fingernails are pointed, hard, and sharp. My jacket is strong enough to keep me from getting shredded to ribbons, but they get a couple of glancing slashes in to my face and neck.

It's a small price to pay since it gives Brohn time to slide his arms under Manthy's legs and neck as he lifts her up and backpedals to safety.

"Safety" turns out to be fleeting.

With the kids pacing on the other side of a low concrete barrier and with our backs literally to the wall, a second group of kids—closer to our age and armed with clunky, wrist-mounted crossbows—emerges from around a corner.

## 8

## SCROUNGERS

B<small>ROHN</small> T<small>UGS</small> at the strap running across his chest. He doesn't unclip his arbalest, but he's definitely making sure this new batch of kids knows it's there.

Although we have guns on us, we know better than to use them here. Guns are strictly forbidden in London and one of a handful of things, so we've been told, that can get a person an instant death penalty.

I don't know who's responsible for leveling those charges, prosecuting violators, or punishing those convicted, and I'm not in a hurry to find out.

My talons—the gloves with five curved and serrated switch-blades built into each wrist guard—are in my satchel. I start to reach for them, but Manthy puts her hand on my forearm.

"Kress. Don't. It's okay."

I can feel my eyes go wide as I keep my attention riveted to the two combined groups—the coyote kids and this new batch of armed teenagers—in front of us. "Um, Manthy. How is *this* okay?"

"They're not going to hurt us."

"And you know this *how?*"

"Danger is either real or it isn't." Brushing back her tangle of auburn, sunkissed hair and looking me square in the eyes, Manthy puts one hand on my shoulder and points over at the scraggly band of new and potentially deadly enemies. "All we are is nightmares in each other's dreams."

"Damn it, Manth! Does that mean we should run or fight?"

"It means we should wake up."

Grunting her impatience at Manthy, Rain shoulders past her to face our foes. She reaches around to rest her fingertips on the gun tucked into the waistband of her skirt, but she doesn't take it out. She's got her dart-drivers on her wrists, but they're not loaded, and she doesn't make a move toward the quiver of arrows slung across her body. Instead, she takes a breath and addresses our adversaries. "Are you the ones they call Scroungers?"

The lead girl's face wrinkles, and the kids milling around her seem to bristle at the suggestion.

The girl raises her hand with the small crossbow attached to her wrist. It's a bigger, clunkier, and deadlier-looking version of the dart-drivers Rain has, and my heart jumps at the thought of one of my Conspiracy being shot before we've had a chance to get our bearings and defend ourselves.

The girl swings her arm around and squeezes her hand into a fist. A black bolt zings out of the crossbow and thunks to a quivering stop in an exposed wooden support beam protruding from a pile of bricks and concrete blocks about twenty feet away.

She gives us a gray-toothed grimace of disgust and spits on the ground. "We's Scroungers sure an' all but ain't skew-whiff scrumpers, us. We's gots inna *pride*, ain't us?"

A buzz and hum of agreement burbles from the other kids around her.

Combined, there are fifteen of them. Six coyote-kids–each nursing various injuries from our scuffle—and nine of this new, older group, all apparently led by the tall girl in front of us.

Her speech is garbled and rapid-fire. One of the only words I'm sure about is "pride."

Only I don't know if she means it like a pride of lions or like the vague sense of guilty pride you get from knowing you survived when so many others died.

I've known both versions.

Brohn puts his hands out, palms up and then pats the pockets of his jacket and combat pants. "We don't want any trouble. We don't have anything worth taking."

"We just need to find someone," Rain says into the darting yellow eyes watching our every move.

"A driver," Brohn explains. "Someone to get us to where we need to go."

"We heard we could find her somewhere around here," I add.

The girl steps forward. She's nearly as tall as Brohn, only very thin and with winding, noodle-y veins and ropey muscles running the length of her oddly long forearms.

She scowls down at Rain before swinging her eyes up to Brohn's.

He steps back when she reaches out to touch his face, but she presses forward until his jaw is cradled in her palm.

I remind myself to start keeping track of how many times his perfect, athletic body, deeply soulful eyes, and ridiculously magnetic good looks either get us into trouble or else out of it.

"You's the bangers we 'eard about, eh?" the tall girl says.

Stepping up next to her, a shorter girl with mangy tufts of hair poking up from her otherwise bald head, scans us up and down. She snaps her fingers twice, and four of the coyote-kids slink around to take up guard-dog positions behind us.

They're not armed, but we've seen them fight with a raw, animalistic abandon I know none of us wants any part of.

"'eard 'awkers was peekin' fer ya."

"How does everyone in this city seem to know so much about us?" Rain asks.

The two girls turn their attention to Rain, and I'm convinced they're going to attack her. Instead, the tall girl walks around her, scanning her up and down like Rain is some alien pod that just beamed down from outer space into the middle of the broken road.

Taking a step back, the tall girl points to herself. "Aussie."

The shorter girls says, "Mooch."

The tall girl, apparently named Aussie, points over to a short, stocky boy behind them. "L'il 'en dere's Dumplet."

"Um…nice to meet you?" I say.

"Nuffin' much nice left an' all, is it?"

"Council'll clinch what ta do witcha, them."

Behind her and responding to some invisible cue, three boys each raise a weapon—a jagged shard of sheet metal tied with wire to the handle end of a cricket bat—and start to edge their way around us.

Aussie instructs us to "Mush da lane 'n tally on," which I'm assuming means she wants us to follow her since she turns and strides through the parting crowd of kids and into the building behind them.

Actually, "building" might be a generous word for the place these kids seem to call home.

With the piles of rocks and fragments of what used to be walls, the space is more of a slant-walled cave than a building. There's no roof at all. Instead, two of the walls have collapsed against each other to form a kind of tall triangular space underneath.

Based on what's left of the square, black and white tiles, a long time ago, the structure might have been a barbershop or a foyer for a business or a lobby in a small hotel.

Despite not having a front wall, it's murky and dark inside. A line of what look like sleeping palettes have been set up along the perimeter of the room.

"Ugh," Cardyn whispers. "Smells like death took a dump in a landfill."

"Nice." I elbow him, and he says, "Ow," but at least that's *all* he says.

A large, graffiti-covered cube of solid stone sits in the middle of the floor under the steep, soaring walls.

The kids file in around us. A few of the ones in the back and around the edges keep slipping in and out of two dark doorways at the back of the room.

Aussie sits on the large square stone with Mooch standing behind her, her hands on Aussie's shoulders. Dumplet squats in front of the stone, his hands on the ground and his knees splayed out like a loyal dog waiting to be thrown a bone.

All of the kids are tangle-haired, snaggle-toothed, and nearly naked with only scraps and shreds of what looks like old jogging pants and plastic garbage bags tied around their chests and waists.

They speak English, but theirs is practically a different language from ours, and it takes a lot of head-scratching and concentration to figure out what they're saying.

Rattling off a series of questions, Aussie and Mooch talk after and over each other in a jumbled overlap none of us could possibly hope to follow.

The way their yellow eyes roam and with their tongues swollen in their mouths, I can't even tell for sure when they're talking to each other or to us.

"Banties, is ya now? Royal toffers, 'em?"

"Barkin' mad C o' E'ers, eh?"

"Bunch o' whingin' chabbies 'avin' a wobbler."

"An' us stupid cows 'ere left shambly arse over tit."

"Strip 'em an' peel 'em, us. Skin o' da big 'un mark a right proper bedsheet."

"Wait," I say. "Were you asking if we're Banters or Royals?"

Aussie and Mooch squint at me like I've just asked for permission to pee on the floor.

"We're not Banters or Royals!" Terk cries out from behind me.

"Forgive our large and very loud friend," I say. "But he's right. We're not Banters, and we're not Royals."

"We're American," Cardyn says, tapping his chest, although I can't tell if that quiver in his voice is fear, pride, or embarrassment.

"Ahhh…," Aussie drawls, standing up and turning on her heel to proclaim to her "pride" of Scroungers. "Them's Yanktopians. Krug Colonoscopies. Spit outta Broken Promiseland, them."

"An' 'ere ta take side fer sure an all," Mooch cries, her high-pitched voice hitting a frequency that actually hurts my ears.

"Banties an' Royals fight, don't they?" Aussie sneers.

Behind her, three of the boys each press their fingers to one nostril in unison and spew a spray of wet mucus to the ground.

"Jammy bastards, them. An' tight as a duck's arse."

"An' gormless us grizzin' in da mid."

"Fightin' an' bitin'—s'all them know."

"Wait. It's not like that," I insist. "Not anymore."

"The Banters and Royals are together now," Rain says. "No more fighting."

Brohn tells Aussie it's true. "They've made their peace."

"No war between them means you don't have to worry about being caught in the middle," I assure her.

Cardyn leaves Manthy's side to stand next to me. He points to Aussie and then at her entire crew. "Maybe you could join them?" At first, I think he's accessing his Persuasion abilities, but then I realize he's not. He's just trying to give these kids an option, a way out.

But Aussie sneers and holds up two fingers. "Tuppence the people, tuppence the power."

This girl is making me feel weirdly offended and defensive. "It's not like that," I nearly shout.

"Crock up, it ain't!"

"They want better lives for themselves. For everyone."

"What 'em gobbin' fat-cat affies say, always an' all."

"An' 'em tell it full from inner 'em stonker palaces an' snookered up, clamped-hand, tight an' tucked 'roundabout 'em 'yde Park walls, don't dey?"

The boys and girls around us growl and paw at the ground with their bare feet like bulls about to charge.

I can feel whatever chances of finding new friends fading fast. The tension in this dark and forsaken place just ramped up from a one to about an eight with a ten well on its way.

We've been in enough scrapes by now and faced enough people who want to kill us to know the signs when we see them: The beads of sweat. The tremble in the lips. The tremor in the voices. The tiny twitches in the hands as our adversaries reach for their weapons. The way a person's eyes narrow and their heels press into the ground when they're ready to pounce.

Fortunately, I'm not the only one who senses it.

From behind us, a black and gold blur plunges from the sky and rockets into the room, kicking up a cloud of dust between us and the advancing Scroungers, who cover their faces and scream at the sudden, explosive intrusion.

## 9

## DEAD

UNDER A SMALL CYCLONE of black feathers, Render alights on my outstretched arm. He leans toward Aussie and Mooch, ruffles his hackles, and barks out a chainsaw chorus of grinding clicks and clacks.

Startled, the Scroungers take a giant step back, their eyes frisbee-wide, their hands clamped hard over their ears.

I don't blame them.

Render loves to make an entrance, and this one is about as aggressive and grand as it gets. He's already big for a raven. With his thin strips of golden filaments and his unblinking, unforgiving black stare, he must seem positively immense.

In the murky shadows of this cramped space, he might as well be a pterodactyl.

With his beak open wide and his wings spread to nearly their full length, he belts out one more intimidating series of gurgling *kraas!*—a sound like a tiger shark chewing on aluminum siding underwater—before settling back onto my arm.

Two seconds ago, I was sure the Scroungers were about to have a go at us. Kind of a pre-emptive strike before we got a chance to do anything to them.

Which we had no intention of doing, of course.

Now, they seem frozen in place with the kids in the back half-turned, as if preparing to take off in terror in the opposite direction if necessary.

Regaining her composure after leaping back several feet, Aussie inches forward. She stabs a jagged-nailed finger toward Render. "No grub faffin' 'round dis un."

I run my finger along Render's smooth head and flight feathers and introduce him to the Scroungers. "This is Render."

Wringing her hands like she's trying to draw water from them and working hard to disguise a seriously visible case of the shakes, Aussie scrunches up her face. "Shouldna plowed 'im a name, ya. Probs call 'im fren fer a hasher, but ravens is horses fer courses, them."

Mooch tucks herself behind Aussie, her patchy head poking out from behind the taller girl's waist. "Worse'n other sulkers. No nesh about 'em, an' they ain't a-feared o' the brown bread."

Crouching next to Mooch, Dumplet shakes his equally patchy-haired head. "Naw. Them comb fer the bread. Fish n' pitch the bread, them."

Aussie nods. "*Gorge* on the bread."

Cardyn leans in to ask me what the hell they mean by "bread," but I cut him off with a single whispered word:

"Dead."

"Oh."

Ravens are famous for a lot of things.

In some North American aboriginal cultures, the raven is a mediator between life and death.

In the biblical story of the Great Flood, Noah sends a raven out to find land. The raven never returns so Noah sends a white dove, instead—the famous one that comes back with an olive branch in its beak. Some people think the raven didn't return because it was feasting on exposed human corpses as the flood waters receded.

In the Qur'an, it's a raven who gives Cain the idea for how to bury his murdered brother, Abel.

Then there's the old Nordic Viking legend of Ragnar Lothbrok whose hoisted and fluttering flag with the image of a raven emblazoned on it predicted victory in battle while the drooping of the raven flag promised suffering and death for Lothbrok's navy.

And, of course, right here in London—not too far on foot from where we are now—the six ravens of the Tower of London are supposedly responsible for the welfare and survival of the entire kingdom. If they go, "the Crown will fall and Britain with it."

The one common trait in nearly every story, legend, myth, experience, and black and white fact is that ravens and death, like happy little kids or reunited lovers, go hand in hand.

It's gruesome but also natural and normal, so my cheeks go defensively red when I square up to face Aussie. "Render's not like that. I mean, yes, he eats carrion. But he's one of us."

Aussie stares at me for so long, I'm not sure she understood what I said. But then she nods like she approves but frowns like she doesn't. "Then 'aps all o' yas got the raven problem, then."

"Raven problem?"

The tremble in her voice and hands is gone. Her words ring through the gloomy air as clear as clinking crystal. "Chance the lotta yas latched up hard n' fast ta da *dead*."

To my surprise, Aussie looks straight at Manthy when she says this. And I mean, a full-on, eye-to-eye stare down.

Obviously, there's no way in the world she could know about Manthy's recent return from the dead. Or how. Or why. But she looks at her like she does.

Next to me, Brohn's hand drops slowly from his chest where it's been hovering over the leather strap holding his arbalest in place.

Rain also drops her hands, and her shoulders relax.

Glancing back and forth between Aussie and the road outside, Terk raises his human hand. "So...um, can we go?"

Aussie laughs. At least, I *think* it's a laugh. Her young face goes wax-paper wrinkly, and she hacks out a gurgling cough that rivals one of Render's. "Sure 'n long as ya keep a keen eye on dis 'un 'ere." She points at Manthy, who doesn't seem to realize or care that she's being singled out. "An' best peep fer 'awkers, an 'em."

My head's spinning from spending the last ten minutes trying to decipher what Aussie's been saying with her slurred slang, stabbing hand gestures, and contorted facial expressions.

With Terk already back out on the road, the rest of us start to follow. Slowly.

Dumplet tilts his head like a feral dog trying to decide if we're competition, friends, or food.

Still in a crouch, he sniffs at the air. Then, he bounds out into the road next to Terk and points his finger to a spot in the distance.

"'ead ta da Oval," he barks.

Brohn turns back to Aussie and asks what that means.

"Oval," she says matter-of-factly. "Where'n ya scurry if yer on ta trundle."

"I think we're supposed to go that way," Terk says, tipping his head down the road in the direction Dumplet is still pointing.

Dumplet gives Terk an aggressive, nearly-neck-snapping nod. "Stay off o' Harleyford, though. Bad booze fer da gaul. Sinister. Dextral. A thirty-two-oh-four."

"What—?"

"He's giving us directions," Rain says as she steps into the road.

Dumplet bounces on all fours and tells Rain, "Yeah, yeah, yeah!"

Brohn, Cardyn, Manthy, and I join Terk and Rain on the road.

Rain shields her eyes with her hands and stares off into the smoldering distance.

Brohn asks her if she knows where we're supposed to go.

Rain tells him, "Yes. And I can get us there." She takes a long look out over the Thames and the red and yellow remnants of what used to a be a bridge. She turns back to Aussie. "If you can get us across."

Aussie pauses, and I get that sinking feeling again. What if Rain's overstepped her bounds? Asking for a favor from these Scroungers seems like a risky move, and I'm half-expecting the small colony of feral, incoherent kids to change their minds and turn on us at any second.

Instead, Aussie breaks into a yellow-toothed smile. She turns and directs a series of triumphant nods at the kids who have gathered around her in the road.

"See, an' yer ol' mates usefuller than the ol' guard." Turning back to Rain, she says, "Sure an' we 'ave a go crosswise."

Cardyn lets out a long, "Ummmm…"

"She's going to help us get across," Rain tells him.

"Oh. Why didn't she just say so?"

## 10

CROSSING

As we approach the rubble at the water's edge, the Auditor tells us about this being the first iron bridge to be built across the River Thames.

"Opened in 1906," she says, "the Vauxhall Bridge is a steel bridge, eight-hundred-nine feet long by eighty feet wide on top of granite piers and consisting of five arched spans." I smile to myself because I swear I hear a hint of pride in her voice about having such quick and thorough access to this kind of knowledge.

Cardyn's not impressed, though. "How can someone who knows so much be so incredibly useless?" he moans to no one in particular.

I've been debating about whether the Auditor is a mindless computer program or if she really possesses human elements and even the consciousness and personality of my mother.

I still don't have an answer, but when she says, "I was just trying to help" in a sad, barely audible voice, I feel terrible.

Cardyn might not be impressed, but what *is* impressive are the eight enormous bronze women—each at least ten or fifteen feet tall—standing on some kind of concrete pontoons in the middle of the river.

Lined up in two rows like pawns on a chessboard, four of the sculptures face upstream, four downstream, with the leftover mountain range of rubble that used to be a bridge running between them.

Aussie catches us gaping at the imposing bronze women with the rancid, debris-infested water oozing around their bases. She shoots us a smile so wide it makes her eyes squint down into nearly nothing.

"See ya see our scheme."

"Saw your...?"

"That then, there them's the Eight Lasses o' the Apocalypse. Tooken us an' all best nigh an a suncycle ta get 'em peeled off the span and barked upright an' uptight deep da Dark Smoothie."

I don't want to embarrass or enrage Aussie by confessing that I don't have any idea what she's talking about. Judging by the baffled looks on the faces of my Conspiracy, I'm not the only one.

Fortunately, the Auditor comes to our rescue.

"They're examples of Edwardian allegorical sculpture," she translates for us, her voice sheepish and slow. "They used to be ornamental additions affixed to the outside of the bridge. The Scroungers must have dislodged them and somehow planted them on those concrete pedestals in the river. An impressive feat of engineering, considering each one of the statues weighs about two tons." The Auditor pauses, and when no one interrupts, she adds, "The four upstream statues were designed and sculpted by F. W. Pomeroy. The four downstream by Alfred Drury."

Raising Terk's modified left arm, the Auditor points one at a time to the eight female figures standing like silent sentinels in the water.

"That's the Statue of Pottery," she tells us, directing our attention to the muscular female sculpture in robes, hand on her hip with a heavy-looking, two-handled pot pressed tight to her shoulder.

"That's the Statue of Engineering."

We follow Terk's synth-steel pincer to the cloaked female statue, her hand resting on the handle of a hammer, which is resting on top of an anvil. She's holding some sort of gear-box flat in one hand.

Next, the Auditor introduces us to the Statue of Architecture. This one has a compass in one hand and, lying flat in the other, a small version of St. Paul's Cathedral—a building I recognize all too well from our rescue of Lucid and Reverie and our harrowing escape from Noxia and the Hawkers.

When I tug at Rain's sleeve and point it out to her, she frowns, crosses her arms hard across her chest, and says, "Don't remind me."

"The last of Pomeroy's upstream sculptures is the Statue of Agriculture."

This one is a hooded woman with one arm curled around some kind of bundle—the Auditor clarifies that it's a sheaf of corn—and the other arm resting along the staff of a long-handled scythe.

Clearly amused now by the Auditor's knowledge, Cardyn laughs and challenges her, pointing to the other row of four female sculptures rising up from the murky river. "And how about those?"

One at a time—and sounding pleased at being asked—she calls out, "Those are the Statues of Education, Fine Arts, Science, and Government."

The first is a cloaked woman with her arm draped around a boy with a book while she cradles a small baby on her other shoulder.

The second is a female figure, also draped in a long cloak. She's holding a painter's palette in one hand. In the other, she's holding up a tiny figure, which the Auditor informs us is a statue of a female nude.

"Meta!" Cardyn gushes. "A statue holding a statue. Let me guess, the little statue is also holding an even littler statue, right?"

The Auditor says she doesn't think so, which makes Cardyn pout and hang his head. I think he had his heart set on seeing an infinite series of statues holding smaller and smaller statues.

The third sculpture—the one the Auditor said represented science—is turbaned, with braids framing her face on either side. She's holding a globe, which she's studying with her eyes as she traces its equator with her finger.

The fourth sculpture is of a woman clasping a book—the Auditor tells us it's a law book—and she's pointing with the other hand as if directing some invisible person to come closer.

"And these kids did all this?" Brohn asks.

Rain shakes her head. "They didn't sculpt those statues. I think they just relocated them from the bridge to the water."

"Still…," Brohn says, "it *is* impressive."

"As far as art installations go," I say, trying and failing to keep the sarcasm out of my voice. "But how do we get across?"

We're all standing there, staring out over the river, the mountainous, impassable span of concrete and steel, and the eight giant statues.

Aussie breaks from her fellow Scroungers and steps up to the entrance of what used to be a bridge. "I kin crisscross ya roundwise."

Terk nudges Rain. "She can get us across."

"I got that," Rain sneers. "But how?"

"Model me," Aussie barks and then leaps from the road onto one of the twisted orange beams rising up from a pile of blistered-black concrete.

One at a time, we follow Aussie, who leads us—skipping and hopping in Billy goat leaps—over the treacherous, half-submerged ridges of distorted steel and buckled asphalt.

It's easy for Rain to keep up. She's light, fast, and strong. Plus, her Culling enables her to make the right choices when it comes to finding the best handholds and footholds.

For me, I'm plugged into Render, so I can practically fly along. *Practically.*

Brohn is strong enough to stay close to Aussie.

Terk is struggling. His Modified gripper of a left hand is good for stability and clamping onto things. But his size, weight, and obvious sense of terror at falling into the brackish, toxic water is clearly holding him back.

Oddly, Manthy is, struggling, too. She's hesitant and keeps falling farther behind. When I turn around, she's hugging a bent black railing and staring down at the churning, polluted water.

"Cardyn," I call back. "Help her!"

Cardyn blushes, and the muscles in his neck tighten—a sure sign he's embarrassed at having accidentally left Manthy behind.

He tries to backtrack, but I can see from here how dangerous that's going to be. It's been hard enough crossing this far. Without Aussie's help on this horizontal rock-climb, I'm pretty sure at least two or three of us would've slipped off and drowned by now.

Render streaks overhead, offering a useless strain of impatient clicks and clucks. He banks around and alights on a steel strut protruding from a thick concrete slab.

I feel him sever his connection with me.

No. That's not it. He doesn't sever it. He *shares* it.

From behind Cardyn, Manthy lifts her head and releases her vice grip on the black railing.

With a deft skip and a series of confident bounds, she glides from one part of the wrecked bridge to the next until she lands on the narrow edge of a steeply angled girder.

She drops down into a gap and disappears for a second before clambering up a cliff of broken concrete and reappearing next to Cardyn.

Seeing she's safe, I exhale enough air to fill a parade balloon.

Startled by her sudden burst of dexterity, Cardyn reaches out to offer her a hand. She's already next to him on a pretty flat part of the bridge, but she accepts his offer, and he draws her further onto a wobbly but relatively safe span of yellow steel.

Without a word, I watch as she skims past him and alights, light as a bird, next to Terk, who looks like he's two seconds away from giving up, falling in, and letting the brownish-red water sweep him away.

Cardyn catches up to her, and the two of them help Terk the rest of the way across.

It takes some coaxing, goading, and some serious heavy lifting, but they manage to help get our giant friend safely over to a solid spot next to me.

"How…?" Cardyn pants, his hands on his knees while Terk gushes his thanks to Manthy.

"We're connected," she tells them—her voice clear and infused with a hint of exasperation—as she edges past me. "We're all connected."

I don't know if she means me, her, and Render. Or our Conspiracy. Or if she's talking about everyone in the world.

I don't have time to ask, one way or the other.

Through cupped hands, Brohn shouts out, "Come on, slow-pokes" and leaps the final ten-foot gap to land on solid ground on the far side of the river.

He stands next to Aussie and Rain, and the three of them urge the rest of us over the last stretch of rubble.

With me in the lead and with Cardyn and Manthy helping Terk inch his way along the last thirty feet, we get to the final part of the crossing.

One by one, we leap over the burbling water to land on the far side.

I can't speak for the others, but I'm a shaking mess.

"On yer way, den," Aussie says with a two-handed shooing

motion. Laughing, she points back across the water and over the broken bridge at her fellow Scroungers who are watching us and waving from the far side. "Scuttle off a-for the wee bairns borque der brains an' 'ave anover go atcha."

Understanding the Scroungers may be a challenge, but there are certain expressions and tones of voice that I think transcend language and culture.

"Get the hell out of here," is one of them.

It seems like good and timely advice, so we say our goodbyes and take it.

## OVAL

Aussie leaps back onto the bridge and begins clambering her way back across the River Thames.

When she's far enough away to be out of earshot, Brohn points out how useless her advice is about watching out for Hawkers. "Hakwers, Roguers, Scroungers…does it really matter? It seems pretty much everyone around here is dead set on killing us."

I agree. "The only advice should be, 'Watch out for everyone, don't go to sleep, and never go anywhere unarmed."

"And don't let anyone know you're an Emergent," Brohn laughs. "For us, the whole world could be the enemy."

Walking along and catching our breath after our harrowing crossing of the river, it's Cardyn who reminds us that we could have said the same about the Banters and the Royal Fort Knights not so long ago, but they wound up being allies.

Brohn shrugs and says, "I guess," but I can tell he's not ready to drop his guard just yet. And it's a good thing, too. His "guard" has kept us alive too many times to count. If it hadn't been for Noxia's influence back in Buckingham Palace, I'm sure he would have single-handedly battled us out of there, too.

I slip my hand into his. He gives it a little squeeze. It's a moment that probably doesn't mean much to him, but it means the world to me.

Following Rain with our eyes peeled for anything or anyone else that might decide to leap out at us, Brohn and I are chatting away about how good it feels to not give up on strangers, or on each other for that matter.

He flicks his thumb back the way we came. "Seriously. Did you understand a word those Scroungers were saying?"

"I understood enough," I laugh. "I wonder if they had as much trouble understanding us?"

"Well, Render definitely has a way of making *his* intentions known."

"That he does. That he does," I giggle but then something more serious occurs to me. "Speaking of Render, can I tell you something weird that happened back there?"

"Weirder than our run-in with the Scroungers?"

I give Brohn's shoulder a playful whack. "Yes, silly. Weirder than that. You know how Render and I connect?"

"Sure."

"He connected with Manthy."

"When?"

"Just now. On the bridge."

"That's not..."

"I know. It shouldn't be possible." I run my hand along my forearm implants. "The connections my dad gave me—they're supposed to be specific to me and Render."

"And you're a hundred percent sure Render and Manthy..."

"Yeah. I'm sure."

Brohn glances back to where Manthy has drifted off to the side of the road and is padding along like a grumpy old bear. "Did you ask her about it?"

"She said we're *all* connected."

Sweeping his hand around to take in our entire Conspiracy, he asks, "All of us, as in, the three of you or as in the six of us?"

"That's what I was wondering. Or did she mean everyone in the world?"

"I think dying did something to her, Kress. Something weird."

"I think so, too. Do you think she'll be okay?"

I'm serious, so I'm surprised and a little embarrassed when Brohn laughs. "I think Manthy'll be way more than 'okay.' Honestly? I think she has the power to save the world."

I look Brohn straight in his playful, sparkling blue eyes, but I can't tell if he's joking, exaggerating, or being dead serious.

A few steps ahead of us, Terk and Rain are guiding us under the shadows of a row of soot-covered, windowless buildings. Like the rest of London, this neighborhood looks like it's had an old, very full ashtray dumped on top of it.

Rain pauses at the opening of a small side street but then continues marching us along the main road.

Terk says it's eerie how few adults there are, and Rain guesses it's partly because of the Cyst Plague.

"Grizzy told me the other day about how kids didn't get nearly as sick as the adults."

Terk points to the crumbling, hollowed out structures looming around us. "I guess it serves them right. The adults, I mean. They built all this. Then they blew it all up."

"Not every adult is evil," Rain reminds him. "Despite how it feels, there are way more saints than sinners. Our parents didn't deserve this."

Terk hangs his head a little, but he's soon back to prodding Rain into friendly banter about everything from the morality of killing in survival situations to how good real food is going to taste when we accomplish our mission and get back to D.C.

Since our run-in with the Scroungers, they've been chatting practically non-stop, and even the Auditor's been chiming in from time to time to answer our questions or to offer suggestions of her own about which of the skimpy roadside weeds are edible and which ones are likely to kill us.

And since the Scroungers' warning about Hawkers, Cardyn's been especially twitchy. Every movement, shadow, or mild breeze causes him to whip around.

Brohn tells him not to be so paranoid.

"Just cause I'm paranoid doesn't mean we're not being followed."

With so many of the buildings around here crushed and emptied out, there aren't a ton of places for Hawkers to hide.

That doesn't stop us from being scared. And wary. Especially now that Cardyn's gloomy comment has kind of put us on edge.

Careful to avoid the craters and the unexploded ordnance we pass from time to time, we walk down the center of a road that seems way too open and wide for safety.

Here and there, the husks of so-called Eastern Order drones lie off-kilter amid the rubble.

At one point, Terk picks one of them up. He holds it up to his eyes with his mechanical hand and mutters something I can't hear.

The drone is different than the ones we used to run from in the Valta. Those were bigger and clunkier.

This one, even though it's been blasted out of shape, is sleeker and more streamlined, like a silver wine bottle with two pairs of armored wings on either side.

Terk gives a grunt of disgust and hurls the drone overhand, sending it spiraling through the air. It crashes with a tinny bang into the charred shell of an old mag-car sitting on its side.

Brohn tells him to take it easy. "We don't need to attract any more attention than we already have."

"I hate the um...anonymity," Terk says. "Drones. Guns." He unclips his flail from the shoulder strap. "Even these things. Weapons just create so much..."

"So much what?"

"I don't know. Distance?"

"I suppose you'd prefer a good ol' fashioned bare-knuckles brawl?"

Terk holds up his human hand in a loose fist. "Technically, I've only got five knuckles to work with. Honestly, though, I'd prefer not to have to fight at all. I guess I just wish it wasn't so easy."

"There's nothing easy about any of this," Rain tells him.

But Terk says he disagrees. "Pulling a trigger's the easiest thing in the world. That's why so many people do it."

"We only fight to survive," Rain snaps back. "We didn't cause all this, and we sure as hell can't cure it."

"Do you think things'll ever be better?" Terks asks.

I can tell he wants Rain to offer him up a reassuring, "Yes," but she doesn't. Instead, she kicks aside a bunch of dried slags of melted plastic—I think they might have been toys or doll houses at one time—and says, "Peace comes at a high price."

"Peace is worth fighting for," I say before realizing how little sense that makes.

Rain and Terk slip back into the lead, with me and Brohn in the back and Cardyn and Manthy in the middle.

"We're close," Rain calls back.

"Close to what?" I mutter to Brohn.

He answers with a squeeze of my hand in his.

We all step out of the shadows of the laneway and follow Rain down a meandering path that ends in a huge ring of rubble.

The barricade is high, higher than the makeshift walls around the Hyde Park Settlement. They're also mostly concrete, synth-steel struts, splintered wood beams, and a massive network of rusted steel supports.

The towering mass of rubble stretches into the distance in either direction in a long, curved arc.

Terk approaches the wall of rubble and presses his human hand to the giant slab of stone rising up like an ancient monolith amid the packed collection of rocks, cinder blocks, and bricks.

He looks up and shakes his head. "No way we can get over this thing."

Cardyn kneels down next to him, peering into the tiny cracks and crevices between the truck-sized chunks of concrete and the ridged, rusted shafts of exposed rebar. "No way under or through."

"Let's go around," I suggest, taking the lead and walking ahead of the others.

On high alert, we follow the curve of the wall. I'm sure there's no way to get to the other side of it, and I'm just about to say so out loud when I notice a shaft of light up ahead.

"Hey!" I call back. "I think I see an opening!"

The others gather around. Sure enough, there's a gap between two stone pillars.

"It's not much," I say, leaning into the narrow opening with my head and shoulders, "but I think we can squeeze through."

Cardyn claps a hand onto Terk's shoulder. "If Big Guy here can get through, then all of us can. I say we let him go first."

"You just don't want to go first and risk getting killed on the other side," Terk says.

"That's not true!" Cardyn objects, his fists on his hips. "I don't want to go *second*, either."

Terk grins and pushes Cardyn hard enough to knock him back two full steps. "Outta the way, shrimp. I've got this."

Squeezing and grunting his way along, Terk leads us through the opening, and the six of us finally wedge our way out into a vast field of…nothing.

Cardyn stops next to Rain, his chin cradled in his hand. "Um…"

Now inside, we see how the endless exterior wall encloses a huge oval arena of dusty-gray dirt. There's no checkpoint. No plants. No people. No rubble. No sign of life. Not even a sign of death, for that matter. It's like someone flew over top of the massive stadium and filled the flat, sprawling space with a thin layer of coarse sand.

"Weird," Brohn says, his hand extended in front of him, his eyes on the ground. "There's not even any shadows."

"Hm. That *is* weird," I agree.

Terk leans low, his face next to Rain's. "You're sure your Culling thing is turned on?"

"It's not a viz-screen," Rain smirks. "It's a *feeling* that guides me and narrows choices for me."

Terk says he gets that but then frowns. "Did the feeling tell you why it guided you to an empty, walled-off desert?"

"Knock it off," Brohn says. "If Rain led us here, it was for a reason."

Manthy puts her hand up and spreads her fingers wide, pressing her palm to the air like she's touching a pane of glass. "It's the right place."

"For what?" Cardyn asks. "A three-on-three game of beach volleyball?"

"There's a Veiled Refractor."

Cardyn's eyes get big. "Really? Like the ones Granden and Wisp installed in D.C.?"

Manthy nods. "I can feel its distortions."

"Can we turn it off somehow?" I ask, pivoting in a small circle as I look for some kind of device that might confirm Manthy's claim.

"No."

"Then how do we—?"

"It's okay," Manthy says evenly. "I can see."

Before any of us has a chance to press her further, Manthy is striding out onto the open space. Only, she doesn't walk in a straight line. She turns, curves, and curls around what must be invisible objects.

It's like she's walking through a maze with walls only she can see.

"Stay close," she calls back.

We don't argue, and I'm hoping Terk and Cardyn's banter about getting killed in here doesn't turn out to be prophetic.

In the weird and total stillness, our boots sound thumpy against the hard layer of packed-down sand.

I tug Brohn's sleeve and draw him down so I can whisper in his ear. "Do you think Manthy's…?"

"A misunderstood genius who knows exactly what she's doing?" he whispers back.

"I was going to say, 'going batcrap crazy.' But sure. Let's go with 'misunderstood genius.'"

Brohn chuckles. Then, without a word, Manthy comes to a sudden stop, with the five of us scrunched up behind her.

A tall glass door, its edges framed with piercing white light, appears from nowhere and slides open in the middle of all the nothingness around us.

Two young men leap out from the doorway, their faces tight with rage, their long-handled broadswords leveled at us.

## CROQUE MADAME

STARTLED, the six of us spring back into a defensive cluster.

A woman strides out of the doorway-to-nowhere and plants herself between the two young men.

Brimming with confidence, like she has *us* outnumbered, the woman stomps forward, her hands clamped into tight fists on her hips. "You've got to the count of one."

Most of us are too stunned to talk. Fortunately, Cardyn's never had that problem.

"We're a Conspiracy," he explains with a rapid-fire burst of exhalations. "We're on a rescue mission. We need transportation. Some people told us we could find help around here."

The woman squints at Cardyn. "People?"

"Ledge. Harah."

The tension in the woman's face loosens a bit, but the two men flanking her keep their swords pointed straight at us.

"Banters and Royals," she nods. "Rumor is they've kissed and made up."

"It's not a rumor," Brohn says, finally finding his voice. "We were there."

"Then you must be rumor number two."

83

"Rumor number two?"

"We heard a batch of kids—maybe even been Mergies—flew in from overseas, riled everything up—"

"We didn't—" I start to say, but the woman cuts me off with an open palm and an icy glare.

"Riled everything up...but then settled things back down again, nicer and neater than before."

Terk pats his chest. "That last part was *definitely* us."

The woman's eyes dart side to side, and the two young men lower their swords, but only part way, and they don't sheath them.

The woman asks Brohn who our shy friend is in the back.

"That's Manthy. I'm Brohn." He gives a half-turn and introduces the rest of us. "Kress. Cardyn. Rain. Terk."

He's about to add the Auditor to the list of intros, but he stops himself.

The woman points to a black spot, cutting a looping circle over us in the sky. "And him?"

"That's Render," I explain. "He's waiting to see if we need help."

The woman nods. "Then you're the Conspiracy I've been hearing about."

"We are."

"Thought you went home."

"We have a mission first."

"I see."

"Are you...?"

"The 'transportation' you heard about? Possibly." The woman gives us a little bow. "They call me 'Croque Madame.'"

"A toasted ham and cheese sandwich topped with a lightly-fried egg."

The woman and the two young men tense up and leap back at the sound of the Auditor's voice.

"What the hell was that?" the shorter boy says, his sword leveled at us but shaking.

Terk turns and lowers his shoulder, gesturing to his back with his thumb. "It's the Auditor," he explains to Croque Madame and the two startled guards.

"I'm an algorithmic techno-consciousness," her voice hums.

Croque Madame makes a circling motion in the air with her finger, and Terk complies by turning around and hiking up his long brown robe.

Glancing at his exposed back and torso, Croque Madame clicks her tongue at the sight of Terk's Modified parts and at the black disk shimmering in liquid-like waves on his back. "And you can talk?" she asks the disk.

The Auditor laughs—a sound I'm still not used to hearing coming from a sophisticated assembly of neuro-digital pathways. "Just because I don't have a mouth, tongue, lips, or larynx doesn't mean I can't talk."

"It damn well *should*," Croque Madame mutters. "And you know my nickname?"

"I know where your nickname comes from."

"Why?" Cardyn asks, looking back and forth between Croque Madame and the Auditor. "What's a croque madame?"

"I told you," the Auditor says with a sigh of exasperation at Cardyn for not paying attention. "It's a toasted ham and cheese sandwich topped with a lightly-fried egg. They used to be quite popular here. Kress's father and I used to get them for lunch when we traveled to France. But, of course, that was a long time ago."

Croque Madame squints at the disk. "You and Kress's father? What *are* you, exactly?"

"I told you. I'm an algorithmic techno-consciousness. Sometimes called a Techno-human. I'm basically an imprint of Kress's mother working as a collective self-aware entity along with several digital networks."

Croque Madame stares for a long time, and I'm tempted to snap my fingers in front of her face. But she breaks out of her daze and chuckles. "Then I guess it's nice to meet you. I'm Croque Madame. Like the sandwich you and Kress's father used to enjoy."

Unfortunately, it's clear where her nickname comes from. Her bald head is pale as an egg-white and speckled with hundreds of raised, peppery-looking freckles. Her jawline is rimmed with a pink, ear-to-ear scar, and she has a swollen, yolk-yellow mole the size of a shot glass jutting out from the middle of her forehead.

My parents may have enjoyed the sandwich she's named after, but this stout woman doesn't exactly look appetizing.

Somehow, though, her teeth are huge and glistening white, and there's something oddly gorgeous about her. Maybe it's her crisp voice. Or the light way she carries her stocky body. Or that weirdly fluorescent smile.

"What *is* this place?" Cardyn asks. He glances back at the empty field Manthy led us through.

Croque Madame tells us to give her a second so she can show us where we are and then slips back through the halo-edged doorway.

I tell Brohn in a side-whisper that I like her teeth, but he whispers back, "I don't think they're real."

The two young men stand at ramrod attention, staring over our heads like we're not even there. I have to admire their self-control. Most people we've run into would either be afraid of us or, more likely, happy to kill us.

Looking past them, I catch a glimpse inside the open doorway. Inside, it's airy and as sparkling clean as an operating room.

Before I have time to process this, Croque Madame bounds back out.

Although she's shorter than I am and nearly as wide as she is tall, she moves with soft, cat-like quickness.

She says, "All done," and an electric buzz rippling through the air causes all of us to whip around.

With the Veiled Refractor off now…we see an expansive parking lot with a dozen, single-story buildings in the middle and a fleet of transport vehicles—mag-trans and gas trucks—along with a fleet of old-style cantaloupe-colored school buses—some rusted out but a few that look brand new—parked in even rows.

Cardyn exhales. "Marvie."

Equally impressed, Brohn asks, "How'd you manage all this?"

"We were lucky to have the tech we do," she explains. "When we got word the Eastern Order was targeting London, a bunch of us hunkered down here. Ellis, the facilities manager who ran the Oval, had family—some rich uncles or something—that owned a tech firm up in Camden. They set us up with the Refractor. Kept us off the radar."

"Are they still here?" Rain asks. "I'd love to talk to them about the technology."

"No one left to meet. Ellis heard his family got hit in one of the first drone strikes. He left to help. Threw his kids in a company mag-car and took off. Never heard from him again."

She directs the two young men to stand down and return to their posts. They give her military style salutes before slipping through the doorway into the spotless room on the other side. The door slides shut behind them, and Croque Madame calls for us to follow her out into the parking lot.

Cardyn's eyes scan the open sky above us. "What about drones? Without the Refractor, anyone up there can see us."

"Don't worry," Croque Madame assures us. "The upper dome level of the Refractor is still engaged. The external ring, too. All anyone outside the Oval will see is one big, boring field of dirt and sand. Now come along."

"What did you do? Before the war I mean?" I ask as we follow her deeper into the giant lot of vehicles and small, square buildings.

"You may find this hard to believe," she grins as we stop in front of one of the whale-sized vehicles, "but I used to drive a bus."

She slaps her hand onto its steel side. "This is mine."

Brohn steps forward. "Listen. Do you think you might be willing to—"

"Give you a ride?"

Croque Madame grins her immaculately white smile. "Depends on when and what for."

"There's a Processor in Valencia, Spain," I explain. "There are Juvens there—kids. Ones like us."

"You're talking about one of those prison-labs, right? Like the one they had here up in St. Paul's."

"Yes. Only our sources say the one we're trying to get to is still operating."

"Valencia, Spain you say?"

We all nod in unison.

"I know the one you mean. I've seen it, myself."

"You have?"

"And it's more than just 'operating.'" We all stare at her, waiting for her to continue. After taking a breath, she does. "At least as of around two years back when I was down there last. It's probably the most heavily-guarded and secure facility in the Western Bloc. I stopped making runs there, though. Too dangerous. Too risky."

Cardyn flicks his thumb back and forth between Brohn and Rain. "Trust me. 'Risk' and 'Danger' are their code names."

"Don't listen to him," Brohn says. "'Annoying' is *his* code name."

"There's a lot of folks between here and there that'd kill us all as soon as look at us. Roguers. Hawkers. Scroungers. Execs. The Eastern Order."

Croque Madame looks skeptical when Rain tells her defiantly, "We don't worry about the Order."

"That so?"

"Absolutely," I tell her, hoping she doesn't press us further. Until we know more about how the Order worked here and who was behind them, it's not a topic we're eager to get into.

"And the rest of 'em?" Croque Madame asks. "Roguers? Hawkers? Scroungers? Execs?"

"We haven't met Roguers," Brohn tells her. "We've escaped Hawkers. We don't know the Execs. And the Scroungers turned out to be kind of friendly. After they attacked us, anyway."

Now Croque Madame looks *beyond* skeptical, and I can tell she thinks Brohn's lying.

"It's true," I insist. "Aussie just helped us get across Vauxhall Bridge."

Her eyes bounce from one of us to the next before locking onto Brohn. "Valencia, Spain, the Processor…it's not an easy place to get to," Croque Madame warns. "Not anymore. Not by a long shot."

"We know how to travel," Brohn assures her.

"And you really want me to take you through places a lot worse than this so you can free a bunch of kids from a government prison?"

"Yes."

"Yes, *please*," Cardyn chimes in.

Croque Madame surveys us once, then twice, and finally, a third time before she finally breaks into another glistening smile that stretches across the entirety of her scarred, heavily-freckled face. "Sure. Why not? I could use the company. And if those unruly Scrounger critters let you live, you must be doing *something* right." She pauses to wipe her forehead with a white cloth she pulls from her back pocket. "And it's true that it's kids you're trying to save?"

"Kids," Brohn confirms. "Probably younger than us."

"They're being held in that Processor," Rain says.

"We were taken to one when we turned seventeen," I add.

Croque Madame squints at me. "What are they for, anyway? The Processors."

"Good question. We *thought* it was to train us."

"Which they did," Rain says.

"We got trained in weapons, unarmed combat, battle scenarios, and military tactics," Cardyn brags.

Croque Madame starts walking around the bus, and we follow. "Sounds like a decent set of skills to have."

"Sure," Brohn agrees. "Only we were being sorted out so they could use us against our own people, study the ones of us who showed special abilities, and kill whoever was left over."

"Special abilities?"

"We're Emergents, as you know."

"So it's true…"

"We're real," Brohn confirms with a nod.

"I've heard the stories. Heard Mergies might've been leading the Eastern Order attacks."

"Unfortunately, that part might've been true."

Croque Madame stops and gives us a wary stare. "You don't say."

"There's a type of Emergent called Hypnagogics," Brohn explains. "They wound up being more powerful than us. They were enhanced somehow. They got turned into weapons."

Croque Madame kneels down and reaches under the bus, her cheek pressed to its metal side. She stands back up and brushes her hands on her pants. "And these were all kids, you say?"

"Yes. Some of us had certain abilities. Just minor things. Kress could communicate with Render early on. But something happened when we turned seventeen."

"We still don't know what," Rain says.

"Or why," I add.

"But it's other kids like us we're trying to track down," Brohn tells her. "According to Granden—he's kind of our general back home—there could still be as many as five or six Processors in operation."

Rain holds up four fingers on each hand. "And if each Processor has eight kids imprisoned like ours did…"

Croque Madame nods as she kicks a clump of brittle red dirt from one of the bus's back tires. "That's close to fifty kids like you they could be turning into weapons."

"There's so much that's been lost," Rain says, her voice laced with equal parts sorrow and insistence. "There are powerful, greedy people out there who are dead-set on making sure they control what's left."

Her arms folded across her round belly, Croque Madame leans back against the bus, her eyes scanning us back and forth. I'm wondering if she believes us. Maybe she thinks we're crazy. Or making it all up. Or maybe she's just unsure where her eyes should settle. We are a pretty odd-looking bunch, after all.

"Never had kids, myself. My old man and me, we kicked that can down the road until it finally disappeared in the distance." She pats the side of the bus with the flat of her hand. It makes a hollow, metallic noise like a steel drum in the otherwise cemetery-still air. "This old girl and I've been together a long time. I lost count of how many kids sat back there on their way to and from school. Those sweet little cherubs never cared one way or the other about anything except what they were doing and thinking at that exact moment."

I smile at the thought, but she brings me back down to earth with her solemn reminder. "Of course, those kids are all dead now."

Brohn steps forward. "We can't guarantee more kids won't die. But we *can* guarantee the ones in Valencia who can't be weaponized will be killed if we don't get to them before it's too late."

"I wasn't planning on making a run until next month. On the

other hand, this old girl's already powered up and loaded. And it sounds like a month might be thirty days too long."

"We don't know what we'll find. But we know how the Processors run. And we know time matters. Granden's intel says we're down to a matter of days. From this point on, every day... every hour...gets those kids one step closer to being programmed to kill or else get killed, themselves."

"I waited too long to have kids of my own. Better not waste any time helping you to save someone else's." Croque Madame taps an input panel on the side of the bus and scans through the scrolling field of green text in the air in front of her. "Inventory's good. Supply bins are already packed up. Power cell's charged." She pivots and steps up through the open door onto the bus.

A second later, she pokes her head back out.

"Well? What are you waiting for? You're not going to save the world standing there with your mouths hanging open."

## 13

## SPYING

TERK RAISES HIS HUMAN HAND. "You mean you want us to go right now?"

Croque Madame sticks her head back out of the bus. "You said it was urgent, right?"

Brohn nods.

"And the lives of those kids depend on you getting there sooner rather than later, right?"

Brohn nods again. "And maybe a lot more lives than theirs."

"Then it seems to me we're wasting time and risking lives hanging around here chatting it up like a clutch of biddy old gossips."

"You're sure this is okay?" Brohn asks. "We can just leave like this?"

"Sure. My crew'll reactivate the Interior Refractor once we're outside the Oval."

She taps a small silver button on the cuff of her oversized military jacket, and a holo-image appears of one of the two young men who first leveled their swords at us.

"Jakob. I'm going to make the Spain run."

"Right now?"

"Unless you have a better offer?"

"Best o' the British to ya, Madame."

Croque Madame taps the silver button again, and Jakob's image pixilates away. She gestures toward the open door of the bus. "Well…on ya go."

"That's it?" I ask. "We can go, just like that?"

"How else would you like to go?" she beams back at me with her toothy, glistening grin.

Rain darts her eyes from Croque Madame and out in the general direction of the huge parking lot with all its smaller kiosks, charging stations, and buildings. "Don't you want to at least, you know, say bye to those guys back there?"

"There are four other drivers like me in the Oval. And there are sixteen of those boys in this facility and twelve girls, none of them much older than you all. And we come and go and do what we can to get supplies to the folks who need them most. But we never say 'Goodbye.'"

When I ask her why not, she tells us, "It's bad luck and an invitation for Fate to make it the last word of your life."

We all turn to Brohn, who stares, squinting up into the air. "Okay. So here we are. An opportunity to launch this mission into high-gear just landed in our laps. Anyone want to let it fall to the floor?"

Cardyn mimics Brohn's squinting stare before giving a vigorous nod. "Stay here under the safety of a Veiled Refractor or ride a school bus into mortal danger with a woman we just met?" He takes a dramatic pause and then marches with high knees and clompy steps up the stairs and into the bus.

Brohn settles any last doubt we might have with a rich, baritone laugh. "I think Cardyn and Croque Madame have spoken for us. Let's go."

The rest of us follow Brohn onto the bus with Render waiting until we're all on board before fluttering in, himself. Sitting on the back of my seat, he *kraas*! his permission for us to be off.

Laughing and throwing the bus into gear, Croque Madame tells us our next stop will be Folkestone. "Barring incident, that is. It'll take some time. A few hours at least. Good chunks of A2 and M20 aren't there anymore."

"A2 and M20?" I ask.

"Parts of the old highway system. I've seen a lot of it. Holes in it the size of a football pitch. Miles and miles of it all lined up and blocked with wrecked mag-cars, transports, and more bodies than I'd care to count. Not exactly the 'pastoral English country-side' you might've heard about."

The Auditor's breathy voice radiates through the front of the bus. "Folkestone boasts the world's highest arched brick viaduct. It's home to the country's first nunnery. The doctor, William Harvey, who discovered blood circulation, was born there in 1578. And Walter Tull, the first Black officer in the British army, was born there, too."

Croque Madame guides the bus out of the Oval and down an ash-covered road. "She always do this?"

"You get used to it," Brohn assures her.

"Sure," Terk groans. "Try carrying her around on your back."

"She's got knowledge," Croque Madame admits. "I'll give her that. But it's *had*."

"What do you mean?" I ask.

"Folkestone *had* the highest viaduct. The Eastern Order blew it up along with the harborfront years back. Cut off supply lines. More important, cut off what could've been a main escape route out of England. Divide and conquer, right?"

"I'll update my data," the Auditor says.

Brohn shakes his head. "I don't think that was the point."

When the Auditor doesn't respond, I thank her for the information but remind her that human lives aren't trivia.

The Auditor is quiet again but then makes a noise that sounds like a sigh. "I understand that, Kress. Your life is more important to me than anything in the world. I was just trying to be helpful."

"It worked," I promise with total sincerity. "That was very helpful information."

She doesn't answer, but I don't think she believes me.

For the next hour or so, we're gathered in the front seats of the bus like kids around a campfire with Croque Madame rattling through story after story about her adventures over the past years.

We're seated in a shoulder-to-shoulder bunch and leaning in, with Terk looming behind us, his human and mechanical hands gripping the grab-bars running along either side of the bus's ceiling.

In between two of Croque Madame's stories, Terk moans and complains his back is hurting.

The Auditor says she can make it up to him by reading him a list of clinically approved back and spinal remedies, an offer which Terk adamantly refuses.

"At least you have someone looking out for you," Croque Madame tells him over her shoulder. "Always good to have a mum on board."

Cardyn elbows me. "See?"

"I'm about to throw you off this bus," I snarl. "*See?*"

Croque Madame taps a static-y holo-panel in the front windshield and explains why we have to take back roads.

"It's not just the highways. There's too many Rovers, Roguers, Hawkers, and Scroungers out and about these days."

"We've had our share of run-ins," Brohn tells her. "With the Hawkers and Scroungers, anyway."

From here, I can see Croque Madame's eyebrow go up. "Not sure if you realize how many 'run-ins' around here end up with a flock of ravens feasting on the leftovers."

"Conspiracy," I say.

"What's that?"

"A group of ravens is called a 'conspiracy.'"

"That's us," Brohn says, flicking his thumb back and forth between the six of us. "We're a Conspiracy."

"Whatever you are, I don't know if it's strength, brains, or luck what's kept you alive, but you're a rare breed. Lucky for us, most of the Rovers and Roguers headed up north. Trying to get scraps from the New Scotland Royals, I suppose."

"The Hawkers...," Rain asks. "How much do you know about them? How afraid should we be?"

"A lot." Croque Madame glances away from the road for a split-second to make eye contact with Rain through the long rear-view mirror running along the top of the windshield. "And a lot."

"We beat them before," I boast over the grinding and rattling of the bus over the uneven road. "And that was just with me, Rain, and Branwynne."

"We *escaped* from them," Rain corrects me. "That's different than beating them."

I respond with a defiant pout. "I don't care. I'm not scared of them."

"That's fine," Cardyn says, his chin on my shoulder. "I'm scared enough for all of us."

Brohn leans forward and rests his forearms on the back of the seat in front of us. "I've got to agree with Card on this one. The Hawkers are an unknown. That makes them dangerous. Noxia is probably a Hypnagogic. That makes her deadly. We've seen what they're capable of." Brohn taps a fingertip to his temple. "I've seen it way too close for comfort."

"We've faced tougher than them," Terk reminds him.

"True. But it's best to err on the side of caution until we can pin down who they're working for and what they want with us."

"One problem with that," Cardyn warns through an embellished sigh. "What if they pin *us* down first?"

Brohn nods but doesn't answer one way or another. That leaves the rest of us fidgeting in silence as we contemplate the terrible possibilities that lie ahead if we run across the mysterious Noxia and her relentless band of bounty hunters again.

Unable to deal with the swirl of foreboding scenarios in my head, I tug on the sleeve of Brohn's jacket and tilt my head toward the back of the bus.

"We're going to go to the back to get some rest," Brohn tells the others.

"Probably a good idea," Croque Madame agrees. "You're going to need all the strength, brains, and luck you've got if you seriously plan on breaking into that Processor."

Rain and Terk both say they'll stay up front.

Brohn and I make our way in a staggering walk along the center aisle and plop down into one of the rear bench seats.

The trip is bumpy and hot, but we're safe, together, and on the move, so I'm willing to overlook the jostles and jolts.

Brohn and I settle in, his arm slung around my shoulders. I'm doing my best to lean my head against his chest despite the constant rumble and grind of the bus tires on the neglected and pitted road leading out of the decimated city.

Eventually, Cardyn and Manthy get up, too, and go to the middle of the bus where they sit on opposite sides of the aisle.

Render is perched on the top of the bench seat next to Manthy. He seems content to stare out the window, occasionally offering up a gurgle-y bark when the bus shudders unexpectedly or dips and bounces as it navigates the winding roadway.

As much as I'd love to see them sitting in the same bench seat and enjoying the luxury of closeness like Brohn and I are doing, I also know that's not Cardyn's style or Manthy's comfort zone.

In the back of the bus, Brohn is chattering away, reminding me about our adventures and all of our narrow escapes in London. He's usually not much of a talker. More the strong, silent type. But he's unusually energized and contemplative at the moment, so I go with it.

Besides, his rhythmic baritone is enough to make my heart

dance a little tango even as the rest of me relaxes against his solid body.

At one point, he asks if I'm okay, and I tell him, "Yes."

He kisses the top of my head and launches into a somber account of how sad it is to see great cities like London reduced to chaos and rubble.

"The parks. Palaces. Museums. All those monuments, the Underground, the culture. I really wish we could've seen it *before*. When it was still *London*, you know? And not the disaster it's become. It's not just losing all those people. Or the buildings, the roads, the homes. It's all the effort from the past and the potential for the future…Gone. Because of what? Greed? Stupidity? Lies? That's why we need to keep spreading the truth as best we can. The truth might only spread half as fast as lies. But it's twice as powerful."

Brohn swings his head around and stares out the window, his voice so low I don't know if he's talking to me or to himself. "Taking down the Processors…freeing the kids, the Emergents… that's a small step in the bigger picture. But it's the right one. The one that can change the pace. Slow the momentum. We might not be able to snap our fingers and make everything better, but as long as someone keeps taking steps down the right path, the path'll keep getting deeper and wider, and it'll be easier for the people who need it to find it and follow it. I really believe that."

I hum my agreement, but my mind is elsewhere. Specifically, it's on how horrible I feel for doing what I've been doing for the past few minutes.

Although Brohn can't see from his angle, I know my eyes have gone black like they always do when I connect with Render.

In the past, I've connected with him to perform reconnaissance missions for our Conspiracy. Sometimes, it's so he can share advice, wisdom, or his signature mysterious prophecies with me. I've even connected with him to channel his unique skill set as an apex predator for my own survival in combat situations.

Not this time.

This time—and I'm embarrassed, and I *know* it's wrong—I've tapped into his consciousness to allow me to hear the whispered conversation between Cardyn and Manthy as they talk across the aisle in the middle of the bus.

Normally, over the rumble of the bus and with the two of them talking back and forth so quietly, I'd barely be able to make out a word.

With my mind mingled in with Render's, it's like I'm sitting right there between the two of them with the perky Cardyn firing questions at the sullen Manthy.

*What was it like being dead?*

*~ I don't know.*

*Come on, Manth. Did it feel weird? Are there days missing like when someone has amnesia? Does it feel strange to be sitting here after Krug shot you like that?*

*~ I didn't know Krug shot me. Not until Wisp told me back in D.C.*

*Well, he did.*

*~ If you say so.*

*Were there...?*

*~ Were there what?*

*You know. Lights. Pearly Gates. Little fat angels with harps on the other side?*

*~ There is no other side.*

*But—*

*~ It's all one side.*

*I don't—*

*~ Here. Like this.*

Through Render's eyes, I watch as Manthy unties the leather bracelet around her wrist. She gives it a half-twist and re-attaches one end to the other.

*That's great! Um...what is it?*

*~ A Möbius Strip.*

*Möbius Strip? Sounds like a woman's dance move in a Gentlemen's Club.*

*~ It's not. And you're an idiot.*

Manthy leans over and shows Cardyn how she can trace her finger infinitely along the entire length of the leather strip, front and back.

*~ See. There's no inside or outside. In the end, just like in the beginning, we're all on the same side. The sides are all the same. We just haven't gotten to the part where we can see that yet. Except in our dreams.*

*Our dreams are the same as being dead?*

*~ No. Our dreams are the opposite of being dead. Our dreams are where we see the other versions of our lives. Where we see the people living those other lives...they're the ones who dream. Only, they dream about us.*

*Can I ask you something?*

*~ Can I stop you?*

*No.*

*~ Then why ask?*

*Good point.*

*~ What do you want to ask?*

*How? How do you know all this?*

*~ Know all what?*

*Don't be like that. You know what I mean.*

*~ I listen.*

*You listen.*

*~ To what the universes are saying when they talk.*

*Universes.*

*~ Universes. Plural. I've been listening to their language. The one all the others evolved from. It's the one that keeps getting lost in translation between one world and the next.*

*And you know where to find it?*

*~ I think maybe it finds me.*

*Well, whatever you do...however you do it, I'm just glad...*

~ *Glad?*

*Glad to have you back. I...we missed you.*

~ *From the little I saw of London and from what you guys told me, a technopath wouldn't have done you much good back there.*

*You got us past that Veiled Refractor in Vauxhall. But that's not what I meant, anyway.*

Manthy is quiet for at least a full minute before she turns away from Cardyn and slides over to face the window. I can't see her lips move from here, but her words are crystal clear in my mind.

~ *No one's ever missed me before.*

That's when Render's voice reverberates in my head, chastising me for eavesdropping.

He severs our connection before I have a chance to do it myself or to come clean and apologize like I know I should.

Not that an apology would do any good. It's too late. And who should I apologize to? To Cardyn and Manthy for invading their private moment? Or to Render because I made him guilty by association?

I have no business listening in, and I definitely shouldn't be using Render to spy on my friends.

But I can't help myself. Cardyn has been my best friend since we were six, and Manthy...well, she was dead a few days ago, and now she's sitting fifteen feet away from me, talking to Cardyn and fiddling with her hair like she's never been anything other than who and what she is right now.

I know this is all just me rationalizing, and I know what Brohn would say if he knew I was using my Emergent ability to stick my big, fat nose where it doesn't belong.

Fortunately, Brohn's fallen asleep, which leaves me alone and wide awake with nothing but my misbehavior and my guilt to keep me company.

A voice in my head tells me what I did was wrong. It tells me doing something like this once, no matter how innocent or accidental, means it'll be easier to do it again later. It also tells me I'm going to have to face consequences for it.

Usually, the wise, prophetic, sometimes scolding voice I hear in my head is Render's.

This time, it's all mine.

## 14

# TIME

BROHN DOESN'T STAY ASLEEP for long.

He stretches himself awake and squeezes me tight, his lips pressed to my cheek in a playful kiss.

"Come on," he urges. "Let's go up front and join the others."

Gathering up Cardyn and Manthy on the way down the aisle, we join Terk and Rain, who are still chatting away with Croque Madame.

Most of the ride through the English countryside is quiet and uneventful.

The roadway we're on right now is tree-lined and slightly wider than the last.

Of course, the road is cratered, and the trees are all dead.

So, it's not exactly paradise.

But at least there aren't skyscraper-sized ranges of rubble, dusty rivers of broken glass, toppled buildings, or bombed out sinkholes blocking our path.

After a few minutes, Terk says "Hey!" and presses his fingertip to the window. Instead of the rocky, ravaged countryside, there are sloping hills and overgrown fields on either side of us.

The fields of debris and red dust have given way to a stretch of hills layered over with jungles of brambles and dense thickets of entangled vegetation.

Giant masses of thorny vines rise in twenty-foot high ridges and run for miles along the roadside and off into the distance.

Here and there, thatched-roof structures, grain silos, and the peaks of barns poke their heads above the rising piles of thickets like baby birds craning their necks skyward for food.

Four huge tractors, rust-red and crushed nearly out of shape, sit on the top of one of the hills.

A long line of dead trees, their spindly branches reaching skyward, leans over at a forty-five-degree angle, dragged low by relentless hordes of strangling, parasitic creeper vines.

In the middle of it all, the tail of an airplane juts up like a giant shark fin.

"Must've been farmland," Rain says. "After all the planting, building, and terraforming, the government probably blew it up in seconds." She snaps her fingers, "And nature comes clawing and crawling back."

"Is that a good thing or a bad thing?" I ask.

"It's a *scary* thing. It means whatever we manage to accomplish here can be undone just as easily."

Terk now has his nose and both palms—his human one and his six-digit mechanical one—pressed to the glass, his eyes wide. "Do you think there were sheep?"

Rain laughs, but I know she's not laughing *at* him. Not really.

Terk has always had a thing for sheep.

Back in the Valta, after the first drone strikes and the initial carnage, while the rest of us six and seven year olds were latching onto the older kids for security and safety, Terk was rummaging through the wreckage of what used to be his house, desperately trying to unearth his favorite stuffie and his precious matching set of "Charlotte the Sheep" pillows and bedsheets.

He slept on the bedsheets every night for the next ten years,

K. A. RILEY

clutching them to his chest, long after they weren't much more than a dirty mesh of peeling threads.

He never did find his stuffie.

Sitting back down next to Rain, Terk swings around to face the rest of us. He beams a blissful smile and gives a happy "thumbs up" with his synth-steel hand.

Brohn and I return the gesture, and I break into a choking laugh I didn't know was coming.

Like Rain, I'm not laughing at Terk.

Okay. Sure. He's big and lumbering. His oatmeal-colored hair is constantly ruffled and spikey. He's usually the last one to get a joke. He suffered horribly in the Processor—physically and emotionally—and now the left side of his body is a mangled, shocking collection of exposed pistons, cogs, and bundles of cables threaded into his skin and connected to a network of angry-looking digi-ports.

But sometimes, like now, he's just really cute.

"How much longer till Folkestone?" Cardyn calls through cupped hands from the seat right behind me. I whip around and glare at him for shouting in my ear.

"Not much longer," Croque Madame calls back without turning around. "Time hasn't meant much around here in years. Not many places to go and no need to hurry to get there one way or the other."

"I guess I never thought about it that way before," I tell Brohn.

"It's nice to have something we don't need to care about."

"It's kind of like being immortal."

"How do you figure?"

"People used to worry about time, right? Remember how the adults in the Valta used to talk about old times, uncertain times, dangerous times?"

Manthy has her eyes fixed on the passing landscape of dense, swarming thickets, decay, and decimation. She says something I can't hear.

"What was that, Manth?"

"I said, the need to pay attention to time is the only difference between us and God."

Brohn says, "Huh" and turns to me like he wants me to decipher that, but I'm as lost as he is.

Still feeling guilty about spying on her and Cardyn earlier, I resist the urge to press Manthy on this one. Instead, I tell Brohn I'm tired. "I'm going to go to the back and lie down."

"I'll come with you."

Cardyn makes smacking kissing sounds through his puckered lips.

By way of response, Brohn cuffs his ear as he stands and follows me to our bench seat at the back of the bus.

Brohn grins and shakes his head as we plop down. "I don't know what's worse: Manthy's mysteriousness or Card's craziness."

"They're both great," I say with a giggle. "And life would be dull as dirt without them."

Manthy's words about time are still floating around like randomly bouncing bubbles in my head when the glass from the back windows comes exploding into the bus.

## 15

## AMBUSH

BROHN and I duck in unison, and the bus swerves, slamming us up against the walls and windows and then down in a heap in the aisle.

A blast of gunfire explodes through the side window right behind Manthy's seat.

The spray of stinging glass swarms against my face, neck, and the back of my head.

Brohn shouts out, "Get down!" as another discharge slams into the bus and bends in the back door.

I roll to my side in the aisle, my arms curled over my head as Brohn ducks down over me to shield me from another spray of glass.

"Stay here!"

He dives over me, sliding to a stop at our black bag of weapons stowed under one of the middle seats.

Bullets ping like metallic bugs off the back doors and the interior ceiling of the bus.

From a crouch Brohn tosses our handguns and assault rifles up to Cardyn, Rain, Terk, and Manthy, who catch them and scuttle toward us, their weapons clutched tight in their hands and pressed hard to their bodies.

Cardyn cries over his shoulder to Croque Madame, asking if she's okay.

"Having the time of my life!" she snaps back, her body leaning with the bus.

The rest of us slam to one side as we whip around a bend in the road.

I slap a magazine into each of my Sig Sauers and join Brohn, who's crouched down and is now peering over the top edge of one of the empty window frames in the back door, which is bowed in.

I look, too, but then we have to duck down after another round of artillery fire sprays into the bus.

"Can you see?" Rain shouts through the smoke.

I tell her, "No. But Render can!"

Anticipating my request, Render has already expanded his wings and slammed them back against his body, propelling himself in a black blur out of one of the bus's shattered windows.

Already elevating and circling us from above, Render sends me images of our pursuers:

Their engines revving, two military jeeps—decked out with reinforced wedges of steel on their fronts and transparent blast shields angled on their hoods—are racing along behind us.

These aren't like the Patriot jeeps, which were mostly polished and pretty high tech. These look like they've been decommissioned, run through a chop-shop, and put back together out of random pieces of military-grade hardware.

The men are dressed in mostly high-density, high-flex, brown and green combat gear. Their weapons—an assortment of top-end precision sniper rifles—are designed for long-range assaults.

These aren't front-line soldiers. They're not even mercenaries. These are hunters.

Over the sounds of the bus's revving engine and another salvo of artillery fire, I describe it all to Brohn and the others.

"Hawkers?" Terk cries.

"Don't know!" Brohn shouts. "Don't care!"

"We need to fire back!" Rain says, raising her 3P20 handgun while Brohn slings a Gen-2030 sniper-rifle of his own onto his shoulder and drops to a knee in the aisle.

Cardyn throws a protective arm around Manthy as they crouch down behind us.

Terk, a FN F2000 assault rifle clutched hard in his hands, steps over them and clomps down the aisle toward me and Brohn at the back of the bus.

He's polite enough to say, "Excuse me, Kress" as he storms past me, his Modified body brimming with size, strength, and raw power.

Shoulder-to-shoulder, Brohn and Terk kneel in the aisle, their bodies forming a barrier between us and the two vehicles of onrushing attackers.

Rain and I take up positions on either side of Brohn and Terk, firing over their shoulders as best we can as volley after volley of bullets peppers the back doors.

It's hard to take good aim with the bus lurching around, and we have to keep ducking down to avoid getting hit, ourselves.

After a few seconds, though, we hit a straight stretch of open roadway. Moving as one, Rain and I leap up and unleash a barrage of gunfire at our assailants.

Our shots explode against the jeeps' blast shields, leaving palm-sized bursts of smoky residue on the glass.

With a few exceptions, Brohn's skin has proven to be pretty much bulletproof. The Modified side of Terk's body is, too, but nothing's going to stop his flesh-and-blood parts from getting ripped to shreds.

Terk doesn't seem to care, though, and he blasts a hail of

cover fire at the two jeeps, preventing the shooters from locking their sights on us.

That gives me and Rain the time we need to take a good long breath, remember our training, and steady ourselves to compensate for the speed of the swerving, break-neck chase.

Normally, Rain is a better shot than I am, but once I tap into Render, I'm flooded with an enhanced field of vision and pinpoint focus.

I don't just see the whites of our enemies' eyes. I can spot their eye color and make out every strand of stray hair fluttering under their Kevlar-coated combat helmets.

Rain tags one of the soldiers in the upper arm, just between his shoulder and chest protector. He falls back into the jeep. His rifle clatters out of his hand and disappears down the road in the vehicle's dusty wake.

That leaves three men firing at us. One of them reaches into the back of the jeep and comes back up with a canon-sized missile-launcher.

"FIM-92X!" Rain cries out.

We all know exactly the weapon she's talking about, and we all know to be very afraid right now.

We've seen one of those things before. A version of it, at least. Anti-munitions, tank and building-busters. The Patriots brought them out sometimes.

The weapon wasn't much use against a rag-tag band of insurgents like us. But against a big yellow bus on a cratered and wide-open road…that's another matter.

Instead of explosive ordnance, the X-version of the FIM's missiles come laced with a molecular degenerator *and* a neurotoxin for good measure.

Which means, if the guy out there gets a shot off, whatever's left of our bodies will wind up fused with whatever's left of the bus. Which won't be much.

"Kress!" Brohn barks. "Take him down!"

But I don't fire right away. I've been in enough fights and combat situations to know the damage rushing can do. Besides, the guy in the jeep still has to prime the thing.

While he scrambles to punch in the activation code, I squint down the barrel of my bronze Sig Sauer. I allow myself a gentle exhalation. I let the rocking of the bus wash over me like gentle waves on a beach. And then I squeeze the trigger.

The single bullet sears through the air and finds its target, slipping through the tiny gap between his face-shield and helmet and shearing off half of his face under a convulsive spray of blood.

He slumps down dead, the FIM missile-launcher cradled heavily in his lifeless lap.

With that threat gone, Rain and I duck down to avoid another volley of gunfire as the two jeeps continue to close in on us.

Brohn and Terk stand as one, their sniper and assault rifles raised to their shoulders. I've fired both of those weapons before, so I know how heavy they are and how hard to control.

Brohn and Terk, though, they make it look easy.

As if they're reading each other's minds, they target the ground in front of the lead jeep.

The road is smoother here than we've seen in other parts of the countryside. At least it *was* smoother.

When the boys' shots hit, the asphalt surface of the road explodes into a giant crater.

It's too late for the front jeep to swerve, and it smashes grill first into the smoldering pit.

The second jeep skirts the hole and flies in overdrive until it's right next to us.

They fire, and we duck, but no bullets enter the bus.

"They're going for the wheels!" Cardyn shouts.

"Let 'em try!" Croque Madame shouts back. "They're reinforced! This beautiful old girl can handle anything!"

Somehow finding time to be flirty in the middle of a crisis

situation, Cardyn asks, "Are you talking about you or the bus?"

Without taking her eyes off the road, Croque Madame calls him a "Cheeky plonker" and gives him the finger before clamping both hands hard back onto the steering wheel.

Out of the corner of my eye, I see Manthy edge over to one of the windows.

I shout at her to get down, but she doesn't. Instead, she presses her palm to the glass.

A swarm of bullets blasts holes in the window next to her, and now I've got dual waves of panic and adrenaline surging through my body.

I crawl down the aisle, one hand over my eyes to protect my face from the slivers and splinters of glass flying all over.

When I get to Manthy, I reach up and grab her by the back of her jacket and try to tug her down to safety.

She pushes me away, though, and I lose my grip and go slamming to the floor.

I scream out to Brohn for help. "Brohn! Get her down!"

Brohn braves the flurry of gunfire raging in through the windows. Hooking his arm around Manthy's waist, he starts to haul her down into the aisle for safety, but Manthy somehow—and I have absolutely no idea how—is unmovable, her hand still plastered to the window.

Brohn strains again to drag her away from the window where she's about a millisecond away from being blasted to a bloody pulp. But it's like she's turned to stone.

I leap up to help Brohn, something I never thought I'd have to do when it comes to moving a hundred-fifteen-pound girl.

Sliding between two seats and pressing himself toward one of the open window frames, Terk squints down the sight of his sniper rifle. Rain slips in right next to him, her body tucked against his, her 3P20 trained on the jeep speeding along next to us.

Before either of them has a chance to fire, Manthy's stone

body goes light, and she tumbles back into Brohn's arms.

The two of them land in a tangled clump right in front of me.

From outside the bus, an explosion rips through the air.

We all bellow out a chorus of "Yays!" and "Woohoos!"

"Did you get them?" I call up to Terk and Rain as I disentangle myself from Brohn and Manthy.

"That wasn't us," Rain says, lowering her weapon and clearly confused.

Cardyn and I join Terk and Rain at the window. We lean our heads out and look back down the road to see the second jeep smoldering and slowing to a stop behind us.

"What the hell?"

Behind us, Brohn helps Manthy to her feet, and the two of them join us at the window to see the disabled, smoking jeep languishing in our wake.

"If you didn't fire at them…," I start to ask. And then, at the same time, we all swing around to face Manthy.

Cardyn smiles and gives her a slightly accusatory squint. "Did you—?"

"There's a variable manifold built into its accelerator board," she says quietly.

We're all just standing there, staring at Manthy, and she's looking right back at us, face in a confused scrunch, like *she's* the sane one who can't figure out why *our* jaws are on the ground.

"I just asked it to stop," she says. She walks down the aisle, brushes a pile of glass from one of the middle seats, and plops down with a weary groan.

Croque Madame has her hands clamped to the steering wheel and doesn't take her eyes off the road. "Not sure what you did back there, but I'm glad you did it."

Terk lets out a long wind-shear of a sigh and lowers his rifle. "At least they're gone."

"They'll be back," Croque Madame says. "They always come back."

16

# BROHN'S BLOOD

Cardyn plunks down next to me on one of the bus's bench seats near the front. He asks Croque Madame if she's okay.

She assures him she's fine, but through a mischievous chuckle, Cardyn tells her he meant, "with the bus."

"It's fine, too, you cheeky twonk," she says, unable to suppress a smile I can see from here.

At the back of the bus, Rain is cleaning up shattered glass while Terk uses his mechanical arm to try to bend and pound the rear door back into shape, so it'll close.

The open door and the eight or nine shattered windows allow blasts of hot air to go wafting through the bus. The breeze is nice, but I could do without the skin-scorching temperatures.

Brohn is collecting our weapons and shoving them all back into the black bag. He's in the middle of telling me we're already running low on ammo when Manthy stands up on the lurching bus and points at his arm. "Um...Brohn..."

"Yeah?"

"Your arm...you've got..."

Brohn raises his arm and inspects the holes in the sleeve of his

115

jacket. "Oh. This? Just some holes. This jacket was already pretty beaten up. It's been through a lot since—"

"No. Not the holes."

Brohn glances over at me like he expects me to translate, but he should know by now that understanding Manthy is a matter of patience and taking a deep breath while you do your best to figure out what crazy thing she's on about—all while resigning yourself to the fact that you may never know.

While Cardyn continues his playful flirtations with Croque Madame, I swing around and follow Manthy's gaze.

She reaches out and slips her finger into one of the jagged holes in Brohn's jacket.

Obviously not used to such a forward gesture from our shy friend, Brohn recoils like he's been mildly electrocuted.

Manthy doesn't seem to register his reaction. Instead, she pulls her finger back and holds it up for me and Brohn to see.

The tip of her finger is coated in blood.

Brohn squints and does a double-take back and forth between his arm and the tip of Manthy's finger.

Slinging off his jacket and chucking it onto the seat next to him, he calls me over to help inspect the damage.

I take his arm in both hands and pivot it around, scanning the area around his triceps and elbow. "She's right," I tell him. "There's blood."

"Mine?"

I nod, and Brohn gives me a slightly dirty look. It's like he thinks Manthy and I have somehow conspired to play a distasteful practical joke.

"But my skin..."

"Maybe isn't as indestructible as we thought?"

Even as I say the words, a lump forms in my throat, and my mind flashes through a dozen scenarios—from being on the run through the woods out west to our life-or-death battles in San Francisco, Chicago, Washington, D.C., and London—where

Brohn, if not for his hyper-dense skin, could have died. *Should* have died, but didn't.

I take a second to calm the storm of fear and doubt raging through my overactive imagination.

While Manthy slips away to sit by herself in one of the seats at the middle of the bus, I remind Brohn about Buckingham Palace. "You got scratched. Remember?"

"Yeah. But I just figured…"

"Figured what? That your skin can deflect bullets and broadswords but not the claws of an eight-pound feral cat?"

"Truth?"

"Yeah."

"I was kind of…um, scared."

"Scared of a cat scratch?"

"No."

"Then what?"

"Scared I might be…that I might not be…"

"What?"

"That I might not be like the rest of you. That I might not be an Emergent anymore."

I sit down and pat the seat next to me. Brohn takes the hint and sits down, his hands hanging between his knees in defeat.

"You just shrugged off some pretty intense ordnance back there," I tell him. "We've seen that caliber of bullet take chunks out of concrete and dent synth-steel. You protected all of us and gave us time to take them down. If not for you, the rest of us wouldn't be much more than blood spatter on the inside walls of this bus."

Brohn torques his arm around and stares at the small red marks on his skin. "It still hurts."

"I'm sure it does."

"But the cat—"

"The cat."

"How come it was able to scratch me like that?" Brohn drags

117

his fingers over the new wounds. They're barely visible, not much more than tiny blisters, but he definitely suffered some damage in the firefight. He shows me the traces of blood on his fingertips. "And how come this?"

"I don't know." I run the tip of my finger along his neck. "You've got a few marks here, too."

"Where?"

"Just above your hip. And here, on the back of your neck." Brohn touches both spots and gives a little cringe as I draw back from my investigation. "You didn't notice?"

"I noticed it hurt a little. I just thought maybe I'd pulled a muscle or something."

"I think these are from the Scroungers."

Brohn's about to object, but a glimmer of realization flickers across his eyes. "When I was helping Manthy."

"They did come at you pretty hard. And their nails were at least as sharp as a cat's."

"Do you think I'm losing it?"

"No."

"What then?"

"You didn't say anything back at the palace, so I didn't either."

"Thanks. I think."

"I just chalked it up to a freak thing."

"But what about just now, Kress? I stood there and let myself get shot, and then Manthy finds blood on me. And you find *more*. What if—"

I cut him off before he has a chance to let his mind wander down that rabbit hole. "I'm not sure what's going on. But I have two theories. Unfortunately, neither of them is very good."

Brohn sighs and clamps his hand onto the back of the seat in front of us like he's bracing himself for bad news or else preparing for the bus to go careening over a cliff. "Okay. Let's have it. What are your theories?"

"Either really small contact with your skin—a cat's claws,

splinters of glass, sharp fingernails, or a really light graze, as opposed to a full-on shot—can somehow affect you."

"Or?"

"Or...nothing."

Brohn holds his fingers up in a "V." "You said you had *two* theories."

"I did?"

"You did."

"Okay," I say with a resigned sigh. "It could mean that our abilities come and go."

"Come and go? How do you mean? You can always connect with Render. You've been doing it since you were six. Rain can always tap into her Culling. Manthy never seems to have a problem talking with tech." He tilts his head toward the window. "You saw yourself what she did back there...And Terk—"

"She has more problems than you think," I interrupt.

"Manthy? Really?"

"Most of us do."

Brohn gives me a puzzled look, turns to see what Rain and Terk are up to at the back of the bus, gives Manthy, Cardyn, and Croque Madame a quick glance—almost like he's reassuring himself that they're all still there—and then turns his attention back to me.

"You have problems with your abilities?" he asks.

I can tell he's a little offended at the thought that maybe I haven't been totally open and honest with him about my recent experiences as an Emergent.

"I get headaches," I confess. "Bad ones. Manthy does, too. And Cardyn." I trace the intricate pattern of black swoops and swirls running along my forearms. "These hurt sometimes."

"What about Rain? Terk?"

I shake my head. "Not that I know of. Not like ours, anyway."

"How come I'm the last one to know this?"

I give him a reassuring nudge. "I think you've had other things on your plate. You know, the whole superheroic leading us into battle stuff."

"There's nothing super about leading someone into battle. Leading someone *out* of battle, now *that's* heroic."

"Well, you've done plenty of that, too. We're here, right?"

"We're here. And I'm still the only one whose Emergent abilities might be...disappearing."

"They're not disappearing. I just think maybe..."

"Maybe what?"

"I'm thinking there's a lot we don't know. We don't know why we can do what we can. We don't know where these abilities come from. And I don't think we really know ourselves as much as we sometimes think we do."

Brohn slumps deeper into his seat, his head back, his eyes riveted to a spot on the ceiling. "That's got to be about the most depressing thing I've ever heard."

I laugh, thinking he's joking or maybe teasing me, but he gives me a serious corner-eyed glance before telling me he needs to take a walk.

"A walk?" I ask with a light snort and with a tilt of my head toward the confined interior of the bus. "Where are you going to go, exactly?"

"Just for a walk, I guess."

I say, "Brohn, wait," but he ignores me.

He stands and strides back toward where Rain and Terk are still busily cleaning up and conducting whatever repairs they can to the rear door.

I watch as he says something to Rain I can't hear and then turns and walks back down the aisle toward where Manthy is sitting.

He sits down in the bench seat behind her, his arms folded over the back of her seat. He starts talking to her, but I can't hear what he's saying.

Render is perched on the back of a seat across the aisle, and I get ready to connect with him so I can hear Brohn and Manthy's muffled conversation, but then it's like a wall goes up in my mind, and I feel barricaded inside of my own head.

Render shakes his head at me and barks out a series of raspy warbles.

~ *You shouldn't do that.*

*I know.*

~ *Then why—*

For reasons I can't explain, I start to cry. I press my cheek to the window and put my arm up next to my face, hoping Cardyn doesn't turn around and catch me. The last thing I need is the attention, pity, and dumb jokes I know he'll tell to try to cheer me up.

~ *What's wrong?*

*We're on our way to do this impossible thing. Find a Processor. Break in. Free a bunch of kids and hope we don't get them or ourselves killed along the way.*

~ *We've faced tougher challenges.*

*But by accident. Because we had to defend ourselves. We fought for survival. Now, we're not just going into the lion's den. We're going in soaked in blood and practically begging to get eaten. And now with Brohn being worried...I just feel like we have more to lose this time.*

~ *What do you mean?*

*Rain and Terk are bonding. We lost Manthy once already. Now, she's acting weird and won't really talk to anyone about what's happening to her. Brohn thinks he's losing his Emergent abilities. What if I'm losing him?*

~ *It's better than losing yourself. Maybe that's what you're most afraid of.*

I'm about to ask him what he means by that, but he severs our connection. I'm left alone in my seat, my face to the window, as the whispers and murmurs of my friends go on without me, like waves lapping throughout the bus.

## 17

# FOLKESTONE

IT CAN'T BE MORE than about twenty minutes later when Croque Madame navigates the bus through a field of military-style outposts and security stations—all abandoned and smashed to pieces.

What must have been road-side checkpoints are now piles of wood, uprooted steel posts, and coils of razor-wire.

With her fingers on the brake activators in the steering wheel, we navigate down a steep road, snaking our way past dozens of historic Victorian-style homes and churches, most with at least half of their tops and sides blasted off.

From the exposed upper levels of some of the buildings, people step toward the edge and stare down at us as we pass.

"Friend or foe?" Terk asks me from his seat right behind mine.

"They haven't shot at us or thrown anything. So that's probably about as friendly as we can hope for."

In the road, all the rubble has been pushed up to the sides, creating steep, tidy banks.

The air is hostile-red, and there's the brine-y smell of seawater on the air, thick with iodine and heavy with the mist of decay.

After a couple of minutes, the road opens up and flattens out. Ahead of us is a crowd of hundreds of people huddled under massive awnings of corrugated steel, encircling an expansive open-air square of hard-packed earth and gathered like they were expecting us.

Croque Madame brings the bus to a throaty stop in the middle of the square. "Welcome to Folkestone."

My Conspiracy and I gather at the windows along each side of the bus to take in the scene.

Other than Grizzy, Branwynne's parents, and now, Croque Madame, I don't think we've seen any adults since we got to England.

From what we've been told, most of them either moved out of the city to take their chances in the countryside, migrated up north to where the Wealthies have taken up shop, or died from starvation, cataclysmic drone attacks, or mob violence. And if those weren't enough, apparently the Cyst Plague did its best to finish off anyone left standing.

Apparently, whoever was left found their way here.

And it's not just people our parents' age, either. There are older people here, too: Hunched women with weathered, leathery skin and balding men with crooked limbs and gray stubble. There are thin, middle-aged men with balloon bellies, teenage girls with dreadlocked hair past their knees, and little boys with ashy skin and bulging, red-rimmed eyes.

I've spent my life assuming each day could be my last.

I don't say it out loud, but it gives me a slight bump of optimism to know that people—even if they're in bad shape under brutal conditions that have been forced on them—can still find a way to stay alive and together this long.

According to the Auditor and confirmed by Croque Madame, Folkestone used to be a pretty quaint harbor town.

"Folkestone has an interesting history," the Auditor tells us. "Is it okay to give you this information?"

I assure her it's okay, and she leaps into her spiel with lilting enthusiasm. "Folkestone was a seaside city favored by British royalty. Agatha Christie wrote *Murder on the Orient Express* here. The Harbour Arm was a popular promenade for locals and tourists. On the other hand, the town was said to lack the aesthetic charm of other port cities such as Broadstairs and Whitstable. In the Second World War, the Nazis used to drop their leftover bombs on it on their way back to Germany. Oh, and it once served as a major shipping and transportation port and as a defense against French invaders."

"The key word is *'served,'*" Croque Madame clarifies. "Past tense. The last express-ferries stopped running across the English Channel in 2029."

Brohn strides down the aisle and grabs our bag of weapons. He holds up one of the assault rifles and his arbalest, the behemoth crossbow Grizzy gave him back in London. He asks Croque Madame, "Which one?"

"Neither."

Brohn pauses, and I'm sure he thinks she must be joking. Whether we're fighting alongside a friend or facing a foe, we don't go anywhere without quick access to weapons.

Manthy's the closest thing I've ever seen to a pacifist. And even she can go mama-bear crazy when she's forced to fight.

Croque Madame advises us all to follow her lead. "People down here aren't killers by nature. But they *can* be by choice."

She presses her thumb to the input panel in front of her, and the bus's door whooshes open.

A man and a woman climb into the bus. The man is average height, but the woman, with long, thin legs and with her spray-painted orange hair piled high on her head, has to duck down as she swings around into the aisle.

"We need you to step out of the bus," she instructs us. Her tone is cheery. Her tight-lipped grimace and the long-handled pickaxe in her hand are *not*.

Behind her, the man tells Croque Madame to disable the bus's security protocols. "Can't 'ave you trying to drive away on us, now, can we?"

His wide, hair-filled nostrils flare. He taps the chainsaw he's carrying against the metal railing next to Croque Madame's seat. From here, I can tell the chainsaw's links are a fused, rusted mess, and I can't imagine the thing works.

Still, I'd rather not be hit with it.

Besides, we're in a bit of a pickle. We can't exactly launch a pre-emptive attack against a bunch of civilians just because we're afraid of what they might try to do to us with their rusted and rustic weapons.

Croque Madame puts her hands up and rises with molasses speed out of her seat. "The kids won't bother you. So maybe take it easy, eh? They don't know the rules."

"If they step out of line, we'll teach 'em," the spidery-limbed woman says, pickaxe as fixed in her hands as her eyes are on us.

The man with the cavernous, oversized nostrils says, "Come along, then."

He and Spider-limbs step aside as we pass. Walking right behind Brohn, I keep my eyes down and don't say anything.

Cardyn isn't as discreet.

"Hiya!" he beams to the two strangers. "I'm Cardyn."

"Nice to meet you," the woman says through squinty eyes and a light smile. "I'll be your murderer today."

I turn in time to see Cardyn's grin fall and his mouth hang open as Manthy pushes him from behind. "Can you at least wait until we're off the bus before you try to get us killed?" she grumbles.

Outside of the bus, the man and woman hand us off to a circle of menacing looking adults, each of them brandishing a hoe, pickaxe, or pitchfork.

They don't say a word as they gather around us.

"What are they looking for?" Rain whispers to Brohn through an annoyed squint.

"Don't know. Don't care. As long as they keep their distance."

Cardyn bites his lip. "They're not going to confiscate our weapons, are they?"

Nearly as nervous as Cardyn, Terks asks, "Can they decide to just not let us go?"

As subtly as possible, I nudge Brohn with my elbow. "Should we try to stop them?"

Croque Madame shushes us all with a finger to her lips. "They're not looking for anything."

"Then why—?"

"Look around. There's not much left of the place these people called home."

"I don't—"

"People need control. If they can't have control over themselves, they'll find a way to get control over someone else."

"And that someone else is us?"

"For now."

My Conspiracy and I exchange an overlapping series of "What should we do?" looks. If Croque Madame is right, this inspection could be nothing more than a minor annoyance.

If she's wrong, things could get a lot worse.

Spider-limbs and Nostrils step down from the bus.

Spider-limbs strides across the dusty field as the hundreds of people around us press forward, eager to see what's going to happen.

She directs an angry glare at me. "Who's yer bird?"

"Render."

"And the rest of ya?"

Brohn introduces us individually, and I add, "We're a Conspiracy."

Spider-limbs sizes us up before planting herself in front of

Croque Madame. "Good to see you, Elisa. Never sure which trip's going to be your last."

"Good to see you, too, Vivia. Never sure when you're going to change your mind about letting me through."

"You two know each other?" Rain asks.

"We've had...dealings in the past."

"Not always friendly," Vivia grins.

"But always fair," Croque Madame counters.

Nostrils turns, drops to the ground, and slips, head-first, under the bus.

"Cargo?" the woman asks.

Croque Madame shrugs. "Nothing that'll ruffle anyone's feathers."

"Anything you can do without?"

Croque Madame gives her a wink and a knowing nod. "Just so happens..." She edges her way past the woman and presses her thumb to one of the small green input panels on the side of the bus.

A small compartment whirs open above one of the rear wheels, and a crate of silver canisters slides out on a narrow metal shelf.

Nostrils clambers out from under the bus and brushes his hands on his pants. "All good. Looks like you took some hits, though."

"Take a wild guess."

"Hawkers?"

"Who else?"

"They haven't bothered you for a while, eh?"

Croque Madame extends her arm toward me and my Conspiracy. "I haven't had company for a while, either. Not like them, anyway."

Spider-limbs and Nostrils give us a long, lingering look, and I'm half-expecting them to unload an avalanche of questions at us about who we are, where we come from...things like that. And I know that conversation is going to end with us being revealed as foreign Emergents. And, after that, well…things tend to go south after that.

But they break their gaze and swing back around to Croque Madame.

"Elisa is known around here as Six-Cats," Spider-limbs says to Brohn.

"Why's that?"

"Because forget *nine* lives. She's got at least fifty-four."

"You're exaggerating," Croque Madame laughs.

Nostrils bounces his eyes between the two women. "She brought rations?"

Spider-limbs nods, and the man signals to two little girls, who make their way over to the canisters and sniff at them like dogs.

"Protein cubes," the first girl says with a smile of crooked, cracked, and missing teeth.

The second one starts slipping the canisters into a gray canvas sack she's dragged over. "More than last time, even!"

"It's too much," Spider-limbs says.

Croque Madame raises a hand. "It's fine. I can afford it."

"There are too many on your route who can't afford to miss out." She whistles to the two little girls through her fingers. "Lea. Ashlynne. Leave five."

"That's human of you," Croque Madame sighs. "But—"

"We horde, we survive. We share…

"You *thrive*. I know."

The woman laughs and throws her arms around Croque Madame, pulling her close in a sisterly embrace. "Then take your Conspiracy here, toodle on, and the best o' the British to ya."

## 18

# WRITHERS

OUR EYES DARTING across the lingering crowd, my Conspiracy and I step backwards to re-board the bus.

"Is that it?" Cardyn asks, glancing back at Spider-limbs, Nostrils, and the rest of the buzzing and twittering Folkestone crowd.

Croque Madame edges past him as she slips into the driver's seat. "What did you want? A bare-knuckles brawl to the death?"

Cardyn makes a dramatic show of flexing his muscles. "I could see the appeal of that."

I pat his cheek. "It would've been an easy fight for a tough guy like you."

"It's true," he says through a playful grin as he launches into another dramatic bodybuilder pose. "I *am* more powerful than anyone we've come across."

"Give me a break."

"Hey," Brohn calls out to Cardyn, dropping down next to me in one of the bench seats. "We don't get that many easy encounters. Let's appreciate them while we can, shall we?"

Cardyn makes a dramatic bow and a flourish of his hand and

arm like he's saluting Brohn with an imaginary hat. "As you command, your majesty."

I start to get mad, but then both boys laugh, and Brohn gives Cardyn a playful swat to the side of the head as Cardyn plops down in front of us.

"I've made this run a dozen times," Croque Madame confides as she drives the bus slowly between the parting crowd. "No matter how many supplies I bring or how much I tell them I'm not out to get them, they always keep their guard up."

"You don't stay alive around here with your guard down," Brohn observes.

Croque Madame says she believes that's true. But then she adds, "It's also hard to help others without dropping your guard from time to time."

As we pass, some of the smaller kids—Neos and Juvens—hide behind their parents. The older ones give us salutes, cheers, whistles, and wild waves. A few of them pat the side of the bus as we trundle along.

Through the open, broken windows, we hear their cries of, "Best o' the British to ya! Best o' the British!"

After clearing the last of the Folkestone crowd, the bus slips into the darkness of the Chunnel's gaping, toothless mouth.

His cheek pressed to a window, his eyes doing a nervous little shimmy, Terk asks the Auditor if it's safe.

"Records are spotty," she informs us as the light dwindles behind us. "Ten workers were killed during construction. There are accounts of six fires—1996, 2006, 2012, 2028, 2030, and 2031 —although I can't locate details about causes or casualties. A complete electrical shut-down has been attributed to an EMP device detonated by the Eastern Order. The entry ports at Folkestone and Coquelles were sealed off in drone attacks in 2035. Loss of life is listed as 'catastrophic.' But no exact records remain. The entry ports were reopened after the People's Excavation Project of 2036."

"There's tracks on the ground," Cardyn says, his face pressed sideways to the window next to Terk.

"Used to be a rail line under the English Channel," Croque Madame tells him.

"What happened to the trains?"

Croque Madame sighs. "Same thing that happens to all the little things you take for granted before a war." Taking her hands off the wheel for a second, she splays her fingers out from her fists and makes an explosion sound with her mouth.

"Graveyard's on the French side," she adds.

Terk bites his lip. "Wait? Graveyard?"

"Don't worry. It's not for *people*," Croque Madame laughs. "It's for the trains."

"Oh."

"There's water above us?" Cardyn asks.

"Two-hundred-fifty feet of it at the Chunnel's deepest depth," the Auditor purrs.

Cardyn slumps low in his seat until all I can see of him are the loops and tangles of his auburn and burgundy-red hair. "Great," he mutters. "We're going to drown underground in a bus."

"Don't worry," Croque Madame assures him. "We'll get through okay."

Illuminated by the bus's front and side-mounted holo-lights, the subterranean, subaquatic Chunnel is a world all its own.

At first, it's just like I'd expect a drive through an old rail tunnel to be: a lot of claustrophobia and a lot of creepy shadows sliding along the curved interior walls.

Then, we start driving past what looks like plywood and pressboard boxes and stretches of fabric on posts angled out away from the walls.

A kind of tent-city has been built up along either side of the rails.

Each side has a narrow trough running its length. Thick, brown water churns and burbles along in the stone gutters.

Terk pinches his nose. "It stinks."

"That's their waste removal system," Croque Madame informs him.

I can't keep the shock from my voice. "Wait. People *live* down here?"

Croque Madame points to a spot somewhere up ahead and then scans her finger back to show us the area we're passing. "Chunnel Writhers. Been camped down here since about 2035, right before it reopened."

"Why don't they live outside like the others?"

"They're scared," Croque Madame explains. "Shell-shocked. PTSD. Fear of drones. Radiation. Scroungers. Roguers. Hawkers. Who knows? Whatever you want to call it, it all comes back to fear. Justified, if you ask me." There's a hint of a quiver in her voice when she says this.

"So they just live down here all the time?" Rain asks.

Croque Madame snaps her thumb back the way we came. "I guess they figured it's safer down here than up there."

"This doesn't feel safe," Cardyn complains.

As we pass, people crawl part way out from under plywood shelters or damp carboard boxes. Others peer out from closet-sized openings in the curved concrete walls.

The only sound we hear, though, is the hollow, rumbling echo of the bus tires.

There's no sign of light or power. "I don't even see where they have fire," I say to Brohn.

"Just as well," he points out. "This doesn't seem to be the most well-ventilated place in the world. I can't imagine any good could come from having fires down here."

"Then what do you think they do for heat. Or for food? Or air, for that matter?" I can't keep the tremble out of my voice.

As more and more of the Writhers emerge—none of them daring to step all the way out of their shelters as we pass—all I can think is that we're witnessing a slow genocide taking place before our eyes.

We know first-hand about what war does: Families suffer. So do all the cities, the jobs, the sense of security, the feeling of hope, and the awareness of your humanity.

This stretch of underground, underwater, underfed Chunnel-dwellers…this is war broken down to nothing but the suffering.

If the Scroungers had developed into some kind of pack of predators, the people we see down here are definitely prey.

Visibly twitching, no one comes all the way out. No one stands up too high to get a closer look at us.

Instead, they cower in the bleak darkness, staring but apparently too afraid or too unable to make more than the slowest, smallest motions.

All we see as we pass are dark heads of crusted hair, pale hands pressed flat to the ground, and burning yellow eyes.

"Their eyes…" I start to stay but then trail off.

"I see it," Brohn says. "It's eerie."

"They're yellow," Cardyn exclaims.

Terk says, "Those poor people. They're scared."

Rain shakes her head. "They're dying."

"They're like us," Manthy mutters. "They're transfigured."

But then she says, "I can't" when I ask her to tell us what she means.

It takes over two hours of rattling along to make it to the end.

The Writhers' huts, tents, crevices, and makeshift shacks run for nearly the entire length of the Chunnel on either side.

The entire way, we see those haunting yellow eyes glowing in the scrolling shadows cast by the bus's lights as we drive along.

The road beneath us is rutted and lined with what's left of the mag-tracks that must've helped carry commuters, travelers, and tourists back and forth for all those years before the invention of the Eastern Order and the pointless, manufactured, and never-ending war.

The underground world of transfigured people eventually thins out, and we finally burst out of the creepy darkness.

Cardyn thrusts his arms in the air and bellows out a celebratory "Woohoo!" when we emerge into the light and then sulks when the rest of us don't join him in his celebration.

After our quick but cool reception in Folkestone and with the images of the Chunnel Writhers haunting our memories, the six of us, plus the Auditor, are happy to be out on the open road again.

With the countryside scrolling by and with no mortal danger in sight, we find plenty to laugh and talk about.

After hours on the road, Brohn and I decide to squirrel away again in the back of the bus.

"I feel good," I tell him. "I don't know why."

"Why wouldn't you?"

"You don't think that was sad back there?"

"The Writhers?"

"What do you think Manthy meant—about them being like us?"

"I've kind of given up trying to figure out what Manthy means about anything."

"It's true," I laugh. "She's working on a whole different level, isn't she?"

Brohn laughs along with me and throws his arm around my shoulders.

Up front, Croque Madame is leading Cardyn, Rain, and Terk in a rousing chorus of "The Wheels on the Bus," which they're all belting out at the top of their lungs. Even Manthy, her forehead pressed to the window, is mouthing the words.

Cardyn whips around and waves for me and Brohn to join in, which we both do for a round or two before settling back into our conversation.

"I feel guilty being comfortable like this."

"Be happy. Comfort's hard to come by."

"Maybe I'm in denial. Or I'm shell-shocked. Or maybe I'm going crazy."

He says he doesn't think it's any of those things. I lean against his shoulder. "What then?"

He presses himself toward me and kisses the top of my head. "We're alive and singing on a school bus. I think maybe this is what it feels like to be normal kids."

I curl up against him, my cheek pressed to his chest as I watch the world outside of the bus go by.

We curve around a bend in the road. In the distance, a dark, low-hanging cloud roils in angry, undulating waves over the haunting, sizzling glow of a huge city on fire.

"Um…I think 'normal' just flew out the window."

## 19

# BIENVENU

"WELCOME TO PARIS," Croque Madame announces. Her loud but somber voice fills the bus.

We press our faces to the windows to get a good look, and Terk asks if this is *really* Paris.

"It is," Croque Madame assures us, although we have to take her word for it.

Except for tiny pinpricks of what look like small fires scattered across the shadowy landscape, there's not much to see under the blanket of black, starless night hanging over the city.

Croque Madame turns off the road we've been on and drives down a narrow, unpaved laneway. The tips of dead tree branches rake and screech like spiked fingernails along the sides of the bus as we bump our way along.

When the laneway levels out, we wind up parked in a cave of damp darkness under a stone bridge.

"No lights in the City of Light for us," Croque Madame says, toggling off the bus's interior and exterior holo-lights. "Hasn't been grid power here in two years now. And we can't afford to be spotted."

"Spotted?" Cardyn asks, giving his lower lip a good chewing.

"Drone patrol. City's run by 'em now."

"Drones?"

Brohn and I exchange a casual, very untroubled look. It's true that our town was destroyed by drone strikes. But we didn't have access to the kinds of weapons we do now. And we definitely weren't trained, experienced, and battle-tested like we are today.

We fought the Patriot Army in San Francisco and in D.C. It wasn't easy and there wasn't a single second when I wasn't scared out of my mind. Machines have a reputation for being cold, ruthless, and relentless in their ability to destroy anything in their path. But that's nothing compared to what *people* are capable of.

Drones, unlike human beings, though, are nice and predictable. They can be shot down, fooled, avoided, taken over, and even re-programmed for good instead of evil.

So when Croque Madame tells us the city is run by drones, we don't worry. In fact, I'd say we're all a bit relieved.

Like Brohn says, it's important to appreciate the easy stuff.

Highlighted by the dim green glow of one of the navigational holo-panels on the windshield, Croque Madame tells us to load up our guns. "But just the handguns. No rifles. No rocket-launchers. Drones are programmed to spot them. Besides, we've got a walk ahead of us, so we need to travel as light as possible from here."

"Travel to where?" Brohn asks, tucking a Desert Eagle handgun into his waistband.

"We're dropping off a batch of Veiled Refractors and some bunker-blasters. We're on foot from here to the Garden."

In the aisle, Terk leans down over Rain's shoulder. "Garden? Sounds nice!"

She reaches back to pat Terk's cheek. "I hate to disappoint you, Big Guy. But I have a feeling it won't be the one from Eden."

"And these?" Cardyn asks, holding up Manthy's twin tomahawk axes.

Croque Madame gives Cardyn an impressed nod. "Might as

well. Just because we have to travel light doesn't mean we can't travel deadly."

Cardyn gives the axes a quick twirl before snapping them into the mag-holster on his back.

Armed now, we follow Croque Madame out of the bus and over to the side where she triggers open a hidden panel next to the one she opened back in Folkestone. This time, a bulky, boulder-sized backpack slides out on a long silver tray.

Croque Madame starts to haul it down, but Brohn steps forward and says he'll get it.

"Thanks," she smiles in the darkness. "My back's not what it used to be. Come on."

With a grunt, Brohn slings the bag onto his back, and we follow Croque Madame out from under the archway of the dark stone bridge.

She clambers up an embankment, and leads us in a low, loping jog through dense thickets on the side of the road until the overgrown path opens up onto a small, elevated clearing overlooking the city.

Render's on my arm, half asleep. He snaps awake, though, when the hot, churning wind kicks up a small vortex of pebbly dust around us.

He bobs his head and *kraas*! With our fingers to our lips, Cardyn and I shush him at the same time.

Croque Madame kneels down and raises a pair of binoculars to her eyes. "I was afraid of this. There's been a new wave of attacks."

Cardyn says, "No kidding."

He's right not to be shocked. All around us, the earth has been fused into rolling mounds of blackened glass. What's left of a row of nearby buildings looks like a line of melted and re-frozen ice cream cones.

"Les Bois de Vincennes," Croque Madame sighs. "This was all forest once. Protected. A few years back, it was burned to the ground. Now, it looks like even that wasn't enough. They had to come back and burn the *ground*, too."

"They?" Brohn asks.

Croque Madame shrugs. "Wealthies. Drones. Eastern Order. Does it matter? Whoever wants power bad enough is going to do what they can to get it."

What Croque Madame points to next and says used to be woods is now a field of petrified tree stumps and heaps of black ash stretching as far as we can see under the bleak light trickling down from the sliver of a crescent moon.

It's at this exact moment that I realize what I miss most about the Valta in the early days: *green*.

I say this out loud to the others, who all mumble their agreement.

"I never really thought about it that way," Rain confesses. "But you're right, Kress. We need more green in the world."

Nodding, Brohn scans the dead woods. "Leaves. Grass. Vegetables and vegetation. Hell, I'd even take weeds that weren't gray and predatory."

"Periwinkle," Cardyn says.

"What?"

"Periwinkle. It's a mixture of lavender and cornflower blue. I think we also need more periwinkle in the world."

"What we need," Manthy grumbles, "is less Cardyn."

I expect Cardyn to be offended, but then I catch what *might* be matching smiles—it's hard to tell in the dark—tugging at the corners of his and Manthy's lips.

Cardyn throws his arm around her shoulders, and to my surprise, she doesn't recoil in disgust. "Green. Periwinkle. Cardyn," he says. "It's all the same. All just splashes of life in an otherwise very bleak world, wouldn't you say?"

"We need to get moving," Croque Madame interrupts. "The longer we're outside of the Garden, the more danger we're in."

"What is the Garden, anyway?" Brohn asks.

"You'll see. If we can get there without triggering any of the motion-detection and infrared sensors the drones've got stationed along the way."

We hustle along, skirting the edges of the smoldering city. Most of the office buildings are cordoned off with floating orange Perimeter Sensor Pylons.

"Don't get too close," Croque Madame warns. "Set one off, and you'll set 'em all off."

Overhead, as if to emphasize her point, plumes of grungy smoke tumble over each other like a bank of angry, low-lying storm clouds.

According to Croque Madame, the deep ravine, the river—littered with old cars and heaps of crusted-over bones—was called the Seine.

"We've heard of it," I tell her. "From our geography lessons in the Valta."

"It was the river running through the city," Croque Madame whispers from up ahead in the darkness. "Now, it's a graveyard."

I pinch my nose against the smell, but it's not enough to keep out the bacterial odors of iodine, sulfur, death, and decay.

We duck into a deep cluster of brittle reeds as a fleet of drones shrieks overhead, their grav-thrusters leaving ripples of shimmering night air in their wake.

The drones don't seem to notice us as they snake along in a high-speed zigzag pattern toward a nearby tall church with a missing roof.

Out of the dim evening haze, a hail of muzzle flashes lights up from the church's open rooftop with the crack of gunfire reaching our ears a split second later.

"There's people firing from up there," Terk tells me.

"At what?"

"At the drones, I think."

Sure enough, several of the strange snake-like drones are hit and go pinwheeling out of the sky.

The rest dodge through a second round of gunfire.

They blast what's left of the rooftop to rubble. The thick stones and girders of wood and steel go crashing down into the middle of the church, which belches a horrific cloud of black dust from its first-floor doors and glass-less windows.

After the echo of the explosions, all that's left in the night air are the fading screams of the people inside.

Those were people up there. Human beings. Now, they're casualties, numbers to be added to the ledger of all the other lives lost in a pointless war against a made-up enemy.

Crouching down, we watch as the drones glide back into formation, each one folding over onto itself until they look like black bowling balls but with alternating rectangular and triangular panels and sharp edges all around.

We watch as they disappear into the distance and bank around a tall, hollowed-out office building.

"We'd better keep moving," Croque Madame says, leading us out of the reeds and down a narrow, uneven cobblestone road.

"They're morphable drones," the Auditor explains from her disk on Terk's back. "A new model to replace the Concussive-Incendiary Generation Sixes."

"Like the ones that destroyed the Valta," I mutter.

"Krug's engineers were working on a prototype in Chicago. More multi-function and designed to replace a lot of the soldiers in the Patriot Army. That's about all I know. I'm sorry. My protocols were limited to the capture and detention of potential Emergents. I never had full access to drone project files."

Manthy mumbles something we don't catch.

Cardyn leans in. "What's that, Manth?"

"They're transformable rhombicuboctahedrons."

"Rhomba-what?"

"They run on anti-grav fields generated by a string of current inductors embedded along each edge of their prisms." Sounding somehow even more remote and robotic than the Auditor, she adds with an annoyed exhalation, "They're a multi-use design called TRIADS: Tracking, Reconnaissance, Infiltration, Assault, Diagnostics, Surveillance..." She trails off, and she looks away, like she's offended by the sound of her own voice.

I'm not sure what the word is for an equal mixture of astonishment, fascination, and irritation. But right now, it's plastered all over Croque Madame's face. "And how do you know this, young lady?"

Manthy flicks her eyes skyward. They told me."

"Manthy's a technopath," I tell her. "She has a...*relationship* with certain forms of digital technology."

I say it like that explains everything even though, really, it's just the tip of the mostly-submerged Manthy iceberg.

Croque Madame squints at me, and I half expect laser beams or something to come zapping out of her eyes. But then her face relaxes into a soft palette of dimples, freckles, crow's feet, and meandering smile lines. "I don't suppose it's a relationship she can use to turn those things off?"

I look over at Manthy, who shakes her head.

"Sorry," I apologize on Manthy's behalf. "I don't think it works like that."

"Too bad. Could have saved a lot of trouble and a lot of lives."

Manthy sounds annoyed when she says, half under her breath, "Then I guess we'll just have to find another way."

# 20

## LE JARDIN

STILL SCUTTLING along the deserted road, we follow Croque Madame along the dry trench of the Seine and deeper into the city of smoke and ash.

She moves fast and barely makes any noise. It's as if midnight reconnaissance operations through Paris are nothing new to her. For someone with such short legs, she's got bunny stealth and cheetah speed.

Just ahead of me, ducked down in a crouch, Rain reaches out to clamp a hand onto Madame's arm. "Not that way."

There's a hint of offense in Croque Madame's voice when she tells Rain, "I've come this way before."

"I know," Rain says. She points up to the roof of a tall building across the way where a tiny and barely visible red light is winking from the underside of one of the hovering Triad Drones. "*They* know it, too."

I ask Rain if she's okay to do this, and she snaps, "Yes" through a feeble smile.

I know that's a lie. I also know if I press her, she's going to get defensive and probably yell at me, so I back down.

She leads us off the street and into a small shell of a building just down the road. We hustle down a flight of crumbling concrete steps, along a narrow hallway framed by graffiti-covered walls, and up another flight of steps. From there, we're back outside where we jog down one cobblestone laneway after another.

I keep looking up, certain we're going to trip a sensor or get spotted by a surveillance drone. But we're either very lucky, or, more likely, Rain, despite what I know must be an excruciating migraine, is very tuned in to her Emergent abilities at the moment.

I think I hear her gasp. I know this isn't easy for her. I whisper her name in the dark, but she hisses a "Shhh!" at me and continues to lead us through more side streets and laneways.

We don't pass a drone or a single person along the way.

As we wind along, though, we *do* pass apartments without rooftops, window-less churches, and other structures with huge sections of their walls missing. We slip by broken fountains, empty foundations, and sections of sidewalk where the pavement has buckled into tall heaps higher than my head.

Powerlines sag from broken wooden posts. Metal pipes, dry and flaked with rust, jut out from under the ground. Even in the gloom of night, we can make out the dark bands along the bottoms of the buildings where flooding from the ground-up meets with searing scorch marks from the top-down.

We all recognize the surface flash burns and the glassy heat residue in the air as signs of overhead plasma strikes. We've seen it firsthand in the Valta.

In the distance, I spot a strange object—a set of thin steel legs jutting into the sky. For a second, I imagine it's some giant, spindly-legged woman in mesh stockings lying on her back, about to give birth. "What's that?"

"The Eiffel Tower," Croque Madame whispers. "It's on its side."

"Frackin' hell," Cardyn mutters.

"It's been like that for four years now. And that," Croque Madame says, pointing down the road past a line of empty, melted mag-cars, is Le Jardin du Luxemburg, the Garden."

Rain tells us to hurry, and we slide, one by one, down an access chute into an empty basement of a building just across the road from the Garden. She leads us over to an opening in the high part of the wall where we can peer out across the road without being seen.

Rain's prediction about the Garden was right. If anything, this is the *opposite* of Eden.

Across the street and surrounded by more orange sensor pylons is a huge expanse of land. The giant plaza is a mini city packed to the edges with hundreds of leafless trees and thousands of aluminum-topped cabins, all crammed together with a grid of narrow walkways in between.

"So this is where everyone is," Brohn says.

"It's the only place anyone's technically allowed to be," Croque Madame tells us.

By "everyone," she must mean practically the entire city. From here, it looks like pretty much every person left alive inside the Paris city limits has gathered or been forced here to live in this tightly packed park.

Croque Madame clamps her hands onto the ledge of cracked and dusty bricks and rises up onto her tiptoes to get a better look. "It's better than when I was here last."

"It was worse than *this*?" Terk asks, incredulous.

"There was a lot more screaming last time."

She drops back down and points to the bag at Brohn's feet. "The supplies we've got there…they may not seem like much, but they could be the difference between life and death for these people."

"So how do we get in there?" I ask.

"There used to be security checkpoints with actual human guards. Some I knew. A few I could bribe. But it looks like it's all automated now." She scans the road to the left and right and shakes her head, her eyes drooped low with helplessness. "I can't exactly pay off a security drone, can I?"

Cardyn smiles. "Manthy can."

We all look at Manthy, who's standing away from us by one of the basement's flaked and peeling support pillars.

She walks up to Terk and cranes her neck to look up at him. Leaning back, his eyes wide, he stares down at Manthy like he's expecting her to leap up and attack him.

Instead, she puts her hand on his broad chest, her thin fingers splayed out like a starfish. "I need the Auditor."

Terk gives a relieved breath and relaxes his shoulders. From his back, the Auditor says she's happy to help.

Manthy calls me over, and I edge between Brohn and Cardyn to stand next to her. She still has one hand on Terk's chest. She takes my hand in her other.

"For moral support," she tells me through a weak smile.

But I know what she really means. She's bracing herself for the pain and asking me to hold her up in case she can't stand on her own.

Although she wobbles a bit and her eyes flutter, whatever she and the Auditor are doing only takes a few seconds. After that, Manthy drops her hands to her sides and says, "Okay."

"Okay, what?" Rain asks, her eyes darting between mine and Manthy's.

"It's a huge network," the Auditor explains. "Almost totally closed. But Manthy can give us a window. It'll last for maybe *ten* seconds. After that, the drone surveillance system will log the disruption, default to a diagnostic and investigation mode, and trace the problem back to me."

"Which means tracing it back to *us*," Brohn says.

"Should I stay behind?" Terk asks nervously. "Me and the Auditor?"

Brohn seems to consider this before saying, "No. We stick together."

Rain seems agitated, only I don't know if it's from the headaches she's been getting or from the general stress of what we're about to do. "So when can we cross over?"

Manthy closes and then opens her eyes. "Now."

Without another word or even a second's pause to tell us what she's about to do, she bounds up the small set of stone steps to street level with the rest of us sprinting along behind her, churning our arms and legs in an effort to keep up.

In a frantic dash and counting down the seconds in our heads, we slip between two of the floating orange pylons just as their sensor rings glow back to life.

Slowing to what we hope looks like a casual walk, we melt into the edge of the crowd, holding our collective breath to see if we've been spotted.

Other than a few annoyed grunts and curious stares from a few of the people ambling around on the perimeter of the Garden, there's no reaction.

Manthy stops, and Cardyn sings out, "Hey! We're not dead!"

Laughing with nervous relief, we gather in a tight space under one of the dead, ash-white trees where we can finally have a better look around.

The Garden isn't tidy and orderly like the Banters' settlement back in Hyde Park. This has become a medical center to treat the victims of whatever war has been fought here.

The place is crowded with everyone scrunching and nudging around each other. It's ironic. Everyone's so close together that, other than a few glances up at Terk, the seven of us go pretty much unnoticed.

Like in London, it's mostly kids our age with a few Neos, Juvens, and older adults sprinkled into the mix.

Unlike London, though, these aren't people playing at being

147

Medieval. And they're not like the small, relatively peaceful community we passed through back in Folkestone.

These are desperate, defeated people. Despair hangs on their bodies like old clothes. Hopelessness is painted on every inch of their faces.

And anger.

Brohn is just asking Croque Madame which way we need to go next when a tall, swarthy young man peels himself out of a line of passing pedestrians.

His eyes lock onto mine, and he charges right at us, advancing through the parting crowd with long, deliberate strides.

# IBRAHIM

WITH A DAZZLING, ear-to-ear smile of perfect teeth, the young man strides up to Croque Madame and plants his hands on her shoulders.

"Madame!"

"Ibrahim!"

Giddy and giggling, she throws her arms around the young man's waist before stepping back to introduce us.

We all shake hands, and I can't help but be impressed by his confidence. He's got thick, shiny black hair, high cheekbones, and a dimpled chin, barely visible under a coat of stubble. His skin is tight and tanned as polished leather, and his broad shoulders and thin waist give him the look of a very symmetrical and, okay, *gorgeous* triangle.

Even his fingernails are nice.

I'd never say it out loud, but looks-wise, he even gives Brohn a run for his money.

After our introductions, he stops, frozen in place like we've just told him we're a family of space aliens. "Wait. How did you get into the Garden?"

Cardyn throws his arm around Manthy. "Our friend here has a special way with machines."

Manthy scowls and takes a full step back, leaving Cardyn's arm to drop limply to his side.

Ibrahim strokes his chin and says, "Hm," but otherwise seems content to let the matter drop.

Instead, he urges us down one of the crowded footpaths and into a small white building not much bigger than one of the Hyde Park garden sheds.

He invites us to sit, his voice an unexpected combination of softness and authority.

Based on the holo-maps on the walls and the table of handguns and comm-links off to the side, I'm assuming this is some kind of command center.

As Ibrahim invites us to sit and begins to pour tea, we meet some of the many residents, who shuffle in and out of the shelter. They ask Ibrahim all kinds of questions about dates, times, supplies, medical equipment, preparedness status, and escape routes.

He answers every question with short, clear answers and a supportive smile.

"Most of the city is too dangerous to live in anymore," he explains. "We're trying to change that."

He goes on to give us a history of the Wealthies, the evolution of the drones, and the years of slow surrender until what was left of the population had been squeezed into the Garden.

At one point, Terk asks him, "Why don't the drones just bomb this entire park?" Rain glares at him and tells him that's a horrible question to ask.

Terk hangs his head and mumbles an apology.

"It's okay," Ibrahim assures him. "We used to wonder the same thing. We waited every day for the end. For the final act of genocide. But it never came."

"That's a good thing, right?" I ask.

"I don't think it was their intention to *effacer*...to *erase* us."

"You're sure?"

"That somehow crossed a line."

"Between?"

"Justifiable acts of cruelty and the loss of any last vestiges of humanity in whoever programs and runs the drones. I suspect keeping at least some of us alive confirms for them how right and just they truly are. So they're content to corral us. Keep us in these pockets."

"Where they can control you."

"We resisted. But how do you fight against an invisible enemy? Where are their leaders? Their troops? Their vulnerabilities? You can't negotiate with a drone."

"You said people program them," Brohn points out. "Where are *they*?"

"They are up there. In their towers. They are the wardens. And this...Le Jardin...this is the world's largest outdoor prison."

It's not walled off like the Banters' compound at Hyde Park in London, so I ask him why the people living here just don't leave.

"And go where?"

"I don't know. Somewhere...safer?"

"Did you ever play tag?"

"What?"

"Tag. The game where kids chase each other all over the place."

"Um. Sure, I guess."

"Remember home base? The safe spot you could get to where no one was allowed to tag you."

"Yeah."

"Well, this is that."

"So the drones don't—?"

"They leave le Jardin alone. The Custodian Drones keep track of who's here and who isn't. The people who live here...we're called Les Mains."

"Les Mains?"

"The Hands." Ibrahim stands, unclips a window panel in the wall, and tells us to have a look outside. He directs our attention to a tall, cylindrical tower of synth-steel and reflective glass, looming nearly invisible in the night sky. It's shimmering silver with thin red rings encircling it at different parts of its immense height. "We work in there."

"It's an arcology," Rain says.

"Oui."

"It looks like the world's largest rectal thermometer," Cardyn quips.

"It's one of two arcologies in the city," Ibrahim informs us with a sad laugh, pointing off into the distance in a different direction. "A third one is being built up on Montmarte. *We* build them." He taps his chest with his thumb. "*They're* the ones who live in them." He grumbles and stands up to pace, his jaw set and chiseled. "Once they defeated the Eastern Order, they said they had to keep us all safe from future attacks."

"Defeated the Order?"

"Drove them out in 2038."

"How do you know?"

"What do you mean?"

"What I mean is, did you ever fight the Order yourself?"

Ibrahim tilts his head back and laughs. "Me? I was just a kid last time the Order set foot in Paris. I don't think I'd even ever held a gun."

"What if we told you that the Order never set foot in Paris?"

We've had to explain the reality behind the propaganda before. It's never fun, and it's never easy. Sometimes we're believed. Other times—like with the Devoteds back home—we're ignored or seen as some kind of threat to world order.

Ibrahim's reaction is surprising.

"Eh bien. I figured as much."

"Really?"

"My mother was a philosopher. When I was little, she used to ask me all kinds of questions. Things that would probably make a grown-up's head spin."

"Like what?"

"Oh…things like, 'How do we know we can trust our senses?' Or, 'What if we're only hours old, and all of our memories have been implanted by God?'"

"Seriously?"

"She was a strange person, I admit. Papa couldn't deal with her half the time. Anyway, she taught me not to believe something just because I see it on a viz-screen. She said since they were broadcasts, they were already a version of a lie."

"Your mother told you this when you were…?"

"About six or so."

"And you understood it?"

"Ha! Not even close. But it made me skeptical. So when I saw rich and powerful people getting more rich and more powerful by telling us how afraid we should be of the Eastern Order, I grew suspicious. And when the military disappeared and the drones came, it started to occur to me that maybe there was more going on behind the scenes than we'd been led to believe."

Ibrahim invites us all to sit down again, and he goes about pouring cold tea into the small cups on the round table between us.

"Years back, before I was born, there was martial law here. Anyone speaking out, standing up, or getting in the way of what the Wealthies wanted got corralled into the parks: Luxembourg, Bois de Boulogne, Parcs des Buttes-Chaumont, Bois de Vincennes, and La Villette up north. They became what you see here: outdoor camps where people could live in peace and poverty."

"Except the Bois de Vincennes," Brohn reminds him. "We just came from there. And that park's been destroyed."

Ibrahim ponders this, as if he's connecting certain dots in his head. "That's true. Which means maybe even home base isn't safe anymore."

Croque Madame clenches and unclenches her fists like she's preparing for a fight. "There's no telling how long before the Wealthies decide their automation is good enough, which would make Les Mains—all of you—expendable."

"I'm surprised that hasn't happened already," Brohn growls.

Ibrahim hangs his head. "We're in a countdown," he says when he finally looks back up. "A race against time. Can we stop them before they cross the line and turn everything over to those Triad Drones? If that happens...*when* that happens, we'll go from being slaves to the Wealthies to being at the total mercy of the machines. And, as I'm sure you know, machines don't have mercy. We'll be a redundancy at best, a threat at worst. Either way, the Garden will go from safe haven to ground zero." Ibrahim gives an almost proud snort. "You could be looking at the last batch of true Parisians. The Wealthies will close their eyes. They will live their lives while they leave the drones out here to end ours."

Ibrahim apologizes for not being a better host. "But Madame and I need to consult with Council about distribution and allocation of the supplies you all so bravely and graciously brought."

Ibrahim and Croque Madame step outside of the cabin where they stand in a tight cluster with seven or eight other people just beyond the open doorway.

While they talk, Rain glances out at them before tugging me and our Conspiracy into a little huddle of our own. It feels kind of rude to lean into this six-person whisper fest, but I don't think I've ever said "No" to Rain before, and I'm not about to start now.

"There might be another way to save some of the people here." She looks up at Brohn. "If we can spare the time before we head out again."

"The Processor in Valencia is our top priority."

Rain frowns. "We can't just leave here without helping."

"That's exactly what we can do," Cardyn chimes in. "I'm all for a good bloodbath of a fight, but are we really going to try to save everyone we run into?"

Rain gives him a low, irritated growl. "Saving the world is possible, Card. We just have to do it one person at a time."

"You're the best one of us at math," Cardyn snaps back with uncharacteristic snark. "How much do the odds of our own survival go down with each one of those rescues?"

"Is there something between doing nothing and jumping into a full-on war?" I ask Rain.

She scowls at me, but then lightens up. She glances over her shoulder and through the open cabin door to where Ibrahim is pointing out through the gloom at the spotty muzzle flashes, the patrolling drones, and the distant explosions we can see from here.

"If we can infiltrate the drone network—"

"We?" Brohn asks.

"Well...the Auditor and Manthy. They got us in here. If they could do on a larger scale what they did with those Perimeter Sensor Pylons back there..."

Shaking her head, Manthy leans behind Cardyn like she's desperate to be as invisible as possible.

"If the two of them can combine their abilities," Rain continues, her voice undulating in an excited whisper, "maybe we can do in a few minutes what the people here haven't been able to do at all."

"I'm not capable of doing what you're asking," the Auditor's voice hums from the disk on Terk's back. "Not without modular root access. It's a lot different than slipping a redirectional protocol into the Perimeter Sensor Pylons."

"I haven't asked you anything yet," Rain snaps before gathering herself with a meditative sigh.

"She's just trying to help," I say. I know the Auditor was created partly out of my mother's consciousness, but I still feel kind of dumb for sticking up for what's essentially a complex, sometimes helpful, and occasionally annoying computer program.

Brohn strokes his finger and thumb along his stubbly jaw and looks up at the ceiling like he's expecting fat raindrops of answers to come plopping down. "Granden, Kella, and Wisp sent us on a very specific mission."

"To free kids from the Processor in Valencia," Terk adds, doing his best to be helpful.

"Right."

"Doing that and trying to help the people here aren't mutually exclusive missions," Rain says through an irritated grimace.

"I'm not disputing that. I just think we need to consider our options. Something's happening here. I don't know what. It smells like a rebellion. A last stand. If we get tangled up in some insurgency…well, let's just say we're not going to be much help to the kids in Valencia if we're dead."

Cardyn raises his hand. "Um. I get the dilemma. But which choice is most likely to wind up with our heads and our bodies being hauled off in different boxes? Because I'd like to vote for the *other* option."

Croque Madame leans her head into the cabin. "Are you all okay in there?"

Rain plasters on a smile and gives her a hearty thumbs up.

"I think Croque Madame is ready to get moving one way or the other," Terk observes.

"I don't know about the rest of you," I say, "but I can't see myself feeling great driving happily on to Spain while people are getting slaughtered in our rearview mirror."

I'm pleasantly surprised when everyone—even Manthy—nods their agreement.

"Fine," Brohn sighs. "Manthy and the Auditor can take *one* shot at this. We'll do what we can. But that's it. One shot. Call it a parting gift. Granden didn't send us on this mission just to give us something to do. Whatever's waiting for us in Valencia is important to him. *Very* important."

"Brohn's right," I tell the others. "Granden could have sent anyone on this mission. But he sent us. He would have given us more intel if he could. But we know it's important. Like, on a global scale. I hate to say it, but the six of us might be all that's stopping our own country, and who knows—maybe the entire world—from collapsing into...*this*."

Through the open window panels on three sides of the cabin, we all look out at the Garden. It's cramped, ringed by the smoky ruins of a once majestic city, and barely hanging onto life.

"So, Manthy?" Brohn asks. "Are you up for one more infiltration?"

"Ugh," Manthy grumbles, heaving herself to her feet. "Life was so much easier when I was dead."

## 22

## REPROGRAM

RAIN SPRINGS to her feet and leaves the cabin. When she comes back, she's practically dragging Ibrahim and Croque Madame back in by their hands.

"I think we can help."

"A *little*," Brohn interjects. "We can't stay here and fight with you. But maybe we can tip the odds a bit more in your favor."

Manthy doesn't look up when she says, "I need an access point."

"For what?" Croque Madame asks.

"We think maybe we can give Les Mains a way to start turning things around," Brohn tells her.

"But for that," Rain adds, "we need a foothold, some way—no matter how small—to patch into the local network."

Ibrahim looks from Brohn to Rain. He runs his fingers through his thick, dark hair. "We have a drone."

Rain squints and bites her lip. "What do you mean?"

"Our people—Les Mains—we've been known to fight back from time to time." Ibrahim walks the length of the cabin and opens up a large metal footlocker. He comes back, holding one of the snakelike Triad Drones in his hands, its diamond-shaped head and multi-faceted tail drooping down. "Will this do?"

Squinting, Rain leans over the drone. "Is it active?"

"They're programmed to self-destruct and basically vaporize themselves in the event they malfunction or get shot down. This one didn't, so we kept it. Call it a souvenir. One of the spoils of war. Not active, unfortunately."

"It doesn't matter," Manthy says evenly, stepping between Ibrahim and Brohn. "It'll do."

She holds her arms out and Ibrahim slides the drone from his hands to hers. It must weigh more than it appears to, because Manthy grimaces with surprise and has to strain a little just to hold it up.

Ibrahim leans in close to me. "And what's she going to do with that thing?"

"She's going to talk to it."

Ibrahim's eyebrow goes up as Manthy lays the drone on the floor and kneels in front of it like she's praying at an altar.

Folding his long legs under him, Terk sits down across from her. The Auditor instructs him to clamp his Modified hand onto the drone, which he does, and Manthy puts both of her hands on top of Terk's six-digit, synth-steel pincer.

Manthy closes her eyes and asks the Auditor if she's connected.

"I am," the Auditor replies. "But not as deeply as you seem to be. I'm afraid I can't find my way past the most surface-level protocols."

"It's okay," Manthy assures her. "I'll show you where to go. But be careful. This isn't like with the Perimeter Sensor Pylons. You can get lost in here."

The Auditor actually sounds nervous when she stammers, "I'll do my best."

Although the drone doesn't spring to life, it *does* give a few little twitches as a cluster of holo-code and 3D schematics appears in fluorescent orange and crackling neon green in the air above it.

On either side of the glitching array of diagrams and graphs, lines of strobing code scroll through the air, far too fast for our eyes to follow.

A muscular man in a tight white tank-top practically hurls himself into the cabin and shouts out for Ibrahim to come outside. "The Escorts and Crowd Controllers!"

In a smooth, casual motion Ibrahim stands and extends a hand, his voice calm in the face of the other man's panting excitement. "Take it easy, Solomon. What about them?"

"They're...they're...just come look!"

While Manthy kneels across from Terk over the trembling drone and continues staring blank-eyed into the scrolling code, the rest of us rush to the doorway to see what all the fuss is about.

Hundreds of people are gathered outside Ibrahim's cabin. They're all looking into the sky, chattering, and tugging on each other's sleeves as they point and stare.

We all look up, too, to see four different clusters of Triad Drones breaking formation overhead at the edges of the Garden. Several of the drones appear to have been frozen in mid-air, their grav-thrusters making feeble ripples in the air around them as they chug and struggle to keep from plunging to the ground. A bunch of other drones have started gliding around in lazy, random directions as if they've been drugged.

From inside the cabin, Manthy calls out to us that she's done.

We tear ourselves away from the odd sight of the aimless, drifting drones and go back in to find Terk helping Manthy, sweaty but smiling, to her feet.

"Those Patrol Drones out there," Ibrahim stammers. "They always run like clockwork. I've never seen them do anything like that before."

"They'll do that every day at exactly this time," the Auditor tells us. "They'll consider it a standard reset. Their diagnostics won't register it as anything other than a scheduled software update."

"The hibernation mode won't last long," Manthy says, her voice distant and frail.

Ibrahim looks far too happy to care, but he asks anyway. "How long?"

When Manthy doesn't answer, the Auditor tells him, "Approximately fifteen minutes."

He bites his lower lip and seems to contemplate this. "And that will happen every day?"

"At the same time. Yes."

"And there's no way they can detect us during that window?"

"That's right."

"Nowhere around the Garden, inside or out?"

"Nowhere in the city limits. That's the best we could do."

Ibrahim beams a glistening white smile, a flash of excitement dancing in his dark eyes. "Then I guess we take back our country. Fifteen minutes at a time."

All giggles and goofy grins, a swarm of Ibrahim's friends come barreling into the cabin. Rolling and tumbling over each other with the bouncy energy of a litter of puppies, they point back toward the open doorway. "Ibrahim! Did you see? The Patrol Drones—!"

"I saw. We have our new friends to thank."

The bouncing group—two older men, three older women, and at least seven or eight teenage boys and girls—swarms us and lock us into tight hugs, hard-pumping handshakes, and double-cheek kisses.

"Okay, okay!" Ibrahim laughs. "Let's not reward them by suffocating them, eh?"

The crowd of happy Hands trickles out, leaving us alone with Ibrahim, who continues to aim his beaming smile and impressed nods in our direction. "You should stay with us. It'd be a shame if you wound up saving our lives but weren't around to see what we do with them."

"As nice as that would be," Brohn tells him, "we're in a bit of a time crunch."

Cardyn compliments Manthy and the Auditor on a job well done but ends his praise with a long, drawn-out, "Only…"

"Only, what?" Rain asks.

"How do we get back out of the Garden? Manthy and the Auditor only put the Patrol Drones into hibernation. Those orange Perimeter Sensor Pylons are still active, right?"

"Could you disable them again?" I ask, but Manthy is quick to shake her head.

It's the Auditor who explains, "They'll track us in a split-second if we try another intrusion like that so soon."

We all swing around as one when Ibrahim laughs. "Don't worry. As admirable as your high-tech entry was, we have a few low-tech ways of our own for moving in and out of the Garden. We may be prisoners, but we're not completely paralyzed. Not yet, anyway. And, thanks to you, maybe not ever. *Viens.* Come. I'll get you back to your bus."

Without any further explanation, he leads us out of his cabin and takes us through the throng of his fellow Parisians, many of them with their eyes still fixed on the dazed drones. He seems to be something of a celebrity, and practically everyone we pass greets him with huge smiles, pumped fists, and claps to the shoulder.

He absorbs it all with grace, deferring any praise they have to Manthy each time.

When the people turn their attention to her, she cringes like their touch is toxic and burrows against Terk for shelter as we weave our way through the crowd.

Ibrahim strides along until we arrive at another cabin similar to his but smaller.

He ushers us inside and leads us to a silver hatch at the back of the dark room. He presses his thumb to a small pad on the wall, and the top of the hatch slides open.

"An old maintenance access port to the park's drainage system," he says, his eyes on the top rung of the rusted ladder leading down into the dark abyss. "Since it's not on any official city schematics, the drones don't know it's here. That's the great thing about machines, eh? Only as smart as their programming."

"Aren't we all," the Auditor sighs.

It takes a second to realize she's joking, and we all share a quick case of the giggles before Brohn breaks us out of our moment of amusement and tells us we need to get going.

"You'll be safe," Ibrahim promises. "Follow this route. It will get you to le Sorbonne. After that, follow the river. But *faites attention*. Be careful. The drones patrol there."

"And our fifteen-minute drone-less window will be long gone," Rain reminds us.

We spend probably a few minutes too long saying goodbye to our charismatic, perpetually-smiling new friend.

With Brohn in the lead and with Manthy bringing up the rear, we climb down the ladder one at a time. After Manthy's down, we embark on a long, dark, and very wet slog through the access tunnel.

Less than an hour later, after some of the creepiest, darkest, and sloshiest underground shuffling we've ever done, we climb a second metal ladder and wind up in what seems to be a building's climate-control room.

From there, we follow Rain down a maintenance corridor and out an old delivery door. Once outside, we scamper along a construction tunnel and then through an abandoned zoo that smells like overcooked bacon and barbecued hair.

Hopping the tall fence on the far side of the old zoo, we dash along the Seine's empty riverbed—ducking into dark alleyways, open doorways, or squatting behind tall piles of rubble as we make our way through the near total darkness.

With our fifteen-minute window long gone, we take extra care to stick close to Rain, stopping and starting again only when she does.

A very long hour later, we cross a bridge, sprint through some decimated woods, and emerge in a clearing.

Croque Madame's bus is sitting right where we left it, and I feel really dumb for being this close to tears. Who would've thought the sight of a twelve-ton, cantaloupe-colored school bus with so many broken windows and too many bullet holes to count could ever look this beautiful?

After Croque Madame scans the doors open, we climb aboard and say our sad goodbyes to the smoking shell of Paris as we continue our way south through the French countryside.

Peering out the bus window into the dark Parisian night, Terk bites his lip. "What if the drones follow us?"

Manthy shakes her head and assures him they won't. "We're outside their patrol range."

Brohn and I drift to the back where we sit across the aisle, facing each other with our backs pressed to the walls on opposite sides of the bus. He's got his legs stretched out and crossed at the ankles. I've got my legs tucked up with my chin resting on my knee.

I ask him if he thinks Ibrahim and Les Mains will be okay.

He shrugs. "Obviously, I *hope* so."

"Obviously. But what do you *think*?"

"I think they're facing a faceless enemy with endless resources and no empathy."

"Ugh. That's not exactly the best prescription for success."

"I also think they're organized, angry, and desperate."

"Definitely a better prescription."

"Plus, Manthy and the Auditor gave them a serious edge. Fifteen minutes a day might not be much, but it's a start. Every revolution has to start with fifteen minutes where someone, *anyone*, makes a very loud, very public choice between the safety of slavery and the demands of freedom."

"And Ibrahim can be that someone?"

"If we could pull off our own revolutions back home, there's no reason they can't do the same here. I don't see that guy settling for slavery. He's too smart. Too stubborn. Besides, it's not like we're the only people in the world who care enough to act."

"I guess."

Exhausted, I fall into a deep sleep. I don't know how long it lasts, but I bolt awake with a scream.

I'm shocked to hear my voice echo inside the bus.

Then I realize it's not an echo. It's Manthy.

From her spot two rows ahead of mine, she's woken up screaming, too. At the exact same time as me.

Brohn, Cardyn, Rain, and Terk cluster around us.

Rain and the boys lean in, their faces contorted with worry.

After I finally get my bearings and catch my breath, I recount my dream:

"I was flying past a long wall with tiny holes in it. Like windows or portals or something. I kept trying to see what was on the other side. There were people and things there. People and things I *kind of* recognized but couldn't quite place. The holes were too small, and I was flying too fast. I couldn't control my speed. I was flying, but it felt like I was falling. Sideways. Over and over in a big, endless loop. Does that make sense?"

"Dreams aren't supposed to make sense," Rain says, swinging around to sit down next to me. "That's why they're dreams."

"I've had dreams like that," Terk assures me, his voice full of comfort and concern. "Dreams about falling. I always wake up right before I land." He looks genuinely relieved about that fact.

"I wouldn't worry about it too much," Cardyn says. He's kneeling on the seat in front of mine, his arms folded along its top, his chin resting on the back of his hands. "Dreams don't mean anything, right?"

165

"Dreams," the Auditor says, "have been speculated about and obsessed over but never conclusively understood."

"Do tell," I say with a smile and an eyeroll.

"The ancient Sumerians believed dreams were windows into other worlds," she continues, apparently not picking up on my weary sarcasm. "The ancient Greeks saw dreams as prophecies or as guidance from the gods. Some early Chinese philosophers saw the soul as two units where one wandered in the dream world while the other slept. Austrian psychoanalyst and neurologist Sigmund Freud speculated that dreams were manifestations of subconscious desires, repressions, and sexual anxieties. Many Indigenous populations see dreams as communication between themselves and their ancestors. Seventeenth-century French philosopher René Descartes believed it was possible that every-thing in the material world was implanted as dreams in our minds. In 'Simulacra and Simulation,' Jean Baudrillard proposed that human reality is all a dream-like imitation of the *real* reality. Nearly twenty-five hundred years ago, the Chinese philosopher Zhuang Zhou dreamed he was a butterfly but then wondered if maybe *he* was the butterfly having a dream about Zhuang Zhou."

The Auditor stops as abruptly as she started.

There's a thick, chunky pause while we let her breathless lecture soak in.

Filling the void of silence, the Auditor adds, "The study of dreams is referred to as 'oneirology.'"

For some reason, we all break out into a burst of eye-watering laughter. Even Manthy tries to clamp her lips down over an insuppressible grin.

To our combined shock and delight, even the Auditor laughs. "I'm sorry," she giggles. "What can I say? I *am* connected, after all."

"I'm jealous," Cardyn admits with a chuckle. "I wish I were."

"Don't worry," the Auditor assures him. "You'll get there."

"Well, whatever dreams are," I say, wiping tears from my eyes with the heels of my hands, "in my dream just now...I don't think I was me."

"Who were you?" Brohn asks.

"I think I was a raven in someone else's dream."

From the front of the bus, Render turns his head around and gurgles and clacks in our direction.

"I think Render's offended," Rain says. "I'm sure he won't want to hear he's really a butterfly who just dreamt he was a raven."

"I won't pretend to know what it means," Brohn says with a shake of his head. "But it sounds like a pretty scary dream."

Terk turns to Manthy. "Hey, Manth. What about yours?"

Manthy fixes her eyes on Terk's for what feels like a long time before she glances over at me from the corners of her eyes and then turns back around and leans her head against the window. "I had the *exact* same dream."

I start to smile, but then I realize she's not joking.

## 23

# BRIDGES

THE TREACHEROUS AND winding road is littered with garbage, fallen trees, remnants of rockslides, and deep, singed-around-the-edges craters.

For the next hour, the bus rumbles over a series of hills and around a long series of tight curves with no guardrail and with what looks like a pretty high probability of death.

Croque Madame shouts out for us to hold on, but we've already got a vice-grip on the backs of the seats in front of us.

The bus leans hard to the side as Croque Madame struggles with the mammoth steering wheel.

The curved and rocky road evens out, and the bus settles at last, its grinding mag-combustion hybrid engine relaxing into a gentle hum.

"Did you see that?" Terk asks.

Wide-eyed and with his nose practically pressed to the window, Cardyn mutters, "Marvie."

We line up along the windows, staring out in disbelief at the metamorphosis happening before our eyes.

It's like the sky changed its mind and, in an instant, went from a stormy red to a peaceful, rolling, ocean blue.

The narrow, cratered road has smoothed out and widened. For the last part of our trip, it was littered with garbage, derelict cars and trucks, and strewn with human and animal bones. Here, the shoulders of the highway are lined with fine white gravel, coffee-colored earth, and deep fields of dainty gold and purple flowers.

There are even trees with living branches and leaves and the splashes of the green we were missing before.

Madame gives us all a coy look from the front of the bus.

When I ask, "How...?" she taps a small translucent tube embedded in the front console next to the steering wheel. "A gift. It lets us see what others can't."

"And what are we seeing, exactly?" Brohn asks.

"The Port of the Moon. The Edge of the Water..." She relaxes her vice-grip on the steering wheel and guides the bus along a glassy, untouched stretch of road. "Welcome to Bordeaux."

We can't believe our ears. Or our noses. Or any of our senses for that matter. This place...this city we're approaching...it looks from here to be intact, quiet, and clean.

*Where are the fallen buildings? The roving gangs of Scroungers? Where are the cratered roads, the scorched ruins, the blood-red sky, the charred piles of human remains, and all the other remnants and reminders of war?*

Brohn has his head out the window. He's taking deep breaths, and I can't tell if he's stunned, relieved, or in shock.

I put my head through the window next to his and ask him what he's feeling.

"I'm hopeful," he sighs into the crisp breeze. "And nostalgic."

"The Valta?"

"Remember the smell?"

"It was clean."

"Right? Even after the attacks. Every time. It's like the air, the woods, something in the mountains wouldn't give up."

My hair is a wild mess in the rolling wind, but I don't tie it back.

"Are you seeing this?" Rain calls out from an open window a few rows behind mine.

"I'm seeing it!" I assure her over the swirling, breezy gusts and the even thrum of the bus tires on the practically frictionless, glistening road. "Seeing it, smelling it, loving it!"

Madame steers the bus past a line of evenly spaced trees, their healthy trunks and leaf-clustered branches casting long, soft shadows over us as we pass.

I duck back into the bus and plop down onto the bench seat. My lungs feel better than they've felt in a long time. "Why can't *every* place look and smell like this?"

Up front, Croque Madame can't seem to stop looking into the sideview mirrors.

"No one's following us," I assure her.

I've just tapped into Render who's been flying high overhead for the past hour or so. Normally, a raven wouldn't be able to keep up with a fast-moving vehicle. In the wild, ravens travel at around twenty-five miles per hour. But deplorable road conditions here combined with his bio-tech enhancements enable him to stay with us and even fly ahead sometimes.

For now, though, he's sending me images from the area we just passed, so I can tell there's nothing behind us but our tire tracks on the open road.

I disconnect from him after a few seconds. This is one of the rare times when I'd rather be cruising along the highway as me than flying up there in the air as *us*.

Cardyn leans forward, his chin on my shoulder as he explains more about my abilities to Croque Madame. "So, Kress here can see from a bird's eye view any time she wants."

Croque Madame's eyes glance skyward. "So I've seen. And you never get dizzy up there?"

"I used to. It's gotten easier over time."

I don't admit to my growing fear that I'll eventually start losing my balance down here.

"How is this happening?" Terk asks, his eyes fixed on the impossible city outside. Even though it looks like paradise out there, he sounds scared.

Croque Madame fiddles with one of the holo-projection ports on the input panel next to the steering wheel. "I'll show you."

She drives us across a bridge. "This is the Pont Jacques Chaban-Delmas. It's the longest vertical lift bridge in Europe."

She must sense something's up with us because she glances over her shoulder to see all of us sitting stock-still and holding our breath.

"We're not used to seeing unbroken bridges," Brohn explains as we reach the other side of what Croque Madame tells us is the Garonne River. "We had to climb over the remains of a badly broken one in London."

"Oh, right. Vauxhall Bridge. Amazing what those kids did with the sculptures, eh?"

"Actually, yes," I admit.

"You know why?"

"Why what?"

"Why the Scroungers re-located those eight sculptures in the river."

"No. Why?"

"Rumor is they believed the only way to stay safe was to have those eight women—four facing upstream, four facing down—watching over them. Protecting them. They said it was men who did the world wrong. Maybe those eight women were all it'll take to do it right."

"The Scroungers are still alive so maybe it worked," Terk suggests.

"I'd hardly call the world out there 'right,'" Rain tells him.

Terk shrugs and takes a long look back at the bridge as we near its end. "This is a start, though, isn't it?"

Croque Madame drums her fingers on the steering wheel. "Bridges are one of the first things the enemy looks to destroy."

"Why? So people can't get to work?" Terk asks.

"No," Cardyn counters. "It's so trucks can't pass over and boats can't pass through. It's all about cutting off supply lines." He taps his temple. "Very clever strategy."

Brohn shakes his head. "It's to destroy morale. Bridges are symbols. They show there's nothing human beings can't do, no distance we can't cross. Destroy that, and you destroy morale. Destroy morale, and you keep everyone afraid and too broken to fight back."

Rain suggests that targeting bridges has to do with a reallocation of resources. "It's like in chess," she says. "If I can get you to dedicate your pieces to defense on one side of the board, I'm free to launch my attack on the other."

I tell them I'm pretty sure I read that the destruction of bridges in war is to prevent the movement of enemy troops.

From a few rows behind us, Manthy's voice is smooth and even. "It's about separation." She seems fixated on something outside the bus—maybe the long green grass along the side of the road or the intact houses and shops up ahead—and doesn't turn to look at us.

We all glance up at Croque Madame who nods her agreement. "She's right. The first step in any war is to separate people from each other. Divide families. Sow discord. Makes it easier to imagine an enemy. Whether the enemy is real or not. Like you guys and Ibrahim said back there in Paris about the Order."

I look back at Manthy who seems relaxed at least, even when she rejects my invitation to join us up front.

Brohn, Cardyn, Rain, Terk, and I all lean forward as we turn onto a narrow road barely wide enough for the bus.

At Brohn's request, the muffled voice of the Auditor tells us about the city. "Bordeaux was built on the right and left banks of the Garonne River. With nearly four hundred historical monuments, it was known as the 'City of Art and History.' In the early part of this century, it became a hub of laser technology. The Fourth Matter Plasma Project of 2028 and the Magnetic-Optical Initiative of 2030 began in Bordeaux and led to many of the advances that made today's drone technologies possible."

"Marvie," Cardyn says with a sarcastic snort. "So this is where they built the drones that destroyed our town."

"Only the technological foundation," the Auditor clarifies. "President Krug and the Deenays in the U.S. built the actual devices used in the attacks on American targets."

"Even marvier," Cardyn grumbles.

"If it makes you feel any better," the Auditor continues, "Bordeaux was also known for its wine production, especially its reds. For a long time, it was the home of Vinexpo, the world's largest wine festival."

"I don't drink," Cardyn boasts, and I whack his shoulder and tell him to stop being such a grump.

"It also has the Rue Saint Catherine, which was Europe's largest shopping center."

"Only one problem with your info," Croque Madame says through a sly, nearly giddy grin.

The Auditor sounds vaguely offended when she asks what problem Croque Madame is referring to.

"You keep saying 'was.' There's no past tense this time. You see, Bordeaux...*is*."

She points through the front windshield at the majestic wood, steel, and stone buildings rising up into a sea-blue sky. Colorful awnings flutter in a light breeze over what must be thousands of balconies overlooking paved roads and glistening cobblestone lanes.

The city we enter is...clean. The buildings are standing. There are people out on the streets. There *are* streets.

Unlike London, where the buildings were piles of rubble, or Paris, which was basically on fire and under constant siege, Bordeaux looks how a city with so much history should look.

Compared to what we've experienced in our travels—from the Valta to Chicago to D.C. to London to Paris—it's practically paradise.

Croque Madame steers the bus into what I'm sure is going to be an impossible turn, but she completes the maneuver with ease, whistling a happy tune as she goes.

After another minute or two, she swings us into a large parking lot where six other buses, similar to ours but empty, are parked in spaces marked off with yellow holo-lights.

"This is it," she calls out. She presses the pad of her thumb to a red gear panel to drop the bus into parking mode. The bus heaves a sigh and goes quiet as Croque Madame stands and bends over to touch her fingertips to her toes. "We'll stop here to refresh and refuel before heading on."

"Seriously?" I ask. "Is it safe?"

"Safest place we're likely to land."

"We have a habit of dragging danger along with us."

"Then we'll try not to stay too long."

"Try?"

"Like beauty," she tells us, "Bordeaux is seductive. Try not to fall in love."

*Too late*, I think, as I breathe deeply and stare around at the ornate sea of stunning gothic and baroque architecture, untouched by war. *Too late.*

## CHOCOLATE

HOPPING down one at a time from the bus, we follow Croque Madame's lead and do a whole series of stretches of our own on the clean cobblestones of the large parking area.

But sore muscles are the last things on my mind. I want to know where we are, exactly, and why this city isn't a smoldering expanse of slag.

Brohn must've been reading my mind because he stops in the middle of a groaning back-stretch, turns to Rain, and laughs. "So...Rain. You're our resident expert in logistics. Is this place real? Or did Noxia get ahold of us and plant this all in our heads?"

"It *does* seem too good to be true," Terk agrees.

Rain takes a second to survey the empty area. The buildings surrounding the open parking lot are a combination of old stone and tidy brick. There are a few signs on some of the shops: "Boulangerie." "Laverie." "Café." "La Boucherie." "Supermarché." "Grand Magasin."

The big storefront windows twinkle under the rays of the crisp yellow sun.

The place is an odd combination of quaint and clean with a

few modern flourishes—strips of holo-lights, automated waste-recycling bins, mag-doors, and floating, apple-sized air purifiers—speckled around for good measure.

Surrounding us are church spires and cathedral tops—fully intact—poking up here and there, happy flowers in a field, all of them getting along like old friends.

Rain swings back around to face Terk and starts ticking names off on her fingers. "There are lots of examples of perfect little places like this hidden away in corners of our world: Xanadu. Brigadoon. Narnia. El Dorado. Wonderland. Atlantis. Shangri-La. Themyscira. Avalon. Wakanda."

"But those are made up," I remind her. "This is real. We're here. We're in it."

Rain shrugs.

From behind me and sounding a little offended, Manthy crosses her arms. "They're not *all* made up."

"Sure," Cardyn scoffs. "Now I suppose you're going to sprinkle some of your magical Manthy-dust on us and fly us home to Neverland."

"Whoa," Brohn says to Cardyn, as if he's calming a wild stallion. "Try not to be such an annoying little Lost Boy."

"I don't care if this is real or an illusion or a figment of our deepest desires planted in our heads," Terk gushes. "It's clean. There's no one chasing us, and it smells like the Valta."

"With a little cedar, prunes, and pepper thrown in," I add, with my headed tilted back, my nose in the air.

Croque Madame gives me an impressed squint. "You know your scents. Wine connoisseur?"

"It's not me," I assure her, pointing up to where Render has settled on a spiked, white metal railing running along the rooftop of a nearby two-story building. "It's him."

"Got a good nose on him, does he?"

"Well," I grin, hoping he doesn't hear me. "He's no turkey vulture, but yeah."

We're all startled to attention as a group of people appear out of nowhere. They're mostly adults with a few kids our age mixed in.

Dressed in a rainbow of linen pants, skirts, and shirts, many of them are carrying some kind of silver cricket bats with a blurry red halo around the edges of the blades.

In a single flowing motion, my Conspiracy and I leap into a defensive half-circle around Croque Madame as the mob approaches.

*I knew this place was too good to be true!*

I do a quick scan and consider our odds. There are twenty-six people approaching. Twelve of them are armed with those glowing, bladed batons. Two of the men have some sort of machete hanging in clenched fists at their sides. The other people could be concealing any number guns, explosives, or bladed weapons.

And we're six teenagers, a grown woman, and an armored raven who've just cruised into their town on a big orange school bus.

Paradise has just turned ugly. We're surrounded, outnumbered, and our weapons—modern and Medieval—are still on the bus.

Taking long, determined strides now, the crowd advances.

Terk asks Rain, "What now?" out of the corner of his mouth.

"We don't panic," Rain whispers back out of the corner of hers.

Next to me, Brohn's muscles tighten, and he takes a half-step forward, ready to plant himself between us and our assailants.

Out of the corner of my eye, I catch Croque Madame making a quick move.

In a smooth, subtle motion, she reaches over and presses her thumb to one of the input pads on the side of the bus. A long panel hisses open, exposing a storage compartment, packed full of silver, cinder block-sized storage boxes.

I start backing up as the crowd continues to advance.

"Those better be weapons you've got in there," Cardyn calls out to Madame over his shoulder.

"They're not," Croque Madame laughs.

I whip my head around to see what she could possibly be laughing at.

In that split second, the crowd surges forward.

They swarm past me and my startled Conspiracy and leap onto Croque Madame.

Buried under the pack of people, she continues to laugh as the noisy throng embraces her or reaches through the swarm to shake her hand.

The rest of us are tensed to the hilt, and I'm wondering why we're not dead.

"This is *l'Équipe de Transfert*. The Transfer Crew," Croque Madame calls out to us from deep within the happy mass of giddy, bouncing bodies. "They're going to ferry some of our cargo from the bus to their distribution center."

A couple of the people give us polite little bows. One of the teenage girls—her hair in long, blond, fairy-tale braids—licks her lips and blows Brohn a kiss. He smiles and gives her a half-wave, and I smack his arm.

"Ouch. What was that for?"

"I have no idea what you're talking about."

Brohn gives me a quick peck on the cheek. "Riiiight."

I smile and whack his arm again, only not as hard this time.

"I thought you were going to whip out a bunch of weapons," Terk admits to Croque Madame.

"I run weapons, but supplies, too."

"Supplies?" Brohn asks.

With a distinct twinkle in her eyes, Croque Madame points to the line of crates in the open bay of the bus. "That the good stuff. Baguettes. Macarons. Cheese. Éclairs. And, of course, chocolate."

At the word "chocolate," my salivary glands shift into over-drive, and I've got to drag my sleeve across my mouth to staunch the flow. "We thought you were just a weapons-runner. You know—supplying the resistance with guns and explosives and swords and such."

"I do that, too. But would you really want to live in a world without bread, cheese, and chocolate?"

"Good point," Cardyn gushes, and I'm afraid he's going to break his neck from snapping his head back and forth so fast.

I tell him to wipe the drool off his mouth before we all step aside to let the Transfer Crew pass.

They lower their silver batons we all thought were weapons. It turns out they're grav-staffs.

Lining up along the side of the bus and with Croque Madame's happy blessing, the men and women approach the cargo hold one at a time and slip the blade end of their devices into slots at the base of each crate. The red halo goes green, and they're able to lift the crates as easily as Render could lift a twig.

They give us curious looks but also smiles and soft "Bonjours" as they pass by, filing out of the parking lot and down a cobblestone laneway, pushing their floating cargo in front of them like a line of victorious army ants bringing home their trophies from war.

"Come on," Croque Madame calls out. "We'll follow them."

"To where?"

"To Martine de la Bourse. She's a friend, kind of. And an innkeeper at the Arc en Rêve."

"What's 'kind of a friend'?" I ask.

Madame tells us not to worry. "You'll love her. Trust me."

His voice gravelly and gruff, Brohn snaps his head around to the bus. "What about our weapons?"

"Won't need 'em. Can't take 'em."

Brohn stops in his tracks. "Why does that make me nervous?"

"Because you're smart, strong, and you've got a protective instinct bigger than my bus." Croque Madame stops and swings her attention from one of us to the other. "It sounds like you've

179

been through a lot. More than anyone should've been through at your age. Trust isn't the enemy of caution. Out there, being careful can keep you alive. But don't let 'out there' also kill your ability to find and trust new friends." Madame gives me a wink. "Even if they're only 'kind of.'"

"You're right," I beam, my mind flashing back to the Insubordinates, War and the Survivalists, Mayla and the Unkindness, the Banters, the Royals.

With all the enemies we've had to overcome—from the invented Eastern Order to Krug and his Patriot Army—it's nice to remember all the friends we've made along the way.

Cardyn cranes his neck forward, his chin practically on Croque Madame's shoulder. "You did say there's chocolate, right?"

"Among other things. Did you think protein cubes were all that's left to eat in the world?"

"Kinda."

"Then I'm happy to report how wrong you were."

Cardyn beams an unreturned smile at Manthy, who seems satisfied to trundle along in Terk's shadow as we follow Croque Madame and the long line of human army ants.

"What do you think?" Brohn asks Rain. "It this a trick?" Then he swings around to me. "A trap?"

"I don't care," I tell him. "It smells like home."

## BORDELAIS AND BORDELAISES

CROQUE MADAME PEELS OFF from the back of the line and raps her knuckles on the polished wooden door of one of the many quaint little shops lining the laneway.

The door swings open to reveal a shortish woman—not much taller than Madame—with silvery, wide-set eyes, full lips, rosy cheeks, and salt-and-pepper hair trimmed into a neat bob.

The woman's face glows with a sunny, open-mouthed smile as she throws her arms around Croque Madame and kisses her on both cheeks. "Bienvenu! Nous saluons le retour! C'est bon de te voir!"

Croque Madame holds the woman at arm's length, matching the woman's cheerful smile with a wide one of her own. "It's good to see you, too, Martine."

Turning to us, she tells us to follow her into the foyer where she introduces us one at a time to this pleasant, gleeful woman.

Martine gives us each a "Bienvenu!" and a double cheek-kiss, which Rain tolerates, which makes Terk giggle, and which Manthy, wide-eyed and tongue-tied, seems too stunned to reject.

Brohn, Cardyn, and I let out a simultaneous breathy whoosh at not being tricked into some life-threatening trap.

*At least not yet.*

"And Render's flying around somewhere," I tell Martine. He's a raven."

"Ah...*le corbeau*. Great intellectuals. Tool-users. And holders of grudges."

"That's only because they're smart enough to remember who's offended them," I offer with my fists on my hips and with more of a defensive pout than I intended.

"Zen I shall be careful not to offend," Martine offers with a pleasant smile.

The clearing of a disembodied throat wafts from the disk on Terk's back. "And *I'm* the Auditor."

"Oh, sorry," Terk blushes, his chin tilted toward his shoulder. "I have the techno-consciousness of Kress's dead mother strapped to my back."

Martine pauses before jutting out her bottom lip and nodding. "Don't we all?" and then she bellows up a hearty laugh. "*Viens, viens*," she squeals. "All of you...Come with me!"

Martine takes us through the back of the building and along a series of cobblestone laneways snaking between rows of bright two and three-story apartments and small cafés with well-populated outdoor patios.

"Sooooo...," Cardyn drawls, looking up, down, and all around at the people and places we pass. "Is anyone going to explain how all of this is even possible?"

Martine laughs. "Bien sûr! How many questions you must 'ave! Where to begin, eh? When ze Eastern Order first attacked London, we grew *inquiet*...um, worried. When zey attacked Paris, we grew scared. We were sure we were next. But nozing 'appened. No bombs rained down from ze sky. We didn't know why. Not at first. Only zat we 'ad become magically overlooked. *Oublié*. Invisible."

"Invisibility," Cardyn sighs. "Now that's a power I'd like to have."

Brohn throws a brotherly arm around Cardyn's shoulders. "Invisibility...it's a power the rest of us wish you had, too."

Cardyn makes a grand show of pushing Brohn's arm off of him like it's an unwelcome giant anaconda.

"Wait," I say. "What do you mean, invisible?"

"I'll show you."

"She's going to show us what's invisible?" Cardyn says. "Isn't that a paradox?"

"*You're* a paradox," I tease.

"Oh. You mean because I'm somehow simultaneously rakishly good-looking, brilliant, *and* unusually modest?"

"Yeah," I say with an eyeroll that makes him laugh. "*That's* what I meant."

Martine waves her hand to get the attention of a young girl at one of the vendor's stalls about a hundred feet away.

The girl—pouty-lipped and with a nearly-shaved head—bounds up to us and throws her arms around Martine's waist.

Dressed in a plum-colored fjord swing dress and white tights, the girl can't be more than ten or eleven years old.

"Zis is my niece. Roxane."

We all say "Hi," but Roxane doesn't answer.

*Great,* I think. *Another mousy and withdrawn girl.*

But then I feel terrible when Martine tells us that Roxane *can't* talk. "She's never said a word her entire life." She hugs the girl close and kisses her on the top of the head. "But she has ways of making herself heard. Oh, and she's ze reason we're all not dead. You see, Roxane can do something no one else can do. She has an *ability.*"

"Like us!" Terk blurts out. "We're Emergents." He blushes and holds up his mechanical arm. "Well, *they* are. I guess I'm technically a Modified now."

"You're *actually* our friend," Brohn declares. "No matter what you are."

"What can she do?" I ask, turning our attention back to this small, innocent looking girl.

Martine shifts her gaze from me to Croque Madame, who gives her a half-nod and an "It's okay. These are friends" look of permission.

"Roxane can...*créer le voile*. She can shift space-time perceptions."

We're quiet for a second before Brohn admits on behalf of all of us, "We don't know what that means."

"It means she can change when and how we're seen."

"We knew a boy like that," I say. "Amani. He could kind of camouflage himself as other people."

Next to me, I feel Brohn blush. As far as we know, he was Amani's last victim. And then, to get taken over by Noxia...I know, as strong as he is, he's been feeling like the weak link lately. And on top of that, now it looks like he might have certain other physical weaknesses we never suspected. I forget sometimes that having tough skin isn't the same as invulnerability.

"She doesn't disguise *herself*," Martine elaborates. "She disguises everything else."

"So...basically a human Veiled Refractor?" Rain asks.

Martine frowns. "I don't know if I'd call her a Veiled Refractor. But yes, she's human."

Reverting to his little-boy-in-school mode, Cardyn raises his hand and makes a circle in the air with his finger. "You mean she disguises all of this?"

"Zat's *exactly* what I mean. Drones, satellites, radar systems— zey see Bordeaux. Only zey see it over fifty miles to ze west from where it really is. She is ze one who saved ze *Bordelais* and *Bordelaises*—ze men and women of Bordeaux."

It sounds like she wants to say more, but Martine is suddenly quiet.

"What is it?" Rain asks.

"Bergerac is gone."

"Bergerac?"

"A wonderful town."

"Gone?"

"Détruit. Bombed. *Éliminé*."

"But you're safe," Croque Madame chimes in.

"Zat we are."

"And this little girl did that?" Brohn asks.

"She's not ze one who shielded us. Not at first. Zat was her mother. My sister. But zis little one, she inherited ze gift. She takes care of us now."

I look around the crowded market. "Where's her mother?"

Martine and Croque Madame both hang their heads, but it's Martine who answers. "How old are you?"

We glance back and forth at each other before Brohn answers. "We're eighteen."

"Eighteen," Martine repeats. "And not from here."

"We're on a mission."

"Not sent by your parents."

"No. We have a team back home. Granden, Wisp, Kella—"

Martine cuts him off with a wave of her hand. "Then I suspect Roxane's parents are in ze same place as yours."

A lump rises in my throat, and I take a full step back along with every member of our Conspiracy. It's like we've been kicked in the chest.

I know Martine isn't trying to hurt us, but her words are a sledgehammer.

The truth always hurts.

Martine's voice goes apologetically soft. "Françoise—Roxane's mother—was killed by Hawkers."

Brohn stares at her for a second before he manages to get his jaw working again. "Hawkers."

"You know zem?"

"We've escaped them."

"Zen count yourselves lucky."

185

"Luck isn't a strategy," Rain says. "We're alive because we've stayed together. We're a Conspiracy."

Martine nods her understanding. "Françoise was alone when she was...when ze Hawkers came. Zey're relentless, you know. Zey never stop."

"So we've heard."

"But zey have one weakness."

"What's that?"

"Zey rely on separating their prey." Martine points directly at each one of us. "Zey don't know what to do when ze ones zey're hunting stick together."

Martine tells Roxane to run off, and the little girl skips away, disappearing into a crowd of older girls at the end of the block.

Cardyn tugs the elbow of Croque Madame's jacket and reminds her about her promise of food.

Overhearing, Martine laughs and tells us she has a feast in store for us. "For the stomach, yes? But also for the eyes. Follow me!" Her long, light skirt whooshing around her legs, she strides off with steps far too fast and long for a woman with legs that short.

I'm just starting to follow her when Rain yanks me back. "Did you hear what Martine said?"

"Sure," I tell her, already anxious to catch up with the others. "We're going on a tour. I'm looking forward to it. This place looks *amazing!*"

"Not that, Kress."

"What then?"

"She said that little girl can change 'when and how we're seen.'"

"Yeah. Sounds like a handy ability to have. You're not jealous, are you?"

"I'm being serious, Kress."

"Fine. So what's the big deal? She has an ability. She's an Emergent. We knew we weren't the only ones out here."

"No." Clearly growing impatient with me, Rain gives a little stomp with her foot. "How can she change *when* they're seen?"

I stare at Rain for a second without an answer. "Maybe she misspoke. Or maybe you misheard her."

"You heard it, too, didn't you?"

"Hey!" Brohn shouts back to us. "Kress! Rain! Try to keep up!"

We shake ourselves out of our discussion and scamper down the street before I have a chance to admit to Rain that maybe she's onto something.

By the time we've caught up to the others, though, the whole idea seems silly, and I scold myself for letting Rain distract me from the incredible beauty of this amazing place.

## TIME OUT

THE TOWN MAY BE invisible from the outside, but from inside, it's a buffet of charm for the eyes.

While Render continues to explore from above, Martine, bouncing and bubbly, shows us around down here at ground level.

We walk for a long time. The whole day, in fact. But none of us seems tired. I keep thinking, after all we've already been through just to get this far, we should be wiped out or passed out unconscious in a bunch of beds somewhere. But whatever second wind I've picked up seems to have found its way into all of us.

"It's got to be the air," I tell Brohn. "Seriously. Have you ever smelled anything like it?"

He makes a big show of taking a deep breath and then clutches me tight and laughs as he kisses the top of my head. "Your hair gives this air a serious run for its money!"

I tell him I can't take credit for that. After all, the sonic wands we've been using to keep ourselves clean can only do so much. Instead, I tell him I think the air here is actually cleansing. "Like it wants us to be at our best."

"Well, whatever it is," he replies, his lips grazing over my fore-head and down my cheek, "Kress...you are *beyond* best."

It's times like this when I'm glad I have a good memory. This is one of those moments I'd better not *ever* forget.

Over to the side of the road, Cardyn's been chattering away to Manthy about all the sights and about how clean everything is. Brohn keeps saying, "Impressive" every time I point out some new monument, church, or park we pass. Terk hasn't been jumping at his own shadow. Even Rain has seemed borderline giddy, which is both a nice and a creepy thing to see. Rain does fighting and logistics. She doesn't do giddy. And yet...here she is.

At one point, Martine leads us into a cathedral and up a spiraling set of stone steps. At the top, she pushes open a thick wooden door, and we step out onto a terrace. "*Voila*! La Cité du Vin."

From up here, the city is even prettier than it looked from the road. There are clusters of buildings in neat rows and large swaths of green space crisscrossed by clean sidewalks and tidy footpaths. The river meanders in a slow, patient arc around the eastern edge of the city.

Martine points up at the sky. "*Voila, mes amis!* Look!"

We all look up to see Render cruising overhead, happily bouncing along on the warm, rolling wind and playing tag with a flock of darting little yellow-beaked birds that Martine tells us split their time between the city and a large bird sanctuary nearby.

We all stand up there for who-knows-how-long with our hands on the railing and our noses in the air. We don't talk, strategize, plot, or plan. We don't joke around, complain, or reminisce.

We just...*breathe.*

Even though breathing is something I've done every second of my entire life, right now, the common, involuntary act feels fresh, new, and oddly exciting.

Grinning ear to ear, Martine shakes us out of our hypnosis. "Zis isn't all zere is. *Allons!*"

She leads us back down the stairs and on what turns out to be a long, blissful walking tour of the city.

"*Voila!* La Grosse Cloche. Armande-Louise. Ze big bell of Bordeaux."

We crane our necks to look up at the two towers, each topped by a copper-green cone. Under the archway between them, a giant bell hangs like a chubby toad.

"You cannot see it from here," Martine says, "but ze inscription at ze base of ze bell reads, 'I ring for ze hours and my voice is a call to arms, I sing for happy events and weep for ze dead.'"

I don't tell her, but thanks to Render who is flitting around under the archway, I *can* see it from here.

Like kids on a field trip, we explore for a while—from the towers and ramparts to the gloomy Medieval dungeons down below—before Martine ushers us along.

We turn a corner, and she announces grandly, "Ici, c'est Porte Cailhau."

Cardyn nudges Rain as we gaze in awe at the thick, stern-looking castle with its conical spires piercing the sky. "Looks like a rook from one of your chess sets."

Staring, Rain hums her agreement. "Mmmm."

We wander the area, circling the castle, sticking our noses into doorways and around corners, and apologizing to the people we pass, although they all seem perfectly pleased to welcome us and encourage us to relax and enjoy ourselves.

"*Voila!* Le Grand Théatre de Bordeaux!" Martine announces at our next stop.

Cardyn rushes to the front of our little sight-seeing procession and points and claps his hands at the massive building and its twelve towering columns, each topped by a statue, which Martine explains are Juno, Venus, Minerva, and the nine muses.

"It looks like one of the government buildings in Washington," Cardyn gushes.

"The style is called 'neo-classical,'" the Auditor informs us.

We all have a good laugh when Martine pretends to snap at her. "*Sacrée mère, Madame Auditrice!* Who's giving ze tour here?"

"Sorry."

I think if the Auditor had hands, she'd be slowly backing away right now, holding them up in embarrassed surrender.

Martine makes a sweeping gesture with her hand, and we pour inside and gape in jaws-to-the-floor awe at the grand stone staircase of polished white blocks and at the majestic curved interior of the auditorium with its orderly levels of posh balconies rising high up to the arches framing what Martine describes as "a fresco for the arts" painted on the ceiling.

We unleash ourselves into the overwhelming space, dragging each other through the opera house, marveling at the one-ton chandelier hanging from the cupola, and touching every seat, wall, and brass banister in an ongoing effort to confirm for ourselves that this isn't a trick, an illusion, or some kind of implanted VR-sim.

Martine practically has to drag us back out onto the street, past a row of bakeries, outdoor pubs, breweries and bridal shops, and into a vast and populated park.

"And here is *Esplanade des Quinconces*, ze largest city square in all of France."

The park is statue-filled and enormous. Surrounded by squat, four-story buildings on three sides and by the Garonne River on the fourth, it's as open and green as the National Mall in Washington. Instead of Patriot soldiers on patrol, though, this place is teeming with happy, running kids, teenagers playing frisbee, and picnicking families sitting cross-legged on striped blankets.

Martine and the Auditor take turns telling us about the statues in honor of Commerce, Navigation, Liberty, History, Eloquence, and Happiness and even something about part of a statue being dedicated to Cambodian grapes, but I'm far too stunned by the totally idyllic, small-town beauty of the place to hear most of the details.

We laugh and chatter as we wind our way through the park and city.

Rain jokes with Terk about "walking way too slow for someone with legs that long."

Cardyn fills Manthy in on more of our adventures from before her miraculous return from the dead.

Manthy tries to be cold and snarky, but every time I turn around to check on her, she's got a thin smile going and an amused sparkle in her dark eyes.

Walking the length of a polished sidewalk, we absorb the fragrances of fresh bread and hot coffee while the Auditor peppers in random historical details to go along with Martine's descriptions of Bordeaux. Between the two of them, we're getting bombarded with information, but it doesn't feel stressful or anything. Something about this place makes everything seem like it's happening in slow-motion, like someone found a dial for the city's mood and set it to "calm."

Brohn bounces back and forth between walking with me and straying off to investigate some building or another. He keeps pressing his hands to the stone walls and calling out how clean and cool to the touch everything is.

When I shout out for the tenth time, "It's real!" he laughs at being caught in a bout of skepticism and strides back over to lift me up and spin me around in the middle of a small, cobblestone plaza.

As we continue along, Render teases me inside from my head for being so carefree and happy.

I ask him, *What's not to be happy about? We could use a little happiness.*

~ *We still have a mission.*

*I know.*

*~ The new Emergents are going to be activated.*

*I know.*

*~ Or else terminated.*

*I know that, too!*

*~ Soon.*

*We'll get there. We have plenty of time.*

*~ All we thought we had is gone.*

Groaning, I sever the connection, and Brohn asks me what's wrong.

"Nothing," I tell him, giving him a reassuring pat on the chest. "Render gets weird sometimes."

As Render shoots me a blitz of angry barks, the rest of us round a corner and step out into an endless avenue of life and color.

Brohn and I stop in our tracks, and he exhales a breathy, "Marvie!"

Our final stop, the Rue Sainte-Catherine—the place the Auditor told us about when we first arrived—turns out to be a practically endless road, lined on both sides with display tables of infinite food and merchandise under colorful awnings.

The street is bustling and busy with happy, laughing people, who are buying, selling, and trading everything from jewelry and clothes to dinners and desserts in an endless loop of friendly commerce.

We bounce from stand to stand, talking over each other with giddy excitement and feasting on canelés—small, scallop-shaped pastries made with vanilla, sugar, and rum—as we go.

At one point, Cardyn stops mid-sentence, his lips and chin speckled with crumbs and powdered sugar from one of the many pastries we've sampled. "Hey! How come it's getting light?"

"Because it's morning, dummy."

"But...we *got* here in the morning. We've been sight-seeing with Martine all day. The sun was just going down five minutes ago." He points up at the warm glow of the gently rising sun. "Now it's going *up*."

I put my hand on Cardyn's chest to stop him in his tracks. While Brohn, Rain, and Terk fool around nearby, trying on a variety of hats, scarves, and linen shirts at one of the hundreds of kiosks, I stop for a few minutes to watch the sun and the shortening shadows it's casting around us. Finally, I whip back to Cardyn. "Holy frack! I think you're right."

Cardyn calls the others over and explains to them through anxious gasps what we just saw.

Brohn leads us over to the side of the road where Martine is talking with a group of Juvens.

Tugging her aside, he asks, "What's happening here?" When she looks confused, Brohn points a stabbing finger at the sun. "What *time* is it?"

Martine takes a long time to answer. Finally, she says one word: "Roxane."

"Roxane?"

"The girl who hides the city?" I ask.

"She keeps the night away."

"How? Why?"

Martine shrugs. "How do any of you do what you do? As for why, you'd have to ask her. Just…don't expect an answer."

Rain scans the sky and doesn't sound nearly as worried as I think she should. "It makes sense."

Terk scratches his head. "I don't get it."

"Veiled Refractors work the same way. They can't have too much variance or else they're open to detection."

"So," Brohn says, "It's like we're in a bubble."

"Kind of."

"Render was telling me we needed to hurry. I thought he was being paranoid about our mission. What if…?" My voice trails off as the possibility hits me full force like a sucker punch to the side of the head.

Asking the question that's burning in my own throat, Cardyn raises his hand. "Um…So how long have we been here?"

When he asks that, I think the sucker punch that nailed me hits everyone else, too. We've done a lot, visited a lot of places, walked too far, eaten too much, and had way too many conversations to fit into a single day.

"We don't measure time here," Martine says slowly, as if she's just now remembering this fact, herself.

Croque Madame's voice goes low and serious. "Martine. These kids are on a mission. There are lives at stake. Possibly lots of them. How long?"

Martine doesn't smile when she says she's not sure, herself. "Maybe a week. Maybe more?"

"A week?" Brohn's cheeks flush red. "We haven't slept."

"Roxane's reality takes some getting used to," Martine admits with a shrug.

She sounds like it's no big deal, but Brohn looks like he's ready to hit her full in the face. Instead, he unclenches his fists and barks out, "We have to go!"

"You really have to go?" Martine asks, her face in a sorrowful slump. "So much danger out there."

"We have a pretty intimate relationship with danger," I tell her.

"And in our experience," Rain adds, "if we run from it, it'll just find us anyway."

"So instead," Cardyn sighs with a grimace and an eye roll, "our brilliant policy is to keep running *toward* it."

"Sounds like a brave policy," Martine admits with an unhappy smile.

"Sure," Cardyn groans. "You know that fine line between 'brave' and 'stupid'? Well, we keep doing our best to erase it."

"Do we really have to go?" Terk asks. "It's so nice here."

"Terk, it's an *illusion*," Brohn barks.

"It's not real," I add.

Martine sounds worried and a little offended when she says, "It's real."

"The place, maybe," I admit. "But not the time."

"This isn't helping," Brohn snaps, casting an accusing glare at Martine. "Enough chitchat. Who knows how much more time is going to pass while we stand here and discuss how much more time is going to pass?"

Croque Madame shakes her head and booms out to us that it's time to get moving. "Martine and her town here may be invisible, but we're not. No one's found this place. Let's not stick around and let the Hawkers be the first."

Martine tries one more time to convince us to stay, but Brohn is locked into a tunnel-visioned state of leaderly focus. Standing toe-to-toe and towering over her, he orders her to take us back to the square where our bus is parked.

Martine hesitates, but only for a second. "*Suivez-moi.* Follow me."

In what feels like maybe ten minutes—but who knows how long it really takes—we're back at the bus.

Through tears, Martine bids us "*Au revoir et bonne chance.*"

And, with that, we pile back in the bus, our stomachs full and our minds in a dizzying tailspin, as we speed through the curving green countryside on our way to Spain, hoping with every hum and bump of the bus tires on the road that we're not already too late.

## SAN SEBASTIAN

FOR THE NEXT SEVERAL HOURS, we take turns either sleeping or driving the bus.

When Croque Madame needs to sleep—which isn't often— one of us takes on the driving responsibilities. We've driven bigger rigs than this, but never over quite so decimated a hellscape.

When Croque Madame resumes her place at the wheel, I sleep and have the dream again, the one where I'm passing through walls and catching glimpses through pinprick holes of what's on the other side.

It's intense like last time but not as terrifying and not nearly as painful.

When my eyes snap open, the first thing I do is glance forward to where Manthy is sitting. She tilts her head around to meet my eyes and nods, so I know she just woke up from the exact same dream.

Groaning awake next to me, Brohn asks if I know where we are.

Rubbing my eyes and looking out the window, I tell him I don't. "But wherever this is, it's pretty dead."

We navigate our way through a wasteland of scorched earth. Patches of the road as long and wide as a football field glisten in waves of black volcanic glass.

When the road becomes too rough to pass, Croque Madame finds narrow paths cutting through forests of dead trees caked in layers of white ash until we find the road again.

I rub a layer of sticky dust from the inside of the window with the heel of my hand. Then, I rub my eyes, but it's still hard to see even though it shouldn't be. There are no big cities in sight. No towering, bombed out buildings or mountain ranges of rubble crowding the horizon. Yet, somehow, a dense, impenetrable fog hangs over this bleached span of the earth in a silvery haze that might as well be raven-black.

At one point, the dead forest thins out, melting away into the foggy distance. We're bombarded through the open bus windows with a metallic smell and a light, almost acidic mist.

"I think it's the Atlantic," Rain tells us, scrunching up her face and holding up her arm to inspect the sheen of water vapor collecting on her sleeve.

"It's the Bay of Biscay," the Auditor corrects her.

"Thanks," Rain sneers.

"We're here," Croque Madame announces. "Welcome to San Sebastian."

We peer out the bus's front and side windows, expecting to see a city but instead seeing pretty much nothing.

"Where is it?" Manthy asks with a puzzled squint through one of the foggy windows. "Where is San Sebastian?"

Croque Madame points to the area laid out in front of us where the edge of the land meets up with the white froth of the rolling water of Biscay Bay.

"Right there."

We look again, but there's nothing but a series of large islands —some flat, others peaked as a pyramid—rising up from the cresting water.

"Are those islands—?" I start to ask.

Croque Madame doesn't answer as she eases the bus into a narrow, wooded turn-off and brings it to a stop in front of a large pedestrian bridge made of lashed-together slats of wood and steel.

I look closer out over the water. The peaked pyramids and squarish islands...they're the tops of buildings. All around them, waves choked full of seaweed-covered timber and the corpses of countless fish, slippery with decay, boil and crash against the rooftops of steel and stone.

"Wait. The city's under water?"

"Most of it. Yes."

"So where do people live?"

"A lot of them don't. Not anymore. A lot of people made it out before the ocean rose. A lot didn't. The ones who couldn't get out or didn't want to...they live on the rooftops, mostly."

"The rooftops?"

"It's what they call the city now. *Las Azoteas*. The Rooftops."

We pad after Croque Madame as she hops to the ground and circles around to the back of the bus. She flips up a small panel, inputs a security code in the exposed holo-pad, and a segmented door rolls up.

Reaching into the deep storage bay, she hauls out six square silver cases for us to carry.

"Ugh," Cardyn complains, his arms pulled down by the weight of one of the cases. "Heavy. What's in these things?"

Pointing from one case to the next, Madame rattles off their contents. "Water purifiers. Hydro enhancers. Desalinizers. Protein cubes. Mag-batteries. First-aid and radiation kits. Static comm-links. And bread."

"Bread?"

"Well, croissants, actually. Can't get them here." Croque Madame points to the case Rain's carrying. I know you're not happy with Roxane—."

"She's a kid," Brohn grumbles. "It's not her fault."

"Okay. Martine, then."

"She cost us days."

"And may have cost lives," Rain snaps.

Croque Madame says she agrees and apologizes on behalf of Martine. She swings around to face Cardyn. "You know that line you said you keep erasing...the one between 'brave' and stupid...?"

"Yeah."

"Well, Martine kind of does the same. Only for her, it's the line between host and overprotective mother. She means well. She really does. And I've never known her to keep anyone for quite that long. She must see something in you. Something special. Something worth protecting. Something worth saving."

Brohn grits his teeth, his voice hollow and deep as a grave. "We're flattered."

"I know she crossed a line. But her people stocked us up. They always share what they can."

Brohn doesn't look appeased, but he doesn't say anything.

"Come on," Croque Madame urges. "Follow me. And don't get too close to the edge. You never know when a good-sized wave might sweep you out to sea."

"You're kidding, right?" Terk asks, hugging the silver case tight against his chest.

She doesn't answer, and we start across the narrow, wobbly bridge. It's got damp wooden planks, many of them squishy and glazed over with coats of slippery moss. The guardrails are thin lengths of braided synth-steel pulled tight through the eyelets at the top of rusted metal posts every ten feet or so. Even without the heavy cases clutched tight against our bodies, this would be a scary, hundred-yard walk.

I envy Render for his ability to fly in safety over it all.

In the distance, weather-beaten shacks lean into the stiff, whirling wind as hundreds of people—their arms shielding their eyes—scurry back and forth along the wobbly, crisscrossed network of rope, wood, and steel bridges spanning the city's rooftops.

What used to be San Sebastian really is now underwater.

Even without getting too close to the edge of our little bridge, we can easily see the remnants of the city stretched out in distorted waves under the foggy, garbage and corpse-filled waves.

"People here live and die on rooftops," Croque Madame says, pointing over the stretch of churning water below. "They have since the Climate Floods nearly twenty years ago."

A flurry of motion in the distance catches our eyes. Maybe a quarter mile away, a group of people is scaling a tall antenna protruding up from one of the rooftop towers.

"One of the engineering crews," Croque Madame explains. "They build and maintain the bridges."

Terk mutters, "Marvie. But sad, too," and I have to agree.

I tell Brohn how much I admire the resilience of the people here, but he says that's not the point.

"Then what is?"

"That people wouldn't *need* to be this resilient if the cruel and selfish people of the world would just stop standing on their necks."

I know he's right, but hearing it said out loud like that deflates me a little.

Whether it's the Hyde Park Settlement, the miles-long tent city in the Chunnel, or Luxembourg Gardens, I don't think I'll ever get used to all the ways people find to stay together and build a place—no matter how fragile—they can call home.

We arrive at a kind of landing, an intersection between our bridge and a larger one, and Croque Madame steers us onto the wider, sturdier bridge.

"I can't figure out if this is depressing or impressive," Rain murmurs.

"Is there a word for being foolishly optimistic?" Brohn asks as he adjusts his grip on the big case he's carrying.

"Yes," the Auditor says from Terk's back. "It's called being a 'Pollyanna.'"

Cardyn scrunches up his face as we walk on, doing our best to keep up with Croque Madame over the lightly shifting bridge. Over the sudden thunder of a wave crashing against a crumbling brick chimney not too far away, Cardyn calls out, "What's a 'Pollyanna'?"

The Auditor's voice rises above the howl of wind and the rumble of waves fighting each other below our feet. "Pollyanna is a character in a series of books first published in 1913. She was known for playing the 'Glad Game' where she learned to see the positive in everything."

"Really? What if something terrible happened?"

"It did. She gets hit by a car at one point and can't walk."

Cardyn offers up a snide laugh. "And she manages to see the positive in *that*?"

"Eventually, yes. She realizes how much she appreciated the time when she *could* walk."

"Sounds dumb," Cardyn gripes.

"It's called looking at the world through rose-colored glasses," Rain tells him.

We follow Croque Madame across another intersection and onto an even wider and, thankfully, even stronger bridge. Cardyn tilts his chin up at the pink-hued sky. "The world's already rose-colored, Rain. I don't see much to be optimistic about out there."

Rain seems to consider this for a minute. Finally, she drums her fingers on the side of the silver case in her arms. "Well...we have chocolate."

"Touché."

Croque Madame calls out, "This way," and we follow her onto what looks like a homemade railroad bridge. The pathway of thick wooden beams is suspended by tall silver towers jutting up on either side from beneath the water's surface.

As we walk along, with the water churning ten feet below us and the mist of the ocean stinging our faces, I can see the orderly way these bridges crisscross what's left of the city.

At first, I thought it was just random. As it turns out, all the rooftops are connected via this huge network of repurposed railroad bridges like the one we're on and by a bunch of shaky-looking footbridges and rope-bridges slung in between to form a grid of walkways with what must be hundreds, or even thousands of intersections.

Rain comments on what she calls, "the neat feat of engineering," and we all have to agree.

It's not exactly paradise. And I don't think I'd enjoy living here. But it's definitely unlike anything we've ever seen before.

As we get deeper into the suspended city, it's easy to see all the silver tarps set up as billowing tents hovering over many of the rooftops. It looks like an armada of sailboats.

"Only thing that helps to keep off the heat," Croque Madame explains.

She ushers us along another wide bridge and then back onto a narrow one, leading us at last to a small but sturdy-looking bungalow in the middle of a flat marble-covered rooftop.

We follow her inside to find a pretty lavish space. There are purple-cushioned couches, a bunch of leather loungers, and a ring of stuffed pillows.

"Now this is the exact kind of comfy we need!" Cardyn beams.

Croque Madame points to a long table and tells us we can drop our cases of supplies there.

We shuffle over as one, grateful to be able to deposit the heavy cases and shake the feeling back into our numb hands and arms.

"Funny," Madame says after a long look around.

"What's that?" Brohn asks.

"*El alcalde*. The mayor. He lives here."

"So? Where is he?"

"Exactly." She shakes her head. "He doesn't leave."

"Maybe he went for a walk?" Rain suggests. "There are a lot of people out and about."

Croque Madame seems oddly nervous when she shakes her head. "Marcelino weighs four hundred pounds. And his legs don't work."

"Like Pollyanna!" Terk beams.

"Yes," Croque Madame agrees with an exasperated sigh. "Like Pollyanna. And he definitely doesn't go for walks."

"It's been a while since you've been here, right?" Terk's voice goes shaky. "Could he have…you know…died?"

"Is there someone else we can—?" I'm interrupted by Render whose voice sears into my brain, screaming out a warning that nearly deafens me from inside my own head.

## PURSUIT

"SOMEONE'S OUT THERE!" I shout.

I whip around and edge back to peek out the door. Rain dashes over to join me as she barks at Croque Madame to stay inside.

Sure enough, way down at the far end of the wide bridge leading up to the mayor's cabin, we see a tall woman and a small battalion of men in slick green and brown combat armor marching right toward us.

"Noxia!" Rain cries out. "And Hawkers!"

"We need to get out of here!" I shout.

Cardyn starts backpedaling deeper into the cabin. "I'm open to suggestions."

With Noxia and the Hawkers closing in fast along the main bridge leading up to the mayor's cabin, our options for escape are supremely limited.

"This way!" Croque Madame calls out from within the cabin. "There's a back way out!"

The Hawkers are just raising their weapons to fire on us when we bolt toward the back of the cabin and follow Croque Madame on a dead run through a thick purple curtain.

The crack of gunfire sounds from behind us, and a chunk of the wood and aluminum frame around the front doorway explodes into the room in a cloud of dust and shards.

Manthy shrieks and covers her face to protect herself from flying splinters and debris.

Urging her along and following Croque Madame, we burst through the purple curtain and wind up on a wide balcony with a cluster of rope and steel bridges splitting off from the mayor's cabin like threads in a spider's web and extending out toward a whole field of the city's rooftops.

All around us, people gathered on nearby rooftops snap their heads up at our sudden presence and at the sound of gunfire ripping through the air.

Another volley rings out from the Hawkers' weapons, and we go diving and ducking for cover.

"Which way?" Cardyn cries out to Rain, but she's flustered—like the rest of us—and is caught in a rare moment of indecision.

With no other options, Brohn dashes into the lead, and the rest of us follow in a random sprint over a series of shaky bridges and across crowded rooftops.

People scream and scatter as we pass. Some leap behind chimneys and vertical exhaust chutes. Others dive into canvas tents or into smaller versions of the mayor's cabin.

*Great. Now we've put their lives in danger, too.*

Moving fast for such a short person, Croque Madame waves her arms frantically at us. "This way! We need to circle around and get back to the bus!"

Shouting our apologies as we plow through the rooftop neighborhood, we go leaping on and off of bridges and skirting our way over the churning ocean water below.

We cross the next roof, past another group of startled people, and cut over to a smaller set of bridges spanning the space between a slanted roof and a flat one where a bunch of men and women seem to be building some kind of intricate metal scaffold.

Dropping their tools, they all shout and leap to the side as we streak past.

In the middle of the next bridge, we slide to a halt.

The Hawkers...Not only did we *not* lose them—there are more of them than we thought.

"Go back! Go back!" Rain shouts.

Following her orders, we double back on the wildly rocking bridge and pile out onto the stability of the rooftop.

But Noxia and her Hawkers have closed in, and we know we're in trouble.

We've got six Hawkers on one side of us now, with Noxia and another six of the armored assassins slowing down to an ominous walk on the other.

We're surrounded and stuck on the wet rooftop with at least twenty of the San Sebastian residents.

Brandishing slats of wood and various tools, the group of men and women step away from their project and stand between us and Noxia.

Slapping a baseball bat sized plank of wood against his palm, one of the men approaches Noxia and slings a string of what must be Spanish profanity at her.

Her eyes narrow, and the man takes a full step back.

Next to me, Rain whispers, "Oh no."

Turning away from Noxia, the man swings the thick slat of wood with full force into the head of the gray-haired woman standing next to him.

The crunch of wood on bone is sickening, and she drops in a broken, bloody heap at the man's feet.

Stunned at this bewildering and brutal betrayal, the other men and women aren't sure where to direct their energy.

In their split second of hesitation, the Hawkers swarm past Noxia and descend on the unsuspecting group, dropping some of them with stun-sticks while the others bound toward the other bridge in terror.

Screaming and shouting for help, they skirt around the Hawkers—who seem content to let the rest of them go by—and scramble across another set of bridges to find safety on the nearby rooftops.

As much as I know we'd like to follow them, our own escape route is cut off.

The Hawkers drag two unconscious men out of their way and step over the body of the gray-haired woman, who is lying, her face caved in and her neck twisted—in a pool of blood.

I'm in shock.

It's Render who snaps me back into action.

~ *The innocents are safe. Escape is blocked. Time to fight.*

## ROOFTOP RUMBLE

THERE'S ONLY one good thing about being surrounded: It limits the Hawkers' use of their deadly, magazine-fired Infantry Automatic Rifles.

But my mental note of that fact is erased as I realize how well trained these men are in hand-to-hand combat.

Breezing over the rooftop, one of the Hawkers leaps onto Brohn's back, his arms wrapped around his neck in a vicious chokehold. Together, they roll to the edge of the roof and nearly tumble into the water. Gagging and clutching at his assailant's arms, Brohn drops down to one knee as his face goes white.

Although his skin has an elevated molecular density, he still has to breathe like anyone else.

Crying out his name, I hurl myself across the length of the rooftop. It's got to be twenty feet but being plugged into Render means it's not much more than a hop for me.

In an urgent panic but landing on light, quiet feet, I snap my talons out and plunge them into the Hawker's sides. He's wearing some kind of Kevlar armor, but there are gaps in the side where the buckles meet, and my razor-sharp blades dig in deep.

Shrieking, he hurls himself wildly to the side, sending me bouncing off the bronze guardrail.

Out of instinct, he glances down to have a look at the deep gashes and the blood spreading a crimson stain down the sides of his combat cargo-pants.

With his head down, he doesn't see Brohn's fist, arcing in a tight uppercut. Brohn's strike connects with the Hawker's chin, and the man's head cracks back in an explosion of splintered jawbone and a spray of blood and broken teeth.

Together, Brohn and I both duck as a swarm of silver throwing-daggers flies through the air over our heads.

The Hawker who threw the knives makes the mistake of running at us too fast in the process. I greet him with a side kick to the midsection that doubles him over. Before the air has left his lungs, Brohn's locked him into a standing arm-bar, which he turns into a quick hip-throw, launching the man over the railing and into the churning whitecaps below.

On the bridge behind us, two Hawkers are closing in on Rain from either side. They've got guns drawn, but I know they can't shoot. One misfire from the shaking rope bridge and they'll wind up killing each other.

The two Hawkers grin, thinking they have her trapped.

Instead, she's lured them into close-quarters, face-to-face combat where their guns are useless, but her reflexes and dart-drivers aren't.

In a single, smooth, and perfectly-choreographed motion, she slides under one punch and dodges another before lunging upward, full-force into one of the men, to deliver a throat-crushing heel-of-the-hand to his neck.

He hasn't even fallen by the time Rain's whipped around to land on one knee right in front of the second Hawker.

He glances down just in time to see her fire her darts upward into his chin.

The thin silver slivers pierce his chin strap and lodge clean through to the roof of his mouth.

As she's reloading her dart-drivers, one of the Hawkers leaps in front of Noxia to defend her. He locks his sights on Cardyn and is a micro-second away taking his chances with his gun in close-quarters when two silver flashes—a second volley of the thin arrows from Rain's dart-drivers—zings through the air and pierces his neck and hand.

He drops in a bloody heap, his gun clattering to the rooftop as another Hawker circles around to try to corner Cardyn.

Cardyn deftly reaches back and unsnaps his twin tomahawk axes.

He pinwheels the bladed weapons in a whirring blur as he strides down the bridge, advancing on the Hawker, who charges forward, a six-inch combat knife in each hand.

Cardyn drops his shoulder to evade one knife-strike and side-steps the next. His blades glint in the sunlight as they ping off his Hawker's forest green shoulder-guards and chest-protector in a furious counterattack.

The Hawker seems startled in the face of Cardyn's relentless strikes, and he stumbles backward and then drops as one of Cardyn's blades finds its mark deep in the man's neck just under his ear.

A shower of blood explodes from the Hawker's carotid artery, and the man topples over the guardrail and splashes into the murky sea below.

It's the last thing I see before Brohn and I are swarmed by at least four or five Hawkers who pile on us, crushing both of us to the ground under a flurry of punches and chokeholds.

I take a barrage of sharp strikes to the side and feel my ribs compress against my lungs.

In the dark chaos of bodies, a man's arm slides around my neck, and I don't have time to stop him from clamping down.

The tendons in my neck tighten against the fierce pressure on my windpipe.

But then, the arm slides off along with the weight of my assailants. When I roll over and look up, Terk is tossing the four men, one after the other, into the water.

On the far side of the roof and with his face contorted in obvious pain, Cardyn is holding his shoulder where he must have gotten hit.

Manthy is making her way over to help him and doesn't see the three menacing Hawkers bearing down on her.

I shout out, "Behind you!"

Wincing, Cardyn manages to toss one of the tomahawk axes to Manthy, who whips around to face the advancing men.

Before our eyes, she transforms from mousy and mysterious to invincible warrior.

I've seen her fight before. A lot of times, actually.

But not like this.

She glides and pirouettes her way through and around the attacking Hawkers. There's three of them and one of her, but it's like she's got them surrounded and outnumbered.

Crouching, she ducks a knife strike, spins, and swings her axe around in a blistering arc. Her blade slices through the back of the first man's knee.

Collapsing, he shrieks an agonizing scream of pain I can hear from fifty feet away.

Manthy's momentum carries both her and her axe right into a second Hawker, so they're practically nose to nose.

The man throws a lightning uppercut followed immediately by a knife thrust. Both attempts miss Manthy by a mile.

She counters with a spinning back elbow that cracks the man's visor and plunges the splintered Plexiglas deep into his face. Blinded by pain and by his own blood, he staggers backward onto one of the smaller rope bridges extending out from the rooftop.

Manthy goes after him, launching herself across the distance with a side kick to the chest that blasts the air out of the man's lungs and sends him flailing and falling backward, his head cracking hard against one of the bridge's steel support posts.

With her sights set on finishing him off, she doesn't notice the third man storming onto the bridge after her.

Before I have a chance to shout out a warning, Terk clomps onto the bridge, his flail in his fist, his arm cranked back and primed like a catapult.

He unleashes a titanic swing. The spikes on the flail dent the man's armor at his ribcage. The force of the strike sends the Hawker sprawling through the air and onto the rooftop where he slides to a stop, coughing out a spray of blood before slumping down, unconscious.

Manthy, her hair sticking to her face in a sweaty, disheveled mess, says, "Thanks!"

Terk beams. "Don't mention it!"

Brohn and Rain have managed to dispatch two more of the Hawkers, but the others are regrouping under Noxia's orders and are working their way around the roof to cut off any escape routes.

"This way!" Rain shouts, vaulting a steel air duct and darting toward the one unguarded bridge left leading off the roof.

Gathered together again, we break into an all-out run.

With Rain in the lead, Manthy and I flank Croque Madame, our arms hooked around her back and shoulders as we go.

Behind us, Terk unleashes his flail on the two posts holding the bridge in place. I glance back just in time to see the entire structure crumble and crack. The bridge plummets into the water, taking two more of the Hawkers with it. Noxia and the remaining Hawkers dart over to one of the other bridges and bolt across.

Sprinting like our lives depend on it—because they *do*—we cut across rooftops, through the open doorways of cabin after cabin, past the startled and terrified residents, and along the wobbly lengths of a zigzagging maze of bridges.

We've got churning sea water below and what would be a completely confusing complex of bridges all around us.

Fortunately, we've also got Rain in the lead, and she doesn't hesitate for a single second.

As if she's lived here all her life, she guides us with confidence and precision.

I risk glancing back at one point and am relieved that Noxia and her Hawkers are nowhere to be seen.

The bridge we're on ends at a field of tall, jagged rocks, each nearly as high as my head.

Rain leads us through this new maze until—panting and sweat-soaked—we burst into a clearing.

"The bus!" Cardyn shouts.

We've come at it from a different direction, but sure enough, our bus is sitting right where we left it, unharmed and unguarded.

Croque Madame swipes the door open, and we all pile in.

Brohn calls out to see if everyone's okay.

With whatever scraps of breath we have left, we all answer, "Yes."

Except for Rain.

She's collapsed down into the aisle, her arm covered in blood and twisted around at a grisly, unnatural angle.

# BROKEN

"Yes, it fracking hurts!"

By accessing ocular sensors in Terk's Modified network, the Auditor is able to scan Rain's arm.

"Your arm is broken."

Sounding rude and seriously thrown off by her obvious agony, Rain snaps, "What do *you* know?"

"I know you have a fractured ulna. A twisted radius. Strained ligaments and cartilage damage. But don't worry. It's fixable. We need a few supplies and some time, and you'll be as good as new before you know it."

Feverish and sweaty, Rain winces and tries to pull her arm out of Terk's, but she goes porcelain-white, and her eyelids flutter as she stammers out her objections. "You seriously...expect me to... to...put myself...in *your* hands?"

"Well, technically, I don't have hands. But yes, I advise you to put yourself into Terk's hands and under *my* care."

"But—"

"Unless you want this lovely and powerful arm of yours to heal up looking like a question mark. And imagine what a drag you'd be on your Conspiracy *then*."

Rain blinks away some of her disorientation and stops squirming. "Fine. Do what you…have to. I don't care, anyway."

"I've got to hand it to the Auditor," Cardyn whispers to me, "she's got some handy medical skills."

"And her bedside manner's not bad, either," Brohn chimes in.

I can't help but offer up my proud agreement.

And then, without warning but with jarring speed, Croque Madame guides the bus over to the side of the road. Rain shrieks, and Terk locks his arm around her to stop her from flying out of her seat.

"Oh, frack," I say, twisting around, my heart in my throat as I glance back the way we came. "What now?"

Brohn pushes himself up and starts scooping up our weapons. He looks bone-weary and hardly ready for another fight.

*That makes all of us.*

"What's wrong?" Cardyn cries out. "Hawkers?"

We all brace ourselves and stare toward the rear doors, sure we're going to see Noxia and her mercenaries marching at us down the center aisle.

Croque Madame shakes her head. "It's Pamplona."

"The city?" Brohn asks, turning back around.

"I was going to drop supplies there."

"So? What's the problem?"

"*That's* the problem."

As Brohn, Cardyn, Manthy, and I gather around her, she points down the length of the road. We all lean forward to peer through the front windshield, but a swirling vortex of gray fog makes it hard to scope out the landscape and the figures in the distance.

I'm about to ask Render to fly a recon mission for us, but Madame cuts me off.

"Here," she says, activating a long-distance ocular array built into the front windshield. The images spring to flickering, full color life in the 3D holo-display projected from the glass in front of us.

Poking her finger into different parts of the digitized scene, Madame directs our attention to the battalions of soldiers clad in red and yellow armor. Above them, Triad Drones—the same angular, snake-like drones we saw back in Paris—hum along in a huge, ominous arc. Beyond the soldiers are two rings of military tanks, the outer circle with their massive gun turrets pointed out toward the road, the inner circle with their turrets pointed inward toward the desolate city. In the middle of it all, the towering black struts, spires, and support beams of a half-built arcology puncture the smoke-filled sky.

Pamplona, as the Auditor informs us, was famous for the Running of the Bulls, an annual festival of San Fermin.

"It was also known for the festivals featuring the *Gigantes*," she adds as an under-the-breath afterthought. "Twelve-foot tall dancing dolls of steel framework bodies and realistic, painted, papier maché heads controlled by a person inside."

"Sounds fun," Cardyn quips, although I can't tell if he's being serious or not.

"We can't get into the city?" Terk calls up to us.

Madame offers up a disgusted grunt. "Forget 'into.' We can't even get *near* it."

Behind us, Rain is leaning against the window, her eyes closed. Terk leaves her side for a minute to come up and peer over my shoulder at the schematic layout of the city. He reaches over with his Modified pincer and taps at the image of a field of slowly marching soldiers. The graphic sizzles in a wavy distortion at his touch. "Who's that?"

"You told me about the Patriot Army," Croque Madame reminds us.

"Yeah."

"They're like that. Only more ruthless than in America and with way more violence crammed into a fraction of the space.

Those troops out there...they're from the Army of the Wealthies. Formally known as the Continental Execs. The same ones Ibrahim and the Hands once fought against. Someday, these soldiers will leave, too, and be replaced by the drones. That's how it goes. The government controls the people with an army. Then the drones replace the army. Pretty soon, even they won't be needed. The Execs out there, those are the ones fighting the Eastern Order...sorry...the ones who *pretend* to fight the Eastern Order. All so the Wealthies can keep building their arcologies in peace while they keep the rest of us at war."

Terk takes a step back and plops down again next to Rain who has drifted into a moaning, squirming sleep, and he holds her securely under his arm. "Um...those Continental Execs...they can't see us, can they?"

"Honestly, I don't know what kind of sensory range their Triad Drones have."

Cardyn slips back into his seat. "May I suggest we don't stick around to find out?"

Madame is frozen in place, her eyes locked onto images of the distant collection of soldiers, weapons, and hovering drones. "I've never failed to make a delivery before."

Brohn reaches over to offer her a consoling hand to the shoulder. With misty eyes, Madame glances up to give him an appreciative, feeble smile.

"It's not a failure," Brohn assures her. "If we can get to Valencia...if we can find and free the Juvens there...well, a success for us there might just translate into a success for the people here."

"For people everywhere," I add.

It takes a full minute before Madame is able to draw her eyes away from the shimmering, haloed images of the besieged city.

With a resigned sigh, she taps her thumb to a small pad on the dashboard, and the schematic pixilates away. As Brohn, Manthy, and I return to our seats, Madame edges the bus away from the side of the road and guides it down a steep, rocky hill, squeezing us between a cluster of dead trees that crack and crumble to dust as we grind our way through.

By the time the wheels hit the relatively even surface of a smaller access road, we're all reeling like we've just been slugged in the face.

A few hours later, we get walloped with what turns out to the second of a one-two punch.

Like Pamplona, Zaragoza is dense with Exec soldiers and encircled by Triad Drones. It also has an arcology—just as bleak and sky-splitting as the one in Pamplona—being erected right in the middle of the smoldering ruins.

Madame steers the bus right into a thicket of strangler vines whose thorns look big enough to puncture our tires. "To keep us out of sight," she explains.

In the holo-images Madame calls up this time, we see the same red and yellow armor of the Execs glinting from turrets of brick and stone built onto the top edges of a ring of high hills encircling the city.

Madame curses under her breath and deactivates the monitor. Backing the bus up the way we came, she steers us back onto what's left of the access road. Her knuckles twitch and bulge from the tight fists she's got clamped onto the steering wheel.

"Twenty years ago," she tells us, her voice breaking as she goes, "this part of the trip would've taken us a few hours. But not anymore. With the detours and backtracking to avoid drones, Execs, and impassable roads, it'll take us nearly a full day. You all should get some rest."

She sniffles, and it kills me to realize how hard she's trying not to cry.

LATER IN THE DAY, Render decides it's time to spread his wings. Giving me the tiniest nod of acknowledgement, he bursts through one of the open windows, launching himself out into the searing red sky.

Jealous, I watch him soar until he's a dot in the distance.

I scrunch my feet up onto the seat and wrap my arms around my knees. Brohn is a few seats up, talking to Madame. Manthy is a few seats back, her bare feet up on the headrest of the seat in front of her.

A few rows in front of me and on the other side of the aisle, Cardyn is tossing and turning—seeming to drift off into sleep one minute and then snapping awake and on high-alert the next. He looks over his shoulder at me and offers up a frail, sad-eyed smile.

I try to give him a comforting smile back, but it's hard to think straight with the swirl of so many calamities churning through my head.

The Valta. Chicago. Washington, D.C. And now, all these great European cities: London, Paris. San Sebastian. Pamplona. Zaragoza. And all the ruined towns and the lost lives in between.

I know the same images, thoughts, and memories are plaguing Cardyn, too. Plaguing all of us.

*We could really use a win.*

For the rest of the day, all the uncomfortable jostling and our constant panic about what—or who—we might run into as we trundle our way along, Terk never leaves Rain's side.

Which means the Auditor never leaves Rain's side.

Despite the sorrow pressing down on my heart at the sight of the cities, towns, and small, empty villages we've passed, an unexpected surge of pride wells up in me to hear the Auditor paying such careful attention to Rain.

She's fully recruited Terk as an impromptu nurse, who works as her hands as she applies various balms to the skin on Rain's arm and continues to monitor her fever and the status of the blue gel-cast.

Drifting in and out of consciousness—I'm not sure if it's from pain, fatigue, or the painkillers the Auditor gave her from the first-aid kit—Rain moans that she wants to know what's happening.

I'm close enough to hear it all. It's not like the Auditor is telling Rain anything secret, so this doesn't count as eavesdropping.

"We were going to stop in Pamplona," the Auditor explains.

"And then Zaragoza," Terk adds.

"I remember...kind of."

"We didn't stop, though."

"Why not?"

"It was too dangerous," the Auditor says.

Terk gives Rain a gentle squeeze. "There were soldiers there. Lots of them."

"Soldiers?"

"Like the Patriot Army."

"They're called the Continental Execs here," the Auditor clarifies. "It's all the same, though. Everywhere we've been, everything we've seen, everything the world has become...it all boils down to the insane, limitless greed of a corrupt few who will stop at nothing, including the invention of an enemy, to elevate themselves as gods."

"Why, though?" Rain asks through clamped teeth.

"Why are they willing to cause so much suffering?"

Rain nods.

"I don't know. I wish I did."

Rain forces her mouth into a strained smile. "It's because they want what they can't have."

"What's that?" Terk asks.

"They want immortality. They want to be gods."

"So they kill everyone until they think they are?"

Rain nods again.

"And to kill," the Auditor says, "whether it's a single person or an entire population, starts with a single act of dehumanization. And once that's been done, it's just a matter of lying."

"Lying?" Rain mumbles, her eyelids drifting closed as she starts to fall asleep again.

"Lying. Lying to the public and to the poor. But the ultimate lie is the one they tell themselves."

"What lie is that?" Terk asks, his hand on Rain's feverish forehead.

"The lie that we're destined to be separate from each other," the Auditor tells him, "that we're better off disconnected than connected. And it takes an army to protect a lie that big."

A few seats behind Rain, Terk, and the Auditor, Manthy is nodding her head in quiet agreement.

## VALENCIA

BY THE TIME the sun goes down and we get our first glimpse of Valencia, Rain is already feeling better.

"Are we here?" she asks, rubbing the grogginess from her eyes and dragging the backs of her fingers along the cool surface of her gel-cast.

Croque Madame assures her we're closing in on our destination.

Rain holds up her arm and asks how much longer she needs to keep the rippling blue cast on. A thin tendril snakes out from a small port in Terk's wrist and slips into the tiny sensory nozzle on the wrist-edge of the bulging blue mold.

The Auditor tells Rain, "One more day."

Rain grumbles under her breath and joins the rest of us in looking out the bus windows at Valencia, our final destination in what's turned out to be more of a perilous pilgrimage than the simple, there-and-back, in-and-out rescue mission I thought and —kind of stupidly, I realize now—*hoped* it would be.

The city is quiet and sparkling clean. Even from here, we can see how nearly every surface looks polished to a high shine.

Unlike our adventures in some of the other cities on this

mission—not counting Bordeaux, of course—Valencia isn't belching toxic smoke into the air. There are no visible armies, no heavy artillery, no looming drones, and no menacing arcologies piercing the sky.

In some ways, though, this is worse.

There's nearly nobody out there.

At least no one we can see from here.

"Where are the people?" Terk asks, his eyes skimming the wide, glistening, and very empty avenues in the distance.

Croque Madame explains to him how this city, over the years, has become the hub of the En-Gene-eers and their Exec armies. "They used to keep what they do here a secret. All hush-hush stuff behind a lot of closed doors. Now, thanks to the Execs, there are no civilians left to stand in their way. So it's not the most ideal city for the average person to live in. But if you're interested in manipulating human genes to create a legion of super-powered slaves or slaughtering anyone who gets in your way, this is the place for you."

As we continue down the road with that menacing warning in our minds, we keep expecting to round a corner and drive head-long into a battalion of the Continental Execs.

The soldiers and drone armies were definitely scary. But Cardyn speaks for all of us when he says this is scarier.

"It's like they're not worried about who enters the city," he mutters. "Which means they probably have even worse ways to kill whoever tries."

Madame drops the bus to a crawl as we climb a steep hill where we get an even better view of Valencia.

With the bus still gliding toward the shimmering metropolis, we take a minute to marvel at the spotless, graceful look of it all. Cardyn says Valencia—with its colossal domes and multi-faceted constructs and monuments—is like "a five-mile wide crystal chandelier that's been dipped in a vat of window-cleaner."

Brohn looks impressed and tells him it's an apt description.

"What can I say?" Cardyn beams. "I'm the master of metaphor."

"I think that was more of a simile," I correct him.

He's just opening his mouth to argue with me when the bus comes to a sudden halt, causing all of us to lurch forward. I stagger in the aisle and regain my balance in time to see a man and a woman in form-fitting red and yellow combat gear marching at us down the center of the road.

I mouth the words, "Oh, frack. Execs," but I don't think any sound comes out.

Croque Madame calls back, telling us not to worry. "I've come through here before. I know the security detail."

I'm just relaxing and releasing the breath I was holding when Croque Madame says, "Uh oh."

"What is it?" Brohn asks.

"Remember the security detail I said I knew?"

"Um. Yes."

"This isn't them."

The man taps the barrel of his rifle on the glass panels, and the woman motions for Madame to open the doors, which she does, although her hands are trembling. The two Execs climb the steps, their visors down and their weapons drawn.

After surveying us, the woman turns back to the open bus door. Through her silvery-white face-shield, she says something in a language I don't understand. Well, I don't understand most of it. One word stands out, though, and we all hear it clear as day:

"Emergents."

Her voice barely audible, Croque Madame gives a half-turn over her shoulder and answers with a single word of her own:

"Brohn."

Brohn gets the hint before the rest of us have even registered Madame's voice.

Rising from his seat in a six-foot two-inch blur of coiled

muscles, he clamps his hands onto the armored shoulders of the woman's yellow tactical vest and jettisons her clean off the bus.

She slams into the man behind her, and we're thrown back as the bus surges forward, leaving a dark cloud of kicked-up dirt in its wake.

The two soldiers fire at us as we try to make our escape.

We duck down and are covered instantly in a spray of broken glass from the few windows that haven't already been blown out.

The bus slams to the side of the road, screeching as the metal sides grind in long gouges against the long steel guardrail.

We're all tossed back and forth across the aisle, tumbling over each other while we try to hang onto the edges of the seats as sparks fly up from outside the bus.

We grind along, and one of the back windows explodes as a grenade comes smashing through. It skitters down the aisle and stops against Manthy's boot.

In a single swift motion, Brohn grabs her by the scruff of her jacket, slings her toward the front of the bus, and collapses down on top of the grenade.

He's curled around it, knees to his chest, when it explodes.

Brohn's body shudders, but he's able to direct the force of the blast downward.

He's saved Manthy, and probably all of us, but the explosion has blown a jagged hole in the floor.

A horrible screech of snapping metal and the grind of steel against the rough pavement screams out from the underside of the bus.

Croque Madame struggles to hold onto the wheel and keep the bus from careening over a cliff.

Out of control now, the bus slams into the railing again, sliding along the curved and narrow highway under a swirling cloud of angry sparks and churning black smoke.

We're all pitched up against the windows. The remaining

glass bursts in and slices through my skin as the bus groans to a horrific stop.

A tremor rumbling through his deep voice, Brohn calls out, "Is everyone okay?"

Even Rain says she is, but we can all tell she's not. I don't think she even realizes how twisted in pain her face is or how gingerly she's holding her arm.

I shift my gaze down the aisle toward the back of the bus.

Out on the road, the two soldiers gallop toward us, their weapons leveled at their shoulders.

The man is just tapping a comm-link on the side of his helmet when an explosive shockwave rips through the air just past my ear.

Out on the road, the man's entire body goes flying backwards before skidding to a stop against what's left of the twisted metal guardrail our bus just destroyed.

The woman Exec dives down as Brohn's second shot goes whizzing through the air just over her head.

"Damn!" Brohn is quick to reload his assault rifle, but he doesn't have time to fire.

Leaping out onto the road, Cardyn has slipped right into his line of sight. He raises his hand, and the Exec drops her gun.

From here, I can't hear what Cardyn says to the woman, but out of nowhere, she rips off her helmet and goes sprinting full-tilt in the opposite direction.

Baffled, we all watch as she disappears around a bend in the road in the direction we just came from.

Cardyn jogs back onto the bus, and I ask, "What did you tell her?"

"I told her to go home."

"Why? What does that mean? What's she going to do?"

Agitated, Terk asks, "What if she calls for help or something?"

Cardyn shrugs. "Don't worry, Big Guy. She won't. She'll go

home. She'll forget about this. She'll live happily ever after with her family."

"And you know this, how?" Rain asks through gritted teeth, her arm cradled against her body.

"Card!" I interrupt. "You're bleeding!"

Cardyn drags his finger under his nose and inspects the smears of blood. "I'm okay."

I've known Cardyn nearly my entire life. One look in his eyes is all I need to tell me he's *not* okay. But he shakes off whatever pain must be searing through his head right now, so I have no choice but to take him at his word.

"So what happened with that Exec?"

"When I connected with her mind just now..."

"Yeah?"

"It's like she connected back."

"Like me with Render."

"I guess so. Anyway, it's kind of like I gave her a suggestion. In return, she gave me a promise."

"To go home and live happily ever after?"

"Yep."

"Well," Brohn sighs, "I think we got them before they were able to contact anyone. So I guess we don't have to worry about anyone calling for help."

"They're a patrol team," I point out. "Someone'll be checking on them before long, right?"

"I know for a fact they're required to check in with their commanders," Croque Madame tells us.

Cardyn laughs. "That's true. And right now, that Exec *is* checking in with her boss. She's telling him everything's all right, and that she and her dead partner over there are fine until the shift-change."

"Which is when?" I ask.

"Two hours."

"Wait. So we only have two hours to find the Juvens, get them out, and get back here without being caught and smeared into paté?"

"And get this bus fixed and road-ready. Yes." Cardyn puts his hands up. "Don't kill the messenger, right?"

Brohn frowns, his face in a knot of annoyed and impatient anger. "I'm rethinking that little saying as we speak."

After a few minutes of anxious negotiation, we agree that Terk will stay behind with Croque Madame to try to fix the bus.

"You should stay, too," Brohn says to Rain. "We're far enough from the road, and it's plenty dark out. I think you all should be safe."

She suppresses a groan and tells him, "No way." Looking wobbly and green, she stands up. "Besides, you need me to get us to where we need to go."

From where he's standing now, just thirty or so feet ahead of us by a bend in the road where the trees thin out, Cardyn shouts out, "Um...maybe not" and calls us over. He directs our attention toward a massive complex of buildings dominating the horizon.

We all look out and know instantly what Cardyn means. We won't need Rain's Culling to direct us. The Processor is the biggest installation any of us has ever seen.

And I mean, it's *huge*. Like, practically blocking out the moon huge.

When we were little, our world was Shoshone High School, at least after the first few waves of drone strikes. The Processor where we were taken on the day we turned seventeen was an enormous compound of eight cube-shaped buildings with a giant silver disk—the Observational and Assessment Halo—rotating slowly overhead. In Chicago, we were confined to small cells, the Bistro, and the Mill for most of our incarceration. In Washington, D.C., we fought on the expansive National Mall. We've been in Hyde Park, Kensington Palace, Buckingham Palace, and St. Paul's Cathedral.

But this place is a whole different level of immense, going on forever and dominating the entire skyline.

When we were held captive in the Mill back in Chicago, I had visions. One of them featured the bones of a partially beached whale made of glass and chrome rising skyward in the middle of a shallow sea. Its body had begun to decay. Its ribs were exposed, bleached under the searing hot sun.

This is my dream turned horrible reality.

Only it's not just a single building. It's a city-sized complex of stadium-sized domes and towering white gates curving in an endless arc around the perimeter of the glistening metropolis. Up close now, this makes the little bit we saw before of Cardyn's "chandelier city" look even *more* impressive. All smooth synth-steel, mirrored chrome, and polished glass, the endless compound of buildings, sculptures, gates, and clusters of surreal, organic-looking structures is an overwhelming sight to behold. My breath catches in my throat just from the effort of trying to take it all in.

Rising over it all is a familiar and bone-chilling sight:

A Halo.

Like the one we got to know in our Processor, it's an enormous, floating, slowly revolving ring. If aliens were going to send a ship, it'd look like this. If the Titans of ancient Greek mythology played with a hollow-centered frisbee, it'd look like this.

"It's like ours," Cardyn mutters.

He doesn't say it in a happy, nostalgic way.

No surprise there. As we found out when we managed to infiltrate it on our last day in the Processor, the Halo was part lab, part observation, part control center, and all keeper-of-terrible-secrets.

At least ours was secluded in the middle of the woods. Getting out was hard. Getting away was harder. Forgetting about why we were there and what we went through was nearly impossible.

Any parts of the experience we might have managed to suppress come flooding back.

The tests. The riddles and puzzles. The physical and psychological challenges.

The so-called "game" that cost Terk his arm, and the ultimate escape that nearly cost the rest of us our lives.

It was all capped off by the discovery that we were nothing but pawns in a game against an invented enemy. It was inside the Halo that Brohn, Manthy, and I first learned the truth about the Eastern Order and began to learn more of the truth about ourselves and our place in the world.

This complex in front of us is a large-scale version of the nightmare we thought we'd finally woken up from.

And we're all standing there, mesmerized by the sight of the intimidating campus but also by the obvious impossibility of what we're about to try to do.

"Okay," Brohn says, assessing the situation. "We can get there without Rain."

"But I don't know how good we'll be in a fight out there if she's stuck back here," I say.

Rain gives me an appreciative wink and then goes quietly serious. "I don't like the idea of staying behind. But you're right." She holds up her arm, which is still yellow, bruised, and a little swollen above and below the blue gel-cast. "I probably can't help much with the bus. But I'll be a total liability in a fight."

I start to object, but she cuts me off. "As much as I'd like to be a hero here, Brohn's right. Logically, I should stay behind. I can help Terk and Croque Madame fix the bus. But the rest of you…"

Brohn says, "Yeah?"

"The rest of you better promise to get yourselves and any kids you find in there back here alive."

"We won't let you down," I promise her.

"You better not. Because if you do…" She raises her good arm and clenches her small fingers into a tight, white-knuckled fist.

We all put our hands up, palms out in surrender. "Don't worry," Cardyn assures her. "We'd rather die than face the wrath of Rain!"

Brohn clamps a hand onto Cardyn's shoulder. "If we do this right, we won't have to worry about either of those outcomes."

Cardyn returns Brohn's brotherly-hand-to-the-shoulder gesture. "Then let's do this right, shall we?"

Rain moans and presses her fingertips to her temple. Before I can ask her what's wrong, she tells us to look for a big white pipe.

"Pipe?" I ask.

"I can see it in my mind's eye," she tells us through a tense squint. "I can't tell you much else. But look for a white pipe. It's a start. I'm sure of it."

"White pipe," Brohn repeats. "Got it."

"Can we stay in touch with comm-links?" I ask.

Croque Madame starts to laugh but then seems to realize I'm serious. "Sorry. That Halo up there doesn't just prevent any outside signals from functioning. It also *traces* them. Three years ago, I found that out the hard way. I was lucky. My friend Deraddo wasn't."

"I'm sorry."

She shakes her head. "I grieved a lot. Not something I'm anxious to repeat."

"It's okay," Brohn assures her. "Rain's given us a starting point, and we have no intention of giving you any more reason to grieve."

"We have two hours," I remind everyone. "The clock is ticking, captive kids could be waiting, and we need to get *moving*!"

32

# DIVING IN

A SCREAM from overhead urges us along, and Render comes parachuting down to land on the bent guardrail on the side of the road.

*Where have you been?*

*~ Flying. The land here is beautiful.*

*Sure. If you ignore all the death and soldiers.*

*~ That's a small part of what's out there.*

*I guess. You missed all the action.*

*~ I saw it.*

*Great. Thanks for all your help.*

*~ Sarcasm. No wonder you humans aren't more evolved.*

*We do just fine, thank you. Hey, can you stay here? Kind of...you know, watch over things while we're gone?*

*~ Where are you going?*

*To find those new Emergents.*

*~ I suppose rescuing little humans is a noble cause, sarcasm and all.*

He doesn't say it, but I know what he's thinking, maybe even more than he does. After all, I can read his mind. It's not just his sense of justice, morality, or his protective instinct.

Render wants to be a father.

In my mind, I tell him, *Someday.*

~ *Someday, what?*

I don't answer. I know he knows what I mean.

"Render's going to stay here," I tell the others.

Croque Madame promises us that Render can be their lookout while the rest of them—her, Rain, and Terk—work together to get the bus up and running again.

That promise has barely left her lips before Brohn, Cardyn, Manthy, and I are in a wind-sprint down the road. After about a half mile, we plunge into a wooded area, scamper over a few hundred yards of sloping, uneven terrain, and slide down to a ravine by the edge of a dark expanse of water.

Breaking through a wall of undergrowth, we step into a small clearing. Built on top of the cliff overlooking the bay, the hunched back of the domed Processor looms above us. The gravity-defying Halo rotates a hundred yards above that. A full moon hangs over it all, soaking the panorama in its reflective, blood-red light.

On the shore, steep cliff walls rise up on either side of us. We can't go left or right, and we sure can't go back. There's no way to climb the rock face to get up to the Processor. Besides, as soon as we got up there, we'd be standing in plain sight at their front door. Not exactly a Stealth 101 recommended course of action.

"So now what?" Cardyn pants, his hands already on his knees.

Brohn points to a spot along the rock face, directing our attention to a large white pipe extending from the cliff's base in the distance.

"Look! There's a water run-off conduit."

"So?"

"So...It's a big white pipe. Sound familiar? Besides, we can't exactly walk in through the front door."

"Right."

"And we can't fly up to the Halo."

Cardyn pushes me hard enough to make me take a full step to keep my balance. "Well, not *all* of us can."

"I can't fly, dummy."

"Since we can't get in by land or by air…we'll get in by sea," Brohn announces with his typical leaderly finality.

"Wait," I say. "You're suggesting we break into the Processor from under water?"

"Sure," Brohn grins. "And we can all swim, right?"

I draw my two gold-plated handguns. "What about these?"

We're each loaded up with our arsenal of guns and Medieval arms—not the lightest or most water-friendly weapons in the world.

Brohn takes a second to consider this, his head tilting back and forth between us and the dark, choppy water.

"We'll need to leave the guns and my arbalest behind."

"That just leaves us with my Talons and the two tomahawk axes," I remind him.

"Then I guess we'll need to pick up the slack ourselves. How are those knuckles of yours, Card?"

Cardyn makes a grand show of kissing the knuckles of his clenched fist. "Lined up and ready to rumble!"

"Great!" Brohn tucks the guns and his enormous crossbow into a cluster of long green reeds hanging over a small outcropping of rock.

Then, the four of us slip down the small embankment until the water is lapping at our boots.

With Brohn in the lead, we walk in a low crouch along the shore. When we run into a dead end where the cliff face blocks our way, Brohn guides us out into the deeper part of the bay, and we trudge along the gravelly bottom, the water soaking us up to our waists.

After a few minutes, Brohn and Cardyn are still able to walk along with their heads above the surface, but Manthy and I aren't as tall as them, and we have to start treading water.

"Are we close?" I gasp through a whisper and a glugging mouthful of water.

In the dark, Brohn nods and points to where the huge white pipe with a metal mesh across its mouth is spitting a stream of foamy water out into the Balearic Sea.

"Follow me."

The water is way too deep now for walking, so taking long, powerful strokes, Brohn starts swimming toward the pipe.

Cardyn and Manthy follow, and I splash along behind them, doing my best to keep up and keep quiet all at the same time.

It's a long swim, but the water gets shallow again as we approach the rocky crag and the wide white pipe. Gasping for breath, I'm grateful when I feel the toes of my boots scrape along the bay's rocky bottom.

On top of a glass and steel wall high above us, three shadowy figures are walking along an elevated pedestrian bridge. Based on their red and yellow armored uniforms, I'm guessing they're part of the Execs. Probably some kind of security detachment. Fortunately, they're going in the opposite direction from us, and we just have to hope they don't hear us splashing around down here and suddenly turn around.

In the dark and in the lapping water, every whisper and movement sounds thunderous to my ears, and I'm fully prepared to dive down and hold my breath for as long as it takes if those guys catch wind of us.

One at a time, we climb out of the water to stand on the slippery concrete platform under the wide mouth of the gurgling pipe.

As quietly as he can, Brohn works the circular grate until it starts wobbling under his back-and-forth effort. With his finger clamped to the steel grille, he manages to tug it a few inches away from the outer edges of the water run-off pipe.

But that's as far as he can get it.

"It's really locked on there," he pants. "If Terk was here…"

"Don't worry," Cardyn says, unclipping one of the tomahawk axes from the mag-holster on his back. He makes a dramatic show of spitting into his hands before clutching the handle, giving the weapon a whirling helicopter spin, and then bringing the blade down just below the head of one of the six big lag-bolts holding the grate in place. The blade slices cleanly through the threaded steel. To our pleasant surprise, Cardyn's axe blade on the steel bolts barely makes a sound over the soft gurgle of foamy water burbling out around our feet. Smiling, Cardyn repeats the effort on the other five bolts until their thick, hexagonal heads are lying in a small cluster on the platform.

With the bolts now decapitated, Brohn hauls the grate off, sets it on the concrete pad with a heavy thud, and the four of us clamber inside the nearly six-foot tall pipe.

Thankfully, we haven't tripped any alarms so far. We hustle down the length of the pipe, which turns out to be well-lit, clean, and high enough for us to scuttle along without having to duck our heads. Well, Brohn has to duck. The rest of us manage in the smallest of crouches. The water churning down the pipe is only ankle deep, and it's relatively clean and odor-free.

"At least we're not going in through a waste run-off," Cardyn says, reading my mind.

I chuckle at that, but Brohn hushes both of us. "There's an access door."

He walks up a short flight of steps and cranks the door's big handle. It swings open, to reveal a small room filled with gears, valves, gauges, dials, and thick, white pipes running from the floor into the ceiling. A metal plaque, faded and dusty, identifies this room as "Tertiary Hydro-Monitoring Port 7."

A square, black-topped table sits mushroom-like in the center of the room.

Manthy pulls the heavy steel door shut behind us as Brohn runs his hand over the table's sleek, glassy surface. "It's a holo-console."

"There's got to be a communications network in this place," I point out.

Cardyn's eyes swing over to Manthy. "Can you tap into it?"

"I can."

At first, I think I must have misheard her. Manthy's favorite phrase these days has been, "I *can't*."

But she brushes her hair back behind her ears and steps up to the holo-console. She gives me a strange, side-eyed glance, like she's about to leap off the top of a building and wants to have a last look at one more living soul before she dies.

I remember the flood of panic and pain I used to get when I first connected with Render. My mind didn't know how to process the foreign emotions, thoughts, and memories. Over time, it's gotten easier. But I also have my forearm implants to help and a lot more experience than Manthy does.

Her face tightens, and she lets out a little moan as she braces herself for what I know must be a painful experience.

Under her flat palms, the glossy black glass lights up into a rainbow array of sparkling indicator lights.

I glance over at the smaller door on the opposite side of the room, but Brohn catches me and tells me not to worry. "Look at the dust in this place. I'm sure the rest of the facility is top-of-the-line, but I don't think anyone's been in this room lately."

"Maybe they've forgotten about it?" I ask with a pleading smile.

"Let's hope."

Hunched over the table, Manthy mutters, "They record their sessions."

"Sessions?"

"It's a lab. In this building. Nine floors up from here."

"And they're doing experiments?"

Manthy nods. "Do you want to see what they're up to?"

"Um...*yeah*."

Manthy slips her hand into mine and closes her eyes.

Above the table, a new set of holo-images springs to life. From this angle, it looks like she must've tapped into one of the lab's overhead security cameras.

Three men and a woman are standing around a wide-armed reclining chair. The men are wearing white lab coats over red scrubs. The woman's got a matching lab coat, but her scrubs are lemon-yellow. All four of them have a symbol on the breast pocket of their lab coats: a stylized double-helix in the shape of a capital "E."

"En-Gene-eers." Brohn grinds his teeth around the word.

My breath catches in my throat when one of the men turns to tap out a flurry of code into a floating display.

When he steps to the side, we can see there's a girl in the chair. A Juven. I don't recognize her, but I know the chair.

We were plugged into ones exactly like it in the Epsilon Cube of our Processor when we were run through an elaborate V-R simulation. That virtual rescue mission only ended when Manthy managed to infiltrate the program. Good thing, too. We might still be locked in there if she hadn't.

The image in front of us flickers as two of the men leave, and the remaining man and the woman launch into what turns out to be a pretty tense conversation.

Their voices have the faintest metallic echo as the two En-Gene-eers amble between the Juven in the chair, the curved bank of holo-projections, and the glass lab table between them.

"Has she found them yet?" the woman asks.

Without looking up from his display, the man mutters, "Give her time."

"I told you we shouldn't have let her out on her own like that."

"She was ready."

"She's a prototype."

"And she's being field tested. What's the problem?"

"The problem is that we threw her to the wolves."

"*She's* supposed to be the wolf. She's the one doing the hunting, right?" The woman doesn't answer, so the man asks again. "Right?"

Now, the woman shrugs and says she doesn't know.

"Krug and the Deenays made those kids what they are. We have a chance to do the same with Noxia and the others. Only better. She's an upgrade. They're all upgrades."

"There's nothing wrong with those kids."

"They're out of control."

"Out of *your* control, you mean."

"Sure," the man snaps. "If that makes you feel better. And now they're out there about to undo everything we've been working on. They're out there right now, ready to evolve the rest of us into extinction. Unless we can control them."

"The Execs won't just catch them, you know."

"They have orders."

"And you think they'll follow them, especially if those kids resist? The Execs aren't known for their overwhelming sense of self-control."

The man stares daggers at the woman, who stares back, her hands clamped onto the edge of the lab table.

The man breaks into a sinister smile and tells the woman she worries too much.

Back in the dusty confines of our monitoring port, Cardyn asks, "Are they talking about *us*?"

Brohn says, "Mm-hmm."

In the holo-projection, the woman sighs, fiddles with a small cluster of blue wires at the back of the Juven's chair and plops down onto a lab stool, her head down, her shoulders slumped. "You know, everyone knows the story of Frankenstein, but no one ever learns the lesson."

"See," the man snorts. "That's the problem with your whole department. Here we are, behind the wheel and heading straight into a whole new era of human evolution, and you want to pump the brakes. Frankenstein created a monster that came back to destroy him." The man clamps both hands onto the back of the Juven's chair. "Those new monsters in the lab and this one here… they're going to *protect* us, not destroy us."

"You can't engineer evolution, Kent."

"Maybe *you* can't, Sadia. But that's exactly what the rest of us have been doing for years now. You really need to get on board."

"Is that a threat?"

"It's a warning. A friendly warning for an old friend."

The man stops fiddling with the holo-display above the console and turns his full attention to the woman, who lifts her head and sneers, "Always so logical."

"It's who I am," the man shrugs. "I'm a scientist. I'm a techno-biogeneticist."

The woman unclips the little girl from the chair and begins to lead her by the hand, dazed and wobbly, from the room.

Before they leave, the woman turns back, and we can see the fusion of fury and sadness in her face from here. "You should try being a human being sometime, Kent. Just for a change."

## 33

REVELATION

CARDYN PUTS both hands on the surface of the table and leans toward Manthy. "Where's she taking that girl? What about the rest of the kids?"

"They're here."

"Where?"

"Give me a second."

Manthy's face goes marshmallow-white, and a horrifying network of blue veins rises up in her face and along both sides of her neck. Her hand slips out of mine. She gasps and falls backward into Brohn's arms.

With whatever strength she has left, she manages to mutter, "I know where they are." She points to a spot where the wall meets the ceiling. "Six floors up and about eight hundred yards in that direction."

I bite my lip. "Eight hundred yards? Six stories? Can we get there? Without being spotted, I mean?"

She waves her hand over the holo-display, and lines of green code scroll through the air above the table. After a few more flicks of her fingers, a complex graph of an interconnected network of pipes, wires, vents, and conduits appears.

"We can get there." She walks over to the wall and pushes aside a small red storage cabinet to reveal a two-foot square vent cover.

"What? Through there?" Brohn asks, sizing up the small opening.

"Don't worry. We won't need to be in it for long."

This cover is much easier for Brohn to remove than the one over the opening of the water run-off pipe.

Crawling, we follow Manthy, who leads us along a system of aluminum air ducts, into a higher and wider conduit, up a snaking series of thin metal stairs, down a narrow maintenance walkway, and, finally, through a long access corridor running behind the facility's walls.

The entire time, we move as fast and quietly as the close confines and our combat boots will allow.

Every thirty or forty feet or so, we're able to peek out through one of the vent grates into the bright hallway. The place is filled with people, mostly Execs and scientists.

The Execs are clad in the yellow and red battle fatigues we're getting used to seeing. Everything about them is familiar: the assault rifles, the thick-soled boots, the chest-protectors, the smoky face-shields, and the battle gear. If they were sporting red, white, and blue, they could just as easily be the Patriot Army.

The scientists, on the other hand, are almost all dressed in matching white lab coats, but they wear four different colors of scrubs underneath: red, lemon-yellow, purple, and hunter green. All of their coats have the stylized "E" patch on their lapels. Most of them walk with their heads down, scanning the holo-images and floating text above their silver lab-tablets.

A few of them stop to compare notes in the middle of the hallway, much to the obvious annoyance of the three Execs clomping along in the opposite direction.

Other than that, though, two groups—the Execs and the En-Gene-eers don't seem to pay much attention to each other and stride down the same hall like they exist in two totally different worlds.

Fortunately, none of them seems to have been alerted to our presence. They march along, in and out of various room, their heels clicking on the glistening white floor, all business as usual.

The crawlspace we're in leads to another duct, which ends at a small ventilation grate. But the winking red lights on the top corners of the grate are bad news.

"Alarms," Manthy whispers back to us.

We all stop, frozen in fear. This tiny dark tunnel is definitely *not* the place to get caught.

But then Manthy assures us it's okay.

Tapping into the security feed, she strains until the little red lights ping to black. I think she must have just used her last drop of strength. She's sweat-soaked and ghost-pale. Her eyes are red and dry.

Honestly, she looked healthier when she was dead.

Cardyn edges past her and pushes the grate open, leading us through the portal and into a large lab with a floor-to-ceiling holo-monitor on one wall and heavy black conduits snaking along the ceiling.

Seated and strapped down in the middle of the lab, the five Juvens are facing each other in a circle of those partially-reclining medical chairs, the ones we got to know so well from our VR-sim in the Processor.

The Juvens, including the little girl we saw earlier, are dressed in identical, loose-fitting powder-blue pants and matching short-sleeved, button-down tops. Their generic walking shoes are vibrant white except for the laces, which are the same powder-blue as their clothes.

All in all, the outfits, plus the dead, glazed-over look in their eyes, give them a creepy appearance, like they're a bunch of very young scrub nurses who just walked out of a psych ward in a horror movie.

We used to think Emergents had to be our age—seventeen-years-old. Knowing that we can be identified, captured, and recruited *this* young is a terrifying thought.

Brohn is quick to unhook the leads running from a long glass console to the base of each chair.

In a shaky whisper, I call out for him to wait. "We don't know what those cords are for. They could be keeping them alive."

Brohn hesitates, but only for a second. "You might be right, Kress. But we don't have time to figure it out. These are the same chairs they had us plugged into in our Processor. I don't think being disconnected will hurt them."

His head whipping back and forth, Cardyn says he doesn't care anymore. "I just really think we ought to grab these kids and get the frack out of here!" He taps his wrist as if he were wearing an old-style wristwatch. "Clock is ticking, people, right?"

Brohn agrees, and he and I start helping the kids out of the reclining chairs and onto their feet.

He asks each of them if they're okay, but they don't answer, and Cardyn guesses maybe they're drugged.

"Then how are we supposed to get them out of here?" I ask.

Brohn starts ushering the Juvens back toward the open air duct we just crawled out of. "We'll manage."

Cardyn leans over my shoulder. "Do you think they really have abilities like us?"

"If they do, it's probably all that's saved their lives so far."

"Until us," he brags.

"Let's pat ourselves on the back *after* we get them and us out of here."

With the kids in tow, we shuffle single file back through the duct and down the narrow access corridor running alongside the long hallway.

We turn a corner and reach the point where we have to start edging our way sideways through the tight space.

"Good thing Terk didn't come," I whisper to Brohn.

Suppressing a chuckle, he agrees, his voice barely a breath. "Just what we'd need, right? He'd get wedged in here, and they'd find our dead bodies three weeks later."

After a few more turns and a six-floor scamper back down the narrow metal stairways, we're finally near the vent leading to the Hydro-Monitoring Port where we started. From behind Cardyn and in the near darkness, Manthy whispers, "Wait."

At first, I think she's scolding me and Brohn for talking too loudly, but then she presses her cheek and both of her palms to the wall.

"There's still an active security feed up ahead."

Cardyn bites his lip and glances back the way we came. "Didn't you disable them back there?"

"Just the local feed. This one's a backup to the primary sensors. It activates when the other systems go down."

"What does that mean?" Cardyn whispers from just behind me. "In English, preferably."

"It means as soon as we pass this junction, the backup sensor is going to detect our motion and body heat and—"

"Set off any active alarms left in the compound," I finish.

Manthy nods. Behind Manthy, the five Juvens start murmuring as they try to figure out what's going on.

Cardyn is twitching around and tugging at his hair so hard I'm afraid he's going to pull himself bald. "So...what? We came to rescue them, and now *we're* stuck, too?"

"We just need to get past this wall," Manthy says, her hand pressed flat to the smooth surface. "The hydro-port room where we first got in here is just on the other side."

"And we can get back out through the water run-off tunnel," Brohn says. He stares up through the darkness at the low ceiling before fixing his eyes onto Manthy's. "Can you...you know—do anything about it?"

"I can't."

"Great, Manthy," Brohn snaps, bent over, his hands on his knees. "Then what are we supposed to—?"

"But Kress can," she says.

"Kress can *what*?" I ask.

In the cramped space, Manthy's voice is low and hollow. "Do you remember when you flew past the walls?"

"What walls?"

"The long ones. The ones with the tiny holes. You said they were like windows with people on the other side."

"Manthy," I say, hoping she can't hear the worry in my voice about her sanity, "that was just a dream."

"Nothing is 'just' a dream, Kress."

Brohn scowls. "We don't have time for—"

Manthy cuts him off with a raised hand. She doesn't look at him, though. In the near darkness, those mysterious eyes of hers are plastered onto mine. "We have all the time Kress can find for us."

She takes my hand in hers, and a specific configuration for my forearm implants flashes in my memory. It's an old one, one my dad taught me in the early days of the first drone strikes. I remember it like it was yesterday: He called it "the Bypass Pattern."

With my fingers flying, I draw the pattern onto my forearm implants:

I trace one of the long lines running from my elbow to the back of my wrist. I do the same on the other arm. Then, three taps on one of the constellations of black dots followed by an arcing swipe of the black spiral at the crook of my arm. I finish by pressing the tips of my fingers to the crescent moon on my inner forearm.

In the millisecond it takes for me to blink, Brohn, Cardyn, Manthy, and the five kids we have in tow fizzle away into a pixilated haze until I'm left alone in darkness.

In my mind, two voices roll over each other like white-capped rapids in a river.

~ *She's not ready.*

*She is...in her dreams.*

~ *Reality and dreams aren't the same.*

*They're not opposites, either.*

~ *She'll need help.*

*Then we'll help her.*

One of the voices, as always, is Render's. The other belongs to Manthy.

"Okay," I say out loud—and at far too high a volume for where we are and for the situation we're in. "Get out of my head and give me two seconds to think!"

Brohn asks me what's going on, and I tell him I think I can get us past this wall and into the hydro-port. "Only...I'm not a hundred percent sure how."

"I don't care about *how*," Brohn snaps, gesturing with a frenzied wave of his hand for me to get on with doing whatever it is I need to do. "I trust you."

I close my eyes again, and I get the terrifying sensation— despite the close confines, our nerve-wracking escape attempt, and the very real possibility of getting caught and killed—that I'm about to fall asleep.

Instead, though, I snap fully alert, opening my eyes to a black wall covered with tiny specks of white paint.

*Wait. That's not paint. It's light. But from where?*

*From the other side.*

And then, I'm stepping forward, into the void.

And I'm not alone.

Brohn, Cardyn, and Manthy are with me. And so are the five Juvens.

Somehow, and I have no idea how, we wind up walking, hand in hand, through what was once a very solid wall but is now a murky space, a state somewhere between a solid, a liquid, and a gas.

Together, we step through the wall and into the Hydro-Port.

His hands on his hips, Cardyn bends over and throws up. "Don't *ever* do that again!"

Breathing hard, Brohn huddles us into a group, does a quick headcount of the Juvens, and takes a deep, quivering breath.

I'm as queasy as Brohn, Cardyn, and the Juvens seem to be, and it's all I can do to choke back the acidic phlegm pooling in the back of my throat.

Over by the door leading out to the water run-off pipe, Manthy is hurrying us along…and *giggling*?

"What the hell…?" I manage to choke out. We all just walked through a wall! And all of us but Manthy look like we just ran headlong *into* one.

Manthy shrugs. "What can I say? It tickled."

She bolts along with the rest of us, queasy and totally disoriented, limping along after her.

The end of the pipe where we snuck in is still barfing up its tumble of water into the burbling black sea.

From the platform at the base of the cliff, Brohn gazes out over the water. "We have to get these kids across."

I ask one of the girls, "Can you swim?"

She doesn't answer. None of the five kids seems to even acknowledge that I've spoken.

From the deep shadow of the open pipe behind us, a voice says, "I can help."

I recognize the voice instantly even though I've never heard it before today.

We spin around and find ourselves face to face with the En-Gene-eer in the lemon-yellow scrubs, the same woman we saw on the holo-monitor arguing with the male scientist in the lab.

Hopping down from the lip of the pipe and onto the concrete platform at its base, she folds her arms across her chest. Even in the dark, her odd smile is clear as day. And it's equal parts impressed, embarrassed, and royally pissed off.

Her eyes soften, though, and she actually looks kind of amused.

"We have Noxia and the Hawkers out looking for you, and here you are…our very own Emergents—right under our noses."

Cardyn unclips his tomahawk axes, and I snap my talons out. Reflecting the moonlight off the water, the blades give off silver winks in the gloom.

The woman doesn't panic or react. Instead, she uncrosses her arms, raises both hands in surrender, and steps toward us.

Brohn orders her to stop where she is, and she complies. "You know us?"

"I'd better. I made you."

## SADIA

"MY NAME IS SADIA. I work here. That's how I know you'll get caught if you try to swim across right now. You've tripped at least two perimeter circuits and the underwater array. They'll be looking for you."

"They?"

Sadia tilts her head back toward the Processor and up at the Halo spinning slowly overhead. "You'll be safe here. For about ten minutes, anyway. And as long as you don't make a lot of noise or move around too much. Each of these kids has a tracking chip implanted. Once the security detail finishes their sensor sweep, the chips'll be reactivated, and you'll be detected."

We must look terrified because Sadia laughs and tells us not to worry. "I'm not here to hurt you. I'm here to help you."

Drawing out a dagger-like weapon, she says, "Here," and steps toward us, and every one of us takes a full step back. "It's for *them*," she tells us with a head-tilt toward the five dazed and swaying Juvens.

Before we can stop her, she steps right between me and Brohn and waves the dagger in a high arc over the kids' heads before stepping back toward the mouth of the water run-off pipe. "It's a Suppressor. It'll neutralize their tracking chips."

"Why?" I ask. I don't believe her for a second, and I'm fully prepared to take her down first and figure out our escape after.

Her eyes widen and then narrow into focused slits, and it looks like she's getting ready to scream at us.

Instead, her face relaxes, and she glances past us and out over the water before taking a deep breath. "There's a crossroads, an intersection where no one's ever stood. It's the meeting place of technology, people, and our dreams. Close to twenty years ago, something happened in our human DNA. Something puzzling. Something transformative. Something potentially deadly. It may have something to do with a certain degree on the earth's latitude. We're still not sure. The two groups of biotech-geneticists you know as the Deenays and the En-Gene-eers were the first to realize what was happening. We called you Emergents. The other ones, the ones we could more easily weaponize, you know them as Hypnagogics. Like Noxia. Way more complex, way more unpredictable, and, frankly, way more powerful than you. There was also a classification called Hypnopompics. They carried a severe genetic defect, though. As far as we know, none of them survived." A gust of wind whips up and blows a thin mist of water over us. Tying her hair back in a ponytail, Sadia pauses for a second and says, "I'm assuming you know the truth about the Eastern Order."

We're all too stunned to do anything other than tip our heads in a weak collection of half-nods.

"Krug and a few others like him—they were already full of themselves. But that wasn't enough. They needed everyone else to be as full of them as they were. They got addicted to themselves. And, like most addicts, eventually they needed more. So they went after money. And power. And when that wasn't enough, they went after immortality. Which meant going after you. When they discovered who you were and how to use you, they built the Processors and started working on well...*manufacturing* you."

"And the Order?" Brohn asks.

"The Eastern Order was a textbook enemy. They kept people scared. No one asked questions. No one challenged the handful of dictators who were running the world. And it gave them the perfect excuse to recruit you, weed you out, and keep the rest of you for themselves. You've seen magic tricks, right? Keep your mark busy with one hand, and they won't see you picking their pocket with the other."

"So you're the bad guy," Cardyn says. It's not a question.

But Sadia looks horrified at the thought and gives her head a vigorous shake. "No, no, no. I only *work* for the bad guys."

"Then you're a bad guy," Brohn insists. Again, not a question.

Her eyes go slack and watery, and she looks genuinely hurt. Biting her lip, she glances out over the water, then into the big white pipe before turning back to us.

"I was one of the ones working from the inside to try to stop what was happening. Or at least guide it. These kids here...they lost *everything*: Home. Family. Freedom. But we needed to allow this amazing evolutionary transfiguration to take place. Only we couldn't afford to let Krug and his gang of Wealthies control it, monetize it, and weaponize it. We were Infiltrators. Krug and the Deenays thought we were working for them, but we were really working *against* them. The Deenays and En-Gene-eers combined their resources to build secret facilities—maybe dozens of them —throughout the U.S. and around the world. We never did find out where or how they hid them from us. Or, honestly, even if they ever existed at all. I was an Infiltrator." Sadia surprises us all by pointing at me. "And so was your father."

"My father..."

I knew my father was involved in programs related to the

Emergents. I knew he was responsible for the Auditor. Now, hearing how deep and global his involvement went makes me feel confused, proud, and betrayed all at the same time.

Leaning forward, Brohn, Cardyn, and Manthy are as eager as I am to hear more, but Sadia jumps at the sound of shouting in the distance. We all look up to see full platoons of Execs charging across a series of elevated walkways between two of the Processor's towering domed buildings.

Her words tumble out with heated urgency. "We're out of time."

"So what now?" I ask. "You wouldn't have told us all that if you were planning on letting us go."

"That's *exactly* why I told you. For decades now, this whole thing has been one giant puzzle. I'm giving you a corner piece. And I'm not 'letting you go,' Sadia says with a wink. "You're escaping 'despite my very best efforts.'" Her eyes linger over the five Juvens clustered together behind us. "All of you."

Despite what she's saying, I'm sure she's going to hit an alarm, scream for help, or whip out a gun and try to kill us all.

But none of that happens.

She glances down at a small holo-monitor on her wrist. "Noxia. She's dangerous."

"We know," Brohn tells her.

Sadia checks the holo-monitor one more time. She nods to herself and then taps out a code. In between us, a hatch in the ground grinds open, and we jump back, startled.

"You can't go through the water," Sadia says. "But you *can* go under. This is an old maintenance access tunnel. It won't be pleasant. But once you're on the other side, you'll be past the perimeter for the primary detection grid." Sadia points to our new batch of young Emergents. "If you make it home, don't waste who you are. *Help* them. Train them the way *you* should have been trained. Your power isn't about your bodies and what you can do. It's about your hearts and who you can help."

And then, without another word, she steps over the lip of the water-run off pipe and slips away into the darkness.

## 35

# INTRODUCTIONS

COLLECTING THE JUVENS, we follow Sadia's directions and make our way through the hatch and down a long, rust-flaked ladder into a tunnel.

By the time we've hit the bottom, the hatch has grumbled closed above us, leaving us in a foul, syrupy darkness.

"Ugh. That Sadia wasn't kidding about this being 'unpleasant,' was she?"

Cardyn's ahead of me so he can't see my eye-roll at his colossal understatement.

The tunnel isn't more than about five feet high and three feet wide. The walls are coated in a disgusting layer of putrid sludge.

It's not literally burning through our jacket sleeves as we slide by, but it sure feels like it might.

I don't think there's any air here except what we brought with us, and I can easily see our heroic rescue mission ending with me, Brohn, Cardyn, Manthy, and the five Juvens suffocating and dropping face-down-dead in the six-inches of dirty, boot-sucking slurry oozing along the tunnel's warped cement floor.

In what must be a pretty painful crouch, Brohn continues to trudge through the passageway with Manthy right behind him.

The Juvens are edging quietly along after them with me and Cardyn in the back of our single-file line.

Just when I'm convinced the next aching breath I draw is going to be my last, Brohn calls back to us from the front of our procession. "There's a ladder here. And another hatch in the ceiling. It's got an input panel, but I don't think it works."

His breath is halting and heavy, and I have no doubt he's summoning whatever strength he's got left just to talk.

Telling us to wait where we are, he clambers up the ladder. In the meager greenish light, I see him tap at the hatch and then swear as he punches it as hard as he can.

His knuckles clang against the small steel door, but—judging by his grunt and a string of profanity—I don't think it's budged.

"I disengaged the primary locks in the Processor," Manthy apologizes through the steamy air. "But that's all I could connect with."

Cardyn whispers up that maybe there's a mechanical lock on the outside of the hatch. "If that's all that's standing between us and getting the hell out of here..."

Brohn says, "It's worth a shot." Bracing his hands on the ladder's rickety rungs, he thrusts himself up, shoulder-first, into the steel door.

We all jump when it smashes open on the first try, and a blast of fresh air whooshes into the tunnel.

We scramble up the ladder with Brohn and Manthy helping to pull the Juvens up one at a time. Cardyn and I are the last ones out.

Recognizing where we are, Brohn leads us back down to the water's edge where he gathers up his arbalest and the guns we stashed before we snuck into the facility. "These may come in handy."

Cutting and dodging through the woods, we practically fall all over each other as we run in a frantic clump. Finally, we slow down for a second to get our bearings.

Cardyn and Manthy urge the kids along and offer them a helping hand over the rough, uneven terrain.

Behind us, the Valencia compound, round and wide and glowing as the moon, rises up over the red-tinged bay and against the raven-black sky.

As we pass through a clearing, we can see the bus up ahead.

"Let's go!" Cardyn urges us through the darkness.

I get dizzy and nearly fall over, but Brohn catches me in time. He grips my arm in his hand and asks if I'm okay. "We're nearly there," he assures me.

I'm halfway between laughing and crying when I confess, "I don't know what's happening to me. That thing I did back there with the wall…"

"I don't know either," Brohn confesses. "But Manthy seems to."

"Whatever it is," Cardyn says, his hand on my other arm as I struggle to stay upright, "it probably saved our lives. As awful as it felt—and please let's *seriously* not do that again—I'd still rather be out here than locked in there."

Shaking off a wave of nausea, I tell the boys I'm okay. "It's like my dreams are answers to questions I haven't asked yet."

Brohn throws his arm around me and draws me into a warm hug. "Hey. I've got my dream come true right here."

Laughing, I push him away and tell him to stop embarrassing me. Inside, though, I'm all melty but refreshingly complete.

Ahead of us, past a thicket of brambles and a thin patch of skeletal-white trees, Terk's waving mechanical arm glints silver-pink in the moonlight.

We rush the last hundred yards up to where he's standing with Rain and Croque Madame over a bunch of tools littered around the ground next to the bus.

Terk takes a full step back as the nine of us come sliding to a frenzied stop.

With all of us panting in a cluster, Cardyn asks if they were able to fix the bus.

"Short answer," Rain says, "Yes."

"And the long answer?" Brohn asks.

"Well…we're not going to be winning any speed contests."

"And there's no guarantee the mag-system's drive-train won't fall to pieces underneath us," Terk adds.

"Will it get us on the road and far away from here?" I ask.

"In theory."

"That's a theory I *really* think we should test out," Cardyn insists. "Like, right now."

While Croque Madame starts gathering up the tools from the ground and tossing them into an open storage bay in the side of the bus, the rest of us make a beeline for the bus door.

The five Juvens don't follow us, though.

"Come on!" I plead, but they're locked in a confused and frightened cluster. "Come on!" I shout again, louder this time, more urgent and insistent.

I'm just asking myself what the hell is wrong with these kids when a thought occurs to me:

*Of course. They have no idea who we are. We could be the Eastern Order for all they know.*

I tug the sleeve of Brohn's jacket as he prepares to board the bus, and I point at the speechless, unmoving Juvens.

Brohn shrugs me off and continues up the bus steps. "We don't have time for introductions."

"And they don't have any reason to believe they're not being kidnapped. *Again.*"

He freezes in place, one foot on the bottom stair, the other on the ground. He looks back the way we came, past the trees and the brambles and out toward the sky-high domes, the illuminated walkways, the thin glass spires, and the glowing, rotating Halo over Valencia. "Fine," he sighs.

In a rapid-fire flurry, Brohn hops down and introduces our Conspiracy to our new friends.

When he gets to Render, it's like the kids have forgotten all about the rest of us. While Brohn was rattling of our names, their eyes skimmed over us, but, now, they lock onto the glistening black raven who's just landed on my outstretched arm.

The girl who introduces herself as Sara finally breaks the moment of hypnosis.

The tallest of the group, she reaches out for a second like she's going to try to pet Render, but then seems to think better of it. Instead, she points one at a time to the rumpled, scraggly band of rescued Juvens.

The slick-haired, olive-skinned girl she introduces as "Mattea" gives us a happy smile. Mattea's top and bottom lips are plump and nearly identical to each other, and she has matching beauty marks on her forehead and chin, giving her face the appearance of being kind of upside-down.

The eyes of the boy Sara calls "Arlo" skip around like he can't decide which one of us to focus on. Pale and doll-faced, he's oddly handsome and weirdly symmetrical, as if he was built instead of born.

"I'm Libra," the next girl beams before Sara has a chance to introduce her. Her head pivots on her swan-like neck as she rattles off a gushing flurry of random greetings to me and my Conspiracy: "I like your bird. You're really tall. How come you all have fancy guns *and* old-timey weapons?"

I giggle at her enthusiasm but then feel bad when she blushes and takes a step back.

"Don't mind Libra," Sara laughs. "She's a chatterbox, but you get used to it."

"The guards never did," the swarthy, curly-haired boy next to her scowls.

"And this handsome, grumpy young man," Sara sighs, "is Ignacio."

Ignacio grunts at us with what somehow manages to be an angry smile.

"And this…," Brohn announces in a rush, "is Croque Madame. Our driver and our savior."

"Your very *impatient* driver and savior," she blurts as she wipes grease from her hands onto a tattered, gray cloth. "So…can we get going or were you interested in waiting around for the En-Gene-eers to figure out what's happened to their little prizes here?" She leaps into the bus and slides behind the wheel. "I'm guessing *someone* in that Processor is going to notice five missing kids and won't be too happy about it."

"Understatement of the century," Cardyn says, leaping into the bus after her.

Rain, Terk, and Manthy follow while Brohn and I stand to either side of the bus doors and usher the kids in. Apparently satisfied that this is, indeed, a rescue and not a trick or a second round of kidnapping, the kids—perking alive for the first time—bound up the steps and file down the aisle.

Render is the last one on board, fluttering to a squawking perch on the back of my seat.

We've all barely sat down when the bus roars to life, and we go blasting down the road with a screech of tires on the rough pavement.

At the back of the bus, the kids turn around to watch the city, the Processor, and the Halo disappear into the gloomy distance.

It's not until the last hint of the hovering Halo is out of sight that they finally turn back around to face front and to sit in a weird, silent stillness.

I can't even begin to imagine what must be going through their minds.

My Conspiracy and I were captive in a Processor. Before that, we lived for ten years trapped in the Valta.

These Juvens seem to have lived the better part of their lives

261

in their Processor. With no family and with nowhere to go, I guess all they have to look forward to now is...*us*.

My Conspiracy and I are used to taking care of each other. Looking out for five new Emergents...well, that's another matter altogether. And, if what Sadia said back there is true, we've got one whale-sized responsibility on our hands.

Brohn must be reading my mind because he leans toward me and says, "From now on, I think we might be all they've got."

"From now on," I reply, "we're going to have to work even harder to make sure we're enough."

## 36

# RETURN TO BORDEAUX

WE DRIVE through the night and deep into the next morning.

In better spirits now that her arm's begun to heal, Rain plies us with questions about our infiltration of the Processor and rescue of the kids.

She and Terk hang on our every word as Brohn, Manthy, and I—but mostly Cardyn—fill them in on everything from our entry into the Processor to our encounter with Sadia and to our ultimate underground, undersea escape.

When we get around to the part where Sadia told us about our past and about being the products of experiments in techno-human transfiguration, Terk's eyes roll back, and I honestly think he's going to pass out right here in the front of the bus. But he shakes off the shock and stares down at his human and Modified hands for a long time before finally turning back to us.

"Who do you think we'd be if we hadn't been…transfigured?"

Brohn sounds annoyed when he tells Terk, "We'd be exactly who we are. Emergent, Modified, Hypnagogic, or anything else for that matter. It's all just labels. They may come with abilities or baggage or problems, but forget about the Deenays, Krug, and the En-Gene-eers. *We're* in charge of being who we are."

Terk tilts his head down like he's been scolded, but when he raises it again, he's got a pleasant smile stretching across his wide face and pushing his rosy cheeks up into smooth, puffy lumps.

WITH THE SUN nudging over the horizon in a shimmering red blob, I stretch and rub my eyes and look back at the kids who are sleeping in a variety of slumped and entangled positions. "Where are we?"

"We're going back a different way," Croque Madame informs us.

Looking worried and rubbing the sleep from his own eyes, Terk asks why.

"If the Hawkers are still out there, they'll be looking for us around San Sebastian. As you saw, Pamplona and Zaragoza aren't exactly the safest places in the world for us right now. Our best strategy is to stay on the access and auxiliary roads running along A23 and N260."

"I don't know if I'd call this a 'road,'" Cardyn complains just in time for all of us to get violently jostled by a series of deep grooves in the bumpy stretch of earth below.

The five Juvens in the back jolt awake and shriek before settling into their seats when Brohn calls back to them that everything's okay.

"You have a funny definition of 'okay,'" Cardyn tells him.

Before Brohn has a chance to respond, Croque Madame points ahead toward the shimmering border between the neglected world around us and the city of Bordeaux.

We're just as amazed as we were last time at the striking transition between one world and the other.

"We're stopping here again?" Terk asks.

Rain tells him it's best. "We need supplies. Food. Those kids back there don't look like they've had a decent meal in…well, ever."

"Remember," Brohn reminds us, "time doesn't work the same here as what we're used to."

"Yet *another* understatement of the century," Cardyn mumbles.

"How will we know?" I ask. "We could wind up here for a month and not know it. And who knows what the world will turn into while we're gone?"

Stroking his jawline with his fingertips and with his eyes on the sky, Brohn seems to consider this. "Rain?"

Rain calls out for Croque Madame to pull the bus over to the side of the road. She gives Rain a puzzled look but complies.

Rain asks me if I can get Render to stay here with the bus.

I tell her, "Sure. I guess. Why?"

"Go into the city but stay connected with him. Ask him to signal you if more than, I don't know…a few hours have passed."

I'm about to say, "Sure. No problem." But then I realize there may be one potentially *huge* problem.

"I've stayed connected with him over distance," I tell her. "But never over time."

Terk asks, "What's the difference?"

"I don't know, really. But he could get disoriented. Or I could. Or we might not be able to stay connected at all."

"In which case we're fracked six ways from Sunday," Cardyn moans unhelpfully.

"We need someone to stay behind," Brohn suggests. "Someone to keep an eye on the kids."

Rain and Terk exchange a look and seem to come to an unspoken agreement.

"We'll stay," Rain volunteers. "We fixed the bus together. My arm's feeling better. I guess we can babysit, too."

"We'll take care of Render and the new Emergents," Terk promises.

"And Manthy," I say.

Manthy scowls at me. "What about Manthy?"

"You should stay, too."

"I can go. I'm fine."

But even those few words barely make it past her lips, and we all know for sure that Manthy is still at least a few days of rest and probably a couple months' worth of serious downtime away from being "fine." We ask a lot of her. She doesn't always cooperate. But when she does, she gives it her all and puts her life on the line every time.

"We won't be long," I promise.

Manthy frowns and clenches her jaw. Rain takes her hand while Terk puts a supporting hand on her shoulder. And it's a good thing, too. Manthy's legs are trembling, and her eyes are unfocused.

Croque Madame seems almost as reluctant as Manthy, and I can't blame her. This bus is just a mode of transportation for us. For her, I think it's kind of her life. The thought of leaving it like this must be painful, but she knows even better than we do how charming Martine and Bordeaux can be. We can't risk *all* of us entering into that same seductive bubble.

"Come with us," Brohn says to her. "You know Martine and the people of Bordeaux way better than we do. Chances are we couldn't get in without you, anyway."

After a long sigh and an equally long look around at the eleven of us on her bus, she agrees. "Take away the drone attacks, the death, the ruined and uninhabitable cities, and you super-powered Emergents, and this would all be—"

"We're not superpowered," I protest.

"Yeah?" Brohn smiles over my objection. "What would all this be?"

"This could be the next best thing to normal: me driving my wee ones to school like I used to love doing for so long."

"Speaking of which," Brohn says with a wink as he steps out of the bus, "I think I hear the school bell ringing."

Cardyn, Croque Madame, and I follow him out. From where we've parked, it's a long but pleasant walk down the side of the road. The gravel under our feet is white and smooth, and there's a deep row of heathery grass swaying on either side of us in the warm breeze.

Despite our nervousness over the possibility of getting sucked into this place forever, our second stop here promises to be every bit as enjoyable as the first.

"This is the closest feeling I've had to coming home," I say out loud, and Brohn, and Cardyn are quick to agree.

But then Brohn reminds us: "Remember, it's *not* home. And we won't get any closer to getting back by pretending that is."

Still following Croque Madame, we walk along the cobble-stone path leading into the city.

To our surprise, Martine, herself, greets us at the city's entrance. We've barely said "Hello" before she's lunging in for double-cheek kisses and bombarding us with open-armed excla-mations of welcome.

"Where's your bus?"

"We left it back on the access road," Croque Madame says. She doesn't elaborate about why, and Martine, thankfully, doesn't ask.

I have a feeling she'd be offended if she knew we planned our departure before we'd even arrived.

Instead, all smiles and without a care in the world, she takes us straight to the Rue St. Catherine and bombards us with an equal bounty of food and questions.

With her blessing, Brohn packs up the black duffel bag he brought with an aromatic variety of food to take back to the others.

As usual, Cardyn's stomach takes priority over all else for him. Martine laughs when Cardyn, from out of a disgustingly full mouth, tries to tell her about our adventures in Spain and about our successful rescue mission with the help of Sadia. Instead of a nicely detailed story, however, he showers her with a misty spray of spittle.

As if this is a common occurrence, she draws out an embroidered lace handkerchief and wipes her face as Cardyn turns red and apologizes, careful to keep his hand over his mouth to avoid bombarding her with a second salvo.

"I'm just glad you're alive!" Martine gushes. "Very few people have found zis place. Even fewer have left." She holds up two fingers, which she waggles back and forth. "You're among ze first to visit us...*twice!*"

"It's quite the paradise you have here," Brohn says.

I glance over at him, but I can't tell if he's being serious or sarcastic.

Martine accepts it as a compliment and blushes, her voice going sadly soft. "We feel bad about what's happening in the world. But zis *bulle*...um, how do you say? Bubble! Zis bubble, zis *utopie*, as you call it...it keeps us hidden. It keeps us safe."

Croque Madame and Martine loop their arms through Cardyn's and guide him deeper into the seemingly endless market.

Brohn sighs. "It really is perfect here in their little *bulle*, isn't it?"

"We can't stay," I remind him.

With his eyes fixed on the beautiful city spread out before us, he sighs again and adjusts the strap from the bulging black bag over his shoulder. "I know."

"The thing about bubbles," I remind him, "is that they're beautiful."

"Yeah?"

"And they're also easy to pop."

Brohn offers up a Cardyn-esque groan. "How come the truth is always so depressing?"

"It doesn't have to be," I assure him with a laugh. Although right now, I only kind of half-believe that, myself.

268

With Brohn shaking himself out of his reverie, we stride forward to join the others.

The market is crowded and bustling but still somehow calm. There's an air of relaxation hanging over the place. Everyone is smiles. No one's in a hurry.

In the distance, clean buildings—many of which I recognize from our earlier tour—rise up, casting warm shadows over the sunny city.

In front of us, the market stalls are lined with sweets or filled to overflowing with robust vegetables in every hue of orange, purple, red, and green.

A group of men and women are standing at a waist-high bistro table, chatting in rapid-fire French over glasses of brick-red wine, a tray of orange and butter-yellow cheeses, and rows of marbled, thinly sliced meats.

"I could get used to this," Brohn confesses.

I tell him, "Don't."

"Okay, okay. I'm just saying…"

From somewhere outside the bubble, Render reaches out, slipping his consciousness into mine.

~ *It's time to go.*

*We just got here.*

~ *You entered the city twenty-four hours ago. Rain and Terk tried to get in but couldn't.*

*You're kidding, right?*

~ *Our thoughts are each other's. What do you think?*

*Um…I think it's time to go!*

~ *Thank you. Why can't more humans think like birds?*

With that, Render severs our connection, and I grab Brohn's arm as firmly as I can without having him think I'm attacking him. "Render says it's already been twenty-four hours."

Brohn smirks at me. "I think your bird is a little bird-brained. It's been *maybe* thirty minutes."

"Unless you're saying we shouldn't trust him."

Brohn seems to contemplate this before calling out to Cardyn and Madame that it's time to go.

"But we just got here!" Cardyn protests, an éclair in one hand, a profiterole in the other.

"And now we just need to get going," Brohn snaps back. "Unless you think Render and Kress are steering us wrong."

During our time growing up in the Valta and over the past year of adventures through our own country and now, halfway around the world, we've had plenty of reason to doubt our missions or each other.

But no one's ever doubted Render.

And I don't think anyone's ready to start now.

Against every logical thought and deeply ingrained instinct, we say our hurried goodbyes to Martine and to the hundreds of vendors and townspeople who have gathered around us in the middle of the market.

"You really should consider staying," Martine suggests.

She sounds relaxed and casual, but there's also an undercurrent of urgency in her voice. And not the good kind. Not the kinds that says, "Stay here so you'll be safe."

More like, "Stay here so *we'll* be safe."

That's when it occurs to me that Martine has a dilemma: She wants visitors, and I think she genuinely wants to keep as many people safe and off the grid as possible. But every person who visits here and leaves is another person who could expose their secret and reveal their hidden location—accidentally or on purpose—to the world.

Or, more precisely, reveal their hidden location to the En-Gene-eers who seem to double as the puppet-masters in the fight against the Eastern Order here and have been responsible for unleashing the Execs and the drone attacks that have turned so much of this part of the world—like our own—into rubble.

I'm no longer sure if the gathered townspeople are going to wish us farewell or try to keep us from leaving.

I'm not even sure if *they* know.

But the little strain in Martine's voice fades away as she kisses each one of us on the cheeks and tells us, "Au revoir, et bonne chance."

As we step out of the city's limits, she pleads, "S'il vous plait, gardez nous et notre secret en sécurité."

*Please keep us and our secret safe.*

Brohn promises we will.

Resisting every natural instinct and the seductive pull of paradise, we turn and march back up the cobblestone path toward the access road, the bus, Rain, Terk, Manthy, and the new Emergents.

Cardyn flicks his thumb back toward the city. "They'll be okay, won't they?"

Brohn tells him, "Absolutely. They have time on their side, right?"

"I guess."

I don't know if it's a gut feeling, if I'm experiencing a waking dream, if Render is doing something weird to my brain, or if I'm just going crazy...but I've got a strange and very strong feeling that Martine and the people of Bordeaux might not be *storing* time as much as they might be *running out of it.*

And even worse, I'm worried that whatever happens might turn out to be our fault.

## STOWAWAY

I DON'T KNOW if they're scared, still in shock, or just naturally
shy. Either way, our new companions seem content to sit quietly
in the back of the bus as we rumble along the nearly impassable
access roads through France on our way back to London.

Of the five of them, only Libra is curious or brave enough to
come up to the front of the bus to talk with me and my
Conspiracy.

Questions cartwheel out of her, but she doesn't seem especially interested in our answers.

"Where are we going?"

"To London first," Brohn says. "Then home. Hopefully."

"Are you really Emergents?"

"We are," I smile.

"How come you didn't take us with you into that city back
there?"

"It's too dangerous," Cardyn explains.

"Why were you gone so long?"

"We didn't know we were."

"Do you speak French?"

"A little," I tell her.

"You should ask Mattea for help. She speaks about every language there is."

"Really?"

Libra waves frantically toward the back of the bus to get Mattea's attention. "Mattea! Come up here and show them!"

Mattea shakes her upside-down face and scrunches deeper into her seat.

"Trust me," Libra gushes, "I've heard her do it. French. Spanish. English. Chinese. Xhosa. If it's a language, she can speak it."

"Most people around here seem to speak English," Cardyn points out.

Libra shrugs. "Doesn't matter. Mattea speaks everything. Do you think it's 'cause she's a Mergie?"

"Could be," Brohn nods. I smile, but I can tell he's not especially happy about having this new young friend of ours chattering away in his ear.

Sara calls up to Libra and tells her to leave us alone.

I tell both of the girls that it's okay, but Libra stands up and sulks down the aisle to return to the back of the bus.

I'm about to go after her, but Cardyn stops me. "She'll be okay. They'll all be okay."

Rain says she agrees. "This has got to be pretty overwhelming for them. I think they could use some down time."

Terk swings around and stretches his long legs across the aisle. "Me, too," he yawns and leans his head against the window.

WE'VE BEEN on the road for a couple of hours when the sound of a light thumping from underneath the bus turns into a dense, steady hammering.

Swearing under her breath, Croque Madame eases the trundling bus to a stop.

Brohn tells the kids to stay put while we follow her out and around the bus as she checks the tires.

Brushing aside a cluster of thorny, head-high weeds, she squats down at one point and comes back up, shaking her head.

"What is it?" Terk asks.

"Not sure. I'll check the magnetic converter on the drive shaft next. But it doesn't sound like—"

"Doesn't sound like what?" Terk asks.

Croque Madame shushes him with a raised hand and tilts her head toward the bus, her eyes in a squint of deep concentration.

"It's one of my stowage bays."

"Where you keep the supplies you transport?" I ask.

"I think I forgot to seal one of them properly. Mag-locks, you know. They're skittish. And this old girl *did* take a beating back there."

"Whatever it is, can we do it fast?" Cardyn asks, dancing in place and looking back the way we came. He scans the overgrown clusters of dried vegetation stretching out along the side of the bus and gazes nervously up at the rockface, towering up to a dizzying height along one side of the narrow road. "I'm feeling kind of surrounded."

Rain tells him to quit being so fidgety. "You're making me nervous."

"We should *all* be nervous."

"We should all be *cautious*," Brohn advises. "Being nervous leads to making mistakes. And we're too close to the end to risk making a mistake."

Croque Madame crawls out from under the bus. "Speaking of mistakes, I might've made one when I didn't double-check the mag-lock on the sixth starboard-side cargo bay before we left."

Before we can ask what she means, she reaches behind her back to drag out...

*Roxane?*

Cramped-up, haggard, and squinty-eyed, Roxane emerges from behind Croque Madame.

I can't speak for myself, but Cardyn's eyes are wide open. "What the frack?"

Croque Madame nudges Roxane into the middle of our circle. "Looks like we have a stowaway."

"What we have is a problem," Brohn growls. "We need to take her back."

Rain gathers up her composure first and asks Roxane if she's okay.

Roxane doesn't answer. Not that any of us expected her to.

"What were you doing in there?" Rain asks.

Again, Roxane doesn't answer.

"You're wasting your time," Cardyn moans.

"And you're wasting mine," Rain snaps before turning to me. "Kress. Can you and Render…?"

"We can try."

Concentrating, I connect with Render, who has just flown up to the top of the bus where he's pacing like a foot soldier on patrol. His sharp claws click against the segmented steel roof.

I feel his consciousness reach out to mine, and I gratefully accept the invitation.

*Can you help us?*

*~ I can help you help her.*

*How?*

In my mind, an elaborate pattern emerges—a series of curved lines, right angles, dime-sized dots, and thick streaks of jet black.

"My tattoos!" I say out loud.

Before anyone from my Conspiracy can distract me with questions, I swipe a new pattern into the black implants in my forearms. It's one I've never tried before, and I hope I got it right.

In a flash, it's like a whole hidden hallway of doors has opened up in my mind.

"Render's inside her head." I inform the others as I cringe against a small wave of pain. "He's in mine, too."

Thanks to Render, I'm able to communicate with Roxane, but it's not easy. It *is* easier than trying to sort out what the Scroungers were saying a few days ago back in Vauxhall. But still…

Roxane seems smart but also kind of invisible, like she's not sure if she even exists. In the conversation bouncing around inside of our heads, she doesn't refer to herself or even use a first-person pronoun.

It's like she's distilled everything in her mind down to its most basic element, which I do my best to translate into words.

*Where did you come from?*

*~ Home.*

*You shouldn't be here.*

*~ Belong.*

*Our lives are…*

*~ Deadly.*

*To say the least. We need to take you back.*

*~ Join?*

*Not with us. We need to get you back to Bordeaux.*

*~ Extreme.*

*Extreme what?*

*~ Pain.*

*I don't understand.*

*~ Protecting.*

*Bordeaux? You protect Bordeaux, right? We know.*

*~ Gone.*

And then it occurs to me: the beauty of Bordeaux, the happy people, the safety…it's all on Roxane's shoulders.

It's a burden she may be too young to bear.

I sever my connection with Render, which severs my connection with Roxane. Giving my head a good shake, I swing around to face my Conspiracy. "We need to take her back. Now!"

## 38

# RETURN

"WHAT'S SHE DOING HERE?" Rain snaps at me. "And why the big hurry?"

It's scary getting yelled at by Rain—especially since I didn't do anything—so it takes me a couple of seconds to respond. "I...I think she's scared. And in pain."

"No wonder. She's been squished down there for hours," Cardyn says.

"Not from that."

"What then?"

"You know my headaches? Or Manthy's? Or yours?"

"Sure," Cardyn shrugs.

"This little girl's head is weighted down with these weird, isolated thoughts of pain and death. She's being asked to shield an entire city. Every life back there is in her hands."

"I still don't understand how she can protect the entire city like that," Terk says.

"I don't either, Big Guy. But she does it. Only..."

"Only what?" Brohn asks.

"Only...I don't think she can do it anymore." Tears well up in my eyes. "And I think it might be too late."

Terk does a little shuffling-in-place dance of nervous impatience. "We can't just leave her here. And she can't come with us."

"So I guess we really do have to take her back," Cardyn suggests.

When I start to hesitate, Manthy asks if I'm okay. Since I can't answer honestly, I don't answer her at all.

I've got a bad feeling. Beyond bad.

Cardyn's protective instinct has kicked in, and he's ready to usher Roxane back onto the bus and get us turned around and headed back to Bordeaux. "You have to admit," he insists, "we've been able to help a lot of people. Why stop now?"

"Card's right," Rain says. "Like it or not, what we have is a gift."

"What if the ability to help others," I say after a quick pause while I try to gauge my friends' reactions, "turns out to be a curse?" When no one responds, I rest a hand on Roxane's small shoulder. "Even worse. What if saving all those lives is slowly costing Roxane her own?"

Terk's shoulders slump, and he runs a hand through his short, bristly hair. "I don't know, Kress…"

"It'll take a while to find a place on this road wide enough to turn the bus around," Croque Madame warns.

Brohn swings around so he's facing me. He bends over a little so our eyes can meet. "You said we might be too late."

I give what I know is a pathetic nod.

Brohn's voice drops to a low rumble. "Too late for what?"

I can only shake my head in response. First, Rain barked at me, and now I know Brohn's getting annoyed that I'm not able to give everyone a more satisfying answer about why this little girl is with us and what we're supposed to do about it.

I also know there's more going on here than just a simple case of a stowaway. Roxane's mind is a scary collection of dark, cramped hallways with a lot of locked doors. It's also a disorienting mess of pain.

Whipping around to face the others, Brohn announces, "We take Roxane back to Bordeaux. But we need to talk with Martine once we get there. We have to let her know what that paradise of theirs is costing."

Cardyn looks glum as he re-boards the bus behind me. "You mentioned Roxane's head being filled with 'pain' and death.'"

"Yeah?"

"What if it's a price Martine's willing to pay for the sake of the city?"

WITH ALL OF us back onboard, Croque Madame starts up the bus and tells at us to, "Sit tight, and hang on!"

As she suspected, it takes a long time for us to find a place in the narrow, pitted road wide enough for us to get the bus turned back around.

When we do break through into a relatively level clearing, Croque Madame performs a scary maneuver with the front wheels of the bus dipping down several inches into the loose ridge of dirt and rocks at the top of a steep drop-off.

She calls out for all of us to go to the back of the bus. "We need to weigh it down back there or else…"

She doesn't need to finish. We can see over the edge of the cliff and down into the dry and rocky ravine below.

We bolt to the back of the bus where the eleven of us, plus Render, huddle as close to the rear door as we can.

*If our survival depends on the weight of six teenagers, six Juvens, and a bird scrunched together in the back of the bus…*

Croque Madame maneuvers the vehicle back on a crazy angle, and I'm convinced we're all going to die in a screaming, blood-curdling freefall.

But by some miracle, she gets us back on solid ground, and we start driving back the way we came.

Although I'm not excited about backtracking, I *am* looking forward to the rush that comes with leaving all this devastation behind.

The others must be on the same page as me because they're all leaning toward the windows, craning their necks in anticipation of the healthy trees, the country-fresh air, and the ocean blue skies of Bordeaux.

*We're not too late,* I assure myself. *We'll get Roxane back to her city, we'll work things out between her and Martine, and everything will be fine. It's paradise, after all, right? Just don't get stuck there!* I add with a little internal laugh.

We round a corner—a familiar one from our first trip here—and I can practically taste it all.

Only nothing happens.

There's no "Wow!" moment this time. The red sky doesn't fade to pink and yield to a crisp expanse of lazily drifting clouds.

Instead, we see a mushroom cloud of churning charcoal gray, tumbling over itself in angry waves on the horizon.

Croque Madame grinds the bus to a screeching stop in the middle of the narrow, rock-filled roadway.

She scans the door open, and Brohn leaps out with the rest of us clambering after him.

He sprints about twenty yards down the narrow, rocky path and then slides to a stop, his hands cupped around his eyes.

I run after him only to stop and stare at the spouts of flame rising into the air over the city no outsider is supposed to be able to see.

A huge flock of birds is fading into the distance.

~ *Those aren't birds.*

I cup my hands around my eyes as Render's senses blend in with my own.

It becomes crystal clear that what I thought were birds are actually a swarm of segmented, sharp-angled machines snaking their way through the sky.

"Triad Drones," I say out loud.

Two words from behind me pierce our stunned silence: "It's gone."

We all turn to face Manthy.

I grab her by the arm and tug her aside. "What the hell do you mean?"

Brohn steps over and takes Manthy's shoulders in his hands. Leaning in close, he points to the flames and the churning thunderclouds over Bordeaux and repeats my question.

Manthy's eyes go wet, and her lip trembles. She starts to say something, but no words come out.

Brohn grips her tighter. He looks like he's two seconds away from losing his temper and shaking an answer out of her.

Rain clamps her hand on the crook of his arm and tells him to take it easy.

"I'm *not* taking this easy, Rain," he barks before swinging around to Roxane. "What did you do?"

Brohn takes Roxane by the collar now, in a half-guiding, half-forceful grip. She's young and small, but she looks even more meek in Brohn's shadow and locked in his fists and in his furious gaze.

He could sling her halfway down the road if he wanted to, and I'm afraid for a second that he might.

"Brohn…"

"What?" he snaps.

"She can't…I mean, she doesn't…"

"What? Are you going to tell us she doesn't know any better? You heard Martine. That whole city, all those people…they counted on her to keep them safe!"

"Brohn," I cry, "you're scaring her!"

He stabs a finger up the road toward Bordeaux. "Better than getting killed like that!"

"We don't know for sure what happened."

"We know enough. You said it yourself. Triad Drones. She

was supposed to be protecting this city, and she left it. And for what? To come joyriding with *us*?" He whips around to glare down at Roxane, who looks even smaller and more helpless than before. "Why did you do this? Why would you let this happen to your own city? To your people?"

I find myself slipping between her and Brohn. I know he won't actually hurt her, but I've seen inside her mind, so I know just as clearly that he'll never actually reach her, either.

"Maybe the people got away," Terk says. It's half question, half hope.

Brohn shakes his head.

"They *did* say they lived underground in the early days of the war," Rain reminds us.

We look down the road.

In that moment, I know there's no doubt in any of our minds about the cost of Roxane's actions or the brutal truth of Manthy's two words. We may not know for sure what happened to the people, but we don't need to get a single inch closer to know that the surface of the city at least—the sunny, safe, and food filled paradise—is gone.

Terk shuffles his feet, his boots kicking up clouds of dust like horse hooves pawing at the dirt-covered road. "We have to go help them!"

Brohn clamps both hands onto Terk's brown robe, gathering up the material under Terk's neck in his clenched fists.

"Go back to what? To that? That city is dead. Do you want us to be, too?"

Terk looks stunned, although I'm not sure if it's at the thought of what's happened to Roxane's city and its people or at being confronted so aggressively by Brohn.

Rain takes a step back toward the bus, then changes her mind and looks like she's about to run toward the town. And then she seems frozen, her eyes red, her face wet, and I don't think I've ever seen her looking so distraught, so vulnerable, or so indecisive.

A chill races through me. Like Rain and Cardyn, I'm teary-eyed, and I can't look away from the smoldering clouds in the distance. The billowing thunderheads are boiling and alive with mini-explosions and flashes of fire, and it's all rumbling in angry waves right toward us.

I glance down at my arm. My tattoos, normally midnight black, are glowing a dull red, and the skin on my hands and in between the implanted digital patterns is starting to blister.

"Radiation," I say out loud.

Rain says, "Oh, frack," and looks down at her own arm, horrified as red ripples run over her skin.

There's no sense trying to get any closer. With the rolling waves of heat already licking at the dried vegetation and raising rippling distortions in the air above the pitted road, we'd be fried in second.

We don't need a thermometer or a radiation detector to know how dangerous the air around us already is.

We're all standing there in the middle of the road, frozen at all the pain, fear, and horror that have crammed themselves into our lives in the space of a few minutes.

Manthy and Rain step in front of Brohn, slip their arms around Roxane's shoulders, and start hustling her back onto the bus.

Cardyn's eyes bounce between me, Brohn, Terk, and Croque Madame. "What are we supposed to do?"

"We get back on the bus," Brohn says, his jaw clenched and his eyes straining against the tears I know are there. "We get back to London. We get the hell home." He starts heading back toward the bus with the rest of us following him in a morbid daze. "And we forget what happened here."

As I step back onto the bus, it occurs to me that this is the first time he's asked the impossible.

283

## 39

BACK TO FOLKESTONE

IT TAKES another bit of skillful maneuvering on Croque Madame's part to get us turned around once again.

For the next several hours, the bus transforms into a torture chamber of helpless, hopeless misery.

No one talks. No one eats. No one sleeps.

Brohn isn't telling us what we should do next. Rain isn't guiding us. The Auditor isn't offering up pointless historical trivia about the scattered ghost towns and overgrown farmland we pass. Terk isn't asking questions. Cardyn isn't joking around.

As for me, I can barely breathe.

Sure, we've got a few more answers now. And we succeeded in the first part of our mission: rescuing potential new Emergents.

But after seeing what happened to Bordeaux, after knowing what part we played in the destruction of paradise, what we *don't* have is peace of mind.

Instead, we have a powerful wave of guilt pushing against us.

We don't talk. We don't even sit next to each other.

The Juvens stay congregated in the back, but the rest of us are spaced throughout the bus. We're little islands of sorrow. Except for Brohn.

He's pure rage.

Even from here, I can see it etched into his face like a carving in stone.

I've seen him angry before, but always in combat or in his tireless pursuit of a just cause. This anger is different. It's darker. Deeper. Scarier.

There's a tension under his surface now. Or a detachment. Or maybe it's the same lurking fear and powerlessness I know we're all feeling. Whatever it is, I've never seen it in him before, and I can't imagine it's going to exactly help our relationship.

I want to reach out to him, but I don't know what to say. I don't feel like his girlfriend right now.

Right now, we barely feel like a Conspiracy.

It's Rain who finally breaks the awkward silence by clearing her throat and asking if she can borrow Croque Madame's first-aid kit.

She uses hydrocortisone cream and something called bethamethasone—the Auditor tells us it's a corticosteroid anti-inflammatory— to treat the radiation burns on our skin.

We're lucky, Rain tells us. We weren't exposed for more than a few seconds. "We should all heal up fine."

She doesn't sound happy about that, and we all know why. We're not complaining about the pain in our skin or the queasiness from the waves of radiation. The knowledge about what's been lost and about the part we played in it: *that's* what's making us sick to our stomachs.

To get us back to London, Croque Madame skirts the edge of the Parisian city limits. It's sad to see the whirling vortex of smoke and dust that seems to have taken up permanent residence over the city.

It's not just the city, either. Even the small surrounding suburbs and towns are belching plumes of putrid smoke into the sky.

The scorched and polluted countryside looks like an array of rooftop chimneys from some Industrial Age skyline.

I turn my head away from the window, so I don't have to see the hellscape. And then I drop my chin to my chest so Cardyn won't tease me for crying.

When I look up, I realize I didn't have anything to worry about. Cardyn is staring out the window from the seat a few rows in front of me. He turns to me and shakes his head, his own eyes filled with tears.

"Look on the bright side," Rain says.

"What bright side?"

She points out the window at the smoke-filled sky above the city.

"No drones over Paris."

Cardyn is slow to nod his agreement, but Rain's right. Things could be worse. They *were* worse before Manthy pulled her stunt with the Triad Drone fleet a few days ago.

"How long before they get those things back online?" Terk asks, his eyes focused on Manthy who doesn't return his gaze.

Instead, she tucks her chin into her chest.

"Manth? How long?"

"Anything I do, they can undo."

Then, she does something we've rarely seen her do, something none of us has done for hours now. She smiles.

When I ask her what's going on, she drops the smile and gives me a little shrug. "I might have tinkered around in there a bit more than I let on."

Brohn leans forward. "Tinkered?" Like the rest of us, he's desperate for some good news right now.

286

The Auditor's voice rings out from Terk's back. "She planted a binary vacillator."

Cardyn raises his hand. "I don't know what that is."

"It's like a computer virus," the Auditor explains. "Only more complex. It doesn't just corrupt or overwrite code. It transfigures it."

"Meaning?"

"Meaning," Rain explains, a glint of realization flashing in her dark eyes, "that the Hands in the Jardin du Luxembourg might be able to reprogram them. Not just disable them but use them to their advantage."

It's potential for a small victory, I guess.

Still, the mood in the bus is as bleak and miserable as the scenes outside.

"Can you do it with all the drone fleets?" Cardyn asks.

Manthy shakes her head. "They're not networked liked that."

"Makes sense," Rain points out. "Each fleet probably has its own network and operators. There's no way we can stop all of them at once."

Brohn grips the back of the seat in front of him so hard I think his fingers might pierce clean through the synthetic green fabric and bend the metal frame underneath. "Then I guess we'll just have to shut them down one fleet at a time."

"And when we're done with them, I say we come back and crush the Execs," Terk snarls. Normally, it'd be an empty threat. A hollow boast. But he says it with all the sincerity in the world.

As much as we would like to sneak back into Paris and check on Ibrahim and Les Mains, we know it's too much of a risk. Not just to our lives but also to our sanity, which, right now, is at a tipping point.

WITH THE NEW Emergents asleep in a tangle of limbs in the rear seats of the bus, we drive back through the Chunnel.

Like before, the tents, shelters, and lean-tos are there. But no people.

With Rain wondering aloud where everyone is, we burst into the light in Folkestone and head straight to the large lot where the hundreds of people in the town had gathered on our last trip through.

The lot—and possibly the entire town—is empty.

Croque Madame glides the bus to a stop in the same spot we parked in before.

Brohn barks at the kids to stay on the bus. When they look shocked, he holds up his finger and softens his tone. "Just give us a minute, okay?"

He doesn't take my hand or guide me off the bus like he's done in the past. All business, he instructs Madame to wait on the bus with the kids and strides out into the big empty lot to survey the area, fists on his hips.

"Noxia?" I ask as I step up next to him.

From behind me, Cardyn asks, "Hawkers?"

Brohn shakes his head. "Maybe Execs?"

Terk still has one foot on the bottom step of the bus entrance. "Could they have followed us?"

"We were away long enough," Rain reminds us. "They could have gotten *ahead* of us."

"And then what?" Terk asks. "They came here and killed everyone?"

"There's no bodies," I observe.

"Maybe the Hawkers *were* here and just scared everyone off?" Cardyn suggests.

Brohn takes another long look around at the deserted square and starts walking a slow, tight circle. "They could be hiding."

I hope he's right, but clearly, even he's not sure. Which makes *me* not sure. Which makes me realize how contagious doubt is.

Cardyn points to where a blue plastic bag is dancing on the wind across the far end of the lot. "Look! If that was tumbleweed, this could be like the Old West."

"Which would mean we're about to get into a shoot-out," I warn him. "A good ol' fashioned showdown."

I know about Westerns from my dad. He used to talk in weirdly romantic tones about men squaring off over a dry patch of worthless land to settle some dispute or another.

"They'd walk out real slow," my father told me, pounding the heels of his hands—thump, thump, thump, one after the other—on the kitchen table to simulate heavy, booted footsteps.

He sounded impressed, like he kind of admired the violent insanity of it all.

"It was always so climactic," he gushed. "There were only two outcomes: one guy died, or else the other did. Somehow, it was always the good guy who got out alive."

My dad was a tech guy. He thought in ones and zeroes. Maybe that's why the idea of life or death disguised as fame or infamy appealed to him.

Either way, the images of combatants squaring off over an open field with nothing to look forward to except horrible pain and a death or two always stuck with me.

A bunch of Hawkers appear on the rooftops surrounding my Conspiracy, and a bunch more step out from the laneways around the lot.

When Noxia, herself, steps out onto the wide open, dirt-covered square, I realize this is exactly like those Westerns my dad used to love so much.

*We just walked into an ambush. An old-fashioned gunfight. And someone's not making it out of this showdown alive.*

## GHOST TOWN SHOWDOWN

I'VE FINALLY FIGURED out why Noxia bothers me so much. It's not just that she's an evil Hypnagogic who turned my boyfriend against us for a brief time. And it's not just how she mysteriously appeared in our lives with the apparent sole purpose of ending them.

It's in her eyes, in her *look*.

Standing here, face-to-face across the distance of the large empty lot, I can see it now. I can see what Sadia was talking about outside of the Valencia Processor.

Noxia doesn't see us as human. She doesn't even see us as Emergents. We're not even prey.

At least prey animals have value to the predator.

Our value to her is nothing more than what we're worth to the En-Gene-eers who hired her.

To her, we might as well be a handful of tap-coins.

The Hawkers—at least a dozen of them this time, not counting the ones stationed on the rooftops—form a circle around us, as Noxia steps forward, ready to collect.

If this is really going to be the final showdown, we're ready for it.

We have our guns *and* our Medieval weapons at the ready. We have Render soaring the skies above us. And we have our Emergent abilities, a life-saving bus driver, and the lives of six Juvens to fight for.

Brohn shouts back toward Croque Madame and the bus. "Don't let those kids come out!"

As if they're answering him, the bus doors whoosh shut, and just like that, we're on our own, the six of us in a half circle with Render circling, vulture-like, overhead.

Brohn has a gun in one hand with his other hand hovering over the quiver of arrows for his arbalest.

Terk's got his flail in the pinchers of his Modified hand and a barbell-sized assault rifle in the other.

Rain's wrist-mounted dart-drivers are primed and ready to fire. And, just for good measure, she's got the AK-84—our eight-and-a-half-pound assault rifle with grenade-launcher, laser-scope, and target-acquisition sensors—clutched tight in both hands and pointed straight at Noxia's head.

Cardyn and Manthy each have a tomahawk axe in one hand and a matching gold-plated fifty-caliber Desert Eagle in the other.

As for me, I snap my Talons out. The ten curved and serrated claws glint in the sun. I tap into Render, and he gives me access to his superior senses and reflexes.

Our Conspiracy is outnumbered, outgunned, cornered, and overmatched.

But Noxia's out of her mind if she expects us to surrender, barter, or beg.

She stands still, her hands clasped gently in front of her.

From under the hood of her cloak, her long hair flutters and snaps around in the wind.

I'm thinking about how peaceful and utterly un-menacing she looks when all of a sudden, the six of us double over, smothered in an instant by the same nightmarish cyclone spinning through our brains.

I clamp my hands to my head. Cardyn and Brohn do the same, staggering and grabbing at each other for balance.

Above us, Render cries out and spirals down. Right before my horrified eyes, he hits the ground hard next to my feet and lies motionless, one wing bent awkwardly over his body.

Next to me, Terk drops to one knee.

Rain and Manthy follow.

Behind Noxia, the Hawkers raise their weapons and step forward.

"Sorry it had to be this way," Noxia apologizes. "The people I work for…the En-Gene-eers…they originally wanted you alive. Then, when they saw what you were capable of, it turned into 'dead or alive.' But now that they know how powerful—and, frankly elusive—you can be and how many of you there are, it's just 'dead.'"

Her voice bombards me from inside and out at the same time, echoing around in dark, rough waves inside my ears.

On the rooftops encircling the parking lot, a team of three Hawkers tilt their heads, squinting down the laser sights of their sniper rifles.

Several of the Hawkers start edging into a shrinking circle around us. They look menacing and practically robotic in their Kevlar armor and brown and green combat gear.

I can't think straight, my eyes are burning, and it's like someone set my brain to a high heat and tumble-dry.

Her eyes sparking with lightning flashes of white and yellow, Noxia grins in triumph. "The Execs are still out there looking for you, you know. Too bad I had to find you first. They might have let you live. The little ones on the bus…they may still be worth something. But I'm afraid the six of you—what do you call yourselves? A Conspiracy? I'm afraid your days of conspiring against the *truly* powerful people of the world are over. And by 'powerful,' I don't mean those power-hungry scientists or the trigger-happy Execs. I mean *me*." Her grin tightens into a tight smirk. "Nothing personal."

I don't know how, but Brohn manages to force himself to his feet. "That's the problem," he says through a strained grimace. "There's not enough 'personal' left in the world."

Under her hood and the snaking strands of hair whipping around in the wind, Noxia rolls her eyes. She curls her hands into fists, her eyes burn brighter, and Brohn gasps and drops to the ground.

"Don't worry, Brohn. I'm not going to take you over this time. There's nothing in that head of yours I want anymore. You lived in that little mountain town for too long," she says with a pretend sad shake of her head. "You need to see how the real world works."

"We've seen enough of it," Brohn growls from his knees.

On my hands and knees, myself, I try to shuffle over to him, but whatever hold Noxia has on us is just too strong. I can barely turn my head.

Noxia steps forward, the smirk now a confident, mocking scowl. "How many dead pacifists and peacemakers will it take for you to realize your side lost? There's no room for you anymore. You're fighting for a world that never existed, never could, and never will. The only thing that matters is what we can still become. Emergents. Hypnagogics. *We're* the future. *We're* the ones who'll be left when all the rest of them have burned each other to the ground. The funny thing is, you're the key to that. You're the answer. And you're too young or maybe just too dumb to know it."

She shakes her head like she's resisting a spell of her own. In a semi-circle around her, the Hawkers' forearms tense up as they prepare to fire, to finish us off once and for all.

That's when I'm startled by the little boy who walks up to stand on one side of me.

It's Ignacio.

I can barely move my jaw enough to tell him to get back to the bus.

Brohn tries, too, waving at him to get the hell away from here.

He ignores both of us.

Instead, he makes a tiny motion with his open hand. The two teams of Hawkers on the roof across from us lower their weapons and snap their heads from side to side.

Then, as if the buildings they're stationed on have suddenly burst into invisible flame, they scream in agony, spinning and slapping at their arms and legs like they were on fire.

And then, they *jump*.

One after the other—ten, eleven, twelve of them—they leap from the tops of the buildings around the parking lot and plummet down, their bodies slamming up clouds of dust and crunching to lifeless heaps on the hard ground.

Still disoriented by whatever Noxia did to us, I can't tell if what I'm seeing is happening or if it's some horrible nightmare come true.

If it *is* a nightmare, at least this time, I don't think it's mine.

Standing between me and Brohn, with the rest of our Conspiracy still on the ground behind us, Ignacio points at Noxia and at the remaining Hawkers.

He's slim and a little above average height for his age. He's got the penetrating eyes of an adult, but his thick, curly hair and boyish face give the rest of his features an air of something eerie, otherworldly, and older than his years.

Like Noxia, his eyes crackle with flecks of electric-yellow.

Standing there with his finger extended toward our enemies, he looks like a little boy showing his parents his selection at an ice cream counter.

But what happens next is beyond age or desire. It's just pure power.

Red tears, which I realize are actually blood, trickle from the outside corners of his eyes. Thin veins spiderweb out from his cheeks and zigzag downward along his neck. His skin goes deathly gray.

Then, his whole body goes into horrifying convulsions.

The Hawkers behind Noxia and the ones surrounding us drop their weapons like they're made of molten lava. Clamping their hands to the sides of their heads, they stagger back, limbs twitching, their eyes wide with confusion and terror.

Then, they go slack, and it's like someone clicked off the light switch to their bodies.

In front of us, Noxia's eyes roll back. She plunges to her knees before twisting to the ground in a shaking wave of violent spasms.

Cardyn, Rain, Terk, and Manthy clamber to their feet behind me and Brohn, and the six of us pivot in a slow circle, wondering what the hell just happened.

I scoop Render up and cradle him in my arms. He's confused, but he's breathing and stirring, and I have to squint hard against the ocean of relieved tears rising up behind my eyes.

All around us, every one of the Hawkers lies dead on the ground. Even some of the ones who jumped from the buildings and who were crying out and writhing in agony just seconds ago have gone stone still.

Ignacio presses a finger to his forehead and mumbles something I realize is Spanish.

"*Toqué sus mentes.*"

The girl named Mattea has come down from the bus. She presses in between us and translates. "He can touch electrical impulses." Like Ignacio, Mattea points to her own forehead. "He says he touched them here, in their minds."

"Touched?" Cardyn asks through a frown, his voice as shaky as my whole body feels.

Mattea looks distressed for a second before her face relaxes as she finds the right words. "Touched. Manipulated. Integrated. He tried to do this in the Processor. One of the times we tried to escape. But they stopped him."

She tugs the collar of her powder blue shirt aside to reveal a set of perfectly concentric circles, raised and red, on her neck. "They inserted disks."

"Contact Coils," I mutter as I touch my own neck where I'd had a similar device implanted in the Mill in Chicago.

Mattea nods. "Only Ignacio figured out how to short-circuit those, too. So they had to take them out."

Terk's voice quivers. "Short-circuit…"

Manthy says something half under her breath about electrical impulses.

Brohn glances over at her, and she meets his eyes. "I said, 'all we are is electrical impulses.'"

Brohn gives Manthy a long look before swinging back to examine our assailants, lying lifeless on the ground or slumped over the rooftop balustrades and railings. "He short-circuited their brains."

Manthy nods.

Now, we all swing around to face Ignacio, whose sparkling, firecracker eyes have gone back to their normal amber-brown. He wipes at the trickles of blood on his face with the tips of his fingers. The smeared droplets leave dark red streaks behind. Before our eyes, the veins in his face and neck recede, and his skin drops in shade from tombstone gray to campfire ash.

Without a word, he turns on his heel and walks back toward the bus. He edges his way past the other Juvens and Croque Madame, who have all just come spilling out into the parking lot.

All around us, the people from Folkestone start edging their way out of their hiding places in laneways, external stairwells, and from inside the ring of buildings surrounding the parking lot. Dozens of them come pouring out of basements and storm cellars.

They inch their way toward us, their mouths open, their eyes wide at the carnage around them.

The Hawkers' bloody bodies litter the ground.

And in the middle of it all, Noxia lies face up, her cowl back, her dark hair splayed out, her lifeless eyes staring up at the red sky.

Vivia, the woman we met a few days ago, finally steps up to us. Flanking her are the woman I think of as "Spider-limbs" and the man I call "Nostrils," their eyes darting around at the gruesome scene.

Croque Madame bounds over to us, sliding to a stop between our Conspiracy and Vivia.

A deep crease forms between Vivia's eyes, which are bouncing from us to the dead bodies and back to us before finally landing on Croque Madame. "What happened here? What did they do?"

"They saved themselves. And they saved us."

I can't tell if Vivia is happy or horrified. Her face remains cloudy and expressionless as she calls out to three of the people behind her to join her in a quiet conversation.

They only talk for a few seconds while the rest of us try to clear our heads of the searing, acidic residue of Noxia's intrusion into our minds.

When Vivia turns back to us, she has the same unreadable expression as before, but at least the deep crease between her eyes has settled into a shallow wrinkle.

"On behalf of the citizens of Folkestone, we thank you for your intervention." She tilts her chin toward Noxia's lifeless form. "If not for you, that woman and the Hawkers might have killed us all."

"We did what we had to do," Brohn starts to say, still struggling to catch his breath. But Vivia stops him mid-thought with an abrupt wave of her hand.

"They might have killed us if you hadn't stopped them. But they wouldn't have been here at all if they hadn't been looking for you."

"But—"

"We appreciate who you are and the good you're able to bring about. But we're scared of what comes with you."

"We were only—"

"I know. We get it. We really do. And maybe one day our world will be better than this. But right now, we have to ask that you continue on your way."

Hanging our heads, defeated despite having survived, we turn and head back to the bus.

Behind us, and just barely loud enough for us to hear, Vivia, through what I know is a sniffle of appreciation and regret, chokes out, "Best o' the British to ya, Loves. Best o' the British."

MY CONSPIRACY and I gather in the front seats as Croque Madame lurches the bus into motion.

Looking up at her, I clamp my teeth tight and try not to think what I'm thinking: Her life has been in danger all this time, too. And it's still in danger. And it's because of us.

Finally, I can't take the stress of my guilt anymore, and I just say what I'm thinking out loud. My throat hurts, and my eyes start to burn when I apologize to Croque Madame for putting her in the Hawkers' sights. "And for what happened in Bordeaux. And in Valencia. We could've gotten you killed. And all you were trying to do was help us." I can't bear to look at her. Instead, I keep my eyes locked on Brohn's hand, which is on my knee. "We seem to keep finding a way to put innocent people at risk."

Croque Madame shakes her head and curls her lip. "You're innocent, too," she reminds me. "You've been putting *yourselves* at risk for a greater good. What you do, you do for people like me. For people like Vivia and the citizens of Folkestone. And I appreciate it. I know she appreciates it. If I can do a small part to help you succeed, we'll all be better for it. Listen, you may be my passengers, but *I'm* the one who's honored to be along for the ride."

She turns and gives us a wink over her shoulder before returning her focus to navigating the bus down the long empty road. She whistles what I think is supposed to be a happy tune, but it's somehow flat and sad until it eventually fades into silence.

"Um...Did you see what Ignacio did back there?" Terk asks, puncturing our haze of shame, relief, and regret.

"We've killed before," Rain says evenly.

"Not like that," Cardyn says, his eyes darting toward the Juvens sitting quietly again at the back of the bus. "Not...short-circuiting someone's brain."

"How's that different from what you do?" Brohn asks. "Or what Kress and Render do?"

"I can persuade people a little. I can nudge them. Kress and Render talk by getting inside each other's heads. That's a *lot* different than shutting off a person's life-switch."

"The way they died," I say, suppressing a shudder. "Rain's right. We've killed in battle, in self-defense, and in defense of others. But, listen...what just happened out there in that lot...that was different. It wasn't just killing. It was more like an assassination."

Brohn nods and glances at the six young potential Emergents, who are all staring out the windows and taking in a world they've never really seen before. "Ignacio...he could potentially be as dangerous as Sheridyn was."

Cardyn shakes his head. "How does someone so young have the ability to do something so...deadly?"

"Who cares how it's done?" Terk asks. "If Ignacio hadn't been there..."

"We wouldn't be *here*," Rain finishes.

Rain's right. We've fought and killed before. We know how much survival costs. But now I'm wondering if instant mass murder is the new price we're preparing to pay.

## 41

# DETOUR

STILL UNDER A WEIGHTY double blanket of relief and worry, we cross into the London city limits on our way back to Hyde Park.

"Can we make one little detour?" I ask Croque Madame.

"You're kidding, right?"

I shake my head.

"Detours around here tend to end with your head taking a sharp detour from your body."

"It's important," I promise. "There's someone we swore we'd check in on."

I don't say it out loud, but after what happened in Bordeaux, there is no way I'm risking heading back to the Arrival Station without making at least this one last stop.

Croque Madame grinds the bus to a halt in the middle of the road. Soot-covered buildings rise up on either side of us. A shopping cart full of bricks is overturned on the wrecked concrete of what used to be a sidewalk. The roof of a small corner store has caved in, causing bricks, splintered wooden joists, and assorted garbage to spew out of its front door in a mass of regurgitated wreckage. A boy and a girl in oversized sunglasses and matching Crystal Palace football jerseys stare down at us from the exposed second story of an apartment building just up the road. Then, in a flash, they're gone.

The Hyde Park Settlement is somewhere to the west of us. The Tower of London is somewhere to the east.

Croque Madame stares through the front windshield for a long time.

In the short time we've been together, I've seen her scared, chatty, happy, angry, and confused like the rest of us. But I think this might be the first time I've really seen her sad. I can tell she's as rattled as we are about what happened in Bordeaux and Folkestone.

She wasn't a participant either time. But she saw it all. At least the aftermath of it. And I'm sure she's heard us talking about it for the few scattered minutes when we could gather ourselves together enough to form words.

She tightens and loosens her grip on the steering wheel a bunch of times before her shoulders slump.

"Where to?"

"The Tower of London?"

"I'm not used to taking requests."

"We're not used to making them."

"This is my bus."

"We know."

"And you're on it. That makes you my kids and my responsibility."

"So…will you take us?"

Croque Madame gives us a weak smile from over her shoulder. "Tell me it's to do that thing where you risk your lives to help others."

"We just have one more person to check in on."

"Another kid?"

"Yes."

"Another one who needs help?"

"Maybe. We've helped each other in the past."

"You say we're your responsibility," Brohn chimes in. "Well, she's ours."

"Well then," Croque Madame sighs, "what are we waiting for?"

She scans the bus into gear, and we grind along an empty street, weaving around husks of stripped down, ash-covered cars and buses.

After only a few minutes, Croque Madame gives us the bad news:

"Bridges are out. London Bridge and the Tower Bridge."

Rain says, "We know" and goes on to tell Croque Madame about how she, Cardyn, and I were imprisoned in Harah Tower. "We got a bird's eye view of the destruction."

"A bird's eye view of London used to be the best view," Croque Madame sighs. "Now, it's the worst."

"We crossed the river at Vauxhall before," Brohn reminds her. "But we had to do that on foot. What about the bus?"

"There's a crossing upriver."

"Is it safe?"

"No."

"Great."

After another few minutes of trundling along, we enter a roundabout and arrive at a five-foot high wall of old tires and long slats of wood painted red and white.

A boy and a girl—maybe fifteen or sixteen years old—hold up their hands and order us to stop. With their rapiers drawn and small shields on their arms, they approach the bus.

Brohn clamps a hand onto Cardyn's shoulder. "You're up."

Cardyn steps down into the stairwell of the bus to stand face to face with the boy and the girl, who are dressed in yoga pants, leather vests, and a set of gloves and boots it looks like they lifted from two of Robin Hood's merry men.

"Ya canna cross 'ere wifout payin'."

Cardyn plants his hands on either side of the bus door. "What's the fee?"

The boy shoulders past Cardyn and points to the back of the bus. "We'll take two o' yer wee ones."

"Um. No."

Bounding onto the bus, the girl whips out a fourteen-inch, black handled serrated dagger and presses it to Cardyn's neck. "Seriously? Yer gonna try ta bargain wit' us, Mate?"

Cardyn swallows hard but doesn't flinch away from the deadly blade. "Bargaining is just a way for two parties to get what they want," he gulps. And then, straightening up and with a weird echo of confidence in his voice, he adds, "We want to cross, and you don't want to get killed trying to stop us."

The girl's eyes twitch hard and glaze over, and the boy's eyes quickly do the same.

"It seems to me," Cardyn says, his voice pulsing out in lilting, hypnotic waves that make me feel half relaxed and half like throwing up, "letting us pass satisfies all conditions, makes everyone happy, and keeps everyone alive. Doesn't that sound like a good bargain to you?"

Breaking into smiles, the boy and the girl are quick to agree.

They hop down from the bus, and the girl whistles through her fingers to a group of five more of their band of merry men standing at the foot of a large, rusted gate between the long row of wood and tires. They unclip a thick link of chain and swing the gate open.

One of the boys waves his hand to Croque Madame, who re-starts the bus and drives us over the makeshift bridge of concrete blocks, railroad ties, junked cars, and thick sheets of synth-steel.

The murky water from the River Thames gurgles along under the crude bridge and occasionally bubbles up over its surface, sloshing against our tires.

In a voice I can barely hear, Manthy asks Cardyn if he's okay, and he laughs and swears he is.

But I know him better than anyone.

When I glance over at him, he averts his eyes, which I can see are wet. He's got grooves of strained lines around his mouth and thin blue veins pressing out from his cheeks and forehead.

I nudge Brohn, who turns around to look at Cardyn.

Turning back to me, he starts to ask, "Is he—?"

But I cut him off with a shake of my head and a hand to his arm. "I think…"

"What is it, Kress?"

"I think it might be killing him," I whisper.

"Killing…?"

"His Emergent ability. I think every time he uses it, he gets a little weaker."

Brohn gets ready to stand up and go over to where Cardyn and Manthy are sitting together a few rows behind us, but I stop him again. "Don't. Not here."

"But—"

"He knows what's happening to him."

"Then he should let us help him," Brohn pleads, his quiet voice matching my own.

"There's nothing we can do. Not right now anyway. Not here."

"Then when? Where?"

"We need to get home."

"One problem."

"I know. We don't have a home to get to. But we've got to try. I think the only thing that could save him…save any of us…"

"Yeah?"

"Brohn. I have this weird feeling that we need to get back to the Valta."

He's about to object, and I know why. There is no Valta. We've seen the pile of rubble and bodies it used to be. But something inside me is tugging me back. I don't know what, and I don't know why. I just know that something—something invisible but powerful—is whispering in my ear and pulling me by the arm at the same time. Brohn says maybe I'm just homesick.

But I tell him, "I think home is where we need to be to *avoid* getting sick."

I don't have a chance to explain or process it any more as the bus rumbles across the bridge and settles into an even ride on the far side.

Croque Madame breathes a relieved sigh and lets out a small laugh I think she's been holding in for the past ten minutes. "You're definitely a handy bunch to have around."

"It's kind of a mixed blessing," Brohn tells her glumly. "You saw what happened in Folkestone. The thing that makes us handy also makes us hurt...and hunted."

When the Tower of London appears, I try to break the tension by saying out loud how it's a welcome sight.

The Auditor reminds me it wasn't always so. "The Tower once served as a prison. Twenty-two people were killed here. It's where Guy Fawkes was interrogated and tortured for his role in the failed Gunpowder Plot of November 5, 1605."

"Still," I sigh. "It's nice to know terrible places can get turned around. And I'm looking forward to seeing Llyr and Penarddunne again."

At that exact moment, Llyr's and Penarddunne's heads appear outside of the window right next to us, startling us and breaking us out of our collective funk.

Leaving the kids in the bus for now, our Conspiracy clambers out, and we exchange hearty greetings.

"What's that look for?" Penarddunne asks me.

"I had just said your names when you magically appeared at our window."

"Like you were expecting us," Brohn observes.

Llyr tilts his head toward the raven on his shoulder. "We *were*. Eastcheap here told us you was back in town."

"So...," Cardyn drawls into my ear, "you're not the only one with a feathered surveillance drone."

Brohn is kind enough to drag Cardyn—who is clearly feeling

better, or at least *pretending* to be feeling better—back by the collar of his jacket as Rain steps forward to give Llyr and Penarddunne a quick summary of our adventures since we saw them last.

"We completed our mission," Terk brags, pointing behind us to where the six Juvens are just taking their first hesitant steps from the bus down to the cobblestone ground. "We freed the Juvens we were sent to find."

"We ran into some problems on the way," I tell Llyr. "Some bad problems. We wanted to check on Branwynne. Make sure she got back to you okay."

"She got back to us…" Llyr says, his eyes roving over the band of milling kids before returning his attention to me.

"But not okay," Penarddunne finishes for her husband.

A million scenarios—none of them good—flash through my mind:

We left Ledge and Harah in charge of Branwynne. Could something terrible have happened? Could they have failed in their promise to get her home safely? Did the Banters and Royals already have another split? And, if so, could Branwynne have been caught in the middle of the beginning of a whole new war?

"She *is* here, though, right?" I ask, looking around the courtyard.

"She is."

"Then what—?"

Llyr smooths down his jacket with the palms of his hands. "She's here, Kress. But she's not here." He taps his finger to his temple. "She's not *happy* here."

"She doesn't belong here," Penarddunne sighs. "Not in the tower. Not anymore. She's seen too much. She knows too much."

"The Order?" I ask.

"She knows the truth now and has too much potential." Llyr points with his chin toward Roxane and the Valencia Juvens who remain gathered in a quiet group of their own by the side of the bus. "She belongs with them."

"We're not staying here," Brohn explains. "Us or the kids."

"We're heading to the Hyde Park Settlement right now," Rain adds. "After that, we're off to the Arrival Station and then home from there."

"We weren't suggesting you stay here with Branwynne," Llyr explains.

"No. We thought you might be able to take her with you."

"With us? Back to the States?"

Llyr and Penarddunne nod in unison.

"We can't take your daughter from you," Brohn says, hands up, the weight of finality in his voice.

"You wouldn't be taking her," Llyr counters. "You'd be *saving* her."

Rain frowns. "Saving her from what? Noxia's dead. The Hawkers won't be after her. There's no Execs in London to worry about."

Penarddunne exhales a whooshy breath. "Thank goodness for that at least."

With his hand on his wife's arm, Llyr gives a little grunt of agreement. "Still, there's no future for Branwynne here. Not yet."

"Yet?" I ask.

"The Banters and Royals have reunited," Cardyn tells them. "Things'll be safer."

"For *all* of you," Terk adds.

"That's true," I tell them. "We ran into the Scroungers."

"And they're kind of nice, actually," Terk grins. "Not that easy to understand, though."

"It's not a question of safety." Penarddunne slips her hand into her husband's. "Not *entirely* a question of safety."

"She can survive here," Llyr says, his voice ping-ponging back and forth with his wife's.

"But she can't *live*," she stresses.

"Not like she needs to, anyway."

"There is more to her than even she knows."

"She needs to know herself."

"But she can't do it here."

"Not with us."

"Not anymore."

Brohn seems like he's going to relent but then shakes his head. "We can't promise her safety."

"We can't even promise our own," I add.

Rain tells them, "Kress and Brohn are right. We get that it's still dangerous here. But at least the dangers are known. Back home, for us, there's no telling how bad things could get. We beat the Patriot Army, but there's still an insane number of people who'd be just as happy to have them and Krug back. We're doing what we can, but it's a big country with a lot of wounds—"

Cutting Rain off, Penarddunne steps forward and startles me by taking both of my hands in hers. "Her future is tied to you."

Llyr points back and forth between me and Manthy. "To the two of you, to be precise."

Rain's mouth hangs open, mid-sentence, while Manthy and I exchange a puzzled look.

For some reason, maybe because he's been my best friend for most of my life, I glance over at Cardyn for some kind of validation. He surprises me by nodding.

After a couple of seconds of quiet contemplation, Brohn sighs. "Okay. What's one more kid to be in charge of?"

It's a rhetorical question. But in my mind, the answer is, *one more kid who can kill or else get killed on our watch.*

At that second, Branwynne bursts from the deep shadow of a door set into a nearby stone wall. With her jet-black eyes and shimmering purplish-black hair, it's like she's six ravens in one. She's all smiles. And she's not alone. She has a raven of her own on her shoulder.

But it's not one of the tower's six ravens we were introduced to when we were here the last time. No. This bird is unlike any I've ever seen. It's nearly as big as Render, and it has his same signature beak and build.

But that's where the resemblance ends.

This raven has blue eyes. And it's all white.

"Marvie," Cardyn gushes. "An albino raven!"

"This is Haida Gwaii," Branwynne beams. "My best friend."

"Technically, it's not an albino," the Auditor tells us. "Its blue eyes classify it as *leucistic*. The phenotype can be accounted for by pigment cell differentiation during its morphogenesis. The whale from Herman Melville's novel *Moby Dick* is perhaps the best-known literary example of the phenomenon. A white raven appears in a very old Greek story of Apollo, who sent the raven to spy on his lover Coronis. When the raven returned to Apollo and told him Coronis had been unfaithful to him, Apollo grew angry and burned the raven, turning its feathers from white to black, which is said to be the reason why ravens are black today. Another raven origin story comes from the Haida people of the Pacific Northwest. I'm assuming this raven is named after them. In that story, the white raven steals the sun, the stars, the moon, fresh water, and fire from the lodge of Grey Eagle who refused to share them with humans. The white raven flies off with the stolen treasures and hangs the sun, the stars, and the moon in the sky. He drops the water and fire to the earth, but the smoke from the fire turned his white feathers black."

For what feels like five full seconds, Llyr and Penarddunne stare at Terk, who offers up a shrug of helplessness and an apologetic smile for the Auditor's know-it-all voice radiating from the disk on his back.

Penarddunne finally breaks into a shoulder-quaking laugh. "That is a lot to process! But yes—it's accurate. It's too bad they don't broadcast gameshows on the viz-screens anymore. Because you'd be a natural!"

K. A. RILEY

Terk blushes on behalf of the Auditor, who, of course, doesn't have one of her own.

Llyr swings his gaze from one of us to the other before finally landing on Brohn. "I think what my wife is saying is that you've proven yourselves a million times over. And, as much as it pains us to part with our daughter, she has more of a future with you than she does with us."

Branwynne zips up her red leather jacket and slicks her hair back into a ponytail, which she ties off with a braided strip of red leather.

Brohn puts his hands up and says, "Okay. Okay."

"If it's okay," Branwynne beams, "can Haida come, too? I think she'd be a good friend for Render."

At first, I'm offended. After all, I've been Render's "good friend" for his entire life.

But then I remember how frustrating it must be for him to have to put up with us wingless, earth-lumbering, featherless freaks, so I tell Branwynne I think maybe she's right.

Perched on our shoulders, the two birds greet each other with a series of light clacks.

After all these years of being inside Render's mind and having him inside mine, it's nice to hear someone else speaking his native language.

## 42

## BACK TO HYDE

CARDYN LEANS BACK in his seat, his eyes on the ceiling, his hands clasped behind his head. "Now this is more like it," he sighs.

When Terk asks what he means, Cardyn doesn't answer at first.

After a series of rapid-fire blinks, though, he sits up straight, and sweeps his hand along the interior of the bus. "Look around us, Big Guy: a tough but friendly bus driver, six surly teenagers, another half-dozen rowdy Juvens, two birds, and a new girl we picked up at the last minute. It's the perfect high school experience, right? The one we always dreamed about but never had."

"We're hardly surly," I tell him, secretly happy to have our somber mood lightened up a bit. "We're sad, maybe. But we're *not* surly." I flick my eyes toward the back seats where Roxane and the Valencia Juvens are sitting quietly, swaying along with the bus. "And they're definitely not rowdy."

"Give them time," Cardyn says.

From her seat right behind mine, Branwynne leans forward and points to Cardyn. "Is he always so...?"

"Perky?"

"No."

"Optimistic?"

I lean against the side of the bus. The dry wind from the open window whips my hair. Cardyn gets up and moves a few seats back where he starts chatting with Manthy in a voice too quiet for me to hear. Unlike last time, I don't try to listen in. Instead, I swing around to face Branwynne.

"Cardyn usually sees the worst that can happen. I used to tease him about it. But now..."

I don't even realize I've trailed off until Branwynne nudges my elbow. "Now, what?"

"Oh. Sorry. Now that the worst really *has* happened—we've seen it with our own eyes—I think maybe he *is* fighting back with a little bit of optimism."

"That's good." Branwynne reaches over and gently, almost absently, twirls a lock of my hair around her finger. It's such a sweet little sister thing to do, and I smile at how nice it feels. But then she bolts up and asks if it's okay if she and Haida Gwaii go over and talk to Render, who is perched and rocking on the back of the seat right behind Manthy.

I laugh and tell her, "Sure."

With the white raven perched on her forearm, Branwynne leaps up and skips down the aisle of the bus toward Render who tilts his beak back and welcomes her with a cluster of polite clacks and chirps.

I turn my attention to the outside even though there's not much I haven't already seen out there.

Except for the hollowed-out, overturned vehicles and the dust-covered dunes of concrete and debris, the roads along the way are mostly empty.

Croque Madame navigates us through a roundabout and turns a corner until we're face to face with the fortified patchwork walls of the Hyde Park Settlement.

Even the Juvens leave their quiet cluster at the back and make their way toward the front of the bus to peer out at the looming walls extending far into the distance.

The bus has barely come to a stop when two huge double gates swing open, and Ledge, looking small in the towering gateway and against the backdrop of the thousands of tents in the compound, beckons the bus inside.

Entering the Hyde Park Settlement is the next best thing to being home.

The second we're off the bus, we're greeted by frenzied, happy waves from the three girls up in the guard towers. The three archers greet us by name as we're swarmed by a multitude of Banters and Royals. Some are familiar faces. Others aren't. But they're all smiles. Even Lost-the-Plot, Ledge's perpetually grumpy lieutenant, has the bright, welcoming eyes of someone reunited with a bunch of old friends.

It's been a long time since we were "regulars" anywhere.

Ledge and Harah, their arms spread wide, try to insert themselves between us and their armies of enthusiastic greeters and curious well-wishers, but the boys and girls and the young men and women surge around them and nearly overwhelm us with their barrages of handshakes, hugs, and overlapping requests to tell them about our adventures.

After everyone's surprise and enthusiasm has been spent, Ledge and Harah lead us deeper into the Settlement until we come to a small, open plaza set up at the intersection where eight of the laneways and dirt footpaths meet up.

As the sun sets, we all take seats in a big circle on a variety of old tree stumps, stacks of cement blocks, flat-topped stones, or just on the ground. There's a wide, deep pit in the center of the plaza where Chunder and Trolley are stoking a crackling fire to life. It's only now that we're finally able to take a breath and tell everyone about our road trip.

I'm so tired I have to lean against Brohn's shoulder. Cardyn and Manthy are sitting quietly on one of the improvised flat stone benches behind us, so it's mostly Rain and Terk who do the talking.

The eyes of the Banters and Royals stay riveted on the two of them as Rain and Terk recount the stories of Paris and the rebel Hands fighting against a deadly network of military drones, the hidden paradise of Bordeaux, our fight and flight from Noxia and the Hawkers in the bridge city of San Sebastian, skirting past the remains of Zaragoza and Pamplona, and our triumphant liberation of the new Emergents from the Valencia Processor.

Rain's voice gets low when she and Terk get to the part about our return to Bordeaux and to the tragedy of Roxane's unfortunate departure when she came to be in our care.

I lift my head from its resting place against Brohn's arm to make sure Roxane isn't listening in.

She, Branwynne, and the Valencia Juvens stuck close to us at first. But fortunately, as the night went on, they began drifting farther and farther away until now when they're off running, exploring, and chitchatting well out of earshot with the younger members of the Banters and the Royal Fort Knights.

"It was hell," Rain tells the attentive audience.

"Did anyone survive?" Harah asks, her eyes misty.

Terk shakes his head. "We don't think so."

"*We* did," Brohn corrects him, pointing over to where the younger members of our extended Conspiracy are scampering around and kicking a half-deflated soccer ball over an open patch of ground. "*We* survived. *They* survived. We can only hope Roxane's people managed to find shelter from that drone attack."

My voice cracks when I explain how the radiation was too intense for us to go back into the city and check.

"Either way," Brohn continues, clearing his throat, "it's up to us to take care of them now."

Everyone offers up slow nods of solemn agreement as Rain and Terk finish telling them about our return to London. Rain skips over the part about Ignacio wiping out Noxia and the

Hawkers in Folkestone. Instead, she offers up a quick, cryptic comment about not having to worry about Noxia anymore, and I'm glad when no one presses her to elaborate.

Between Roxane and Ignacio—all they've been through, suffered, and all the lives they've been responsible for—I doubt anyone's heart could take too much detail right now.

When Rain and Terk get everyone caught up, the Banters and Royals take turns telling us about what life is like now that they're no longer at war with each other.

We also hear stories about what life was like here years ago. They tell us about how cooperation turned into competition for disappearing resources. And then how that competition turned into fear, distrust, animosity, and war.

All-to-Pot and Bob's-yer-Uncle take turns telling us about how guns and rifles and other modern weapons came to be banned. We hear about the raids on museums and department stores that led to their reversion to a Medieval kind of lifestyle.

It's all super interesting, but I'm also exhausted, so I catch myself drifting off from time to time. Every time I open my eyes, it's to a new and fascinating story of war, adaptability, and survival.

As much as we might like to, we don't stay long.

Before we know it, the steamy quiet of the lightless night has started to surrender to the wispy bits of pink and crimson dancing on the horizon.

Brohn nudges me, and I nod. We need to get going.

Feeling more like a mom than I ever imagined I would, I call out to Branwynne, Roxane, and the Valencia Juvens. "Come on! It's time to go!"

And, just like the kind of kids I imagine we all used to be, they groan and make an exaggerated show of feeling punished as we herd them away from their new friends and back onto the bus.

"Sure you can't stay?"

Brohn extends his hand to shake Ledge's. "That's the problem. We *can* stay. We just *shouldn't*."

Rain steps forward to shake Ledge's hand and then Harah's. "We finished our mission. Thanks to you."

"Not the last part of our mission," I remind her. "We still need to get back home."

"Safely, right?" Terk asks.

"That would be nice," Rain says with a lilting laugh.

"I'm sorry about…" Harah's voice trails off, and she blushes crimson, but it's Cardyn who saves her.

"Nothing to be sorry about. We may have gotten off to an, um…rocky start. But we don't hold grudges. You've set an example more people should follow. You forgave us and each other and started over. That's all that matters."

Ledge doesn't look too pleased when Harah kisses Cardyn on the cheek. But whatever jealousy he's feeling doesn't last long.

He takes my hand in his. "I 'ope we see each other again."

"We will."

He realizes it wasn't me who said that, and we all look around. The voice was quiet and seemed to have come out of nowhere and everywhere all at once. At first, I think it was the Auditor. But it's not.

It's Manthy.

A chill runs up and down the back of my neck. By now, we've all noticed how Manthy's been a little…different…since her return from the dead.

She's still quiet. Still mysterious. Still Manthy. Only now, when she *does* speak, it's not with mousy shyness or hesitant uncertainty. It's with the knowing confidence of a prophet.

## 43

# RETURNS AND DEPARTURES

LEDGE AND HARAH invite us to drive the bus all the way through the Settlement, which we do.

With what I figure must be the entire population of the Hyde Park Settlement lined up on either side of the road and cheering us on, I feel like we're royalty or celebrities cruising along on a float in a parade.

It's embarrassing. Well, for me, anyway. Brohn has his eyes fixed forward and doesn't seem to notice the clamor and applause from outside the bus. Rain and Terk are debating about how easy or hard it will be to get back home without getting lost or shot down over the Atlantic. Manthy seems to be sleeping.

Cardyn, Terk, and the Juvens, on the other hand, are lapping up the attention. Leaning out of the windows, they wave and cheer back at the crowds jogging alongside us. Even Roxane, still quiet and seeming to live inside of herself, peers out her window.

We arrive at last at the West Gate and wave our final goodbyes.

The massive double doors crank shut behind us. Three archers salute us from their post on top of one of the turrets.

With the sun rising in the red sky behind us, we make our way west.

After a couple of hours of careful driving over some rocky roads and after several detours around terrain that's simply impassable, Croque Madame parks the bus in front of the Arrival Station.

The Juvens may not be recovered yet, but at least they're rested, and they pile off the bus in an energetic swarm.

Lumbering out into the heat, her fur coat billowing out around like a superhero's cape, Grizzy greets us with smothering bear hugs.

"An' who's yer wee ones?"

Gathered around the front of the bus, we introduce her to Sara, Mattea, Arlo, Libra, Ignacio and Roxane. She already knows Branwynne and gushes about how happy she is to see her again.

"And how's the communications network running?" Rain asks. "Please tell me it hasn't gone glitchy again."

"On the contrary, Love," Grizzy says through a robust laugh. "Your mate Granden got in touch just the other day. Was askin' about you, an' all."

"Did he say anything about arranging to get us back?"

"He did."

"And…?"

"Well, it's not like the old days with time schedules and easy bookings and such."

"But…?"

Grizzy scans us all and clamps her hands together. "He says he's already made the arrangements. Now, it's just a matter o' timing an' security."

"Security?" Cardyn asks, the tendons in his neck strained from anxiety.

"So you don't get shot down."

"Yeah," Terk agrees. "That would be bad."

"So would stayin' out 'ere in this heat. Come inta the station.

The lot o' ya. No sense dyin' o' heatstroke before ya get a chance to get shot down over the Atlantic."

"Not funny," Cardyn grumbles, but I can tell he's secretly amused.

At this point, anything other than random death and random destruction feels like a cause for celebration.

Once inside the station, Grizzy morphs into the excellent and tireless host we've gotten to know. She sets all of us up with beds and clean clothes.

As it turns out, she and Croque Madame actually knew each other years ago, so they wind up sitting in the Canteen, swapping stories over cup after cup of weak but pleasant-smelling herbal tea.

The Juvens have taken to exploring the nooks and crannies and the ins and outs of the Arrival Station.

Sara, Ignacio, and Roxane tend to stick together, while Mattea and Libra seem to like being around us.

Libra, especially, is a bundle of energy. Slender, bright-eyed, and lithe as an Olympic gymnast, she bounces around every room she's in, giggling to herself, inspecting everything she can get her hands on, and prattling on endlessly to anyone within earshot.

At one point, Cardyn pulls me aside and asks if I've ever seen the girl actually take a breath.

"She's been in captivity for most of her life," I remind him. "Can you blame her for wanting to vent a little energy?"

Cardyn says he supposes that makes sense. "But why does she have to vent all over *me*?"

"Admit it. You love it."

"Sure. I just *love* being the center of that little chatterbox's attention and being asked all kinds of questions like I'm a celebrity and being followed and worshipped as some sort of heroic savior..." He stops mid-sentence and nods to himself. "Now that you mention it, I guess it *is* pretty marvie!"

I answer him with a laugh and a whack to his shoulder with the back of my hand.

Arlo, the curiously handsome doll-faced boy, prefers to be by himself. Not as shy as Manthy or as mute as Roxane, he nevertheless avoids everyone and won't speak unless spoken to first.

It's nice to see them scampering and cavorting like the kids they are instead of suffering like the human lab-rats they were forced to be.

Sprinting around the Arrival Station, they explore and play tag and hide-and-seek as if they were normal kids on a glorious field trip without a care in the world.

Even Roxane joins in from time to time. But then it's like she realizes she's having fun and splits off to be by herself.

Unfortunately, the rest of them eventually find their way down the narrow corridor leading into the storage room Brohn and I have been using as our own personal hiding spot.

"So much for our secret getaway room," Brohn sighs as the Juvens go bouncing back out.

"There'll be more rooms," I promise him, my arms wrapped around his waist, my face pressed to his chest.

It takes him a second, but he returns my embrace. I smile, happy to have the old Brohn back.

Still, there's a tension in his voice when he sighs and says he expects we'll need to be here for weeks. "It's not like there are regular flights back and forth between here and home."

I know he's right.

But the next day, we're able to communicate with Granden, Kella, and Wisp back in D.C. The conversation is short, static-filled and fuzzy, but they promise they'll get us home.

Three days after that, Rebekah Bezra, Lieutenant Junior Grade and Lieutenant Commander Carl Fredericks—the two pilots who brought us here—step into the Canteen where we've all gathered for a breakfast of croissants, baguettes, cheese, strawberry jam, and bulging glass jars of golden honey, leftover supplies from the storage bays in Croque Madame's bus.

"We've got instructions from Granden," Bezra says, her voice practically a schoolgirl-giddy squeal. "There's a window where we think we can get you back safely."

"But if we're going to go, we need to go now," Fredericks barks.

Cardyn has his head down, his nose practically plunged into a bowl of half-synthetic coconut yogurt, and he doesn't look up from the table. "Define, 'now.'"

"*Yesterday*," Fredericks says, and Cardyn snaps his head up, joining the rest of us in a moment of hyper-alertness.

Looking crestfallen, Grizzy says, "Well, I guess it's time ta pack ya up and see ya on yer way."

We spend the next hour gathering our things. After that, we say a round of very sad goodbyes and very grateful "Thanks!" to Grizzy and Croque Madame. There's not a dry eye in the room.

We may not have an official home anymore, but with the memories of Sadia and the Infiltrators, the new knowledge about my father, and the deaths in Bordeaux and Folkestone smoldering in our minds, we're more than ready to be somewhere else.

LESS THAN TWENTY-FOUR HOURS LATER, our plane lands with a horrific shudder and a mechanical shriek. But at least it lands.

We make our way down the steps, single file.

Me, Brohn, Cardyn, Rain, Terk, Manthy, the five Valencia Juvens, Roxane, and Branwynne.

And, of course, two ravens—one white, one black.

We're greeted by Granden and Sirella, one of the many Insubordinates who've taken a fancy to Cardyn.

She's hilariously flirty. I'm getting a kick out of watching him squirm. She's all over him like he's a celebrity, which, in some ways, I guess he is. I guess we all are.

We're not exactly conquering heroes, but I guess we have reason to be proud.

We're the ones who led the overthrow of Krug and the Patriots. We're the ones who traveled overseas and risked life and limb to find and free what could turn out to be fellow Emergents.

We're the ones who made it back alive. We're the ones who succeeded.

We're also the ones who failed.

All anyone will see is *us*. They won't see the innocents of Bordeaux or the bystanders who died along the way at the hands of Noxia and the Hawkers. They won't see the smoldering ruins of the defeated towns, villages, and cities the Execs left in their wake. And they won't see the self-contained arcologies of the Wealthies or the prison-labs run by the En-Gene-eers.

But Sirella, her hand on Cardyn's shoulder as she giggles at every word he says, isn't interested in any of that.

"Hero worship." That's what I once called it. It didn't occur to me at the time that worship could be a one-way street. But here we are, with Sirella, batty-eyed and flushed-cheeked, bouncing around Cardyn and plying him with questions with the kind of reverence usually reserved for royalty and gods.

Cardyn does his best to ignore her.

He only has eyes for Manthy.

Granden, meanwhile, tells us how happy he is to see us. We introduce him to our new batch of young friends and to Haida Gwaii, who barks friendly greetings to everyone through her white, pink-lined beak.

Standing in Terk's shadow, Roxane is the only one who doesn't make eye contact.

"And you know Branwynne," I tell Granden.

He says, "Of course," but his eyes linger over her like she's a distant cousin at a family reunion or someone important whose name he can't quite place.

Under the guidance of a heli-barge pilot we don't know, we're all flown to the rooftop landing pad of the Old Post Office Building.

From there, we follow Granden and Sirella on foot toward the Capitol Building.

Rain tugs at the sleeve of my jacket, and I lean over to hear her. "Is it just me, or does he seem sad to you?"

"Who? Granden?"

"Yeah."

"Tired, maybe."

"I've seen tired," Rain whispers. "We've *been* tired. Something's up with him."

I get ready to laugh her off and tell her she's imagining things. But then I remember, Rain doesn't imagine. She plans. She observes, strategizes, and takes decisive action.

It's her specialty. It's what she does. It's what she's best at.

I've grown fond of Granden since we first met him in our original Processor, so I can't help hoping that for once, Rain is wrong.

## 44

## MISSION

WITH RENDER and Haida Gwaii looping around overhead, the rest of us hop off the moving sidewalk and continue our way along the Mall.

"Things have changed since you've been gone," Granden tells us.

"What do you mean?" Cardyn asks, sweeping his eyes across the pristine grounds of the National Mall as we pass. "This place looks great!"

He's right. In the weeks we've been gone, the streets have been resurfaced and polished until they practically shine.

The greenspace, the statues and monuments, and the storefronts lining these streets suffered terrible damage in our final, all-out battle against the Patriot Army. But many of the buildings have already been refurbished in a clean aesthetic of polished marble, glass, and a network of thin, synth-steel structural supports.

Transparency seems to be the driving force.

When we left, most of these buildings were red brick and white marble façades with a patchwork of small windows. Now, they're *mostly* windows.

Even the day care center across the street from us is a big cube of glass. Inside, little Neos are skipping and hopping around, laughing and leaping after each other through a maze of lime-green foam pads, carpeted bridges, braided rope-ladders, and interconnected, see-through tunnels.

Happy, well-dressed people glide by on the moving sidewalks or zip along on zero-emission mag-bikes.

"Is it my imagination?" I ask Brohn. "Or is literally *everyone* here smiling?"

"They're either genuinely happy," he says through a smile of his own. "Or else Granden slipped something into all of their drinks."

I put a congratulatory hand on Granden's shoulder. "You really didn't waste any time, did you?"

Granden shrugs. "With the Patriot Army gone and with most of the layers of bureaucracy stripped away, getting things done turns out to be kind of easy."

"But...?"

"The Devoteds remain a problem."

Cardyn slaps a fist into his open palm. "Don't worry. We'll take care of them."

I roll my eyes at his smirky bravado as Granden tells us about other cities, here and out west, that his newly formed government have already been able to turn around.

"And the rest?" Terk asks.

Granden shakes his head. "A lot of them don't want to be turned around. All they want to do is turn *back*."

Brohn scowls. "Back? Back to what?"

"Not to Krug?" I ask.

Granden nods. "Back to Krug. Back to fear and ignorance. Back to chaos."

Rain looks distressed, teetering somewhere between sobbing with sorrow and screaming in anger. "But why? What good could possibly come of that?"

"I promise, if I knew, I'd tell you."

Manthy sighs. "For some people, getting themselves to 'good' depends on how bad they can make things for everyone else."

Granden's eyes skip from one of us to the other. He glances at the ground and then at the sky like he can't decide where to look while he prepares to deliver what my gut tells me is going be terrible news.

He's not halfway through his next sentence when I realize Rain was right. Something's wrong.

"We better keep moving. I need to get you back to base."

Then, going oddly quiet, Granden picks up the pace and continues leading us toward the Capitol Building.

I figured the Valencia Juvens, Roxane, and Branwynne would be obsessed with plying us with questions about this sparkling city, the rest of the country, how we got to this point, and what they should expect going forward.

But I think maybe they're too stunned to form words.

Lagging a little behind, they seem shell-shocked.

I hear their whispered overlap of English, Spanish, and French as they marvel at our nation's capital and at all the freedom and luxuries they've imagined but have been deprived of for most, if not all, of their lives.

I don't blame them for being impressed, although I do kind of wish this city came with a price tag on it to show how much it cost—in tears, blood, and human life—to get to where we are.

After only a few more minutes, we arrive at the Capitol Building.

Teams of landscapers are hard at work, planting flowers, securing saplings with stakes and wire, trimming the larger trees, and dropping coils of black irrigation hoses into trenches dug into the lawn.

Security is okay but not great. Now that we've broken into so many places, I automatically start looking for weaknesses whenever I approach a building. Sure, there are some posted sentries: a few men and women I recognize from the Insubordinates, War's Survivalists, and Mayla's Unkindness.

A bunch of them wave at us from their stations along the perimeter of the building.

There's a line of thin pillars with sensor ports and activity feeds posted behind softball-sized globes of black glass.

There's even a small fleet of surveillance drones buzzing overhead in a predictable grid pattern. I know getting the drone fleet recalibrated and back on-line was a high priority. It was supposed to make it easier to maintain security in what are bound to be turbulent times. But I can't help cringing, knowing this is the same generation of militarized drones that Krug sent in to destroy the Valta.

At least they're not those snaky-looking Triad Drones. Those really creeped me out.

I like the way the Banters did things: Kensington Palace was neutral ground. They used it for meetings and planning sessions, but no one was allowed to live there, and no one could claim it as their own.

I make a mental note to remind Granden that overthrowing a dictator is a lot easier than not becoming one yourself.

But then I remember who this is. Granden was Krug's son and had everything to gain by riding out his father's evil reign and everything to lose by challenging it. He's one of the good ones. He may even be one of the *great* ones someday.

I take a leap of faith and erase my mental note.

Render blends his consciousness with mine to tell me he and Haida Gwaii are going to fly around the city for a bit.

*Like a date?*

~ *It's not a date.*

In my mind, I can both see and feel him blush.

*It is totally a date, isn't it? Admit it!*

~ *I admit nothing. Only that I'm going to show this city off to my new friend.*

*So...a date.*

~ *No!*

*Don't be so uptight. You have feelings for her. If you push those feelings away, you'll just end up pushing her away as well.*

~ *I hate you.*

*No, you don't.*

~ *You're right. I don't. But sometimes I wish...*

*What?*

~ *That you weren't so right all the time!*

He severs our connection, and I send him one last mental gloat that for once, he was the novice, and I was the one with all the wisdom.

Once inside the building, Granden escorts the rest of us down the same hallway where Brohn and I nearly got crushed by a falling ceiling not that long ago.

It's all been repaired. There's not a trace of the damage the Devoteds did here.

From the newly immaculate corridor, we enter the Central Operations Room.

"Where is everyone?" Brohn asks, looking around with an eager smile.

I know that look. Brohn and I have been a couple for over a year now. We've kissed more times than I can count, bared our souls to each other, saved each other's lives. More than once. But that look...I saw it on the day we turned seventeen. The day the Recruiters came to take us away. That special, I'll-do-anything-for-you look...

The one reserved for his sister.

The holo-monitors and input panels are alive with streams of camera-feeds, flashing indicator lights, and 3D holo-projections of various tasks being performed on, in, and around the Capitol Building.

Granden invites us all to sit around the black glass conference table.

Easing himself into his mag-chair, he announces, "I have one last trip I need you to take."

Brohn puts up his hand. "I think I speak for all of us when I say…um…no. Forget it."

The rest of us offer up a chorus of nods and grunts of agreement with Brohn.

"We *just* got off of a plane," Rain reminds him.

Our seven new young friends, huddled in a bunch in front of the room's primary input panel, look back and forth between us and Granden. Their faces are a patchwork of glimmering green light from the holo-projections behind them. I'm sure they're trying to process what's happening, an exercise in futility without knowing the history of what got us here.

"This is a different kind of trip," Granden says. I think he's trying to be soothing, but he can't hide the ominous undercurrent in his voice. "I need you to get to the Valta."

"There is no Valta," Cardyn reminds him. "Not anymore."

"That's not entirely true. The Valta was more special than you realize." Granden's eyes swing away from Cardyn's and lock onto mine. "It wasn't a coincidence that your parents moved there from Boston when you were little. Your father's work there didn't happen by chance, Kress." He surveys us. "*None* of you happened by chance."

"My father…," I start to say. "The Infiltrators…"

"And Sadia," Granden completes for me. "Yes. I know. I'm sure it's a lot to take in. And I promise to fill in as much as I can. It's just that right now…"

My Conspiracy and I exchange a glance. We've been together long enough to know when something's up. And something is definitely up with Granden.

He drums his fingers on the table. "You remember Mammoth Mountain."

"Of course," Brohn says. "The town was built into the side of it."

"Not just your *town*." He pauses, scans the ceiling again, and sighs. "Hidden in the mountain, not far from the Valta, is...a lab."

Rain's ears perk up. "Like...a science lab?"

"Yes. A big one. An important one. A potentially world-changing one. It's five floors of chambers, research rooms, security systems, sleeping quarters, dining and workout facilities—"

Terk's eyes go wide. "Inside the mountain?"

"It's not complete, and it's not fully stocked. Or powered. Not anymore. It was going to be a special place. A special place for extraordinary people in extraordinary times. It's where you were going to be trained. *Properly* trained, not Processor-trained. Until Krug started to get suspicious. He blew up the Valta. Burned it to the ground looking for the source of...well...*you*. I don't need to go into detail. I know you've seen it. Krug never knew about the hidden facility."

"The lab?" Cardyn asks through an annoyed squint. "How did *we* not know about this?"

"It wasn't up and running yet. We didn't even know it was still there until just over a week ago. We got a report of an active status beacon in one of the monitoring systems we took over here in D.C. Once we saw that, we knew we had to find out if there was anything left."

Brohn frowns. "This facility...it's *that* important?"

"More important that you can imagine. It was going to be more of a training ground. Kind of *half* lab. But also, half school." Granden's eyes narrow. "I was part of an underground committee. Caldwell, too. There were others. Good people lurking around in Krug's government—engineers, combat specialists, geneticists, Techies—working right under his nose, to try to make it happen."

"Sadia?" I ask. "The Infiltrators?"

Granden nods as Rain leans toward him, a knot of suspicion on her face.

"Make *what* happen, exactly?

"The place. The lab. The school. It was going to be for you and others like you. We were going to call it 'the Emergents Academy.'"

The Auditor's voice wafts from the disk on Terk's back. "It was my first home." Granden nods as the Auditor continues. "My basic protocols were designed in Boston. But the Valta is where your father first activated me, Kress, along with the techno-interfaces you call your 'tattoos.' The work he did started in the unfinished complex Granden is describing."

"It's just outside of the Valta. But you never would have found it," Granden assures us. "It's concealed by a Veiled Refractor and hidden behind a false rockface in the mountain." A breathy urgency slips into his voice. "We need you to get there before someone else figures it out and finds it first. If they haven't already."

"You said it's not complete," Cardyn reminds him.

"*Not complete* isn't the same thing as harmless. If it really is still active, it has resources, information, and the groundwork for some of the most advanced biogenetic and techno-evolutionary integration systems in the history of humankind. Things that in the wrong hands could be catastrophic for all of us."

"But if it's not complete..." Brohn starts to say.

Granden seems to have anticipated his thought. "It's *not* complete. It never was. But what it *did* have was some of the tech Kress's father used to identify Emergents."

"That doesn't sound so bad," Cardyn says.

"It's not. Not by itself. But the tech doesn't just identify. It can also create and...*corrupt*."

"Corrupt?"

"It's the same tech Krug and the Deenays and the En-Geneers used to enhance the abilities of people like Sheridyn, Noxia, and the Hypnagogics."

At the word, "Hypnagogics," I tense up, my eyes wide and my heart racing.

"Imagine a factory," Granden says. "It can create a global contagion or a universal cure. The Emergents Academy is like that. It has both capabilities. Which way it goes depends on who's in charge. And who's in charge depends on who finds it first."

Cardyn covers his nose and mouth with his hands like he's trying to keep himself from breathing in toxic fumes. Terk looks faint. Rain and I are both wide-eyed. Manthy is staring at Granden in silence. I can't speak for the others, but I'm equal parts shocked, curious, and terrified out of my mind. Even Brohn looks a little woozy as he tries to process this bombardment of new bombshells.

The seven Juvens, Branwynne included, have their mouths open as they look back and forth at each other and then over to us. I don't know if there's a word to describe a "what-did-we-get-ourselves-into?" look, but these kids have it plastered all over their faces.

"I think our traveling days might be over," Brohn says at last and on behalf of all of us. "If this lab is there, why not just send out a scouting party? Let *them* track it down and report back what they find."

"That was our thought, too," Granden says solemnly, his eyes going dark. "We even put together a team. Sent them on their way in one of our recommissioned Patriot Transport Trucks."

I remember the exact type of truck he's talking about. We drove one from San Francisco to Chicago. The truck had every luxury we could ask for, but that trip...it didn't end well.

"Great!" Cardyn beams as he starts to stand, his knuckles pressed to the tabletop. "You sent a team. Then you don't need us!"

Granden shakes his head, and Cardyn plops back down into his seat. "The team we sent...they, um, *disappeared.* Six days ago."

Brohn leans forward. "Disappeared?"

"We lost contact with them. Last we heard, they were somewhere in Illinois. Emiquon National Wildlife Refuge," Granden adds, confirming my worst fears.

"The Processor," Terk says, his eyes darting down to his left side of synthetic parts. "The one where we first..."

"Unfortunately. Yes. That's the one."

"We went back there already," Brohn reminds him. "It's been destroyed. There's nothing left."

"I would've agreed with you. But *something* happened to our team. And it seems to have happened there."

"Are they experienced at least?" Brohn asks. "Your scouting team?"

Granden doesn't answer.

On the tabletop, Brohn's fingers curl into fists. "Granden?"

Granden is still silent. And I have a terrible feeling I know why.

I have an even worse feeling that Brohn does, too.

"Who...," he stammers. "Who was in the scouting team?"

Granden runs a finger along his stubbled jaw. With his broad shoulders and proper posture, he looks like a true leader: strong, confident, in control.

Except he's...*crying*?

He shakes his head and doesn't bother wiping away the tears pooling in the corners of his eyes when he tells us who was in the scouting party. "Kella was leading it. She had the twins with her. Lucid and Reverie. War and Mayla were with them for security."

"War and Mayla," Rain repeats out loud, although I don't think she's aware of having said it.

Granden swings his head around, his red-rimmed eyes riveted to Brohn's. "And Wisp. Brohn...Wisp was with them."

There are no questions. There's no second-guessing what Granden is telling us. Brohn's entire body—from his face to his feet—seems to melt all at once. He leans forward and then slumps back in his seat, and I think he would have just as easily collapsed onto the floor if his shoulder hadn't hit mine.

The contact seems to have startled him alert.

We're sitting there, frozen, unable to process this. Unwilling to accept what Granden is telling us, even though we know it's the absolute truth.

It's Manthy who stands and is the first to break the silence. "Then I guess we've got a rescue mission to complete before we head home."

Brohn has always been our leader. Rain has been our guide. Terk has been our muscle. Cardyn helps keep things light, and I'm our resident raven-whisperer.

But Manthy...Manthy is—and I realize now has always been —our hope for better things to come.

Now, as we prepare to leap back into action, we just have to hope that hope is enough.

# EPILOGUE

BANKING, tilting, and swooping high overhead, Render and Haida Gwaii rain down an impatient refrain of hacking barks as they urge us along the silvery-smooth access road leading to the boarding terminal where our transportation is waiting.

Glancing skyward, Cardyn asks me, "What's up with them?"

"I'm not sure. But they seem to know something."

"You're saying they know something about this rescue mission we don't?"

"Yes. That's what I'm saying."

"Is it um...good knowledge or bad?"

I look Cardyn square in the eye and don't blink when I tell him, "Bad."

His mouth hangs open, and I know he wants me to laugh and say I'm joking.

But now's not the time for the reassurance of lies.

"This is it," Granden announces, escorting us into the cavernous hangar where an array of military vehicles—including small, single-rider mag-scooters and newly-painted, high-speed tactical mag-jeeps—are parked at designated charging ports.

In the middle of the open, high-ceilinged depot is a massive truck, solid and powerful but also sleek and streamlined, as if someone attached a bunch of thick, studded wheels to a gray whale.

The rig—a behemoth of a vehicle—is a modified and updated model of the P2040 Military Tender we took to get from San Francisco to Chicago. Part recreational camper, part personnel transport, and part battlefield tank, it somehow makes Croque Madame's twelve-ton school bus look like a cute, cantaloupe-colored toy by comparison.

"It's an eight by eight, armed and armored troop carrier," Granden explains. "Roomier and more sophisticated than your P2040. Just got its latest updates yesterday. It'll hold the seven of you plus the six-person crew you're going to find and rescue."

He says this casually, like it's the easiest job in the world and like he has no doubt about our ultimate success.

"It's got double suspension and a mag-propulsion system with triple redundancy. The communications array is top of the line. Of course, with the network still so fragmented…well, let's just say our ability to stay in touch will be spotty, at best."

Terk's face is a mishmash of worry. "We won't be able to stay in touch with you?"

Slumping a little, Granden confesses that they're still working on rebuilding the nation's communication infrastructure. "The networks get compromised, infiltrated, or taken down as fast as we can repair them and get them up. Throw in all the atmospheric interference and…unfortunately, you'll mostly be on your own."

"What about weapons?" Rain asks, her eyes scanning the enormous rig.

"It's outfitted with a magnetic stun cannon, thermal cameras, a solar-cell regeneration bank, mine-detection system, an array of python rockets, and dual forty-millimeter grenade launchers. Oh, and it's amphibious and has a stealth-mode light refractor."

Granden reaches up and slaps his hand flat against the gunmetal gray door. "We call this one 'Terminus.'"

Next to me, Brohn gives an impressed whistle.

On my other side, Cardyn wags his head, clucks his tongue, and raises his hand. "Ahhh...But what about *cupholders?*"

I elbow him, but Granden manages a light laugh. "Eight in the cab, twelve in the back."

"Satisfied?" Manthy sneers.

Cardyn throws his arm around her and says, "Very!" as she grimaces in disgust.

Clambering up onto the loading platform next to the big military transport rig, Brohn and Terk dig through two silver trunks and give us a thumbs up, confirming we're fully stocked with guns, rifles, and ample ammo.

We also have our stash of Medieval-style weapons: Brohn's arbalest, Terk's flail, Rain's dart-drivers, Cardyn and Manthy's shared twin tomahawk axes, my talons, and a couple of daggers, longbows, broadswords, and battle axes—souvenirs gifted to us by Ledge and Harah after our last day at the Hyde Park Settlement.

Granden wishes us the best of luck as we make our final preparations to board the Terminus.

"That makes me nervous," Cardyn says to me.

"What does?"

"Having Granden wish us luck like that."

"What are you talking about? Luck is good."

"If we're going somewhere where we need luck, maybe we shouldn't be there."

"So you're suggesting we abandon Wisp and the others? Maybe let them fend for themselves out there and hope things turn out okay?"

Cardyn puts his hands up. "Come on, Kress. You know I'm not saying that. Just...I don't like relying on luck."

Overhearing us as she walks past, Rain slaps a magazine into her gun. "Me, neither."

Brohn gives Granden a firm handshake before turning to the rest of us. "It's time."

Render and Haida Gwaii are hopping around on the steel rafters high overhead. I whistle for them to come join us, and they flutter down, leaving a flurry of tiny black and white feathers in their wake.

Render lands on my shoulder. Haida lands on Branwynne's.

In this moment, I'm filled with a weird combination of hope, nervousness, and pride.

Our Conspiracy has grown. We now have Sara, Mattea, Arlo, Ignacio, Libra, Roxane, and Branwynne to take care of. But only Branwynne will be coming with us.

Despite their potential, they're still kids, and we have a responsibility to keep them safe.

"Which is why you need to stay here," I remind the ones we're leaving behind, feeling like an overprotective mother but hoping I'm coming across as a well-meaning older sister.

"How come Branwynne gets to go?" Mattea asks with a pout.

"It's not a *privilege*," Brohn tells her. "What we're about to do..."

"It's dangerous," Rain says.

"You'll be safe here with Granden," Terk promises the six Juvens. "We'll see you again before you know it."

They nod. After all, we explained this to them yesterday. And again this morning.

"I need Render with me," I told them at the time. "He won't go without Haida Gwaii. Haida won't go without Branwynne."

They've bought the explanation.

*Reluctantly.*

What we left out, though, is the fact that they've been imprisoned in a high-tech biogenetic prison for most of their lives with no combat experience and without weapons or survival training.

That makes them ill-prepared for the dangers we're about to face. We also don't mention that we know Branwynne a little better. We've fought alongside her, and we promised her parents we'd take care of her.

And then there's the one other thing we *definitely* don't mention, the one other truth:

Ignacio and Roxane—after the displays of power and impulsivity they showed back in Bordeaux and Folkestone—might very well prove, no matter how accidentally, too dangerous to themselves and, possibly, to *us*.

Still, as we say our last goodbyes, I can't help but beam with pride at the faces of these restless, eager, and anxious kids.

But as I board the rig, I'm not thinking about the potential teammates we've gained, what we had to do to free them, or what we owe them now that they're here. I'm not even thinking about finding and excavating this mysterious, unfinished Emergents Academy.

No. I'm thinking about the six friends we're going to find and rescue:

Kella. Wisp. War. Mayla. Lucid. Reverie.

I'm thinking about the possibility of seeing the Valta again. Seeing what's salvageable and what we might one day, once again, call home.

And I'm thinking—very seriously, through clamp-jawed determination—about what we're going to do to anyone who stands in our way.


END OF *TRANSFIGURED* – **Book 2 of the *Transcendent Trilogy***

# UP NEXT: TERMINUS

After their overseas missions, Kress and her Conspiracy return home to a divided nation.

The East and West Coasts have become fragile havens from a dystopian middle America, which remains mired in fear, poverty, and the most sadistic brands of vigilante violence.

All Kress and her Conspiracy have to do is embark on a cross-country road-trip from Washington, D.C. to the Valta in Colorado, dodge the deadly Cult of the Devoted and the Army of the Unsettled—two groups battling for control over a land that might not be worth saving—and complete a perilous rescue mission along the way.

What could possibly go wrong?

Join Kress and her friends—new and old—for one last adventure of sad losses, happy reunions, deadly encounters, and heartbreaking departures.

The end is here!

But what new beginnings will the finale inspire…?

*Terminus is available for pre-order until its release in autumn 2020.*

SEEKER'S WORLD

ALSO BY K. A. RILEY

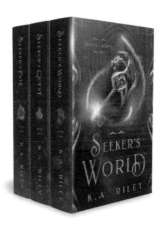

What readers are saying about K. A. Riley's Fantasy series:

*"This book will keep you riveted..."*

*"A page turner. It stirred up memories of how I felt reading the Twilight Series..."*

On her seventeenth birthday, Vega Sloane receives a strange and puzzling gift: a key in the shape of a dragon's head, along with a note that claims she's destined to save the world.

When the handsome and mysterious Callum Drake enters her life, she finds herself inextricably drawn to him, and more questions begin to arise. Who is the boy beyond the exquisite façade and charming smile?

Get the books here:

*Seeker's World*
*Seeker's Quest*
*Seeker's Fate*
*Seeker's Promise*

ALSO BY K. A. RILEY

## Resistance Trilogy

*Recruitment*

*Render*

*Rebellion*

## Emergents Trilogy

*Survival*

*Sacrifice*

*Synthesis*

## Transcendent Trilogy

*Travelers*

*Transfigured*

*Terminus*

## Seeker's World Series

*Seeker's World*

*Seeker's Quest*

*Seeker's Fate*

*Seeker's Promise*

## Athena's Law Series

Book One: *Rise of the Inciters*

Book Two: *Into an Unholy Land*

Book Three: *No Man's Land*

# K. A. RILEY ON SOCIAL MEDIA

If you're enjoying K. A. Riley's books, please consider leaving a review on Amazon or Goodreads to let your fellow book-lovers know about it. And be sure to sign up for my newsletter at www. karileywrites.org for news, quizzes, contests, behind-the-scenes peeks into the writing process, and advance info. about upcoming projects!

# FOLLOW K. A. RILEY

Website: https://karileywrites.org/

facebook.com/karileywrites

Instagram.com/karileywrites

Printed in Great Britain
by Amazon

72440164R00215